I0784588

B. M. Bower

The Ranch At The Wolverine
(Western Adventure Novel)

OK Publishing 2021

B. M. Bower

The Ranch At The Wolverine

(Western Adventure Novel)

Adventure Tale of the Wild West

Published by

Books

- Advanced Digital Solutions & High-Quality book Formatting -

musaicumbooks@okpublishing.info

2021 OK Publishing

ISBN 978-80-272-7565-6

Contents

Chapter I. Let us Start at the Beginning — 11

Chapter II. A Storm and a Stranger — 19

Chapter III. A Book, a Bannock, and a Bed — 23

Chapter IV. "Old Dame Fortune's Used me for a Football" — 29

Chapter V. Marthy Buries Her Dead and Greets Her Nephew — 34

Chapter VI. A Matter of Twelve Months or so — 41

Chapter VII. Ward Hunts Wolves — 48

Chapter VIII. Help for the Cow Business — 53

Chapter IX. When Emotions are Bottled — 56

Chapter X. This Pal Business — 61

Chapter XI. Was it the Dog? — 67

Chapter XII. The Little Devils of Doubt — 72

Chapter XIII. The Corral in the Canyon — 78

Chapter XIV. Each in his Own Trail — 84

Chapter XV. "You Won't get me Again" — 88

Chapter XVI. "I'm Going to Take You Out and Hang You" — 92

Chapter XVII. "So-Long, Buck!" — 97

Chapter XVIII. Fortune Kicks Again — 100

Chapter XIX. The Brave Buckaroo — 105

Chapter XX. "We Been Sorry for You" — 108

Chapter XXI. Seven Lean Kine — 112

Chapter XXII. The Billy of Her — 116

Chapter XXIII. Billy Louise Gets a Surprise — 120

Chapter XXIV. The Hookin'-Cough Man — 123

Chapter XXV. The Wolf Joke — 128

Chapter XXVI. "Hm-Mm!" — 132

Chapter XXVII. Marthy — 136

Chapter XXVIII. All Right and Comfy — 142

Chapter I. Let us Start at the Beginning

Four trail-worn oxen, their necks bowed to the yoke of patient servitude, should really begin this story. But to follow the trail they made would take several chapters which you certainly would skip-unless you like to hear the tale of how the wilderness was tamed and can thrill at the stern history of those who did the taming while they fought to keep their stomachs fairly well filled with food and their hard-muscled bodies fit for the fray.

There was a woman, low-browed, uncombed, harsh of voice and speech and nature, who drove the four oxen forward over lava rock and rough prairie and the scanty sage. I might tell you a great deal about Marthy, who plodded stolidly across the desert and the low-lying hills along the Blackfoot; and of her weak-souled, shiftless husband whom she called Jase, when she did not call him worse.

They were the pioneers whose lurching wagon first forded the singing Wolverine stream just where it greens the tiny valley and then slips between huge lava-rock ledges to join the larger stream. Jase would have stopped there and called home the sheltered little green spot in the gray barrenness. But Marthy went on, up the farther hill and across the upland, another full day's journey with the sweating oxen.

They camped that night on another little, singing stream, in another little valley, which was not so level or so green or so wholly pleasing to the eye. And that night two of the oxen, impelled by a surer instinct than their human owners, strayed away down a narrow, winding gorge and so discovered the Cove and feasted upon its rich grasses. It was Marthy who went after them and who recognized the little, hidden Eden as the place of her dreams-supposing she ever had dreams. So Marthy and Jase and the four oxen took possession, and with much labor and many hard years for the woman, and with the same number of years and as little labor as he could manage on the man's part, they tamed the Cove and made it a beauty spot in that wild land. A beauty spot, though their lives held nothing but treadmill toil and harsh words and a mental horizon narrowed almost to the limits of the grim, gray, rock wall that surrounded them.

Another sturdy-souled couple came afterwards and saw the Wolverine and made for themselves a home upon its banks. And in the rough little log cabin was born the girl-child I want you to meet; a girl-child when she should have been a boy to meet her father's need and great desire; a girl-child whose very name was a compromise between the parents. For they called her Billy for sake of the boy her father wanted, and Louise for the girl her mother had longed for to lighten that terrible loneliness which the far frontier brings to the women who brave its stern emptiness.

Do you like children? In other words, are you human? Then I want you to meet Billy Louise when she was ten and had lived all her life among the rocks and the sage and the stunted cedars and huge, gray hills of Idaho. Meet her with her pink sunbonnet hanging down the back of her neck and her big eyes taking in the squalidness of Marthy's crude kitchen in the Cove, and her terrible directness of speech hitting squarely the things she saw that were different from her own immaculate home. Of course, if you don't care for children, you may skip a chapter and meet her later when she was eighteen-but I really wish you would consent to know her at ten.

"Mommie makes cookies with a raising in the middle. She gives me two sometimes when the Bill of me has been workin' like the deuce with dad; one for Billy and one for Louise. When I'm twelve, Mommie's goin' to let the Louise of me make cookies all myself and put a raising on top. I'll put two on top of one and bring it over for you, Marthy. And —" Billy Louise was terribly outspoken at times —"I'll put four raisings on another one for Jase, 'cause he don't have any nice times with you. Don't you ever make cookies with raisings on 'em, Marthy? I'm hungry as a coyote-and I ain't used to eating just bread and the kinda butter you have. Mom says you don't work it enough. She says you are too scared of water, and the buttermilk ain't all worked out, so that's why it tastes so funny. Does Jase like that kind of butter, Marthy?"

"If your mother had to do the outside work as well as the inside, mebbe she wouldn't work her butter so awful much, either. I dunno whether Jase likes it or not. He eats it," Marthy stated grimly.

Billy Louise sighed. "Well, of course he's awful lazy. Daddy says so. I guess I won't put but one raising on Jase's cookie when I'm twelve. Has Jase gone fishing again, Marthy?"

A gleam of satisfaction brightened Marthy's hard, blue eyes. "No, he ain't. He's in the root suller. You want some bread and some nice, new honey, Billy Louise? I jest took it outa the hive this morning. When you go home, I'll send some to your maw if you can carry it."

"Sure! I can carry anything that's good. If you put it on thick, so I can't taste the bread, I'll eat it. Say, you like me, don't you, Marthy?"

"Yes," said Marthy, turning her back on the slim, wide-eyed girl, "I like yuh, Billy Louise."

"You sound like you wish you didn't," Billy Louise remarked. Even at ten Billy Louise was keenly sensitive to tones and glances and that intangible thing we call atmosphere. "Are you sorry you like me?"

"No-o, I ain't sorry. A person's got to like something that's alive and human, or —" Marthy was clumsy with words, and she was always coming to the barrier between her powers of ex-pression and the thoughts that were prisoned and dumb. "Here's your bread 'n' honey."

"What makes you sound that way, Marthy? You sound like you had tears inside, and they couldn't get out your eyes. Are you sad? Did you ever have a little girl, Marthy?"

"What makes you ask that?" Marthy sat heavily down upon a box beside the rough kitchen table and looked at Billy Louise queerly, as if she were half afraid of her.

"I dunno-but that's the way mommie sounds when she says something about angel-brother. Did you ever —"

"Billy Louise, I'm going to tell you this oncet, and then I don't want you to ast me any more questions, nor talk about it. You're the queerest young one I ever seen, but you don't hurt folks on purpose —I've learnt that much about yuh." Marthy half rose from the box, and with her dingy, patched apron shooed an investigative hen out of the doorway. She knew that Billy Louise was regarding her fixedly over the huge, uneven slice of bread and honey, and she felt vaguely that a child's grave, inquiring eyes may be the hardest of all eyes to meet.

"I never meant —"

"I know yuh never, Billy Louise. Now don't tell your maw this. Long ago-long before your maw ever found you, or your paw ever found your ranch on the Wolverine, I had a little girl, 'bout like you. She was a purty child-her hair was like silk, and her eyes was blue, and-we was Mormons, and we lived down clost to Salt Lake. And I seen so much misery amongst the women-folks —you can't understand that, but mebby you will when you grow up. Anyway, when little Minervy kep' growin' purtyer and sweeter, I couldn't stand it to think of her growin' up and bein' a Mormon's wife. I seen so many purty girls... So I made up my mind we'd move away off somewheres, where Minervy could grow up jest as sweet and purty as she was a mind to, and not have to suffer fer her sweetness and her purtyness. When you grow up, Billy Louise, you'll know what I mean. So me and Jase packed up-we kinda had to do it on the sly, on account uh the bishops-and we struck out with a four-ox team.

"We kep' a-goin' and kep' a-goin', fer I was scared to settle too clost. I seen how they keep spreadin' out all the time, and I wanted to git so fur away they wouldn't ketch up. And we got into bad country, where there wasn't no water skurcely. We swung too fur north, and got into the desert back there. And over next them three buttes little Minervy took sick. We tried to git outa the desert-we headed over this way. But before we got to Snake river she-died, and I had to leave 'er buried back there. We come on. I hated the church worse than ever, and I wanted to git clear away from 'em. Why, Billy Louise, we camped one night by the Wolverine, right about where your paw's got his big corral! We didn't stay there, because it was an Injun camping-ground then, and they wasn't no use getting mixed up in no fuss, first thing. In them days the Injuns wasn't so peaceable as they be now. So we come on here and settled in the Cove.

"And so —I like yuh," said Marthy, in a tone that was half defiance, "because I can't help likin' yuh. You're growin' up sweet and purty, jest like I wanted my little Minervy to grow up. In some ways you remind me of her, only she was quieter and didn't take so much notice of things a young one ain't s'posed to notice. Now I don't want you askin' no more questions about her, 'cause I ain't going to talk about it ag'in; and if yuh pester me, I'll send yuh home and tell your maw to keep yuh there. If you're the nice girl I think yuh be, you'll be good to Marthy and not talk about —"

Billy Louise opened her eyes still wider, and licked the honey off one whole corner of the slice without really tasting anything. Marthy's square, uncompromising chin was actually quivering. Billy Louise was stricken dumb by the spectacle. She wanted to go and put her arms around Marthy's neck and kiss her; only Marthy's neck had a hairy mole, and there was no part of her face which looked in the least degree kissable. Still, Billy Louise felt herself all hot inside with remorse and sympathy and affection. Physical contact being impossible because of her fastidious instincts, and speech upon the subject being so sternly forbidden, Billy Louise continued to lick honey and stare in fascinated silence.

"I'll wash the dishes for you, Marthy," she offered irrelevantly at last, as a supreme sacrifice upon the altar of sympathy. When that failed to stop the slow procession of tears that was traveling down the furrows of Marthy's cheeks, she added ingratiatingly: "I'll put six raisings on the cookie I'm going to make for you."

Whereupon Marthy did an unprecedented, an utterly amazing thing. She got up and gathered Billy Louise into her arms so unexpectedly that Billy Louise inadvertently buried her nose in the honey she had not yet licked off the bread. Marthy held her close pressed to her big, flabby bosom and wept into her hair in a queer, whimpering way that somehow made Billy Louise think of a hurt dog. It was only for a minute that Marthy did this; she stopped almost as suddenly as she began and went outside, wiping her eyes and her nose impartially upon her dirty apron.

Billy Louise sat paralyzed with the mixture of unusual emotions that assailed her. She was exceedingly sticky and uncomfortable from honey and tears, and she shivered with repugnance at the odor of Marthy's unbathed person. She was astonished at the outburst from phlegmatic Marthy Meilke, and her pity was now alloyed with her promise to wash all those dirty dishes. Billy Louise felt that she had been a trifle hasty in making promises. There was not a drop of water in the house nor a bit of wood, and Billy Louise knew perfectly well that the dishpan would have a greasy, unpleasant feeling under her fastidious little fingers.

She sighed heavily. "Well, I s'pose I might just as well get to work at 'em," she said aloud, as was her habit-being a child who had no playmates. "I hate to dread a thing I hate."

She looked at the messy slice of sour bread and threw it out to the speckled hen that had returned and was standing with one foot lifted tentatively-ready for a forward step if the fates seemed kind-and was regarding Billy Louise fixedly with one yellow eye. "Take it and go!" cried the donor, impatient of the scrutiny. She picked up the wooden pail and went down to the creek behind the house, by a pathway bordered thickly with budding rosebushes and tall lilacs.

Billy Louise first of all washed her face slowly and with a methodic thoroughness which characterized her-having lived for ten full years with no realization of hours and minutes as a measure for her actions. She dried her face quite as deliberately upon her starched calico apron. Then she spent a few minutes trying to catch a baby trout in her cupped palms. Never had Billy Louise succeeded in catching a baby trout in her hands; therefore she never tired of trying. Now, however, that rash promise nagged at her and would not let her enjoy the game as completely as usual. She took the wooden pail, and squatting on her heels in the wet sand, waited until a small school swam incautiously close to the bank, and scooped suddenly, with a great splash. She caught three tiny, speckled fish the length of her little finger, and she let the half-full pail rest in the shallow stream while she watched the fry swimming excitedly round and round within.

There was no great fun in that. Billy Louise could catch baby trout in a pail at home, from the waters of the Wolverine, whenever she liked. Many a time she had kept them in a big bottle until she tired of watching them, or they died because she forgot to change the water often enough. She could not get even a languid enjoyment out of them now, because she could not for a minute forget that she had promised to wash Marthy's dishes-and Marthy always had so many dirty dishes! And Marthy's dishpan was so greasy! Billy Louise gave a little shudder when she thought of it.

"I wish her little girl hadn't died," she said, her mind swinging from effect back to cause. "I could play with her. And she'd wash the dishes herself. I'm going to name my new little pig Minervy. I wish she hadn't died. I'd show her my little pig, if Marthy'd let her come over to our place. We could both ride on old Badger; Minervy could ride behind me, and we'd go places together." Billy Louise meditatively stirred up the baby trout with a forefinger. "We'd go up the canyon and have the caves for our play-houses. Minervy could have the secret cave away up the hill, and I'd have the other one across from it; and we'd have flags and wigwag messages like daddy tells about in the war. And we'd play the rabbits are Injuns, and the coyotes are big-Injun-chiefs sneaking down to see if the forts are watching. And whichever seen a coyote first would wigwag to the other one..." A baby trout, taking advantage of the pail tipping in the current, gave a flip over the edge and interrupted Billy Louise's fancies. She gave the pail a tilt and spilled out the other two fish. Then she filled it as full as she could carry and started back to pay the price of her sympathy.

"I don't see what Minervy had to go and die for!" she complained, dodging a low-hanging branch of bloom-laden lilac. "She could wash the dishes and I'd wipe 'em-and I s'pose there ain't a clean dish-towel in the house, either! Marthy's an awful slack housekeeper."

Billy Louise, being a young person with a conscience-of a sort-washed the dishes, since she had given her word to do it. The dishpan was even more unpleasant than experience had foretold for her; and of Marthy's somewhat meager supply there seemed not one clean dish in the house. The sympathy of Billy Louise therefore waned rapidly; rather, it turned in upon itself. So that by the time she felt morally free to spend the rest of the afternoon as she pleased, she was not at all sorry for Marthy for having lost Minervy; instead, she was sorry for herself for having been betrayed into rashness and for being deprived of a playmate.

"I don't s'pose Marthy doctored her right, at all," she considered pitilessly, as she returned down the lilac-bordered path. "If she had, I guess she wouldn't have died. I'll bet she never gave her a speck of sage tea, like mommie always does when I'm sick-only I ain't ever, thank goodness. I'm just going to ask Jase if Marthy did."

On the way to the root cellar, which was dug into the creek-bank well above high-water mark, Billy Louise debated within herself the ethics of speaking to Jase upon a forbidden subject. Jase had been Minervy's father, and therefore knew of her existence, so that mentioning Minervy to him could not in any sense be betraying a secret. She wondered if Jase felt badly about it, as Marthy seemed to do. On the heels of that came the determination to test his emotional capacity.

At the root cellar her attention was diverted. The cellar door was fastened on the outside, with the iron hasp used to protect the store of vegetables from the weather. Jase must be gone. She was turning away when she heard him clear his throat with that peculiar little hacking, rasping noise which sounded exactly as one would expect a Jase to sound. Billy Louise puckered her eyebrows, pressed her lips together understandingly-and disapprovingly-and opened the door.

Jase, humped over a heap of sprouting potatoes, blinked up apathetically into the sudden flood of sweet, spring air and sunshine. "Why, hello, Billy Louise," he mumbled, his eyes brightening a bit.

"Say, you was locked in here!" Billy Louise faced him puzzled. "Did you know you was locked in?"

"Yes-s, I knowed it. Marthy, she locked the door." Jase reached out a bony hand covered with carrot-colored hairs and picked up a shriveling potato with long, sickly sprouts proclaiming life's persistence in perpetuating itself under adverse circumstances. He broke off the sprouts with a wipe of his dirty palm and threw the potato into a heap in the corner.

"What for?" Billy Louise demanded, watching Jase reach languidly out for another potato.

"She seen me diggin' bait," Jase said tonelessly. "I did think some of ketchin' a mess of fish before I went to sproutin' p'tatoes, but Marthy she don't take no int'rest in nothin' but work."

"Are the fish biting good?" Billy Louise glanced toward the wider stream, where it showed through a gap in the alders.

"Yes-s, purty good now. I caught a nice mess the other day; but Marthy, she don't favor my goin' fishin'." The lean hands of Jase moved slowly at his task. Billy Louise, watching him, wondered why he did not hurry a little and finish sooner. Still, she could not remember ever seeing Jase hurry at anything, and the Cove with its occupants was one of her very earliest memories.

"Say, I'll dig some more bait, and then we'll go fishing; shall we?"

"I —dunno as I better —" Jase's hand hovered aimlessly over the potato pile. "I got quite a lot sprouted, though-and mebby —"

"I'll lock you in till I get the bait dug," suggested Billy Louise craftily. "And you work fast; and then I'll let you out, and we'll lock the door agin, so Marthy'll think you're in there yet."

"You're sure smart to think up things," Jase admired, smiling loose-lipped behind his scraggly beard, that was fading with the years. "I dunno but what it'd serve Marthy right. She ain't got no call to lock the door on me. She hates like sin t' see me with a fish-pole in m' hand-but she's always et her share uh the messes I ketch. She ain't a reasonable woman, Marthy ain't. You git the bait. I'll show Marthy who's boss in this Cove!"

He might have encouraged himself into defying Marthy to her face, in another five minutes of complaining. But the cellar door closed upon him with a slam. Billy Louise was not interested in his opinion of Marthy; with her, opinions were valueless if not accompanied by action.

"I never thought to ask him about Minervy," occurred to her while she was relentlessly dragging pale, fleshly fishworms from the loose black soil of Marthy's onion bed. "But I know she was mean to Minervy. She's awful mean to Jase-locking him up in the root cellar just 'cause he wanted to go fishing. If I was Jase I wouldn't sprout a single old potato for her. My goodness, but she'll be mad when she opens the cellar door and Jase ain't in there; I —guess I'll go home early, before Marthy finds it out."

She really meant to do that, but the fish were hungry fish that day, and the joy of having a companion to exclaim with her over every hard tug-even though that companion was only Jase-enticed her to stay on and on, until a whiff of frying pork on the breeze that swept down the Cove warned Billy Louise of the near approach of supper-time.

"I guess mebby I might as well go back to the suller," Jase remarked, his defiance weakening as he climbed the bank. "You come and lock the door agin, Billy Louise, and Marthy won't know I ain't been there all the time. She'll think you caught the fish." He looked at her with a weak leer of conscious cunning.

Billy Louise, groping vaguely for the sunbonnet that was dangling between her straight shoulder-blades, stared at him with wide eyes that held disillusionment and with it a contempt all the keener because it was the contempt of a child, whose judgment is merciless.

"I should thing you'd be ashamed!" she said at last, forgetting that the idea had been born in her own brain. "Cowards do things and then sneak about it. Daddy says so. I don't care if Marthy is mad 'cause I let you out, and I don't care if she knows we went fishing. I thought you wanted Marthy to see she ain't so smart, locking you up in the cellar. I ain't going to bake you a single cookie with raisings on it, like I was going to."

"Marthy's got a sharp tongue in 'er head," Jase wavered, his eyes shifting from Billy Louise's uncompromising stare.

"Daddy says when you do a thing that's mean, do it and take your medicine," Billy Louise retorted. "The boy of me that belongs to dad ain't a sneak, Jase Meilke. And," she added loftily, "the girl of me that belongs to mommie is a perfeck lady. Good day, Mr. Meilke. Thank you for a pleasant time fishing."

Whereupon the perfect lady part switched short skirts up the path and held a tousled head high with disdain.

Jase, thus deserted, went shambling back to the cellar and fell to sprouting potatoes with what might almost be termed industry.

It pained Jase later to discover that Marthy was not interested in the open door, but in the very small heap of potatoes which he had "sprouted" that afternoon. There was other work to be done in the Cove, and there were but two pairs of hands to do it; that one pair was slow and shiftless and inefficient was bitterly accepted by Marthy, who worked from sunrise until dark to make up for the shirking of those other hands.

It was the trail experience over again, and it was an experience that dragged through the years without change or betterment. Marthy wanted to "get ahead." Jase wanted to sit in the sun with his knees drawn up, just —I don't know what, but I suppose he called it thinking. When he felt unusually energetic, he liked to dangle an impaled worm over a trout pool. Theoretically he also wanted to get ahead and to have a fine ranch and lots of cattle and a comfortable home. He would plan these things sometimes in an expansive mood, whereupon Marthy would stare at him with her hard, contemptuous look until Jase trailed off into mumbling complaints into his beard. He was not as able-bodied as she thought he was, he would say, with vague solemnity. Some uh these days Marthy'd see how she had driven him beyond his strength.

When one is a Marthy, however, with ambitions and a tireless energy and the persistence of a beaver, and when one listens to vague mutterings for many hard laboring years, one grows accustomed to the complainings and fails to see certain warning symptoms of which even the complainer is only vaguely aware.

She kept on working through the years, and as far as was humanly possible she kept Jase working. She did not soften, except toward Billy Louise, who rode sometimes over from her father's ranch on the Wolverine to the flowery delights of the Cove. The place was a perfect jungle of sweetness, seven months of each year; for Marthy owned and indulged a love of beauty, even if she could not realize her dream of prosperity. Wherever was space in the house-yard for a flower or a fruit tree or a berry bush, Marthy planted one or the other. You could not see the cabin from April until the leaves fell in late October, except in a fragmentary way as you walked around it. You went in at a gate of pickets which Marthy herself had split and nailed in place; you followed a narrow, winding path through the sweet jungle-and if you were tall, you stooped now and then to pass under an apple branch. And unless you looked up at the black, lava-rock rim of the bluff which cupped this Eden incongruously, you would forget that just over the brim lay parched plain and barren mountain.

When Billy Louise was twelve, she had other ambitions than the making of cookies with "raisings" on them. She wanted to do something big, though she was hazy as to the particular nature of that big something. She tried to talk it over with Marthy, but Marthy could not seem to think beyond the Cove, except that now and then Billy Louise would suspect that her mind did travel to the desert and Minervy's grave. Marthy's hair was growing streaked with yellowish gray, though it never grew less unkempt and dusty looking. Her eyes were harder, if anything, except when they rested on Billy Louise.

When she was thirteen, Billy Louise rode over with a loaf of bread she had baked all by herself, and she put this problem to Marthy:

"I've been thinking I'd go ahead and write poetry, Marthy —a whole book of it with pictures. But I do love to make bread-and people have to eat bread. Which would you be, Marthy; a poet, or a cook?"

Marthy looked at her a minute, lent her attention briefly to the question, and gave what she considered good advice.

"You learn how to cook, Billy Louise. Yuh don't want to go and get notions. Your maw ain't healthy, and your paw likes good grub. Po'try is all foolishness; there ain't any money in it."

"Walter Scott paid his debts writing poetry," said Billy Louise argumentatively. She had just read all about Walter Scott in a magazine which a passing cowboy had given her; perhaps that had something to do with her new ambition.

"Mebby he did and mebby he didn't. I'd like to see our debts paid off with po'try. It'd have to be worth a hull lot more 'n what I'd give for it."

"Oh. Have you got debts too, Marthy?" Billy Louise at thirteen was still ready with sympathy. "Daddy's got lots and piles of 'em. He bought some cattle and now he talks to mommie all the time about debts. Mommie wants me to go to Boise to school, next winter, to Aunt Sarah's. And daddy says there's debts to pay. I didn't know you had any, Marthy."

"Well, I have got. We bought some cattle, too-and they ain't done 's well 's they might. If I had a man that was any good on earth, I could put up more hay. But I can't git nothing outa Jase but whines. Your paw oughta send you to school, Billy Louise, even if he has got debts. I'd 'a' sent —"

She stopped there, but Billy Louise knew how she finished the sentence mentally. She would have sent Minervy to school.

"Your paw ain't got any right to keep you outa school," Marthy went on aggressively. "Debts er no debts, he'd see 't you got schoolin' —if he was the right kinda man."

"Daddy is the right kinda man. He ain't like Jase. He says he wishes he could, but he don't know where the money's coming from."

"How much's it goin' to take?" asked Marthy heavily.

"Oh, piles." Billy Louise spoke airily to hide her pride in the importance of the subject. "Fifty dollars, I guess. I've got to have some new clothes, mommie says. I'd like a blue dress."

"And your paw can't raise fifty dollars?" Marthy's tone was plainly belligerent.

"Got to pay interest," said Billy Louise importantly.

Marthy said not another word about debts or the duties of parents. What she did was more to the point, however, for she hitched the mules to a rattly old buckboard next day and drove over to the MacDonald ranch on the Wolverine. She carried fifty dollars in her pocket-and that was practically all the money Marthy possessed, and had been saved for the debts that harassed her. She gave the money to Billy Louise's mother and said that it was a present for Billy Louise, and meant for "school money." She said that she hadn't any girl of her own to spend the money on, and that Billy Louise was a good girl and a smart girl, and she wanted to do a little something toward her schooling.

A woman will sacrifice more pride than you would believe, if she sees a way toward helping her children to an education. Mrs. MacDonald took the money, and she promised secrecy-with a feeling of relief that Marthy wished it. She was astonished to find that Marthy had any feelings not directly connected with work or the shortcomings of Jase, but she never suspected that Marthy had made any sacrifice for Billy Louise.

So Billy Louise went away to school and never knew whose money had made it possible to go, and Marthy worked harder and drove Jase more relentlessly to make up that fifty dollars. She never mentioned the matter to anyone. The next year it was the same; when, in August, she questioned Billy Louise clumsily upon the subject of finances, and learned that "daddy" still talked about debts and interest and didn't know where the money was coming from, she drove over again with money for the "schooling." And again she extracted a promise of silence.

She did this for four years, and not a soul knew that it cost her anything in the way of extra work and extra harassment of mind. She bought more cattle and cut more hay and went deeper into debt; for as Billy Louise grew older and prettier and more accustomed to the ways of town, she needed more money, and the August gift grew proportionately larger. The mother was thankful beyond the point of questioning. An August without Marthy and Marthy's gift of money would have been a tragedy; and so selfish is mother-love sometimes that she would have accepted the gift even if she had known what it cost the giver.

At eighteen, then, Billy Louise knew some things not taught by the wide plains and the wild hills around her. She was not spoiled by her little learning, which was a good thing. And when her father died tragically beneath an overturned load of poles from the mountain at the head of the canyon, Billy Louise came home. The Billy of her tried to take his place, and the Louise of her attempted to take care of her mother, who was unfitted both by nature and habit to take care of herself. Which was, after all, a rather big thing for anyone to attempt.

Chapter II. A Storm and a Stranger

Jase began to complain of having "all-gone" feelings during the winter after Billy Louise came home and took up the whole burden of the Wolverine ranch. He complained to Billy Louise, when she rode over one clear, sunny day in January; he said that he was getting old-which was perfectly true-and that he was not as able-bodied as he might be, and didn't expect to last much longer. Billy Louise spoke of it to Marthy, and Marthy snorted.

"He's able-bodied enough at mealtimes, I notice," she retorted. "I've heard that tune ever since I knowed him; he can't fool me!"

"Not about the all-goneness, have you?" Billy Louise was preparing to wipe the dishes for Marthy. "I know he always had 'cricks' in different parts of his anatomy, but I never heard about his feeling all-gone, before. That sounds mysterious, don't you think?"

"No; and he never had nothin' the matter with his anatomy, neither; his anatomy's just as sound as mine. Jase was born lazy, is all ails him."

"But, Marthy, haven't you noticed he doesn't look as well as he used to? He has a sort of gray look, don't you think? And his eyes are so puffy underneath, lately."

"No, I ain't noticed nothing wrong with him that ain't always been wrong." Marthy spoke grudgingly, as if she resented even the possibility of Jase's having a real ailment. "He's feelin' his years, mebby. But he ain't no call to; Jase ain't but three years older 'n I be, and I ain't but fifty-nine last birthday. And I've worked and slaved here in this Cove fer twenty-seven years, now; what it is I've made it. Jase ain't ever done a hand's turn that he wasn't obliged to do. I've chopped wood, and I've built corrals and dug ditches, and Jase has puttered around and whined that he wasn't able-bodied enough to do no heavy lifting. That there orchard out there I planted and packed water in buckets to it till I got the ditch through. Them corrals down next the river I built. I dug the post-holes, and Jase set the posts in and held 'em steady while I tamped the dirt! In winter I've hauled hay and fed the cattle; and Jase, he packed a bucket uh slop, mebby, to the pigs! If he ain't as able-bodied as I be, it's because he ain't done nothing to git strong on. He can't come around me now with that all-gone feeling uh his; I know Jase Meilke like a book."

There was more that she said about Jase. Standing there, a squat, unkempt woman with a seamed, leathery face and hard eyes now quite faded to gray, she told Billy Louise a good deal of the bitterness of the years behind; years of hardship and of slavish toil and no love to lighten it. She spoke again of Minervy, and the name brought back to Billy Louise poignant memories of her own lonely childhood and of her "pretend" playmate.

Half shyly, because she was still sometimes touched with the inarticulateness of youth, Billy Louise told Marthy a little of that playmate. "Why, do you know, every time I rode old Badger anywhere, after that day you told me about Minervy, I used to pretend that Minervy rode behind me. I used to talk to her by the hour and take her places. And up our canyon is a cave that I used to play was Minervy's cave. I had another one, and I used to go over and visit Minervy. And I had another pretend playmate —a boy-and we used to have adventures. It's a queer place; I just found that cave by accident. I don't believe there's another person in the country who knows it's there at all. Well, that's Minervy's cave to me yet. And, Marthy —" Billy Louise giggled a little and eyed the old woman with a sidelong look that would have set a young man's blood a-jump —"I hope you won't be mad; I was just a kid, and I didn't know any better. But just to show you how much I thought: I had a little pig, and I named it Minervy, after you told me about her. And mommie told me that was no name for it; it was-it wasn't a girl pig, mommie said. So I called it Man-ervy, as the next best thing." She gave Marthy another wasted glance from the corners of her eyes. "Oh, Marthy!" she cried remorsefully, setting down the gravy bowl that she might pat Marthy on her fat, age-rounded shoulder. "What a little beast I am! I shouldn't have told that; but honest, I thought it was an honor. I —I just worshiped that pig!"

Jase maundered in at that moment, and Marthy, catching up a corner of her dirty apron-Billy Louise could not remember ever seeing Marthy in a perfectly clean dress or apron-wiped away what traces of emotion her weathered face could reveal. Also, she turned and glared at Jase with what Billy Louise considered a perfectly uncalled-for animosity. In reality, Marthy was covertly looking for visible symptoms of the all-goneness. She shut her harsh lips together tightly at what she saw; Jase certainly was puffy under his watery, pink-rimmed eyes, and the withered cheeks above his thin graying beard really did have a pasty, gray look.

"D' you turn them calves out into the corral?" she demanded, her voice harder because of her secret uneasiness.

"I was goin' to, but the wind's changed into the north, 'n' I thought mebby you wouldn't want 'em out." Jase turned back aimlessly to the door. His voice was getting cracked and husky, and the deprecating note dominated pathetically all that he said. "You'll have to face the wind goin' home," he said to Billy Louise. "More 'n likely you'll be facin' snow, too. Looks bad, off that way."

"You go on and turn them calves out!" Marthy commanded him harshly. "Billy Louise ain't goin' home if it storms; I sh'd think you'd know enough to know that."

"Oh, but I'll have to go, anyway," the girl interrupted. "Mommie can't be there alone; she'd worry herself to death if I didn't show up by dark. She worries about every little thing since daddy died. I ought to have gone before-or I oughtn't to have come. But she was worrying about you, Marthy; she hadn't seen or heard of you for a month, and she was afraid you might be sick or something. Why don't you get someone to stay with you? I think you ought to."

She looked toward the door, which Jase had closed upon his departure. "If Jase should-get sick, or anything —"

"Jase ain't goin' to git sick," Marthy retorted glumly. "Yuh don't want to let him worry yuh, Billy Louise. If I'd worried every time he yowled around about being sick, I'd be dead or crazy by now. I dunno but maybe I'll have somebody to help with the work, though," she added, after a pause during which she had swiped the dish-rag around the sides of the pan once or twice, and had opened the door and thrown the water out beyond the doorstep like the sloven she was. "I got a nephew that wants to come out. He's been in a bank, but he's quit and wants to git on to a ranch. I dunno but I'll have him come, in the spring."

"Do," urged Billy Louise, perfectly unconscious of the potentialities of the future. "I hate to think of you two down here alone. I don't suppose anyone ever comes down here, except me-and that isn't often."

"Nobody's got any call to come down," said Marthy stolidly. "They sure ain't going to come for our comp'ny and there ain't nothing else to bring 'em."

"Well, there aren't many to come, you know," laughed Billy Louise, shaking out the dish towel and spreading it over two nails, as she did at home. "I'm your nearest neighbor, and I've got six miles to ride-against the wind, at that. I think I'd better start. We've got a halfbreed doing chores for us, but he has to be looked after or he neglects things. I'll not get another chance to come very soon, I'm afraid; mommie hates to have me ride around much in the winter. You send for that nephew right away, why don't you, Marthy?" It was like Billy Louise to mix command and entreaty together. "Really, I don't think Jase looks a bit well."

"A good strong steepin' of sage'll fix him all right, only he ain't sick, as I see. You take this shawl."

Billy Louise refused the shawl and ran down the twisted path fringed with long, reaching fingers of the hare berry bushes. At the stable she stopped for an aimless dialogue with Jase and then rode away, past the orchard whose leafless branches gave glimpses of the low, sod-roofed cabin, with Marthy standing rather disconsolately on the rough doorstep watching her go.

Absently she let down the bars in the narrowest place in the gorge and lifted them into their rude sockets after she had led her horse through. All through the years since Marthy had gone down that rocky gash in search of Buck and Bawley, no human being had entered or left the Cove save through that narrow opening. The tingle of romance which swept always the nerves of the girl when she rode that way fastened upon her now. She wished the Cove belonged to her; she thought she would like to live in a place like that, with warlike Indians all around and that gorge to guard day and night. She wished she had been Marthy, discovering that place and taming it, little by little, in solitary achievement the sweeter because it had been hard.

"It's a bigger thing," said Billy Louise aloud to her horse, "to make a home here in this wilderness, than to write the greatest poem in the world or paint the greatest picture or-anything. I wish..."

Blue was climbing steadily out of the gorge, twitching an ear backward with flattering attention when his lady spoke. He held it so for a minute, waiting for that sentence to be finished, perhaps; for he was wise beyond his kind-was Blue. But his lady was staring at the rock wall they were passing then, where the winds and the cold and heat had carved jutting ledges into the crude form of cabbages; though Billy Louise preferred to call them roses. Always they struck her with a new wonder, as if she saw them for the first time. Blue went on, calmly stepping over this rock and, around that as if it were the simplest thing in the world to find sure footing and carry his lady smoothly up that trail. He threw up his head so suddenly that Billy Louise was startled out of her aimless dreamings, and pointed nose and ears toward the little creek-bottom above, where Marthy had lighted her camp-fire long and long ago.

A few steps farther, and Blue stopped short in the trail to look and listen. Billy Louise could see the nervous twitchings of his muscles under the skin of neck and shoulders, and she smiled to herself. Nothing could ever come upon her unaware when she rode alone, so long as she rode Blue. A hunting dog was not more keenly alive to his surroundings.

"Go on, Blue," she commanded after a minute. "If it's a bear or anything like that, you can make a run for it; if it's a wolf, I'll shoot it. You needn't stand here all night, anyway."

Blue went on, out from behind the willow growth that hid the open. He returned to his calm, picking a smooth trail through the scattered rocks and tiny washouts. It was the girl's turn to stare and speculate. She did not know this horseman who sat negligently in the saddle and looked up at the cedar-grown bluff beyond, while his horse stood knee-deep in the little stream. She did not know him; and there were not so many travelers in the land that strangers were a matter of indifference.

Blue welcomed the horse with a democratic nicker and went forward briskly. And the rider turned his head, eyed the girl sharply as she came up, and nodded a cursory greeting. His horse lifted its head to look, decided that it wanted another swallow or two, and lowered its muzzle again to the water.

Billy Louise could not form any opinion of the man's age or personality, for he was encased in a wolfskin coat which covered him completely from hatbrim to ankles. She got an impression of a thin, dark face, and a sharp glance from eyes that seemed dark also. There was a thin, high nose, and beyond that Billy Louise did not look. If she had, the mouth must certainly have reassured her somewhat.

Blue stepped nonchalantly down into the stream beside the strange horse and went across without stopping to drink. The strange horse moved on also, as if that were the natural thing to do-which it was, since chance sent them traveling the same trail. Billy Louise set her teeth together with the queer little vicious click that had always been her habit when she felt thwarted and constrained to yield to circumstances, and straightened herself in the saddle.

"Looks like a storm," the fur-coated one observed, with a perfectly transparent attempt to lighten the awkwardness.

Billy Louise tilted her chin upward and gazed at the gray sweep of clouds moving sullenly toward the mountains at her back. She glanced at the man and caught him looking intently at her face.

He did not look away immediately, as he should have done, and Billy Louise felt a little heat-wave of embarrassment, emphasized by resentment.

"Are you going far?" he queried in the same tone he had employed before.

"Six miles," she answered shortly, though she tried to be decently civil.

"I've about eighteen," he said. "Looks like we'll both get caught out in a blizzard."

Certainly, he had a pleasant enough voice-and after all it was not his fault that he happened to be at the crossing when she rode out of the gorge. Billy Louise, in common justice, laid aside her resentment and looked at him with a hint of a smile at the corners of her lips.

"That's what we have to expect when we travel in this country in the winter," she replied. "Eighteen miles will take you long after dark."

"Well, I was sort of figuring on putting up at some ranch, if it got too bad. There's a ranch somewhere ahead, on the Wolverine, isn't there?"

"Yes." Billy Louise bit her lip; but hospitality is an unwritten law of the West —a law not to be lightly broken. "That's where I live. We'll be glad to have you stop there, of course."

The stranger must have felt and admired the unconscious dignity of her tone and words, for he thanked her simply and refrained from looking too intently at her face.

Fine siftings of snow, like meal flung down from a gigantic sieve, swept into their faces as they rode on. The man turned his face toward her after a long silence. She was riding with bowed head and face half turned from him and the wind alike.

"You'd better ride on ahead and get in out of this," he said curtly. "Your horse is fresh. It's going to be worse and more of it, before long; this cayuse of mine has had thirty miles or so of rough going."

"I think I'd better wait for you," she said primly. "There are bad places where the trail goes close to the bluff, and the lava rock will be slippery with this snow. And it's getting dark so fast that a stranger might go over."

"If that's the case, the sooner you are past the bad places the better. I'm all right. You drift along."

Billy Louise speculated briefly upon the note of calm authority in his voice. He did not know, evidently, that she was more accustomed to giving commands than to obeying them; her lips gave a little quirk of amusement at his mistake.

"You go on. I don't want a guide." He tilted his head peremptorily toward the blurred trail ahead.

Billy Louise laughed a little. She did not feel in the least embarrassed now. "Do you never get what you don't want?" she asked him mildly. "I'd a lot rather lead you past those places than have you go over the edge," she said, "because nobody could get you up, or even go down and bury you decently. It wouldn't be a bit nice. It's much simpler to keep you on top."

He said something, but Billy Louise could not hear what it was; she suspected him of swearing. She rode on in silence.

"Blue's a dandy horse on bad trails and in the dark," she observed companionably at last. "He simply can't lose his footing or his way."

"Yes? That's nice."

Billy Louise felt like putting out her tongue at him, for the cool remoteness of his tone. It would serve him right to ride on and let him break his neck over the bluff if he wanted to. She shut her teeth together and turned her face away from him.

So, in silence and with no very good feeling between them, they went precariously down the steep hill (the hill up which Marthy and the oxen and Jase had toiled so laboriously, twenty-seven years before) and across the tiny flat to where the cabin window winked a welcome at them through the storm.

Chapter III. A Book, a Bannock, and a Bed

Blue led the way straight to the low, dirt-roofed stable of logs and stopped with his nose against the closed door. Billy Louise herself was deceived by the whirl of snow and would have missed the stable entirely if the leadership had been hers. She patted Blue gratefully on the shoulder when she unsaddled him. She groped with her fingers for the wooden peg in the wall where the saddle should hang, failed to find it, and so laid the saddle down against the logs and covered it with the blanket.

"Just turn your horse in loose," she directed the man shortly. "Blue won't fight, and I think the rest of the horses are in the other part. And come on to the house."

It pleased her a little to see that he obeyed her without protest; but she was not so pleased at his silence, and she led the way rather indignantly toward the winking eye which was the cabin's window.

At the sound of their feet on the wide doorstep, her mother pulled open the door and stood fair in the light, looking out with the anxious look which had lived so long in her face that it had lines of its own chiseled deep in her forehead and at the sides of her mouth.

"Is that you, Billy Louise? Oh, ain't Peter Howling Dog with you? What makes you so terrible late, Billy Louise? Come right in, stranger. I don't know your name, but I don't need to know it. A storm like this is all the interduction a fellow needs, I guess." She smiled, at that. She had a nice smile, with a little resemblance to Billy Louise, except that the worried, inquiring look never left her eyes; as if she had once waited long for bad news, and had met everyone with anxious, eager questioning, and her eyes had never changed afterwards. Billy Louise glanced at her with her calm, measuring look, making the contrast very sharp between the two.

"What about Peter?" she asked. "Isn't he here?"

"No, and he ain't been since an hour or so after you left. He saddled up and rode off down the river-to the reservation, I reckon."

"Then the chores aren't done, I suppose." Billy Louise went over and took a lantern down from its nail, turning up the wick so that she could light it with the candle. "Go up to the fire and thaw out," she invited the man. "We'll have supper in a few minutes."

Instead he reached out and took the lantern from her as soon as she had lighted it. "You go to the fire yourself," he said. "I'll do what's necessary outside."

"Why-y —" Billy Louise, her fingers still clinging to the lantern, looked up at him. He was staring down at her with that intent look she had objected to on the trail, but she saw his mouth, and the little smile that hid just back of his lips. She smiled back without knowing it. "I'll have to go along, anyway. There are cows to milk and you couldn't very well find the cow-stable alone."

"Think not?"

Billy Louise had been perfectly furious at that tone, out on the trail. Now that she could see his lips and their little twitching to keep back the smile, she did not mind the tone at all. She had turned away to get the milk pails, and now she gave him a sidelong look, of the kind that had been utterly wasted upon Marthy. The man met it and immediately turned his attention to the lantern wick, which needed nice adjustment before its blaze quite pleased him; he was not a Marthy to receive such a look unmoved.

Together they went out again into the storm they had left so eagerly. Billy Louise showed him where was the pitchfork and the hay, and then did the milking while he piled full the mangers. After that they went together and turned the shivering work horses into the stable from the corral where they huddled, rumps to the storm; and the man lifted great forkfuls of hay and carried it into their stalls, while Billy Louise held the lantern high over her head like a western Liberty. They did not talk much, except when there was need for speech; but they were beginning to feel a little glow of companionship by the time they were ready to fight their way against the blizzard to the house, Billy Louise going before with the lantern, while the man followed close behind, carrying the two pails of milk that was already freezing in little crystals to the tin.

"Did you get everything done? You must be half froze-and starved into the bargin." Mrs. MacDonald, as is the way of some women who know the weight of isolation, had a habit of talking with a nervous haste at times, and of relapsing into long, brooding silences afterwards. She talked now, while she pulled a pan of hot, brown biscuits from the oven, poured the tea, and turned crisp, browned potatoes out of a frying-pan into a deep, white bowl. She wondered, over and over, why Peter Howling Dog had left and why he did not return. She said that was the way, when you depended on Indians for anything. She did wish there was a white man to be had. She asked after Marthy and Jase and gave Billy Louise no opportunity to tell her anything.

Billy Louise glanced often at the man, who did not look in the least as she had fancied, except that he really did have a high nose and terribly keen eyes with something behind the keenness that baffled her. And his mouth was pleasant, especially when that smile hid just behind his lips; also, she liked his hair, which was thick and brown, with hints of red in it here and there, and a strong inclination to curl where it was longest. She had known he was tall when he stepped into the light of the door; now she saw that he was slim to the point of leanness, with square shoulders and a nervous quickness when he moved. His fingers were never idle; when he was not eating, he rolled bits of biscuit into tiny, soggy balls beside his plate, or played a soft tattoo with his fork.

"I didn't quite catch your name, mister," her mother said finally. "But take another biscuit, anyway."

"Warren is my name," returned the man, with that hidden smile because she had never before given him any opportunity to tell it. "Ward Warren. I've got a claim over on Mill Creek."

Billy Louise gave a little gasp and distractedly poured two spoons of sugar in her tea, although she hated it sweetened.

I've got to tell you why, even at the price of digression. Long ago, when Billy Louise was twelve or so, and lived largely in a dream world of her own with Minervy for her "pretend" playmate, she had one day chanced upon a paragraph in a paper that had come from town wrapped around a package of matches. It was all about Ward Warren. The name caught her fancy, and the text of the paragraph seized upon her imagination. Until school filled her mind with other things, she had built adventures without end in which Ward Warren was the central figure. Up the canyon at the caves, she sometimes pretended that Ward Warren had abducted Minervy and that she must lead the rescue. Sometimes, when she rode in the hills, Ward Warren abducted her and led her into strange places where she tried to shiver in honest dread. Often and often, however, Ward Warren was a fugitive who came to her for help; then she would take him to Minervy's cave and hide him, perhaps; or she would mount her horse and lead him, by devious ways, to safety, and upon some hilltop from which she could point out the route he must follow, she would bid him a touching adieu and beseech him, in the impossible language of some old romancer, to go and lead a blameless life. Sitting there at the table opposite him, stirring the sugar heedlessly into her tea, one favorite exhortation returned from her dream-world, clear as if she had just spoken it aloud. "Go, and sin no more; and if perchance you will in some distant far land send me a kind thought, that will be reward enough for what I have done this day. Farewell, Ward Warren-Kismet."

The lips of Billy Louise smiled and stopped just short of laughter, and she looked across at Ward Warren as if she expected him to laugh also at that frightfully virtuous though stilted adieu. She found him looking straight at her in that intent fashion that seemed as if he would see through and all around her and her thoughts. He was not smiling at all. His mouth was pulled into a certain bitter understanding; indeed, he looked exactly as if Billy Louise had dealt him a deliberate affront which he could neither parry nor fling back at her, but must endure with what stoicism he might.

Billy Louise blushed guiltily, took an unpremeditated swallow of tea, and grimaced over the sickish sweetness of it. She got up and emptied the tea into the slop bucket, and loitered over the refilling of the cup so that when she returned to the table she was at least outwardly calm. She felt another quick, keen glance from across the table, but she helped herself composedly to the cream and listened to her mother with flattering attention.

"Jase has got all-gone feelings now, mommie," she remarked irrelevantly during a brief pause and relapsed into silence again. She knew that was good for at least five minutes of straight monologue, with her mother in that talking mood. She finished her supper while Warren listened abstractedly to a complete biography of the Meilkes and learned all about Marthy's energy and Jase's shiftlessness.

"Ward Warren!" Billy Louise was saying to herself. "Did you ever in your life-it's exactly as if Minervy should come to life and walk in. Ward Warren! There couldn't possibly be two Ward Warrens; it's such an odd name. Well!"

Then she went mentally over that paragraph. She wished she did not remember every single word of it, but she did. And she was afraid to look at him after that. And she wanted to, dreadfully. She felt as though he belonged to her. Why, he was her old playmate! And she had saved his life hundreds of times, at immense risks to herself; and he had always been her devoted slave afterwards, and never failed to appear at the precise moment when she was beset by Indians or robbers or something, and in dire need. The blood he had shed in her behalf! At that point Billy Louise startled herself and the others by suddenly laughing out loud at the memory of one time when Ward Warren had killed enough Indians to fill a deep washout so that he might carry her across to the other side!

"Is there anything funny about Jase Meilke dying, Billy Louise?" her mother asked her in a perfectly shocked tone.

"No —I was thinking of something else." She glanced at the man eyeing her so distrustfully from across the table and gurgled again. It was terribly silly, but she simply could not help seeing Ward Warren calmly filling that washout with dead Indians so that he might carry her across it in his arms. The more she tried to forget that, the funnier it became. She ended by leaving the table and retiring precipitately to her own tiny room in the lean-to where she buried her face as deep as it would go in a puffy pillow of wild duck feathers.

He, poor devil, could not be expected to know just what had amused her so; he did know that it somehow concerned himself, however. He took up his position-mentally-behind the wall of aloofness which stood between himself and an unfriendly world, and when Billy Louise came out later to help with the dishes, he was sitting absorbed in a book.

Billy Louise got out her algebra and a slate and began to ponder the problem of a much-handicapped goat's feeding-ground. Ward Warren read and read and read and never looked up from the pages. Never in her life had she seen a man read as he read; hungrily, as a starved man eats; rapidly, his eyes traveling like a shuttle across the page; down, down-flip a leaf quickly and let the shuttle-glance go on. Billy Louise let her slate, with the goat problem unsolved, lie in her lap while she watched him. When she finally became curious enough to decipher the name of the book-she had three or four in that dull, brown binding-and saw that he was reading *The Ring and the Book*, she felt stunned. She read Browning just as she drank sage tea; it was supposed to be good for her. Her English teacher had given her that book. She never would have believed that any living human could read it as Ward Warren was reading it now; avidly, absorbedly, lost to his surroundings-to her own presence, if you please! Billy Louise glanced at her mother. That lady, having discovered that her guest's gloves needed mending, was working over them with pieces of Indian-tanned buckskin and beeswaxed thread, the picture of domestic content.

Billy Louise sighed. She shifted her chair. She got up and put a heavy chunk of wood on the fire and glanced over her shoulder at the man to see if he were going to take the hint and offer to help. She came back and stood close to him while she selected, with great deliberation, a book from the shelf beside his head. And Ward Warren, perfectly normal and not over twenty-five or so, pushed his chair out of her way with a purely mechanical movement, and read and read, and actually was too absorbed to feel her nearness. And he really was reading *The Ring and the Book*; Billy Louise was rude enough to look over his shoulder to make sure of that. She gave up, then, and though she picked a book at random from the shelf, she did not attempt to read it. She went to her room and made it ready for their guest, and after that she went to bed in her mother's room; and she thought and thought and did a lot of wondering about Life and about Ward Warren. She heard him go to bed, after a long while, and she wondered if he had finished the book first.

The next morning the blizzard raged so that he stayed as a matter of course. Peter Howling Dog had not returned, so Warren did the chores and would not let Billy Louise help with anything. He filled the wood-box, piled great chunks of wood by the fireplace, and saw that the water-pails were full to the icy brims. He talked a little, and Billy Louise discovered that he was quick to see a joke, and that he simply could not be caught napping, but had always a retort ready for her. That was true until after dinner, when he picked up a book again. When that happened, he was dead to the world bounded by the coulee walls, and he did not show any symptoms of consciousness until he had reached the last page, just when the light was growing dim and blurring the lines so that he must hold the pages within six inches of his eyes. He closed the book with a long breath, placed it accurately upon the shelf where it had stood since Billy Louise came home from school, and picked up his hat and gloves. It was time to wade out through the snow and feed the stock and bring in more wood.

"I wish we could get him to stay all winter, instead of that Peter Howling Dog," Mrs. MacDonald said anxiously, after he had gone out. "I just know Peter's off drinking. I don't think he's a safe man to have around, Billy Louise. I didn't when you hired him. I haven't felt easy a minute with him on the place. I wish you'd hire Mr. Warren, Billy Louise. He's nice and quiet —"

"And he's got a ranch of his own. He doesn't strike me as a man who wants a job milking two cows and carrying slop to the pigs, mommie."

"Well, I'd feel a lot easier if we had him instead of that breed; only we ain't even got the breed, half the time. This is the third time he's disappeared, in the two months we've had him. I really think you ought to speak to Mr. Warren, Billy Louise."

"Speak to him yourself. You're the one that wants him," Billy Louise answered somewhat sharply. She adored her mother; but if she had to run the ranch, she did wish her mother would not interfere and give advice just at the wrong time.

"Well, you needn't be cross about it; you know yourself that Peter can't be depended on a minute. There he went off yesterday and never fed the pigs their noon slop, and I had to carry it out myself. And my lumbago has bothered me ever since, just like it was going to give me another spell. You can't be here all the time, Billy Louise-leastways you ain't; and Peter —"

"Oh, good gracious, mommie! I told you to hire the man if you want him. Only Ward Warren isn't —"

Ward Warren pushed open the door and looked from one to the other, his eyes two question marks. "Isn't —what?" he asked and shut the door behind him with the air of one who is ready for anything.

"Isn't the kind of man who wants to hire out to do chores," Billy Louise finished and looked at him straight. "Are you? Mommie wants to hire you."

"Oh. Well, I was just about to ask for the job, anyway." He laughed, and the distrust left his eyes. "As a matter of fact, I was going over to Jim Larson's to hang out for the rest of the winter and get away from the lonesomeness of the hills. The old Turk's a pretty good friend of mine. But it looks to me as if you two needed something around that looks like a man a heap more than Jim does. I know Peter Howling Dog to a fare-you-well; you'll be all to the good if he forgets to come back. So if you'll stake me to a meal now and then, and a place to sleep, I'll be glad to see you through the winter-or until you get some white man to take my place." He took up the two water-pails and waited, glancing from one to the other with that repressed smile which Billy Louise was beginning to look for in his face.

Now that matters had approached the point of decision, her mother stood looking at her help-lessly, waiting for her to speak. Billy Louise drew herself up primly and ended by contradicting the action. She gave him the sidelong glance which he was least prepared to withstand-though in justice to Billy Louise, she was absolutely unconscious of its general effectiveness-and twisted her lips whimsically.

"We'll stake you to a book, a bannock, and a bed if you want to stay, Mr. Warren," she said quite soberly. "Also to a pitchfork and an axe, if you like, and regular wages."

His eyes went to her and steadied there with the intent expression in them. "Thanks. Cut out the wages, and I'll take the offer just as it stands," he told her and pulled his hat farther down on his head. "She's going to be one stormy night, lay-dees," he added in quite another tone, on his way to the door. "Five o'clock by the town clock, and al-ll's well!" This last in still another tone, as he pushed out against the swooping wind and pulled the door shut with a slam. They heard him whistling a shrill, rollicking air on his way to the creek; at least, it sounded rollicking, the way he whistled it.

"That's *The Old Chisholm Trail* he's whistling," Billy Louise observed under her breath, smil-ing reminiscently. "The very song I used to pretend he always sang when he came down the canyon to rescue Minervy and me! But of course —I knew all the time he's a cowboy; it said so —"

The whistling broke and he began to sing at the top of a clear, strong-lunged voice, that old, old trail song beloved of punchers the West over:

"Oh, it's cloudy in the West and a-lookin' like rain,

And my damned old slicker's in the wagon again,

Coma ti yi youpy, youpy-a, youpy-a,

Coma ti yi youpy, youpy-a!"

"What did you say, Billy Louise? I'm sure it's a comfort to have him here, and you see he was glad and willing —"

But Billy Louise was holding the door open half an inch, listening and slipping back into the child-world wherein Ward Warren came singing down the canyon to rescue her and Minervy. The words came gustily from the creek down the slope:

"No chaps, no slicker, and a-pourin' down rain,

And I swear by the Lord I'll never night-herd again,

Coma ti yi youpy, youpy-a, youpy-a,

Coma ti yi youpy, youpy-a!
"Feet in the stirrups and seat in the saddle,

I hung and rattled with them long-horn cattle,

Coma ti yi —"

"Do shut the door, Billy Louise! What you want to stand there like that for? And the wind freezing everything inside! I can feel a terrible draught on my feet and ankles, and you know what that leads to."

So Billy Louise closed the door and laid another alder root on the coals in the fireplace, the while her mind was given over to dreamy speculations, and the words of that old trail song ran on in her memory though she could no longer hear him singing. Her mother talked on about

Peter and the storm and this man who had ridden straight from the land of daydreams to her door, but the girl was not listening.

"Now ain't you relieved, yourself, that he's going to stay?"

Billy Louise, kneeling on the hearth and staring abstractedly into the fire, came back with a jerk to reality. The little smile that had been in her eyes and on her lips fled back with the dreams that had brought it. She gave her shoulders an impatient twitch and got up.

"Oh —I guess he'll be more agreeable to have around than Peter," she admitted taciturnly; which was as close to her real opinion of the man as a mere mother might hope to come.

Chapter IV. "Old Dame Fortune's Used me for a Football"

Ward Warren sat before the fireplace with a cigarette long gone cold in his fingers and stared into the blaze until the blaze died to bright-glowing coals, and the coals filmed and shrank down into the bed of ashes. Billy Louise had spoken to him twice, and he had not answered. She had swept all around him, and he had shifted his feet out of her way, and later his chair, like a man in his sleep who turns from an unaccustomed light or draws the covers over shoulders growing chilled, without any real consciousness of what he does. Billy Louise put away the broom, hung the dustpan on its nail behind the door, and stood looking at Ward curiously and with some resentment; this was not the first time he had gone into fits of abstraction as deep as his absorption in the books he read so hungrily. He had been at the Wolverine a month, and they were pretty well acquainted by now and inclined to friendliness when Ward threw off his moodiness and his air of holding himself ready for some affront which he seemed to expect. But for all that the distrust never quite left his eyes, and there were times like this when he was absolutely oblivious to her presence.

Billy Louise suddenly lost patience. She stooped and picked up a bit of bark the size of her thumb and threw it at Ward, with a little, vexed twist of her lips. She had a fine accuracy of aim-she hit him on the nape of the neck, just where his hair came down in a queer little curly "cow-lick" in the middle.

Ward jumped up and whirled, and when he faced Billy Louise he had a gun gripped in the fingers that had held the cigarette so loosely. In his eyes was the glare which a man turns upon his deadliest enemy, perhaps, but seldom indeed upon a girl. So they faced each other, while Billy Louise backed against the wall and took two sharp breaths.

Ward relaxed; a shamed flush reddened his whole face. He shoved the gun back inside the belt of his trousers-Billy Louise had never dreamed that he carried any weapon save his haughty aloofness of manner-and with a little snort of self-disgust dropped back into the chair. He did not stare again into the fire, however; he folded his arms upon the high chairback and laid his face down upon them, like a woman who is hurt to the point of tears and yet will not weep. His booted feet were thrust toward the dying coals, his whole attitude spoke of utter desolation-of a loneliness beyond words.

Billy Louise set her teeth hard together to keep back the tears of sympathy. Suffering of any sort always wrung the tender heart of her. But suffering like this-never in her life had she seen anything like it. She had seen her father angry, discouraged, morose. She had seen men fight. She had soothed her mother's grief, which expressed itself in tears and lamentations. But this hidden hurt, this stoical suffering that she had seen often and often in Ward's eyes and that sent his head down now upon his arms — She went to him and laid her two hands on his shoulders without even thinking that this was the first time she had ever touched him.

"Don't!" she said, half whispering so that she would not waken her mother, in bed with an attack of lumbago. "I —I didn't know. Ward, listen to me! Whatever it is, can't you tell me? You —I'm your friend. Don't look as if you-you hadn't a friend on earth!"

Still he did not move or give any sign that he heard. Billy Louise had no thought of coquetry. Her heart ached with pity and a longing to help him. She slid one hand up and pinched his ear, just as she would playfully tweak the ear of a child.

"Ward, you mustn't. I've seen you think and think and look as if you hadn't a friend on earth. You mustn't. I suppose you've got lots of friends who'd stand by you through anything. Anyway, you've got me, and —I understand all about it." She whispered those last words, and her heart thumped heavily with trepidation after she had spoken.

Ward raised his head, caught one of her hands and held it fast while he looked deep into her eyes. He was searching, questioning, measuring, and he was doing it without uttering a word. The plummet dropped straight into the clear, sweet depths of her soul. If it did not reach the bottom, he was satisfied with the soundings he took. He drew a deep breath and gave her hand a little squeeze and let it go.

"Did I scare you? I'm sorry," he said, speaking in a hushed tone because of the woman in the next room. "I was thinking about a man I may meet some day; and if I do meet him, the chances are I'll kill him. I —didn't —I forgot where I was —" He threw out a hand in a gesture that amply completed explanation and apology and fumbled in his pocket for tobacco and papers. Abstractedly he began the making of a cigarette.

Billy Louise put wood on the fire, pulled up a square, calico-padded stool, and sat down. She waited, and she had the wisdom to wait in complete silence.

Ward leaned forward with a twig in his hand, got it ablaze, and lighted his cigarette. He did not look at Billy Louise until he had taken a whiff or two. Then he stared at her for a full minute, and ended by flipping the charred twig playfully into her lap, and laughing a little because she jumped.

"What made you catch your breath when I told my name that night I came?" he asked quizzically, but with a tensity behind the lightness of his tone and behind the little smile in his eyes as well. "Where had you ever heard of me before?"

Billy Louise gasped again, sent a lightning-thought into the future, and answered more casually than she had hoped she could.

"When I was a kid I ran across the name-somewhere-and I used it to play with —"

"Yes?"

"You know —I was always making believe different things. I never had anyone to play with in my life, so I had a pretend-girl, named Minervy. And I had you. I used to have you rescue us from Indians and things, but mostly you were a road-agent or a robber, and when you weren't holding me or Minervy for ransom, I was generally leading you over some most ungodly trails, saving you from posses and things. I used," said Billy Louise, forcing a laugh, "to have some wild old times with you, believe me! So when you told your name, why-it was just like-you know; it was exactly like having a doll come to life!"

He eyed her fixedly until she tingled with nervousness.

"Yes-and what about-understanding all about it? Do you?" He drew in his under lip, let it go, and drew it again between his teeth, while he frowned at her thoughtfully. "Do you understand all about it?" he insisted, leaning toward her and never once taking that boring gaze from her face.

"I —well, I —do-some of it anyway." Billy Louise lifted a hand spasmodically to her throat. This was digging deeper into the agonies of life than she had ever gone before. "What was in the paper," she whispered later, as if his eyes were drawing it from her by force.

"What was that? What did it say?"

"I —I —what difference does it make, what it said?" Billy Louise turned imploring eyes upon him. Her breath was coming fast and uneven. "It doesn't matter-to me-in the least. It-didn't say much. I —can't tell exactly —" She was growing white around the mouth. The horror of being compelled to say, out loud-and to him!

"I didn't know there was a woman in the world like you," Ward said irrelevantly and looked into the fire. "I thought women were just soft things a man had to take care of and carry along through life, a dead weight when they weren't worse. I never knew a woman could be a friend-the kind of friend a man can be." He threw his cigarette into the fire and watched the paper shrivel swiftly and the tobacco turn into a thin, blue smoke-spiral.

"Life's a queer thing," he said, taking a different angle. "I started out with big notions about the things I'd do. Maybe I started wrong, but for a kid with nobody to point the trail for him, I don't think I did so worse-till old Dame Fortune spotted me in the crowd and proceeded to use me for a football." He leaned an elbow on one knee and stared hard at a burning brand that was getting ready to fall and send up a stream of sparks. Then he turned his head quite unexpectedly and looked at Billy Louise. "What was it you read?" he asked abruptly.

"I —don't like to-say it," she whispered unsteadily.

"Well, you needn't. I'll say it for you, when I come to it. There's a lot before that."

Ward Warren had never before opened his soul to any human; not completely. Perhaps, sitting that evening in the deepening dusk, with the firelight lighting swiftly the brooding face of the girl and afterward veiling it softly with shadows, perhaps even then there were desolate places in his life which his words did not touch. But so much as a man may put into words, Ward told her; more, a great deal more, than he would ever tell to any other woman as long as he lived. More perhaps than he would ever tell to any man. And in it all there was no word of love. It was of what lay behind him that he talked. The low, even murmur of his voice was broken by long, brooding silences, when the two stared into the shifting flames and saw there the things his words had conjured. Sometimes the eyes of Billy Louise were soft with sympathy. Sometimes they were wide and held the light of horror. Once, with a small sob that had no tears, she reached out and clutched his arm. "Oh, don't!" she gasped. "Don't go on telling—I—I can't bear to listen to that!"

"It isn't nice for a woman to listen to, I guess," Ward gritted. "I know it was hell to stand, but—" He was silent so long after that, and his eyes grew so intent and so somber while he stared, that Billy Louise pulled at his sleeve to recall him.

"Skip that part and tell me—"

Ward took up the story and told her much; more than she had ever dreamed could be. I can't repeat any of it; what he said was for Billy Louise to know and none other.

It was late when she finally rose from the stool and lighted the lamp because her mother woke and called to her. Ward went out to turn the horses into the stable and fasten the door. He should have sheltered them two hours before. Billy Louise should long ago have made tea and toast for her mother, for that matter. But when life's big, bitter problems confront one, little things are usually forgotten.

They came back to everyday realities, though the spell which Ward's impulsive unburdening had woven still wrapped them in that close companionship of complete understanding. They played checkers for an hour or so and then went to bed. Billy Louise lay in a waking nightmare because of all the hard things she had heard about life. Ward stared up into the dark and could not lose himself in sleep, because he had opened the door upon the evil places in his memory and let out all the trooping devils that lived there.

After that, though there was never any word of love between them, Billy Louise, with the sure instinct of a woman innately pure, watched unobtrusively for signs of those fits of bitter brooding; watched and drove them off with various weapons of her own. Sometimes she cheerfully declared that she was bored to death, and wasn't Ward just dying for a game of "rob casino"? Sometimes she simply teased him into retaliation. Frequently she insisted that he repeat the things he had learned by heart, of poetry or humorous prose, for his memory was almost uncanny in its tenacity. She discovered quite early, and by accident, that she had only to shake her head in a certain way and declaim: "Ah, Tam, noo, Tam, thou'lt get thy faring-In hell they'll roast thee like a herring,"—she had only to say that to make him laugh and repeat the whole of *Tam O'Shanter's Ride* with a perfectly devilish zest for poor Tam's misfortunes, and an accent which made her suspect who were his ancestors.

Billy Louise meant only to wean him from his bitterness against Life, and to convince him, by a somewhat roundabout method since at heart she was scared to death of his aloofness, that he was not "old lady Fortune's football" as he sometimes pessimistically declared. At thirteen she had mixed him with her dreams and led him by difficult trails to safety from the imaginary enemies that pursued him. At nineteen she unconsciously mixed him with her life and led him-more surely than in her dreams, and by a far more difficult trail, had she only known it-safe away from the devils of memory and a distrust of life that pursued him more relentlessly than any human foe.

She only meant to wean him from pessimism and rebuild within him a healthy appetite for life. If she did more than that, she did not know it then; for Ward Warren had learned, along with other hard lessons, the art of keeping his thoughts locked safely away, and of using his face as a mask to hide even the doorway to his real self. Only his eyes turned traitors sometimes when he looked at Billy Louise; though she, being a somewhat self-centered young person, never quite read what they tried to betray.

She took him up the canyon and showed him her cave and Minervy's. And she had the doubtful satisfaction of seeing him doubled over the saddle-horn in a paroxysm of laughter when she led him to the historical washout and recounted the feat of the dead Indians with which he had made a safe passing for her.

"Well, they did it in history," she defended at last, her cheeks redder than was perfectly normal. "I read about it-at Waterloo when the Duke of Wellington-wasn't it? You needn't laugh as if it couldn't be done. It was that sunken-road business put it into my head in the first place; and I think you ought to feel flattered."

"I do," gasped Ward, wiping his eyes. "Say, I was some bandit, wasn't I, William Louisa?"

Billy Louise looked at him sidewise. "No, you weren't any bandit at all-then. You were a kind scout, that time. I was here, all surrounded by Indians and saying the Lord's prayer with my hair all down my back like mommie's Rock of Ages picture-will you shut up laughing? —and you came riding up that draw over there on a big, black horse named Sultan (You needn't snort; I still think Sultan's a dandy name for a horse!). And you hollered to me to get behind that rock, over there. And I quit at 'Forgive us our debts' —daddy always had so many! —and hiked for the rock. And you commenced shooting — Oh, I'm not going to tell you a single other pretend!" She sulked then, which was quite as diverting as the most hair-raising "pretend" she had ever told him and held Ward's attention unflaggingly until they were half way home.

"Sing the *Chisholm Trail*," she commanded, when her temper was sunshiny again. This had been a particularly moody day for Ward, and Billy Louise felt that extra effort was required to rout the memory-devils. "Daddy knew a little of it, and old Jake Summers used to sing more, but I never did hear it all."

"Ladies don't, as a general thing," Ward replied, biting his lips.

"Why? I know there's about forty verses, and some of them are kind of sweary ones; but go ahead and sing it. I don't mind damn now and then."

This sublime innocence was also diverting, even to a man haunted by the devils of memory. Ward's lips twitched, and a flush warmed his cheek-bones at the mere thought of singing it all in her presence. "I'll sing all of *Sam Bass*, if you like," he temporized, with a grin.

"Oh, I hate *Sam Bass*! We had a Dutchman working for us when I was just a kid, and he was forever bawling out: 'Sa-am Pass was porn in Injiany, it was-s hiss natiff ho-o-ome!'"

Billy Louise was a pretty good mimic. She had Ward doubled over the horn again and shouting so that the canyon walls roared echoes for three full minutes. "I've always wanted to hear the *Chisholm Trail*. I know how it was sung from Mexico north on the old cattle-trails, and how every ambitious puncher who had enough imagination and could make a rhyme, added a verse or so, till it's really a —a classic of the cow-camps."

"Ye-es —it sure is all that." Ward eyed her furtively.

"And with that memory of yours, I simply know that you can sing every single word of it," Billy Louise went on pitilessly-and innocently. "You're a cowpuncher yourself, and you must have heard it all, at one time and another; and I don't believe you ever forgot a thing in your life." She caught her breath there, conscience-stricken, and added hastily and imperiously, "So go on-begin at the beginning and sing it all. I'll keep tab and see if you sing forty verses." And she prompted coaxingly:

"Come along, boys, and listen to my tale,

I'll tell you of my troubles on the old Chisholm trail,

Coma ti yi —"

and nodded her head approvingly when Ward took up the ditty where she left off and sang it with the rollicking enthusiasm which only a man who has soothed restless cattle on a stormy night can put into the doggerel.

He did not sing the whole forty verses, for good and sufficient reasons best known to punchers themselves. But, with swift, shamed skipping of certain lines and some hasty revisions, he actually did sing thirty, and Billy Louise was so engrossed that she forgot to count them and never suspected the omissions; for some of the verses were quite "sweary" enough to account for his hesitation.

The singing of those thirty verses brought a reminiscent mood upon the singer. For the rest of the way, which they rode at a walk, Ward sat very much upon one side of the saddle, with his body facing Billy Louise and his foot dangling free of the stirrup, and told her tales of trail-herds, and the cow-camps, and of funny things that had happened on the range. His "I remember one time" opened the door to a more fascinating world than Billy Louise's dream-world, because this other world was real.

So, from pure accident, she hit upon the most effective of all weapons with which to fight the memory-devils. She led Ward to remembering the pleasanter parts of his past life and to telling her of them.

When spring came at last, and he rode regretfully back to his claim on Mill Greek, he was not at all the morose Ward Warren who had ridden down to the Wolverine that stormy night in January. The distrust had left his eyes, and that guarded remoteness was gone from his manner. He thought and he planned as other men thought and planned, and looked into the future eagerly, and dreamed dreams of his own; dreams that brought the hidden smile often to his lips and his eyes.

Still, the thing those dreams were built upon was yet locked tight in his heart, and not even Billy Louise, whose instinct was so keen and so sure in all things else, knew anything of them or of the bright-hued hope they were built upon. Fortune's football was making ready to fight desperately to become captain of the game, that he might be something more to Billy Louise.

Chapter V. Marthy Buries Her Dead and Greets Her Nephew

Jase did not move or give his customary, querulous grunt when Marthy nudged him at daylight, one morning in mid-April. Marthy gave another poke with her elbow and lay still, numbed by a sudden dread. She moved cautiously out of the bed and half across the cramped room before she turned her head toward him. Then she stood still and looked and looked, her hard face growing each moment more pinched and stony and gray.

Jase had died while the coyotes were yapping their dawn-song up on the rim of the Cove. He lay rigid under the coarse, gray blanket, the flesh of his face drawn close to the bones, his skimpy, gray beard tilted upward.

Marthy's jaw set into a harsher outline than ever. She dressed with slow, heavy movements and went out and fed the stock. In stolid calm she did the milking and turned out the cows into the pasture. She gathered an apron full of chips and started a fire, just as she had done every morning for twenty-nine years, and she put the coffee-pot on the greasy stove and boiled the brew of yesterday-which was also her habit.

She sat for some time with her head leaning upon her grimy hand and stared unseeingly out upon a peach-tree in full bloom, and at a pair of busy robins who had chosen a convenient crotch for their nest. Finally she rose stiffly, as if she had grown older within the last hour, and went outside to the place where she had been mending the irrigating ditch the day before; she knocked the wet sand off the shovel she had left sticking in the soft bank and went out of the yard and up the slope toward the rock wall.

On a tiny, level place above the main ditch and just under the wall, Marthy began to dig, setting her broad, flat foot uncompromisingly upon the shoulder of the shovel and sending it deep into the yellow soil. She worked slowly and methodically and steadily, just as she did everything else. When she had dug down as deep as she could and still manage to climb out, and had the hole wide enough and long enough, she got awkwardly to the grassy surface and sat for a long while upon a rock, staring dumbly at the gaunt, brown hills across the river.

She returned to the cabin at last, and with the manner of one who dreads doing what must be done, she went in where Jase lay stiff and cold under the blankets.

Early that afternoon, Marthy went staggering up the slope, wheeling Jase's body before her on the creaky, home-made wheelbarrow. In the same harsh, primitive manner in which they both had lived, Marthy buried her dead. And though in life she had given him few words save in command or upbraiding, with never a hint of love to sweeten the days for either, yet she went whimpering away from that grave. She broke off three branches of precious peach blossoms and carried them up the slope. She stuck them upright in the lumpy soil over Jase's head and stood there a long while with tear-streaked face, staring down at the grave and at the nodding pink blossoms.

Billy Louise rode singing down the rocky trail through the deep, narrow gorge, to where the hawthorn and choke-cherries hid the opening to the cove. Just on the edge of the thickest fringe, she pulled up and broke off tender branches of cherry bloom, then went on, still singing softly to herself because the air was sweet with spring odors, the sunshine lay a fresh yellow upon the land, and because the joy of life was in her blood and, like the birds, she had no other means of expression at hand. Blue's feet sank to the fetlocks in the rich, black soil of the little meadow that lay smooth to the tumbling sweep of the river behind its own little willow fringe. His ears perked forward, his eyes rolling watchfully for strange sights and sounds, he stepped softly forward, ready to wheel at the slightest alarm and gallop back up the gorge to more familiar ground. It was long since Billy Louise had turned his head down the rocky trail, and Blue liked little the gloom of the gorge and the sudden change to soft, black soil that stopped just short of being boggy in the wet places. Where the trail led into a marshy crossing of the big, irrigating ditch that brought the stream from far up the gorge to water meadow and orchard, Blue halted and cast a look of disapproval back at his rider. Billy Louise stopped singing and laughed at him.

"I guess you can go where a cow can go, you silly thing. Mud's a heap easier than lava rock, if you only knew it, Blue. Get along with you."

Blue lowered his head, snuffed suspiciously at the water-filled tracks, and would have turned back. Mud he despised instinctively, since he had nearly mired on the creek bank when he was a sucking colt.

"Blue! Get across that ditch, or I'll beat you to death!" The voice of Billy Louise was soft with a caressing note at the end, so that the threat did not sound very savage, after all. She sniffed at the branch of cherry blossoms and reined the horse back to face the ditch. And Blue, who had a will of his own, snorted and wheeled, this time in frank rebellion against her command.

"Oh, will you? Well, you'll cross that ditch, you know, sooner or later-so you might just as well —" Blue reared and whirled again, plunging two rods back toward the cherry thicket.

Billy Louise set her teeth against her lower lip, slid her rawhide quirt from slim wrist to firm hand-grip, and proceeded to match Blue's obstinacy with her own; and since the obstinacy of Billy Louise was stronger and finer and backed by a surer understanding of the thing she was fighting against, Blue presently lifted himself, leaped the ditch in one clean jump, and snorted when he sank nearly to his knees in the soft, black soil beyond.

From there to the pink drift of peach bloom against the dull brown of the bluff, Blue galloped angrily, leaving deep, black prints in the soft green of the meadow. So they came headlong upon Marthy, just as she was knocking the yellow clay of the grave from her irrigating shovel against the pole fence of her pig-pen.

"Why, Marthy!" Once before in her life Billy Louise had seen Marthy's chin quivering like that, and big, slow tears sliding down the network of lines on Marthy's leathery cheeks. With a painful slump her spirits went heavy with her sympathy. "Marthy!"

She knew without a word of explanation just what had happened. From Marthy's bent shoulders she knew, and from her tear-stained face, and from the yellow soil clinging still to the shovel in her hand. The wide eyes of Billy Louise sent seeking glances up the slope where the soil was yellow; went to the long, raw ridge under the wall, with the peach blossoms standing pitifully awry upon the western end. Her eyes filled with tears. "Oh, Marthy! When was it?"

"In the night, sometime, I guess." Marthy's voice had a harsh huskiness. "He was-gone-when I woke up. Well-he's better off than I be. I dunno what woulda become of him if I'd went first." There, at last, was a note of tenderness, stifled though it was and fleeting. "Git down, Billy Louise, and come in. I been kinda lookin' for yuh to come, ever sence the weather opened up. How's your maw?"

Spoken sympathy was absolutely impossible in the face of that stoical acceptance of life's harsh law. Marthy turned toward the gate, taking the shovel and the wheelbarrow in with her. Billy Louise glanced furtively at the raw, yellow ridge under the rock wall and rode on to the stable. She pulled off the saddle and bridle and turned Blue into the corral before she went slowly-and somewhat reluctantly-to the cabin, squat, old, and unkempt like its mistress, but buried deep in the renewed sweetness of bloom-time.

"The fruit's comin' on early this year," said Marthy from the doorway, her hands on her hips. "They's goin' to be lots of it, too, if we don't git a killin' frost." So she closed the conversational door upon her sorrow and pointed the way to trivial, every-day things.

"What are you going to do now, Marthy?" Billy Louise was perfectly capable of opening a conversational door, even when it had been closed decisively in her face. "You can't get on here alone, you know. Did you send for that nephew? If you haven't, you must hire somebody till —"

"He's comin'. That letter you sent over last month was from him. I dunno when he'll git here; he's liable to come most any time. I ain't going to hire nobody. I kin git along alone. I might as well of been alone —" Even harsh Marthy hesitated and did not finish the sentence that would have put a slight upon her dead.

"I'll stay to-night, anyway," said Billy Louise. "Just a week ago I hired John Pringle and that little breed wife of his for the summer. I couldn't afford it," she added, with a small sigh, "but Ward had to go back to his claim, and mommie needs someone in the house. She hasn't been a bit well, all winter. And I've turned all the stock out for the summer and have to do a lot of riding on them; it's that or let them scatter all over the country and then have to hire a rep for every round-up. I can't afford that, I haven't got cattle enough to pay; and I like to ride, anyway. I've got them pretty well located along the creek, up at the head of the canyons. The grass is coming on fine, so they don't stray much. Are you going to turn your cattle out, Marthy? I see you haven't yet."

"No, I ain't yit. I dunno. I was going to sell 'em down to jest what the pasture'll keep. I'm gittin' too old to look after 'em. But I dunno — When Charlie gits here, mebby —"

"Oh, is that the nephew? I didn't know his name." Billy Louise was talking aimlessly to keep her thoughts away from the pitifulness of the sordid little tragedy in this beauty-spot and to drive that blank, apathetic look from Marthy's hard eyes.

"Charlie Fox, his name is. I hope he turns out a good worker. I've never had a chance to git ahead any; but if Charlie'll jest take holt, I'll mebby git some comfort outa life yit."

"He ought, to, I'm sure. And everyone thinks you've done awfully well, Marthy. What can I do now? Wash the dishes and straighten things up, I guess."

"You needn't do nothin' you ain't a mind to do, Billy Louise. I don't want you to think you got to slop around washin' my dirty dishes. I'm goin' on down into the medder and work on a ditch I'm puttin' in. You jest do what you're a mind to." She picked up the shovel and went off down the jungly path, herself the ugliest object in the Cove, where she had created so much beauty.

Again the sympathetic soul of Billy Louise had betrayed her into performing an extremely disagreeable task. Shudderingly she looked into the unpleasant bedroom, and comprehending all of the sordidness of the tragedy, spent half an hour with her teeth set hard together while she dragged out dingy blankets and hung them over the fence under a voluptuous plum-tree. The next hour was so disagreeably employed that she wondered afterward how even her sympathy could have driven her to the things she did. She carried more water, after she had scrubbed that bedroom, and opened the window with the aid of the hammer, and set the tea-kettle on to heat the dish-water. Then, because her mind was full of poor, dead Jase, she took the branches of wild cherry and hawthorn blossoms she had gathered coming down the gorge and went up the slope to lay them on his grave.

She sat down on the rock where Marthy had rested after digging the grave, and with her chin in her two cupped palms, stared out across the river at the heaped bluffs and down at the pink-and-white patch of fruit-trees. She was trying, as the young will always try, to solve the riddle of life; and she was baffled and unhappy because she could not find any answer at all that pleased both her ideals and her reason. And then she heard a man's voice lifted up in riotous song, and she turned her head toward the opening of the gorge and listened, her eyes brightening while she waited.

"Foot in the stirrup and hand on the horn,

Best damn cowboy ever was born,

Coma ti yi youpy, youpy-a, youpy-a,

Coma ti yi youpy, youpy-a!"

Billy Louise, with her chin still in her palms, smiled and hummed the tune under her breath; that shows how quickly we throw off the burdens of our neighbors. "Wonder what he's doing down here?" she asked herself, and smiled again.

"I'll sell my outfit soon as I can,

I won't punch cattle for no damn' man,

Coma ti yi youpy, youpy-a, youpy-a,

Coma ti yi youpy, youpy-a!
    "I'm goin' back to town to draw my money,

I'm going back to town to see my honey,

Coma ti yi —"

Ward came into sight through the little meadow, riding slowly, with both hands clasped over the horn of the saddle, his hat tilted back on his head, and his whole attitude one of absolute content with life. He saw Billy Louise almost as soon as she glimpsed him-and she had been watching that bit of road quite closely. He flipped the reins to one side and turned from the trail to ride straight up the slope to where she was.

Billy Louise, with a self-reproachful glance at the grave, ran down the slope to meet him-an unexpected welcome which made Ward's heart leap in his chest.

"Oh, Ward, for heaven's sake don't be singing that come-all-ye at the top of your voice, like that. Don't you —"

"Now I was given to understand that you liked that same come-all-ye. Have you been educating your musical taste in the last week, Miss William Louisa?" Ward stopped his horse before her, and with his hands still clasped over the saddle-horn, looked down at her with that hidden smile-and something else.

"No, I haven't. I don't have to educate myself to the point where I know the *Chisholm Trail* isn't a proper kind of funeral hymn, Ward Warren." Billy Louise glanced over her shoulder and lowered her voice instinctively, as we all do when death has come close and stopped. "Jase died last night; that's his grave up there. Isn't it perfectly pitiful? Poor old Marthy was here all solitary alone with him. And-Ward! She dug that grave her own self, and took him up and buried him-and, Ward! She-she wheeled him up in the —*wheelbarrow*! She had to, of course. She couldn't carry him. But isn't it awful?" Her hands were up, patting and smoothing the neck of his horse, and her face was bent to hide the tears that stood in her eyes, and the quiver of her mouth.

Ward drew in his lip, bit it, and let it go. He was a man, and he had seen much of tragedy and trouble; also, he did not know Marthy or Jase. His chief emotion was one of resentment against anything that brought tears to Billy Louise; she had not hidden them from him; they were the first and most important element in that day's happenings, so far as he was concerned. He leaned and flipped the end of his reins lightly down on her bare head.

"William Louisa, if you cry about it, I'll-do something shocking, most likely. Yes, it's awful; a whole lot of life is awful. But it's done, and Mrs. Martha appears to be a woman with a whole lot of grit, so the chances are she'll carry her load like a man. She'll be horribly lonesome, down here! They lived alone, didn't they?"

"Yes, and they didn't seem to love each other much." Billy Louise was not one to gloss over hard facts, even in the face of that grave. "Marthy was always kicking about him, and he about her. But all the same they belonged together; they had lived together more years than we are old. And she's going to miss him awfully."

Several minutes they stood there, talking, while Billy Louise patted the horse absently, and Ward looked down at her and did not miss one little light or shadow in her face. He had been alone a whole week, thinking of her, remember, and his eyes were hungry to the point of starvation.

"You saw mommie, of course; you came from home?"

"No, I did not. I got as far as the creek and saw Blue's tracks coming down; so I just sort of trailed along, seeing it was mommie's daughter I felt most like talking to."

"Mommie's daughter" laughed a little and instinctively made a change in the subject. She did not see anything strange in the fact that Ward had observed and recognized Blue's tracks coming into the gorge. She would have observed and recognized instantly the tracks made by his horse, anywhere. Those things come natural to one who has lived much in the open; and there is a certain individuality in the hoof-prints of a horse, as any plainsman can testify.

"I've got to go in and wash the dishes," she said, stepping back from him. "Of course nothing was done in the cabin, and I've been doing a little house-cleaning. I guess the dish-water is hot by this time-if it hasn't all boiled away."

Ward, as a matter of course, tied his horse to the fence and went into the cabin with her. He also asked her to stake him to a dish-towel, which she did after a good deal of rummaging. He stood with his hat on the back of his head, a cigarette between his lips, and wiped the dishes with much apparent enjoyment. He objected strongly to Billy Louise's assertion that she meant to scrub the floor, but when he found her quite obdurate, he changed his method without in the least degree yielding his point, though for diplomatic reasons he appeared to yield.

He carried water from the creek and filled the tea-kettle, the big iron pot, and both pails. Then, when Billy Louise had turned her back upon him, while she looked in a dark corner for the mop, he suddenly seized her under the arms and lifted her upon the table; and before she had finished her astonished gaspings, he caught up a pail of water and sloshed it upon the floor under her. Then he grinned in his triumph.

"William Louisa, if you get your feet wet, your mommie will take a club to you," he re- minded her sternly. Whereupon he took the broom and proceeded to give that floor a real man's scrubbing, refusing to quarrel with Billy Louise, who scolded like a cross old woman from the table-except when she simply had to stop and laugh heartily at his violent method of cleaning.

Ward sloshed and swept and scrubbed. He dug into the corners with a grim thoroughness that won reluctant approbation from the young woman on the table with her feet tucked under her, and he made her forget poor old Jase up on the hillside. He scrubbed viciously behind the door until the water was little better than a thin, black mud.

"You want to come up to my claim some time," he said, looking over his shoulder while he rested a minute. "I'll show you how a man keeps house, William Louisa. Once a week I pile my two stools on the table, put the cat up on the bunk-and she looks just about as comfortable and happy as mommie's daughter looks right now-and get busy with the broom and good creek water." He resettled his hat on the back of his head and went to work again. "Mill Creek goes dry down below, on the days when little Wardie cleans his cabin," he assured her gravely, and damming up a muddy pool with the broom, he yanked open the door and swept out the water with a perfectly unnecessary flourish, just because he happened to be in a very exuberant mood.

Billy Louise gave a squeal of consternation and then sat absolutely still, staring round-eyed through the doorway. Ward stepped back-even his composure was slightly jarred-and twisted his lips amusedly.

"Hello," he said, after a few blank seconds. "You missed some of it, didn't you?" His tone was mildly commiserating. "Will you come in?"

"N-o-o, thank you, I don't believe I will." The speaker looked in, however, saw Billy Louise perched upon the table, and took off his hat. He was well plastered with dirty water that ran down and left streaks of mud behind. "I must have gotten off the road," he said. "I'm looking for Mr. Jason Meilke's ranch."

Billy Louise tucked her feet farther under her skirts and continued to stare dumbly. Ward, glancing at her from the corner of his eyes, stepped considerately between her and the stranger so that his broad shoulders quite hid her from the man's curious stare.

"You've struck the right place," he said calmly. "This is it." He picked up another pail of water and sloshed it upon the wet floor to rinse off the mud.

"Is-ah-Mrs. Meilke in?" One could not accuse the young man of craning, but he certainly did try to get another glimpse of the person on the table and failed because of Ward.

"She's down in the meadow," Billy Louise murmured.

"She's down in the meadow," Ward repeated to the bespattered young man. "You just go down past the stable and follow on down —" he waved a hand vaguely before he took up the broom again. "You'll find her, all right," he added encouragingly.

"Oh, Ward! That must be Marthy's nephew. What will he think?"

"Does it matter such a h — a deuce of a lot what he thinks?" Ward went on with his interrupted scrubbing.

"His name is Charlie Fox, and he's been to college and he worked in a bank," Billy Louise went on nervously. "He's going to live here with Marthy and run the ranch. What must he have thought! To have you sweep all that dirty water on him —"

"Oh, not all!" Ward corrected cheerfully. "Quite a lot missed him."

Billy Louise giggled. "What does he look like, Ward? You stood squarely in the way, so I —"

"He looked," said Ward dispassionately, "like a pretty mad young man with nose, eyes, and a mouth, and a mole in front of his left ear."

"He was real polite," said Billy Louise reprovingly, "and his voice is nice."

"Yes? I mind-read a heap of cussing. The politeness was all on top." Ward chuckled and swept more water outside. "I expect you saved me a licking that time, Miss William the Conqueror."

"Can you think of any more names to call me, besides my own, I wonder?" Billy Louise leaned and inspected the floor like a chicken preparing to hop off its roost.

"Heaps more." The glow in Ward's eyes was dangerous to their calm friendship. "Want to hear them?"

"No, I don't. I want to get off this table before that college youth comes back to be shocked silly again. I want to see if he's really-got a mole in front of his ear!"

"You know what inquisitiveness did to old lady Lot, don't you? However —" He lifted her in his arms and set her down outside the door. "There, Wilhemina; trot along and see the nice young man."

Billy Louise sat down on the wheelbarrow, remembered its latest service, and got up hastily. "I won't go a step," she asserted positively.

Ward had not wanted her to go. He gave her a smile and finished off his scrubbing with the mop, which he handled with quite surprising skill for a young man who seemed more at home in the saddle than anywhere else.

"I'm awfully glad he came, anyway." Billy Louise pulled down a budded lilac branch and sniffed at it. "I won't have to stay all night, now. I was going to."

"In that case, the young man is welcome as a gold mine. Here they come-he and Mrs. Martha. You'll have to introduce me, Bill-the-Conk; I have never met the lady." Ward hastily returned the mop to its corner, rolled down his sleeves, and picked up his gloves. Then he stepped outside and waited beside Billy Louise, looking not in the least like a man who has just wiped a lot of dishes and scrubbed a floor.

The nephew, striding along behind Marthy and showing head and shoulders above her, seemed not to resent any little mischance, such as muddy water flirted upon him from a broom. He grinned reminiscently as he came up, shook hands with the two of them, and did not let his glance dwell too long or too often upon Billy Louise, nor too briefly upon Ward.

"You've got a splendid place here, Aunt Martha," he told the old woman appreciatively. "I'd no idea there was such a little beauty-spot down here. This is even more picturesque than that homey-looking ranch we passed a few miles back, down in that little valley. I was hoping that was your ranch when I first saw it; and when I found it wasn't, I came near stopping, anyway. I'm glad I resisted the temptation, now. This is worth coming a long way to see."

"I ain't never had a chance to do all I wanted to with it," said Marthy, with the first hint of apology Billy Louise had ever heard from her. "I only had one pair of hands to work with —"

"We'll fix that part. Don't you worry a minute. You're going to sit in a rocking-chair and give orders, from now on. And if I can't make good here, I ought to be booted all the way up that spooky gorge. Isn't that right?" He turned to Warren with a certain air of appraisement behind the unmistakable cordiality of his voice.

"A man ought to make good here, all right," Ward agreed neutrally. "It's a fine place."

"It ain't as fine as I'd like to see it," began Marthy depreciatingly.

"As you will see it, let's say-if that doesn't sound too conceited from a tenderfoot," supplemented the nephew, and laid his hand upon her shoulder with a gentle little pat. "Folks, I don't want to seem too exuberantly sure of myself, but —" he waved a carefully-kept hand eloquently at the luxuriance around him, " —I'm all fussed up over this place, honest. I thought I was coming to a shack in the middle of the sage-brush; I was primed to buckle down and make good even in the desert. And bumping into this sort of thing without warning has gone to my alleged brain a bit. What I don't know about ranching would fill a library; but there's this much, anyway. There won't be any more ditch-digging for a certain game little lady in this Cove." He gave the shoulder another pat, and he smiled down at her in a way that made Billy Louise blink. And Marthy, who had probably never before been called a game little lady, came near breaking down and crying before them all.

When Ward went to the stable after Blue, half an hour later, Charlie Fox went with him. His manner when they were alone was different; not so exuberantly cheerful-more frank and practical.

"Honest, it floored me completely to see what that poor old woman has been up against down here," he told Warren, stuffing tobacco into a silver-rimmed, briar pipe while Ward saddled Blue. "I don't know a hell of a lot about this ranch game; but if that old lady can put it across, I guess I can wobble along somehow. Too bad the old man cashed in just now; but Aunt Martha as good as told me he wasn't much force, so maybe I can play a lone hand here as easy as I could have done with him. Live near here?"

"Fifteen miles or so." Ward was not in his most expansive mood, chiefly for the reason that this man was a stranger, and of strangers he was inclined to fight shy.

"Oh, well-it might have been fifty. I know how you fellows measure distances out here. I'm likely to need a little coaching, now and then, if I live up to what I just now told the old lady."

"From all I know of her, you won't need to go out of the Cove for advice."

"Well, that's right, judging from the looks of things. A woman that can go up against a proposition like she did to-day and handle it alone, is no mental weakling; to say nothing of the way this ranch looks. All right, Warren; I'll make out alone, I reckon."

Afterwards, when Ward thought it over, he remembered gratefully that Charlie Fox had refrained from attempting any discussion of Billy Louise or from asking any questions even remotely personal. He knew enough about men to appreciate the tactful silences of the stranger, and when Billy Louise, on the way home, predicted that the nephew was going to be a success, Ward did not feel like qualifying the verdict.

"He's going to be a godsend to the old lady," he said. "He seems to have his sights raised to making things come easier for her from now on."

"Well, she certainly deserves it. For a college young man-the ordinary, smart young man who comes out here to astonish the natives-he's almost human. I was so afraid that Marthy'd get him out here and then discover he was a perfect nuisance. So many men are."

Chapter VI. A Matter of Twelve Months or so

Out in the wide spaces, where homes are but scattered oases in the general emptiness, life does not move uniformly, so far as it concerns incidents or acquaintanceships. A man or a ranch may experience complete isolation, and the unbroken monotony which sometimes accompanies it, for a month at a time. Summer work or winter storm may be the barrier temporarily raised, and life resolves itself into a succession of days and nights unbroken by outside influences. They leave their mark upon humans-these periods of isolation. For better, for worse, the man changes slowly with the months; he grows more bovine in his phlegmatic acceptance of his environment, or he becomes restless and fired with a surplus energy of ambition, or he falls to dreaming dreams; whatever angle he takes, he changes, imperceptibly perhaps, but inevitably.

Then the monotony is broken and sometimes with violence. Incident rushes in upon the heels of incident, and life becomes as tumultuous as the many moods of nature when it has a wide, open land for a playground.

That is why, perhaps, so much of western life is painted with broad strokes and raw colors. You are given the crowded action, the unleashing of emotions and temperaments that have smoldered long under the blanket of solitary living. You are shown an effect without being given the cause of that effect. You pronounce the West wild, and you never think of the long winters that bred in silence and brooding solitude those storm-periods which seem so primitively savage; of the days wherein each nature is thrown upon its own resources, with nothing to feed upon but itself and its own personal interests. And so characters change, and one wonders why.

There was Billy Louise, with her hands and her mind full of the problems her father had died still trying to solve. She did not in the least realize that she was attempting anything out of the ordinary when she took a half-developed ranch in the middle of a land almost as wild as it had been when the Indians wandered over it unmolested, a few cattle and horses and a bundle of debts to make her head swim, and set herself the problem of increasing the number of cattle and eliminating the debts, and of wresting prosperity out of a condition of picturesquely haphazard poverty. She went about it with the pathetic confidence of youth and ignorance. She rode up and down the canyons and over the higher, grassier ridges, to watch the cattle on their summer range and keep them from straying. She went with John Pringle after posts and helped him fence certain fertile slopes and hollows for winter grazing. She drove the rickety old mower through the waving grass along the creek bottom and hummed little, contented tunes while she watched the grass sway and fall evenly when the sickle shuttled through. She put on her gymnasium bloomers and drove the hay wagon, and felt only a pleasurable thrill of excitement when John Pringle inadvertently pitched an indignant rattlesnake up to her with a forkful of hay. She killed the snake with her pitchfork and pinched off the rattles, proud of their size and number.

When she sold seven fat, three-year-old steers that fall and paid a note twice renewed, managing besides to buy the winter supply of "grub" and a sewing-machine and a set of silver teaspoons for her mother, oh, but she was proud!

Ward rode down to the ranch that night, and Billy Louise showed him the note with its red stamp, oblong and imposing and slightly blurred on the "paid" side. Ward was almost as proud as she, if looks and tones went for anything, and he helped Billy Louise a good deal by telling her just how much she ought to pay for the yearlings old Johnson, over on Snake River, had for sale. Also he told her how much hay it would take to winter them-though she knew that already-and just what percentage of profit she might expect from a given number in a given period of time.

He spoke of his own work and plans, as well. He was going into cattle, also, as fast as possible, he said. In a few years the sheep would probably come in and crowd them out, but in the meantime there was money in cattle-and the more cattle, the more money. He was going to work for wages till the winter set in. He didn't know when he would see Billy Louise, he said, but he would stop on his way back.

To them that short visit was something more than an incident. It gave Ward new stuff for his dreams and new fuel for the fire of ambition. To Billy Louise it also furnished new dream material. She rode the hills and saw in fancy whole herds of cattle where now wandered scattered animals. She dreamed of the time when Ward and Charlie Fox and she would pool their interests and run a wagon of their own, and gather their stock from wide ranges. She was foolish, in that; but that is what she liked to dream.

Mentioning Charlie Fox calls to mind the fact that he was changing more than any of them. Billy Louise did not see him very often, but when she did it was with a deepening impression of his unflagging tenderness to Marthy—a tenderness that manifested itself in many little, unassuming thoughtfulnesses-and of his good-humor and his energy and several other qualities which one must admire.

"Mommie, that nephew goes at everything just as if it were a game," she said after one visit. "You know what that cabin has always been: dark and dirty and not a comfortable chair to sit down in, or a book or magazine or anything? Well, I'm just going to take you over there some day and let you see the difference. He's cut two more windows and built on an addition with a porch, if you please. And he has a bookcase he made himself, just stuffed with books and magazines. And he made Marthy a rocking-chair, mommie, and-she wears a white apron, and has her hair combed, and sits and rocks! Honest to goodness, you wouldn't think she was the same woman."

"Marthy always seemed to me more like a man than a woman," said her mother. "She didn't have nothing domestic in her whole make-up, far as I could see. Her cooking—"

"Well, mommie, Marthy cooks real well now. Charlie praises up her bread, and she takes lots of pains with it. And she just fusses with her flowers and lets him run the ranch; and, mommie, she just worships Charlie! The way she sits and looks at him when he's talking-you can see she almost says prayers to him. She does let her dishpan stay greasy—I don't suppose you can change a person completely-but everything is lots cleaner than it used to be before Charlie came. He's going to buy more cattle, too, he says. Young stock, mostly. He says there's no sense in anybody being poor, in such a country as this. He says he intends to make Marthy rich; Aunt Martha, he calls her. I'm certainly going to take you over to see her, mommie, the very first nice day when I don't have a million other things to do." Billy Louise sighed and pushed her hair back impatiently. "I wish I were a man and as smart as Charlie Fox," she added, with the plaintive note that now sometimes crept into her voice when she realized of a sudden how great a load she was carrying.

"A man can get out and do things. And a woman-why, even Ward seems to think it's perfectly wonderful, mommie, that we don't just about starve, with me running the ranch! I know he does. Every time I do a thing right or pay off a note or anything, he looks as if—"

"I wouldn't be a mite surprised, Billy Louise," said her mother, with a flash of amused comprehension, "if you kinda misread Ward sometimes. Them eyes of his are pretty keen, and they see a whole lot; but they ain't easy to read, for all that. I guess Ward don't think it's anything surprising that you're getting along so well, Billy Louise. I surmise he knows you're a better manager than a lot of men are."

"I'm not the manager Charlie Fox is, though." Billy Louise was frankly envious.

"He didn't have any more to do with than I've got, and he's accomplished a lot more. And, besides, he started in green at the whole business." She rested her chin in her cupped palms and stared disconsolately at the high-piled hills behind which the sun was setting gloriously. "He's going to pipe water into the house, mommie," she observed, after a silence. "I wish —"

"Well, he's welcome. I don't want no water piped in here, Billy Louise, and tastin' of the pipe. I'd rather carry it and have it sweet and fresh. Don't you go worrying because you can't do everything Charlie Fox does. Likely as not he's pilin' up the debts instead of payin' 'em off as you're doing."

"I don't know; I don't believe he is, though. I think he's just managing right and making every dollar count. He got calves from Seabeck, up the river, cheaper than I did from Johnson, mommie. He rode all over the country and looked up range conditions and prices. He didn't say so, but he made me feel foolish because I just bought the first ones I saw, without waiting to look around first. But-Ward said it was a good buy, and he ought to know; only, the fact remains that Charlie has done better. I guess it isn't experience that counts, altogether. Charlie Fox has got brains!"

"Land alive! I guess he ain't the only one, Billy Louise. You're doing better than your father done, and he wasn't any Jase Meilke kind of a man, but a good, hard worker always. You don't want to get all outa conceit with yourself just because Charlie Fox is gitting along all right. I don't know as it's so wonderful. Marthy was always forehanded, and she made money there and never spent any to speak of. Though I shouldn't carry the idea she's stingy, after the way she —"

If Billy Louise had not been so absorbed with her own discontent, she might have wondered at her mother's sudden silence. But she did not even notice it. She was comparing two young men and measuring them with certain standards of her own, and she was not quite satisfied with the result. She had seen Charlie Fox spring up with a perfectly natural courtesy and hand Marthy a chair when she entered the room where he had been discussing books with Billy Louise. She had seen him stand beside his own chair until Marthy was seated and then had heard him deftly turn the conversation into a channel wherein Marthy had also an interest. Parlor politeness-and something more; something infinitely finer and better than mere obedience to certain conventional rules.

She had seen that and more, and she had a vivid picture of Ward, sitting absorbed in a book which he never afterwards mentioned, and letting her or her mother lift heavy pieces of wood upon the fire within arm's reach of him; sitting with his hat tilted back upon his head and a cigarette gone cold in his fingers, and perhaps not replying at all when he was spoken to. She had never considered him uncouth or rude; he was Ward Warren, and these were certain individual traits which he possessed and which seemed a part of him. She had sensed dimly that some natures are too big and too strong for petty rules of deportment, and that Ward might sit all day in the house with his hat on his head and still be a gentleman of the finer sort. And yet, now that Charlie Fox had come and presented an example of the world's standard, Billy Louise could not, for the life of her, help wishing that Ward was different. And there were other things; things which Billy Louise was ashamed to recognize as influencing her in any way, and yet which did influence her. For instance, Ward lived to himself and for himself, and not always wisely or well. He was arrogant in his opinions-Billy Louise had rather admired what she had called his strength, but it had become arrogance now-and his scorn was swift and keen for blunderings. And there was Charlie, always thinking and planning for Marthy and putting her wishes first; wanting to make sure that he himself had not blundered, and with a conservative estimate of himself that was refreshingly modest. And —

"Ain't that Ward coming, Billy Louise? Seems to me it looks like him-the way he rides."

Billy Louise started guiltily and looked up toward the trail, now piled deep with shadows. It was Ward, all right, and his voice, lifted in a good-humored shout, brought Billy Louise to her feet and sent her down the slope to the stable, where he had stopped as a matter of course.

When he turned and smiled at her through the dusk and said, "'Lo, Bill," in a voice that was like a spoken kiss, a certain young woman hated herself for a weak-souled traitor and mentally called Charlie Fox a popinjay, which was merely shifting injustice to another resting-place.

"Are you plumb tickled to death to see me, William?"

"Oh, no; but I guess I can stand it!"

A smile to go with both sentences, and a strong undercurrent of something unnamed in their tones-who wanted the pasteurized milk and distilled water of a perfectly polite form of greeting? Not Billy Louise, if one might judge from that young woman's face and voice and manner. Not Ward, though he was perfectly unconscious of having been weighed or measured or judged by any standard at all.

And yet, when Charlie Fox rode down to the Wolverine a week or so later, tied his horse under the shed, and came up to the cabin as though he knew of no better place in all the world; when he greeted mommie as though she were something precious in his sight, and talked with her about the things she was most interested in, and actually made her feel as if he were immensely interested also, Billy Louise simply could not help admiring him and liking him for his frank good-nature and his kindness. She had never before met a man just like Charlie Fox, though she had known many who were what Ward once called "parlor-broke." She felt when she was with him that he had a strength to match Ward's strength; only, this strength was tamed and trained and smoothed so that it did not obtrude upon one's notice. It was not every young man who would come out into the wilderness and roughen his hands on an irrigating shovel and live a cramped, lonely life, for the sake of a harsh, illiterate old woman like Marthy Meilke. She did not believe Ward would do that. He would have to feel some tie stronger than the one between Marthy and her nephew before he would change his life and his own plans for anyone.

It was not until Charlie was leaving that he gave Billy Louise a hint that his errand was not yet accomplished. She walked down with him to where his horse was tied and so gave him a chance to speak what was in his mind.

"You know, I hate to mention little worries before your mother," he said. "Those pathetic eyes of hers make me ashamed to bother her with a thing. But I am worried, Miss Louise. I came over to ask you if you've seen anything of four calves of ours. I know you ride a good deal, through the hills. They disappeared a week ago, and I can't find any trace of them. I've been looking all through the hills, but I can't locate them."

Billy Louise had not seen them, either, and she begged for particulars. "I don't see how they could get away from your Cove," she said, "unless your bars were down."

"The bars were all right. It was last Friday, I think. I'm not sure. They were in the little meadow above the house, you see. I was away that night, and Aunt Martha is a little hard of hearing. She wouldn't hear anything unless there were considerable noise. I came home the next forenoon —I was over to Seabeck's —and the bars were in place then. Aunt Martha had not been up the gorge, nor had anyone come to the ranch while I was gone. So you see, Miss Louise, here's a very pretty mystery!"

He laughed, but Billy Louise saw by his eyes that he did not laugh very deeply, and that he was really worried. "I must have made a mistake and bought mountain sheep instead of calves," he said and laughed again. "They couldn't have gone through those bars or over them; and I did have a spark of intelligence and looked along the river for tracks, you know. They had not been near the river, which has soft banks along there. They watered from the little creek that comes down the gorge. Miss Louise, do you have flying cattle in Idaho?"

"You think they were driven off, don't you?" Billy Louise asked a question with the words, and made a statement of it with her tone, which was a trick of hers.

Charlie Fox shook his head, but his eyes did not complete the denial. "Miss Louise, I'd work every other theory to death before I'd admit that possibility! I don't know all of my neighbors so very well, but I should hesitate a long, long time —"

"It needn't have been a neighbor. There are lots of strange men passing through the country. Did you look for tracks?"

"I —did not. I didn't want to admit that possibility. I decline to admit it now." The chin of Charlie Fox squared perceptibly, so that Billie Louise caught a faint resemblance to Marthy in his face. "I saw a man accused of a theft once," he said. "The evidence was-or seemed-absolutely unassailable. And afterward he was exonerated completely; it was just a horrible mistake. But he left school under a cloud. His life was ruined by the blunder. I'd have to know absolutely before I'd accuse anyone of stealing those calves, Miss Louise. I'd have to see them in a man's corral, with his brand on them —I believe that's the way it's done, out here-and even then —"

"Where have you looked?" There were reasons why this particular subject was painful to Billy Louise. "And are you sure they didn't get out of that pasture and wander on down the Cove, among all those willows? It's a perfect jungle, away down. Are you sure they aren't with the rest of the cattle? I don't see how they could leave the Cove, unless they were driven out." She caught a twinkle of amusement in his eyes and stopped short. Of course, a mere girl should not take it for granted that a man had failed to do all that might be done. And Billy Louise had a swift conviction that she would never think of talking like this to Ward. She flushed a little; and still, Charlie Fox was a tenderfoot. She was justified in asking those questions, and in her heart she knew it.

"Yes, I thought of that-strange as it may seem." Charlie's voice was unoffended. On the contrary, he seemed glad that she took so keen an interest in his affairs. "It has been a week, you know, since they flew the coop. I did hunt every foot of that Cove, twice over. I drove every hoof of stock up and corraled them, and made sure these four were not in the herd. Then I hunted through every inch of that willow jungle and all along the bluff and the river; Miss Louise, I put in three days at it, from sunrise till it was too dark to see. Then I began riding outside. There isn't a trace of them anywhere. I had just bought them from Seabeck, you know. I drove them home, and because they were tired, and so was I, I just left them in that upper meadow as I came down the gorge. I hadn't branded them yet. I —I know I've made an awful botch of the thing, Miss Louise," he confessed, turning toward her with an honest distress and a self-flaying humility in his eyes that wiped from Billy Louise's mind any incipient tendency toward contempt. "But you see I'm green at this ranch game. And I never dreamed those calves weren't perfectly safe in there. The fence was new and strong; I built it new this fall, you know. And the bars are absolutely bars to any stock larger than a rabbit. Of course," he added, with a deprecating note, "four calves are only four calves. But-it's the sense of failure that gets me hardest, Miss Louise. Aunt Martha trusted me to take care of things. Her confidence in me fairly takes my nerve. And losing four fine, big heifer calves at one whack is no way to get rich; is it, Miss Louise?" He laughed, and again the laugh did not go deep, or reach his eyes.

"I hate to bother you with this, and I don't want you to think I have come whining for sympathy," he said, after a minute of moody silence. "But seeing they were not branded yet-with our brand —I thought perhaps you had run across them and paid no attention, thinking they belonged to Seabeck."

Billy Louise smiled a little to herself. If he had not been quite so "green at the ranch game," he would have mentioned brands at first, as the most important point, instead of tacking on the information casually after ten minutes of other less vital details.

"Were they vented?" she asked, suppressing the smile so that it was merely a twitch of the lips which might mean anything.

"I —yes, I think they were. That's what you call it when the former owner puts his brand in a different place to show that his ownership has ceased, isn't it? Seabeck puts his brand upside down —"

"I know Seabeck's vent," Billy Louise cut in. There was no need of letting such a fine fellow display more ignorance on the subject. "And I should have noticed it if I had seen four calves vented fresh and not rebranded. Why in the world didn't you stick your brand on at the same time?" Billy Louise was losing patience with his greenness.

"I didn't have my branding iron with me," Charlie answered humbly. "I have done that before, when I bought those other cows and calves. I —"

"You'd better pack your iron, next time," she retorted. "If you can't get a little bunch of calves ten miles without losing them —"

"But you must understand, I did! I took them home and turned them into the Cove. I know —I'm an awful chump at this. There are things that I can do," he declared whimsically, "or I should want to kick myself to death. I can ladle out money the year round through a bank wicket and not be shy a cent at the end of the year. And I can strike out man after man-when I'm in good form; why, I've pitched whole games and never walked a man! And I can-but what's the use? I can't drive the cows up from pasture, it seems, without losing all the milk. And I can make a little, gray-eyed girl out here in the sagebrush look upon me with pitying contempt for my asinine ignorance. Hang it, why does a fellow have to learn fresh lessons for everything he undertakes? Why can't there be a universal course that fits one for every trade?"

"There is," said Billy Louise dryly. "You take that in the School of Experience, don't you?"

He laughed ruefully. "Horatio! It certainly does cost something, though. I've certainly paid enough —"

"In worry, maybe. The calves may not be absolutely lost, you know. Why, I lost a big steer last spring and never found him till I was going to sell a few head. Then he turned up, the biggest and fattest one in the bunch. You can't tell; they get themselves in queer places sometimes. I'll come over to-morrow, if I can, and take a look at that pasture and all around. And I'll keep a good lookout for the calves."

Many men would have objected to the unconscious patronage of her tone. That Charlie Fox did not, but accepted the spirit of helpfulness in her words, lifted him out of the small-natured class.

"It's awfully good of you," he said. "You know a lot more about the bovine nature than I do, for all I put in every spare minute studying the subject. I'm taking four different stock journals now, Miss Louise. I'll bet I know a lot more about the different strains of various breeds than you do, Miss Cattle-queen. But I'm beginning to see that we only know what we learn by experience. I've a new book on the subject of heredity of the cattle. I'm going home and see if Seabeck hasn't stumbled upon a strain that can be traced back to your native mountain sheep."

Billy Louise laughed and said good-by, and stood leaning over the gate watching him as he zigzagged up the hill, stopping his horse often to breathe. The wagon road took a round-about course, longer and less steep. At the top, just before he rounded a huge pimple on the face of the bluff, he stopped and looked down, saw her standing there, and waved his hat. His horse stood sidewise upon the trail for easier footing, and the man's head and shoulders were silhouetted sharply against the deep, clear blue of the sky. Billy Louise felt a little, unnamed thrill as she stared up at him. Her lips curved into tenderness. Clean, frank, easy-natured he was, as she had come to know him. It was like coming into a sunny spot to be with him. And then she sighed, with that vague feeling of dissatisfaction with herself. She felt crude and awkward and dull of wit. Her mother, Marthy, Ward-all the persons she knew-were crude and awkward and ignorant beside Charlie Fox. And she had had the temerity, the insufferable effrontery, to criticize him and patronize him over those four calves!

"He can strike out three men in succession," she murmured. "And he pitched whole games and never walked a man." She gave him a final wave of the hand, as he turned to climb on out of sight. "And I don't even know what he was talking about-though I think it was baseball. And I was awfully snippy about those calves he lost."

She began to wonder, then, about those calves. Vented and not rebranded, they would be easy game for any man who first got his own brand on them. She meant to get a description of them when she saw Charlie again-it was like his innocence to forget the most essential details! —and she meant to keep her eyes open. If Charlie were right about the calves not being anywhere in the Cove, then they had been driven out of it, stolen. Billy Louise turned dejectedly away from the fence and went down to a shady nook by the creek, where she had always liked to do her worrying and hard thinking.

She stooped and tried to catch a baby trout in her cupped palms, just as she used to try when she was a child. If those four calves were stolen, then there was a "rustler" in the country. And if there were, then no one's stock was safe. The deduction was terribly simple and as exact as the smallest sum in addition. And Billy Louise could not afford to pay toll to a rustler out of her forty-seven head of cattle.

The next day she rode early to the Cove and learned some things from Marthy which she had not gleaned from Charlie. She learned that two of the calves were a deep red, except for a wide, white strip on the nose of one and white hind feet on the other; that another was spotted on the hindquarters, and that the fourth was white, with large, red blotches. She had known cattle all her life. She would know these, if she saw them anywhere.

She also discovered for herself that they could not have broken out of that pasture, and that the river bank was impassable, because of high, thick bushes and miry mud in the open spaces. She had a fight with Blue over these latter places and demonstrated beyond doubt that they were miry, by getting him in to the knees in spite of his violent objections. They left deep tracks behind them when they got out. The calves had not gone investigating the bank, for there was not a trace anywhere. And the bluff was absolutely unscalable. Billy Louise herself would have felt doubtful of climbing out that way. The gray rim-rock stood straight and high at the top, with never a crevice, so far as she could see. And the gorge was barred, so that it was impossible to go that way without lifting heavy poles out of deep sockets and sliding them to one side.

"I've got an idea about a gate here," Charlie confided suddenly. "There won't be any more mysteries like this. I'm going to fix a swinging gate in place of these bars, Miss Louise. I shall have it swing uphill, like this; and I'll have a weight arranged so that it will always close itself, if one is careless enough to ride on and leave it open. I have it all worked out in my alleged brain. I shall do it right away, too. Aunt Marthy is rather nervous about this gorge, now. Every evening she walks up here herself to make sure the bars are closed."

"You may as well make up your mind to it," said Billy Louise irrelevantly, in a tone of absolute certainty. "Those calves were driven out of the gorge. That means stolen. You needn't accuse anyone in particular; I don't suppose you could. But they were stolen."

Charlie frowned and glanced up speculatively at the bluff's rim.

"Oh, your mountain-sheep theory is no good," Billy Louise giggled. "I doubt if a lizard, even, would try to leave the Cove over the bluff." Which certainly was a sweeping statement, when you consider a lizard's habits. "A mountain sheep couldn't, anyway."

"They're hummers to climb —"

"But calves are not, Mr. Fox! Not like that. You know yourself they were stolen; why not admit it?"

"Would that do any good-bring them back?" he countered, looking up at her.

"N-o, but I do hate to see a person deliberately shut his eyes in front of a fact. We may as well admit to ourselves that there is a rustler in the country. Then we can look out for him."

Charlie's eyes had the troubled look. "I hate to think that. Aunt Martha insists that is what we are up against, but —"

"Well, she knows more about it than you do, believe me. If you'll let down the bars, Mr. Fox, I'll hit the trail. And if I find out anything, I'll let you know at once."

When she rode over the bleak upland she caught herself wishing that she might talk the thing over with Ward. He would know just what ought to be done. But winter was coming, and she would drive her stock down into the fields she had ready. They would be safe there, surely. Still, she wished Ward would come. She wanted to talk it over with a man who understood and who knew more about such things than she did.

Chapter VII. Ward Hunts Wolves

The fate of the four heifer calves became permanently wrapped in the blank fog of mystery. Billy Louise watched for them when she rode out in the hills, and spent a good deal of time heretofore given over to dreaming in trying to solve the riddle of their disappearance. Charlie Fox insisted upon keeping to the theory that they had merely strayed. Marthy grumbled sometimes over the loss, and Ward-well, Ward did not put in an appearance again that fall or winter and so did not hear of the incident.

November brought a long, tiresome storm of snow and sleet and chill winds, which even the beasts would not face, except when they were forced. After that there were days of chilly sunlight, nights of black frost, and more wind and rain and snow. Each little ranch oasis withdrew into itself and settled down to pass the winter in physical comfort and mental isolation. Even Billy Louise seldom rode abroad unless she was compelled to, which was not often. The stage which passed through the Wolverine basin twice a week left scanty mail in the starch-box which Billy Louise had herself nailed to a post nearest the trail. Now and then a chance traveler pulled thankfully out of the trail, stopped for a warm dinner or a bed, and afterwards went his way. But from October until the hills were green, there was never a sight of Ward, and Billy Louise changed her mood and her opinion of him three or four times a week.

Ward, as a matter of fact, had a very good reason for his absence. He was working for a rancher over on the other side of the mountains, and when he got leave of absence, it was merely that he might ride to his claim and sleep there a night in compliance with the law, and see that nothing was disturbed. He was earning forty dollars a month, which he could not afford to jeopardize by any prolonged absence; and he was to take part of his pay in cows. Also, he had made arrangements to keep his few head of stock with the rancher's for a nominal sum, which barely saved Ward from the humiliation of feeling that the man was giving him something for nothing. Junkins, the rancher, was a good fellow, and he had a fair sense of values. He knew that he could pay Ward these wages and let him winter his stock there —I believe Ward had seven or eight head at that time-and still make a fair profit on his labor. For Ward stuck to his work, and he worked fast, with the drive of his nervous energy and the impatience he always felt toward any obstacle. Junkins considered privately that Ward was giving him the work of two men, while he had the appetite of one. So that it was to his interest to induce Ward to stay until spring opened and gave him plenty to do on his own claim; and such was Ward's anxiety to acquire some property and a certain financial security, that he put behind him the temptation to ride down to the Wolverine until he was once more his own master. He had sold his time to Junkins. He would not pilfer the hours it would take to ride twenty miles and back again, even to see Billy Louise; which proves that he was no moral weakling, whatever else he might be.

Then, in April, he left Junkins and drove home a nice little bunch of ten cows and a two-year-old and two yearlings. One of the cows had a week-old calf, and there would be more before long. Ward sang the whole of *Chisholm Trail* at the top of his voice, as he drifted the cattle slowly up the long hill to the top of the divide, from where he could look down over lower hills into his own little creek-bottom.

"With my knees in the saddle and my seat in the sky,

I'll quit punching cows in the sweet by-and-by,"

he finished exuberantly and promised himself that he would ride down to the Wolverine the very next day "and see how the folks came through the winter." He wanted to tell William Louisa that he was some cowman himself, these days. He thought he had made a pretty good showing in the last twelve months; for when he first met her, at the Cedar Creek ford, he hadn't owned a hoof except the four which belonged to Rattler, his horse. He thought that maybe, if the play came right and he didn't lose his nerve, he might tell William Louisa something else! It seemed to him that he had earned the right now.

He rode three miles oblivious to his surroundings, while he went carefully over his acquaintance-no, his friendship-with Billy Louise and tried to guess what she would say when he told her what he had wanted to tell her for a year; what he had been hungry to tell her. Sometimes he smiled a little, and sometimes he looked gloomy. He ended by hurrying the cattle down the canyon so that he might ride on to the Wolverine that night. It would be tough on Rattler, but then, what's a range cayuse made for, anyway? Rattler had had a snap, all winter; he could stand a hard deal once, for a change. It would do the old skate good to lift himself over fifty miles once more.

Whether it did Rattler any good or not, it put new heart into Ward to ride down the bluff and see the wink of the cabin window once more. He smiled suddenly to himself, threw back his shoulders, and lifted up his voice in the doggerel that had come to be a sort of bond between the two.

> "I'm on my best horse and a-comin' on the run,

> Best blamed cowboy that ever pulled a gun,"

he shouted gleefully. A yellow square opened in the cabin's side, and a figure stood outlined against the shining background. Ward laughed happily.

"Coma ti yi youpy, youpy-a, youpy-a," he sang uproariously.

Billy Louise turned her head toward the interior of the cabin and then left the light and merged into the darkness without. Ward risked a broken neck and went down the last bit of slope as if he were trying to head a steer. By the time he galloped up to the gate, Billy Louise was leaning over it. He could see her form dimly there.

"'Lo, Bill," he said softly and slid out of the saddle and went up to her. "How you was, already?" Again his voice was like a kiss.

"'Lo, Ward!" (in a tone that returned the kiss). "Don't know whether the stopping's good to-night or not. We've quit taking in tramps. Where the dickens have you been for the last ten years?" And that, on top of a firm conviction in Billy's Louise's mind that she did not care whether Ward ever crossed her trail again, and that when he did, he would have to do a lot of explaining before she would thaw to anything approaching friendliness. Oh, well, we all change our minds sometimes.

"I felt like it was twenty," Ward affirmed. "Do I get any supper, William? I like to have ridden my horse to a standstill getting here to-night; know that? I hope you appreciate the fact."

"It's a wonder you wouldn't have started a little sooner, then," Billy Louise retorted. "Along about Christmas, for instance."

"Wasn't my fault I didn't, William. Think I've got nothing to do but chase around the country calling on young ladies? I've been a wage slave, Bill-Loo. Come on while I put up my horse. Poor devil, I drove cattle from Junkins' place with him, and they weren't what you could call trail-broke, either. And then I came on down here. I've been in the saddle since daylight, young lady; and Rattler's been under it."

"Well, I'm very sure that it is not my fault," Billy Louise disclaimed, as she walked beside him to the stable.

"I'm not so sure of that! I might produce some pretty strong evidence that the last twenty miles is your fault. Say, you didn't know I've gone into the cow business myself, did you, William? I've been working like one son-of-a-gun all fall and winter, and I'm in the cattle-king class-to the extent of twelve head. I knew you were crazy to hear the glad tidings, so I tried to kill off a horse to get here and tell you. You and me'll be running a wagon and full crew in another year, don't you reckon? And send reps over into Wyoming and around, to look after our interests!" He laughed at himself with a perfect understanding of his own insignificance as a cattle-owner, and Billy Louise laughed with him, though not at him, for it seemed to her that Ward had done well, considering his small opportunities.

To be sure, in these days when civilization travels by million-dollar milestones, and the hero of a ten-dollar story scorns any enterprise which requires less than five figures to name its profits,

Ward and Billy Louise and Charlie Fox-and all their neighbors-do not amount to much. But it is a fact that real men and women in the real world beyond the horizon work hard and fight real battles for a very small success compared with Big Interests and the modern storyman. And I'm telling you of some real people in a real world out in the sagebrush country, where not even a story hero may consistently become a millionaire in ten chapters. There is no millionaire material in the sagebrush country, you know, unless it is planted there by the Big Interests; and the Big Interests do not plant in barren soil. So if twelve head of cattle look too trifling to mention, I can't help it. Ward worked mighty hard for those few animals, and saved and schemed, and denied himself much pleasure. Therefore, he did as well as any man under the circumstances could do and be honest.

He did not do so very well when it came to telling Billy Louise something. Twice during his visit he had to admit to himself that the play came right to tell her. And both times Ward shied like a horse in the moonlight. For all that he sang about half the way home, the next day, and for the rest of the way he built castles; which proves that his visit had not been disappointing.

He rode out into the pasture where his cattle were grazing and sat looking at them while he smoked a cigarette. And while he smoked, that small herd grew and multiplied before the eyes of his imagination, until he needed a full crew of riders to take care of them. He shipped a trainload of beef to Chicago before he threw away the cigarette stub, and he laughed to himself when he rode back to the log cabin in the grove of quaking aspens.

"I'm getting my money's worth out of that bunch, just in the fun of planning ahead," he realized, while he whittled shavings from the edge of a cracker-box to start his supper fire. "A few cows and calves make the best day-dream material I've struck yet; wish I had more of the same. I'd make old Dame Fortune put a different brand on me, pronto. She could spell it with an F, but it wouldn't be football. If the cards fall right," he mused, when the fire was hot and crackling, and he was slicing bacon with his pocket-knife, "I'll get the best of her yet. And —" His coffee-pail boiled over and interrupted him. He burned his fingers before he slid the pail to a cooler spot, and after that he thought of the joys of having a certain gray-eyed girl for his housekeeper, and for a time he forgot about his newly acquired herd.

And then his day-dreams received a severer jolt, and one more lasting. He began to realize something that he had always known: that there is something more to the cattle business than branding the calves and selling the beef.

When the first calf went to dull the hunger of the wolves that howled o'nights among the rocks and stunted pines on Bannock Butte, Ward swore a good deal and resolved to ride with his rifle tied on the saddle hereafter. Also, he went back immediately, got a little fat, blue bottle of strychnine, and returned and "salted" the small remnant of the carcass. It was no part of his dreams to have the profit chewed off his little herd by wolves.

When the second calf was pulled down in spite of the mother's defense, within half a mile of his cabin, Ward postponed a trip he had meant to make to the Wolverine and went out on the trail of the wolves. In the loose soil of the lower ridge he tracked them easily and rode at a shuffling trot along the cow-trail they had followed, his eyes keen for some further sign of them. He guessed that there would be at least one den farther up in the gulch that opened out ahead, and if he could find it and get the pups-well, the bounty on one litter would even his loss, even if he were not lucky enough to get one of the old ones. He had a shovel tied to the saddle under his left leg, to use in case he found a den.

So, planning a crusade against these enemies to his enterprise, he picked his way slowly up the side of the deep gully that had a little stream wandering through rocks at the bottom. His eyes, that Billy Louise had found so quick and keen, noted every little jutting shelf of rock, every badger hole, every bush. It looked like a good place for dens of wolf or coyote. And with the sun shining down warm on his shoulders, and the meadow larks singing from swaying weeds, and rabbits scuttling away through the rocks now and then, Ward began to forget the ill-luck that had brought him out and to enjoy the hunt for its own sake.

Farther along there were so many places that would bear investigation that he left Rattler on a level spot, and with his rifle and six-shooter, went forward on foot, climbing over ledges of rock, forcing his way through green-budded, wild-rose bushes or sliding down loose, gravelly slopes.

One place—a tiny cave under a huge bowlder-looked promising. There were wolf tracks going in and out, plenty of them. But there were no bones or offal anywhere around, and Ward decided that it was not a family residence, but that the wolves had perhaps invaded the nest of some other animal. He went on hopefully. That side of the gulch was cobwebbed with tracks.

Then, quite accidentally, he glanced across to the far side, his eyes attracted to something which had moved. He could see nothing at first, though from the corner of his eye he had certainly caught a flicker of movement over there. Yellow sand, gray rocks and bushes, and above a curlew circling, with long beak outstretched before, and long, red legs stretched out behind. He almost believed he had but caught the swift passing of a cloud shadow over there and was on the point of climbing farther up his own slope, to where a yawning hole in the hill showed signs of being pawed and trampled. Then an outline slowly defined itself among a jumble of rocks; head, sloping back, two points for ears. It might be a rock, but it began to look more and more like a wolf sitting up on its haunches watching him fixedly.

Even while Ward lifted his rifle and got the ivory bead snugly fitted into the notch of the rear sight with his eye, he would not have bet two-bits that he was aiming at an animal. He pulled the trigger with a steady crooking of his forefinger and the whole gulch clamored with the noise. The object over there leaped high, came down heavily, and rolled ten feet down the hill to another level, where it bounded three or four times convulsively, slid a few feet farther, and lay still behind a bush.

"Got you that time, you old Turk, if you did nearly fool me playing you were part of the scenery." Ward slid recklessly down to the bottom, sought a narrow place, jumped the creek, and climbed exultantly to where the wolf lay twisted on its back, its eyes half open and glazed, its jaws parted in a sardonic grin. Ward grinned also as he looked at it. He gave the carcass a poke with his boot-toe and glanced up the hill toward the rocks.

"Maybe you were playing lookout for the bunch," he said, "and then again, maybe you ain't hooked up with a family; though from the looks, you ain't weaned your pups yet-till just now." Leaving the wolf where she lay, he climbed to the rocks where he had first seen her. They lay high piled, but he could see daylight through every open space and so knew there was no den. The base rested solidly on the yellow earth.

Ward stood and looked at the slope below. To the right and half-way down was a ten-foot ledge, and below that outcropped a steep bank of earth. He could not see what lay immediately below, but while he was still staring, a pointed, gray nose topped by pert, gray ears poked cautiously over the bank, hovered there sniffing, and dropped back out of sight.

"You little son-of-a-gun!" he exclaimed and dug in his heels on the sharp descent. "I've got you right where I want you, now."

The den was tunneled into the earth just over another ledge, which underlay the bank there, and gave a sheer drop of ten or fifteen feet to the slope below, where a thick fringe of blossoming cherry bushes grew close and hid the ledge so completely that the den had been perfectly concealed from across the gulch. It was a case where the shovel was needed. Ward "flagged" the den by throwing his coat down before the opening and went back to where Rattler waited. He was jubilant over his good luck. With an average litter of pups, and the old wolf besides, the bounty would make those two calves the most profitable animals in the bunch, reckoned on the basis of money invested in them.

With the shovel he enlarged the tunnel, and between strokes he heard the whimpering of the pups. The sound sobered his face to a pitying determination. Poor little devils, it was not their fault that they were born to be a menace rather than a help to mankind. He was sorry for their terror, while he dug back to where they huddled against the farthest wall of their nest. He worked fast that he might the sooner end their discomfort, and his forehead was puckered into a frown at the harsh law of life that it must preserve its existence at the expense of some other life. Yet he dug back and back, burrowing into the bank toward the whimpering. It was farther than he had thought, but the soil was a loose sand and gravel, and he made good headway.

Then, laying down his shovel, he reached into a hysterical squirm of soft hair and sharp little teeth that snapped at his gloved hand. One by one he hauled them out, whining, biting, struggling like the little savages they were. One by one he sent them into oblivion with a sharp tap of the shovel. There were eight, just big enough to make little, investigative trips outside the den when all was quiet. Ward was glad he had found them and wiped them out of existence, but it had not been pleasant work.

He wiped the perspiration off his face with his handkerchief, pushed his hat to the back of his head, and sat down on the ledge beside the pile of dirt he had thrown out. He felt the need of a smoke, after all that exertion.

It was while he was smoking and resting that he first became conscious of the pile of dirt as something more than the obstacle between himself and the wolf-pups. He blew a little cloud of smoke from his mouth, leaned and lifted a handful of sand, picked something out of it, and looked at it intently. He said "Humph!" skeptically. Then he turned his head and stared at the ledge above and to the right of him, twisted half around and scanned the steep slope immediately above the earth bank, and then looked at the gulch beneath him. He took his cigarette from his lips, said, "Well, I'll be darned!" and put it back again. With his forefinger he turned over a small, rusty lump the size of a pea, wiped it upon his sleeve, and bent over it eagerly, holding it so that the light struck it revealingly. His face glowed. Save the want of tenderness in his eyes, he looked as though Billy Louise stood before him; the same guarded gladness, the same intent eagerness.

Ward sprawled over that pile of gravel and sand and searched with his fingers, as young girls search a thick bank of clover for the magic four leaves. He found one other small lump that he kept, but beyond that his search was barren of result. Still, that glow remained in his face. Finally he roused himself as though he realized that he was behaving foolishly. He made himself another cigarette and smoked it fast, keeping pace with his shuttling thoughts. And by the time the paper tube was burned down to an inch-long stub, he had won back his manner of imperturbable calm; only his eyes betrayed a hidden excitement.

"Looks like there's money in wolves," he said aloud and laughed a little. "Old Lady Fortune, you want to watch out, or I'm liable to get the best of you yet! Looks like I've got a hand to draw to, now. Youp-*ee-ee*!" His forced imperturbability exploded in the yell, and after that he moved briskly.

"I've got to play safe on this," he warned himself, while he scalped the last of the pups. "No use getting rattled. If she's good as she looks, she's fine. She'll help boost my little bunch of cattle, and that's all I want. I ain't going to go hog-wild over it, like so many do."

He went over and skinned the mother wolf, and with the pelts in a strong-smelling bundle, returned to the sand pile and filled his neckerchief as full as he could tie it. Then he went down into the gulch, jumped the creek with his load-and got a foot wet where his boot leaked along the sole-and climbed hurriedly up to where Rattler waited and dozed in the sunshine, with the reins dropped to the ground.

Rattler objected to those fresh wolf-skins, and Ward lifted a disciplinary boot-toe to his ribs. His mood did not accept patiently any unnecessary delay in getting home, and he succeeded in making Rattler aware of his mood. Rattler laid back his ears and took the trail in long, rabbit-jumps for spite, risking his own and his master's bones unchecked and unchided. The pace pleased Ward, and to the risk he gave no thought. He was reconstructing his air-castles on broader lines and smiling now and then to himself.

Chapter VIII. Help for the Cow Business

He had no goldpan of his own, since this was not a mining country, and his ambition had run in a different channel. He, therefore, took the tin washbasin down to the creek and dumped the sand into it. Then, squatting on his boot-heels at the edge of the stream, he filled the basin with water and rocked it gently with a rotary motion that proved him no novice at the work. His eyes were sharper and more intent in their gaze than Billy Louise had ever seen them, and, though his movements were unhurried, they were full of eagerness held in leash.

Several times he refilled the basin, and the amount of sand grew less and less, until there remained only a few spoonfuls of coarse gravel and a sediment that clung to the bottom of the basin and moved sluggishly around and around. He picked out the tiny pebbles one by one and threw them in the creek. He peered sharply at a small bit and held it in his fingers, while he bent his face close to the pan, his eyes two gimlets boring into the contents.

He got up stiffly, backed, and sat down upon the low bank with his feet far apart and his shoulders bent, while he stared at the little bit of mineral in his fingers.

"Coarse gold, and not such a hell of a lot," he pronounced to himself with careful impartiality. "But it's pay dirt, and if there's enough of it, it'll help a lot at this end of the cow business." He sat there a long time, thinking and planning and holding himself sternly to cold reality, rejecting every possibility that had the slightest symptom of being an air-castle. He did not intend to let this thing turn his head or betray him into any foolishness whatsoever. He was going to look at the thing cold-bloodedly and put his imagination in cold storage for the present.

His first impulse-to ride straight to the Wolverine and show Billy Louise these three tiny nuggets-he rejected as a bit of foolishness. He was perfectly willing to trust Billy Louise with any secret he possessed, but he knew that he would be feeding her imagination with dangerous fuel. She would begin dreaming and building castles and prospecting for herself, very likely; and that trail led oftenest to black disappointment. If he made good, he would tell her-when he told her something else. And if the whole thing were just a fluke, a stray deposit of a little gold that did not amount to anything, then it would be best for her to know nothing about it. Ward felt in himself, at that moment, the keen foretaste of bitter disappointment which would follow such a certainty. He did not want Billy Louise exposed to that pain.

He would tell her about the wolves, of course. It was pretty hard not to tell her everything that concerned himself, but the streak of native reticence in his nature had been strengthened by the vicissitudes of the life he had lived. While Billy Louise had found the sole weak point which made that reticence scarcely a barrier to full confidence, still he knew that he would keep this from her if he made up his mind to it.

He would not tell anybody. He raised his head and looked at the hills where his cattle would feed, and pictured it cluttered with gold-hunters, greedy, undesirable interlopers doomed to disappointment in the long run. Ward had seen the gold fever sweep through a community and spoil life for the weak ones who took to chasing the will-o'-the-wisp of sudden wealth. Tramps of the pick-and-pan brigade-they should not come swarming into these hills on any wild-goose chase, if he could help it. And he could and should. This was not, properly speaking, a gold country. He knew it. The rock formations did not point to any great deposit of the mineral, and if he had found one, it was a fluke, an accident. He resolved that his first consideration should be the keeping of his secret for the mental well-being of his fellows.

Ward did not put it quite so altruistically. His thoughts formed into sentences.

"This is cattle country. If men want to hunt gold, they can do their hunting somewhere else. They can't go digging up the whole blamed country just on the chance of finding another pocket like this one. I'm in the cattle business myself. If I find any gold, it'll go into cattle and stay there; and there won't be any long-haired freaks pestering around here if I can help it, and I reckon maybe I can, all right.

"I'd sure like to talk it over with Billy, but what she don't know won't worry her; and I don't know yet what I've gone up against. Maybe old Dame Fortune's just played another joke on me-played me for a fool again. I'll take a chance, but I won't give that little girl down below there anything to spoil her sleep."

Ward's memory was like glue, and while it held things he would give much to forget, still it served him well. He had ridden past a tiny, partly caved-in dugout, months ago, where some wandering prospector had camped while he braved the barrenness of the bills and streams hereabout. Ward had dismounted and glanced into the cavelike hut. Now, after he had eaten a few mouthfuls of dinner, he rode straight over to that dugout and got the goldpan he remembered to have seen there. It was not in the best condition, of course. It was battered and bent, but it would do for the present.

By the time he reached the wolf den, the sun was nearing the western rim of hills, but Ward had time to examine the locality more carefully than he had done at first and to wash a couple of pans of gravel. The test elated him perceptibly; for while there did not seem to be the makings of a millionaire in that gravel bank, he judged roughly that he could make a plumber's wages if he worked hard enough-and that looked pretty good to a fellow who had worked all his life for forty dollars a month. "Two-bits a pan, just about," he put it to himself. "And I'll have to pack the dirt down here to the creek; but I'll dig a nice little bunch of cattle out of that gravel bank before snow flies, or I miss my guess a mile."

As nearly as he could figure, he had chanced upon a split channel. For ages, he judged, the water had run upon that ledge, leaving the streak of gravel and what little gold it had carried down from the mountains. Then some freshet had worn over the edge of the break in the rock until the ledge and its deposit was left high and dry on the side of the gulch, while the creek flowed through the gully it had formed below. It might not be the correct explanation, but it satisfied Ward and encouraged him to believe that the streak of pay gravel lay along the ledge within easy reach.

He tried to trace the ledge up and down the gulch and to estimate the probable extent of that pay streak. Then he gave it up in self-defense. "I've got to watch my dodgers," he admonished himself, "or I'll go plumb loco and imagine I'm a millionaire. I'll pan what I can get at and let it go at that. And I've got to count what gold shows up in the sack-and no more. Good Lord! I can't afford to make a fool of myself at this stage of the game! I've got to sit right down on my imagination and stick to hard-boiled facts."

He went home in a very good humor with himself and the world, for all that. So far as he could see, the thing that had been bothering him was settled most satisfactorily. He had wanted to spend the summer on his claim, making improvements and watching over his cattle. There was fence to build and some hay to cut; and he would like to build another room on to the cabin. Ward had certain fastidious instincts, and he rebelled inwardly at eating, sleeping, and cooking all in one small room. But he had not been able to solve the problem of earning a living while he did all this-to say nothing of buying supplies. And he really needed a team and tools, if he meant to put up any hay.

Now, with that pay gravel within reach, and the gold running twenty-five cents to the pan, and the occasional tiny nuggets jumping up the yield now and then, he could go ahead and do the things he wanted to do. And he could dream about having a certain gray-eyed girl for his wife, without calling himself names afterward.

So he set to work the next morning in dead earnest with pick, shovel, and pan, to make the most of his little find. He shoveled the dirt and gravel into a gunny sack, threw the sack as far as he could over the ledge at the end, where it was not hidden and cluttered with the cherry-trees and service berries below, and when it stopped rolling, he carried it the rest of the way. Then he panned it in the little creek, watching like a hawk for nuggets and the finer gold. It was back-breaking work, and he felt that he earned every cent he got. But the cents were there, in good gold, and he was perfectly willing to work for what he received in this world.

After a couple of weeks he stopped long enough to make a hurried trip to Hardup, a little town forty miles farther up in the hills. In the little bank there he exchanged his gold harvest for coin of the realm, and he was well satisfied with the result. It was not a fortune, nor was he likely to find one in the hills. But he bought a team, wagon, and harness with the money, and he had enough left over for a two-months' grubstake and plenty of Durham and papers and a few magazines. That left him just enough silver to pay Rattler's bill at the livery stable. Nothing startling, but still not bad-that wolf-den find.

He had a lot of trouble getting his wagon to his claim, but by judicious driving and the liberal use of a log-chain for a rough lock, he managed to land the whole outfit in the little flat before the cabin without any mishap. After that he settled down to work the thing systematically.

One day he would pan the sandy gravel, and the next day he would rest his back digging post-holes or something comparatively easy. He worked from daybreak until it was too dark to see, and he never left his claim except when he went to wash gold up in the gulch. The world moved on, and he neither knew nor cared how it moved; for the time being his world had narrowed amazingly. If Billy Louise had not been down there in that other world, he would scarcely have given it a thought, so absorbed was he in the delightful task of putting a good, solid foundation under his favorite air-castle. That fascinated him, held him to his work in spite of his hunger to see her and talk with her and watch the changing lights in her eyes and the fleeting expressions of her face.

Some day he hoped he would have her with him always. He put it stronger than that: Some day he would have her with him, there in that little valley he had chosen; riding with him over those hills that smiled and seemed to stand there waiting for their invasions, with the echoes ready to fling back his exultant voice when he called to her or sang for her or laughed at her; ready to imitate enviously her voice when she laughed back at him. He wanted that day to come soon, and so with days and hours and minutes he became a miser and would not spend them in the luxury of a visit to her. It seemed to him that his longing for her measured itself by the enormous appetite he had for work, that summer.

Week followed week as he followed that thin, fluctuating streak of pay gravel along the ledge. Sometimes it was rich enough to set the pulse pounding in his temples; sometimes it was so poor that he was disgusted to the point of abandoning the work. But every day he worked, it yielded him something-though there was a week when he averaged about fifty cents a day and lived with a scowl on his face-and he kept at it.

He went out in June and bought a mower and rake and then spent precious days getting them into his valley. There was no road, you see, and he was compelled to haul them in a wagon, through country where nature never meant four wheels to pass. He hired a man for a month-one of those migratory individuals who works for a week or a month in one place and then wanders on till his money is spent-and he drove that man as relentlessly as he drove himself. Together they accomplished much, while the goldpan lay hidden under a buck brush and Ward's waking moments were filled with an uneasy sense of wasted time. Still, it was for the good of his ranch and his cattle and his air-castle that he toiled in the gulch, and it was necessary that he should put up what hay he could. There would be calves to feed next winter, he hoped; and when the hardest storms came, his horse would need a little. The rest of the stock would have to rustle; and that was why he had chosen this nook among the hills, where the wind would sweep the high slopes bare of snow, and the gulches would give shelter with their heavy thickets of quaking aspens and willow and alder.

He was thankful when the creek bottom was shaved clean of grass, and the stack beside his corral was of a satisfying length and height. The summer had been kind to the grass-growth, and his hay crop was larger than he had expected. A few days had remained of the month, and Ward had used them to extend his fence so as to give more pasturage to his calves in mild weather. After that he paid the man, directed him to the nearest point on the stage road, and breathed thanks that he was alone again, and could go back to his plan of digging a nice little hunch of cattle out of that bank before snow flew.

Chapter IX. When Emotions are Bottled

One day, when the sun was warm and the breeze that filtered down the gorge was pleasantly cool, Ward straightened his aching back, waded out to dry ground, and sat down to rest a few minutes and make a smoke. His interest in the work had oozed steadily since sunrise, and left nothing but the back-breaking toil. He had found a nugget the size of a hazelnut in the second pan that morning, so it was not discouragement that had made his monotonous movements grow slow and reluctant. Until he had smoked half the cigarette, he himself did not know what it was that ailed him. Then he flung up his head quite suddenly and gave a snort of understanding.

"Hang the gold! I'm going visiting for a change."

He concealed the goldpan and his pick, shovel, and sacks in the clump of service berries and chokeberries that grew at the foot of the ledge and hid from view the bank where he dug out his pay dirt. That did not take more than two or three minutes, and he made them up after he had swung into the saddle on the farther hillside. It was not a good trail, and except for his first exultant ride home that way, he had ridden it at a walk. Now he made Rattler trot where loping was too risky; and so he came clattering down the steep trail into the little flat beside his cabin. He would have something to eat, and feed Rattler a little hay, and then ride on to the Wolverine. And now that he had yielded to his hunger to see the one person in the world for whom he felt any tenderness, he grudged every minute that separated him from her. He loosened the cinch with one or two yanks and left the saddle on Rattler, to save time. He turned him loose in the hay corral with the bridle off, rather than spend the extra minutes it would take to put him in a stall and carry him a forkful of hay. He thought he would not bother to start a fire and boil coffee; he would eat the sour-dough bread and fried rabbit hams he had taken with him for lunch, and he would start down the creek in half an hour. He imagined himself an extremely sensible young man and considerate of his horse's comfort, to give him thirty precious minutes in which to eat hay. It was not absolutely necessary; Rattler could travel forty miles instead of twenty without another mouthful, so far as that was concerned. Ward was simply behaving in a perfectly normal manner and was not letting his feelings get the better of him in the slightest degree. As to his impromptu vacation, he was certainly entitled to it; he ought to have taken one long ago, he told himself virtuously. He had panned dirt all day, the Fourth of July; that was last week, he believed. And he had not made more than two dollars, either. No, he was not behaving foolishly at all. He had himself well in hand.

Then he flung open the door of his cabin and went white with sheer astonishment.

"Lo, Ward!" Billy Louise had been standing behind the door, and she jumped out at him, laughing, just as if she were ten years old instead of nearly twenty.

Ward tried to say, "Lo, Bill," in return, but the words would not come. His lips trembled too much, and his voice was pinched out in his throat. His mind refused to tell him what he ought to do; but his arms did not wait upon his paralyzed mental processes. They shot out of their own accord, caught Billy Louise, and brought her close against his pounding heart. Ward was startled and a little shocked at what he had done, but he held her closer and closer, until Billy Louise was gasping from something more than surprise.

Next, Ward's lips joined the mutiny against his reason, and laid themselves upon the parted, panting lips of Billy Louise, as though that was where they belonged.

Billy Louise had probably not expected anything like that, though of a truth one can never safely guess at what is in the mind of a girl. She tried to pull herself free, and when she could make no impression upon the grip of those arms-they had been growing muscles of iron ma-nipulating that goldpan, remember! —she very sensibly yielded to necessity and stood still.

"Stop, Ward! You —I —you haven't any right to —"

"Well, give me the right, then." Ward managed to find voice enough to make the demand, and then he kissed her many times before he attempted to say another word. Lord, but he had been hungry for her, these last three months!

"You'll give me the right, won't you, Wilhemina?" he murmured against her ear, brushing a lock of hair away with his lips. "You know you belong to me, don't you? And I belong to you-body and soul. You know that, don't you? I've known it ever since the world was made. I knew it when God said, 'Let there be light,' and there was light. You were it."

"You sill-y thing." Billy Louise did not seem to know whether she wanted to laugh or cry. "What do you think you're talking about, anyway?"

"About the way the world was made." Ward loosened his clasp a little and looked down deep into her eyes. "My world, I mean." He bent and kissed her again, gravely and very, very tenderly. "Oh, Wilhemina, you know —" he waited, gazing down with that intent look which had a new softness behind it —"you know there's nothing in this world but you. As far as I'm concerned, there isn't. There never will be."

Billy Louise reached up her hands to his shoulders and tried to give him a shake. "Is that why you've stuck yourself in these hills for three whole months and never come near? You fibber!"

"That's why, lady-girl. I've been sticking here, working like one son-of-a-gun-for you. So I could have you sooner." He lifted his bent head and looked around the little cabin like a man who has just wakened to his surroundings. "I knocked off work a little while ago, and I was going to see you. I couldn't stand it any longer. And-here you iss!" he went on, giving her shoulders a little squeeze. "A straight case of 'two souls with but a single thought,' don't you reckon?"

Billy Louise, by a visible effort, brought the situation down to earth. She twisted herself free and went over to the stove and saved a frying-pan of potatoes from burning to a crisp.

"I don't know about your soul," she said, glancing back at him. "I happen to have two or three thoughts in mine. One is that I'm half starved. The second is that you're not acting a bit nice, under the circumstances; no perfectly polite young man makes love to a girl when she is supposedly helpless and under his protection." She stopped there to wrinkle her nose at him and twist her mouth humorously. "The third thought is that if you don't behave, I shall go straight home and never be nice to you again. And," she added, getting back of the coffee-pot —which looked new —"the rest of my soul is one great big blob of question-marks. If you can eat and talk at the same time, you may tell me what this frantic industry is all about. If you can't, I'll have to wait till after dinner; not even my curiosity is going to punish my poor tummy any longer." She pulled a pan of biscuits from the oven, lifted them out one at a time with dainty little nabs because they were hot, and stole a glance now and then at Ward from under her eyebrows.

Ward stood and looked at her until the food was all on the table. He was breathing unnaturally, and his jaws were set hard together. When she pushed a box up to the table and sat down upon it, and rested her elbows on the oilcloth and looked straight at him with her chin nested in her two palms, he drew a long breath, hunched his shoulders with some mental surrender, and grinned wryly.

"So be it," he yielded, throwing his hat upon the bunk. "I kinda overplayed my hand, anyway. I most humbly ask your pardon!" He bowed farcically and took up the wash-basin from its bench just outside the door.

"You see, William Louisa," he went on quizzically, when he had seated himself opposite her and was helping himself to the potatoes, "when a young lady invades strange territory, and hides behind strange doors, and jumps out at an unsuspecting but terribly well-meaning young man, she's apt to get a surprise. When emotions are bottled —"

"Never mind the bottled emotions. I'd like some potatoes, if you don't want them all. I see you haven't the faintest idea how to treat a guest. Charlie Fox would have died before he would help himself and set down the dish away out of my reach. You could stick pins into him till he howled, but you couldn't make him be rude to a lady."

"I'd sure like to," muttered Ward ambiguously and handed her every bit of food within his reach.

"You can talk and eat at the same time, I see. So tell me what you've been doing all this while." Billy Louise spoke lightly, even flippantly, but her eyes were making love to him shyly, whether she knew it or not.

"Working," answered Ward promptly and briefly. He was thinking at the rate of a million thoughts a minute, it seemed to him, and he was afraid to let go of himself and say what he thought. One thing he knew beyond all doubt, and that was that he must be careful or he would see his air-castle blow up in small fragments and come down a hopeless ruin. He needed time to think, and Billy Louise was not giving him even a minute. So he clutched at two decisions which instinct told him might help him win to safety: He would not make love, and he would not tell Billy Louise about the gold.

"Working! Well, so have I. But working at what? Did you hire out to Junkins again? I thought you said you wouldn't till fall." Billy Louise was watching Ward rather closely, perhaps to see how far she might trust his recovered inscrutability. "Why don't you show some human inquisitiveness about my being here?" she asked irrelevantly, just as Ward was hastily choosing how he would answer her without saying too much.

"It wouldn't be polite to be inquisitive about a lady, would it?" Ward retorted, thankful for the change of subject.

"N-no-but, then, you never bother about being just polite! Charlie Fox would —"

"Charlie Fox would think you came to see him," Ward asserted uncharitably. "My head isn't swelled to that extent. Why did you come, anyway?"

"To see you." Billy Louise lost her nerve when she saw the light leap into his eyes. "To see whether you were dead or not," she revised hastily, "so mommie would stop worrying about you. Mommie has pestered the life out of me for the last month, thinking you might be sick or hurt or something. So —I was riding up this way, anyway, and —"

"I see I'll have to ride down and prove to mommie that I'm very much alive. I'm sure glad to know that somebody takes an interest in me-as if I were a real human." Ward's eyes watched furtively her face, but Billy Louise refused even to nibble at the bait.

"Why didn't you come before, then? You know mommie likes to have you."

"How about mommie's child?" Ward's look was dangerous to his good resolutions.

"Listen here, Ward." Billy Louise took refuge behind her terrible frankness. "If you make love, I won't like you half as well. Don't you know that all the time when I used to play with my pretend Ward Warren, he-he never made love?" A dimple tried to show itself in her cheek and was sent about its business with a twist of her lips. "My pretend Ward was lovely; he liked me to pieces, but he never came right out and said so. He-he skated around the subject —" Billy Louise illustrated the skating process by drawing her forefinger in a wide circle around her cup. "He made love-with his eyes-and he kissed me with his-voice-but he never spoiled it with words."

Ward grunted a word that sounded like "damchump."

"Nothing of the kind!" Billy Louise flew to the defense of her "pretend." "He knew just exactly how a girl likes to be made love to. And, anyway, you've been doing the selfsame thing yourself, Ward Warren, till just now. And —"

"Oh, have I?"

"Yes, you have. And I might have known better than to-to startle you. You always, eternally, do something nobody'd ever dream of your doing. The first time, when I threw that chip, you pulled a gun on me —" The voice of Billy Louise squeezed down to a wisp of a whisper. Her eyes were remorseful. "Oh, Ward, I didn't mean to-to —"

"It's all right. I've got it coming." It was as if a mask had dropped before Ward's features. Even his eyes looked strange and hard in that face of set muscles, though the thin, bitter lips and quivering nostrils showed that there was feeling behind it all. "I see where you're right, William. You needn't be afraid; I won't make love again."

Billy Louise looked as though she wanted to beat something-herself, most likely. She stared as they stare who watch from the dock while a loved one slips farther and farther away on a voyage from which there may be no return; only Billy Louise was not one to watch and do nothing else.

"Now, Ward, don't be silly." The fright in her voice was overlaid with a sharpened tenderness. "You know perfectly well I didn't mean that. You're only proving that in the human problem you're raised to — Stop looking darning-needles at that coffee-pot and listen here!" Billy Louise leaned over the table and caught at his nearest hand, which was a closed fist. With her own little fingers digging persistently into the tensed muscles, she pried the fist open. "Ward, behave yourself, or I'll go straight home!" She held his straightened fingers in her own and drew a sharp breath because they lay inert-dead things so far as any response came to her clasp; the first and middle fingers yellowed a little from cigarettes, the nails soft and pink from much immersion in water. A tale they told, if Billy Louise had been paying attention.

"Ward, you certainly are-the limit! You know as well as I do that that doesn't make a particle of difference. If I had been a boy instead of a girl, and had bucked the world for a living, I'd probably have done worse; and, anyway, it doesn't matter!" Her voice rose as if she were growing desperate. "I —I —like you-to pieces, Ward, and I'd —I'd rather marry you-than anyone else. But I don't want to think about that for a long while. I don't want to be engaged, or-or any different than the way we've been. It was good to be just pals. It was like my pretend Ward. I —I always wanted him-to love me, but I wouldn't play that he-told me, Ward. Oh, don't you see?" She shut her teeth hard together, because if she hadn't she would have been crying in another ten seconds.

"I see." Ward spoke dully, evenly, and he still stared at the coffee-pot with that gimlet gaze of his that made Billy Louise want to scream. "I see a whole lot that I'd been shutting my eyes to. Why don't you feel insulted —"

"Ward Warren, if you're going to act like a —a —" I suspect that Billy Louise, in her desperation, was tempted to use a swear word, but she resisted the temptation. She got up and went around to him, hesitated while she looked down at his set face, drew a long breath, and blinked back some tears of self-reproach because of the devils of memory she had unwittingly turned loose to jibe at this man.

"This is why," she said softly; and leaning, she pressed her lips down upon his bitter ones and let them lie there for a dozen heart-beats.

Ward's face relaxed, and his eyes went to hers with the hungry tenderness she had seen so often there. He leaned his head against her and threw up an arm to clasp her close. He did not say a word.

"After I have kissed a man," said Billy Louise, struggling back to her old whimsical manner, "it won't be a bit polite for him to have any doubts of my feelings toward him, or my belief in him, or his belief in himself." Her fingers tangled themselves in his hair, just where the wave was the most pronounced.

She had drawn the poison. Now she set herself to restore a perfectly normal atmosphere.

"He's going to be just exactly the same good pal he was before," she went on, speaking softly. "And he's going to bring some water so I can wash the dishes, and then bring Blue so I can go home, and he isn't going to say a single thing more about-anything that matters two whoops."

Ward's clasp tightened and then grew loose. He drew a long breath and let her go.

"You do like me —a little bit, don't you?" His eyes were like the eyes of the damned asking for water.

"I like you two little bits." Billy Louise took his face between her two palms and smiled down at him bravely, with the pure candor that was a part of her. "But I don't want us to be anything but pals; not for a long while. It's so good, just being friends. And once we get away from that point, we can't go back to it again, ever. And I'm sure it's good enough to be worth while making it last as long as we can. So now —"

"It's going to be quite a contract, Wilhemina." Ward still looked at her with his heart in his eyes.

"Oh, no, it won't! You've had lots of practice," Billy Louise assured him confidently and began putting the few dishes in a neat little pile. "And, anyway, you are perfectly able to handle any kind of a contract. All you need do is make up your mind. And that's made up already. So the next thing on the programme is to bring a bucket of water. Did you notice anything different about your cabin? I thought you bragged to me about being such a good housekeeper! Why, you hadn't swept the floor, even, since goodness knows when. And I've made up a bundle of your dirty shirts and things that I found under the bed, and I'm going to take them home and let Phoebe wash them. She can do them this evening and have them ready for you to bring back to-morrow. When I was a kid and went to see Marthy and Jase, I used to promise them cookies with 'raisings' in the middle. I thought there was nothing better in the world. I was just thinking —I'll maybe bake you some cookies with raisings on top, to bring home. You don't seem to waste much time cooking stuff. Bacon and beans, and potatoes and sour-dough bread: that seems to be your regular bill of fare. And tomatoes for Sunday, I reckon; I saw some empty cans outside. Don't you ever feel like coming down to the ranch and getting a square meal?"

"Oh, you William the Conqueror!" Ward stood with the water bucket in his hand, and looked at her with that smile hidden just behind his lips and his eyes. "You sure sabe how to make things come your way, don't you?" He started for the door, stopped with his toes over the threshold, and looked back at her. "If I knew how to get what I want, as easily as you do," he said, "we'd be married and keeping house before to-morrow night!" He laughed grimly at the start she gave. "As it is, you're the doctor, William Louisa. We remain mere friends!" With that he went off to the creek.

He was gone at least four times as long as was necessary, but he came back whistling, and he did not make love to her except with his eyes.

Chapter X. This Pal Business

"You've got quite a lot of hay put up, I see," Billy Louise remarked, when they were leaving.

"Sure. I told you I've been working." Ward's tone was cheerful to the point of exuberance. He felt as though he could work day and night now, with the memory of Billy Louise's lips upon his own.

"You never put up that hay alone," she told him bluntly, "and you needn't try to make me believe you did. I know better."

"How do you know?" Ward glanced over his shoulder at the stack, then humorously at her. He recognized the futility of trying to fool Billy Louise, but he was in the mood to tease her.

"Humph! I've helped stack hay myself, if you please. I can tell a one-man stack when I see it. Who did you get to help? Junkins?"

"No, a half-baked hobo I ran across. I had him here a month."

"Oh! Are those your horses down there? They can't be." Last April, Billy Louise had been very well informed as to Ward's resources. She was evidently trying to match her knowledge of their well-defined limitations with what she saw now of prosperity in its first stages.

"They are, though. A dandy span of mares. I got a bargain there."

Billy Louise pondered a minute. "Ward, you aren't going into debt, are you?" Her tone was anxious. "It's so beastly hard to get out, once you're in!"

"I don't owe anybody a red cent, William Louisa. Honest."

"Well, but —" Billy Louise looked at him from under puckered brows.

Ward laughed oddly. "I've been working, William. Last spring I —hunted wolves for awhile; old ones and dens. They'd killed a couple of calves for me, and I got out after them. I —made good at it; the bounty counts up pretty fast, you know."

"Yes-s, it does." Billy Louise bit her lips thoughtfully, turned and looked back at the haystack, at the long line of new, wire fence, and at the two heavy-set mares feeding contentedly along the creek. "There must be money in wolves," she remarked evenly.

"There is. At least, I made good money hunting them." The smile was hiding behind Ward's lips again and threatening to come boldly to the surface. "They haven't bothered you any, I hope?"

"No," said Billy Louise, "they haven't. I guess they must be all up your way."

For the life of him Ward could not tell to a certainty whether there was sarcasm in her tone or whether she spoke in perfect innocence. The shrewdest of us deceive ourselves sometimes. Ward might have known he could not fool Billy Louise, who had careworn experience of the cost of ranch improvements and could figure almost the exact number of wolf-bounties it would take to pay for what he had put into his claim. Still, he was right in thinking she would not quiz him beyond a certain point. She seemed to have reached that point quite suddenly, for she did not say another word about Ward's affairs.

"What all's been happening in the world, anyway?" he asked, when they had exhausted some very trivial subjects. "Your world, I mean. Anything new or startling taken place?"

"Not a thing. Marthy was down last week and spent the day with us. I never saw anybody change as much as she has. She looks almost neat, these days. And she can't talk about anything but Charlie and how well he's doing. She lets him do most of the managing, I think. And he had some money left to him, this spring, and has put it into cattle. He bought quite a lot of mixed stock from Seabeck and some from Winters and Nelson, Marthy says. I passed some of his cattle coming up."

"Going to have a rival in the business, am I?" Ward laughed. "I was figuring on being the only thriving young cattle-king in this neck of the woods, myself."

"Well, Charlie's in a fair way to beat you to it. I wish," sighed Billy Louise, "some kind person would leave me a bunch of money. Don't you? Cattle are coming up a little all the time. I'd like to own a lot more than I do."

"Well, we —" Ward stopped and reconsidered. "If wolfing continues to pay like it has done," he said, with a twitch of the lips, "I intend to stick my little Y6 monogram on a few more cowhides before snow flies, William. And when you've had enough of this friend business —"

"Oh, by that time we'll all be rich!" Billy Louise declared lightly, and for a wonder Ward was wise enough to let that close the subject.

"We're getting neighbors down below, too," she observed later. "I didn't tell you that. Down the river a few miles. The country is settling up all the time," she sighed. "Pretty soon there won't be any more wilderness left. I like it up where you've located. That will stay wild forever, won't it? They can't plant spuds on those hills, anyway.

"And-did you hear, Ward? Seabeck and some of the others have been losing stock, they say. You know Marthy lost four calves last fall, by some means. Charlie Fox was terribly worried about it, though it was his own fault, and-well, I thought at the time someone had taken them, and I think so still. And just the other day one of Seabeck's men stopped at the ranch, and he told me they're shy some cows and calves. They can't imagine what went with them, and they're lying low and not saying anything much about it. You haven't heard or seen anything, have you, Ward?"

"I've stuck so close to the hills I haven't heard or seen anything," Ward affirmed. "It's amazing, the way the days slip by when a fellow's busy all the time. Except for two trips out the other way, to Hardup, I haven't been three miles from my claim all spring."

"Hardup! That's where the bank was robbed, a few weeks ago, isn't it? The stage-driver told me about it."

"I don't know; I hadn't heard anything about it. I haven't been there for a month and more," said Ward easily. "Nearer two months, come to think of it. I was there after a mower and rake and some wire."

"Oh!" Billy Louise glanced at him sidelong and added several more wolves to the number she had mentally put down to Ward's credit.

Ward twisted in the saddle so that he faced her, and his eyes were dancing with mischief. "Honest, William, I'm not wading into debt. Every cent I've put into that place this summer I made hunting wolves. That's a fact, Wilhemina."

"I wish you'd tell me how, so I can do it, too," Billy Louise sighed, convinced by his tone and flat statement, yet feeling certain there was some "catch" to it, after all. It was exactly like a riddle that sounds perfectly plain and simple to the ears, and to the reason utterly impossible.

"Well, I will-when you're through playing pals," he assured her cruelly. Ward did not know women very well, but he believed curiosity to be one of the strongest traits in the sex. "That's a bargain, William Louisa, and I'll shake hands on it if you like. When you've had enough of this just-friend business, I'll show you how I dig dollars outa wolf-dens." He grinned at the puzzled face of her. It was a riddle, and he had practically put the answer before her, and still she could not see it. There was a little streak of devilment in Ward, and happiness was uncovering the streak.

"I never said I was crazy to know," Billy Louise squelched him promptly. "Not that crazy, anyway. I'll live quite as long without knowing, I reckon."

She almost won her point-because Ward did not know women very well. He hesitated, gave her a quick, questioning glance, and actually opened his lips to tell her all about it. He got as far as, "Oh, well, I suppose I'll have to —" when Billy Louise saw a rattlesnake in the trail ahead and spurred up to kill it with her rope. She really was crazy to know the answer to the riddle, but a rattlesnake will interrupt anything from a proposal of marriage to a murder.

Ward's fingers had gone into the pocket in his shirt where the nugget he had found that morning was sagging the cloth a little. He had been on the point of giving it to Billy Louise, but he let it stay where it was and instead took down his own rope to get after the snake, that had crawled under a bush and there showed a disposition to fight. And since Blue was no fonder of rattlesnakes than he was of mud, Billy Louise could not bring him close enough for a direct blow.

"Get back, and I'll show you why I named this cayuse Rattler," Ward shouted. "I'll bet I've killed five hundred snakes with him —"

"Almost as many as you have wolves!" Billy Louise snapped back at him and so lost her point just when she had practically gained it. Ward certainly would not tell her, after that stab.

Rattler perked his ears forward toward the strident buzzing which once heard is never forgotten, and which is never heard without a tensing of nerves. He sighted the snake, coiled and ready for war in the small shade of a rabbit-bush. He circled the spot warily, his head turned sidewise, and his eyes fixed upon the flattened, ugly head with its thread of a darting tongue.

Ward pulled his gun, "threw down" on the snake, and cut off its head with a bullet.

"I could have done that myself," Billy Louise asserted jealously.

"Well, I forgot. Next time I'll let you do the shooting. I was going to show you how Rattler helps. He'll circle around just right so I can make one swing of the rope do. But Mr. Snake stuck too close to that rabbit brush; and I was afraid if I drove him out of there with my rope, he'd get under those rocks. I'm sorry, Wilhemina. I didn't think."

"Oh, I can get all the snake-shooting I want, any time." Billy Louise laughed good-humoredly. "I wish you'd give Blue a few lessons-the old sinner!"

"Not on your life, I won't." Ward leaned from the saddle, picked up the snake by the tail, pinched off the rattles, and dropped the repulsive thing to the ground with a slight shiver of relief. He gave the rattles to Billy Louise. "I'm glad Blue does feel a wholesome respect for rattlers; he'll take better care of himself-and his mistress. With me it doesn't matter."

"Oh-doesn't it?" asked Billy Louise, and there was that in her tone that made Ward's heart give a flop. "There's some of Marthy's cattle right ahead," she added hurriedly, seizing the first trifle with which to neutralize the effect of that tone.

"MK monogram," said Ward absently, reading the brand mechanically, as is the habit of your true range man. "Pretty fresh, too. Must have just bought them."

"He got them a month or so ago," said Billy Louise. "Marthy says —"

"A month?" Ward turned and gave the cow nearest him a keener look. "Pretty good condition," he observed, quite idly. "Say, William, when these hills get filled up with Y6es and big Ds, all these other scrub critters will have to hunt new range, won't they?"

"It will be a long while before the big Ds crowd out so much as a crippled calf," Billy Louise answered pessimistically. "I lost two nice heifers, a week or so ago. They broke through the upper fence into the alfalfa and started to fill up, of course. They were dead when I found them."

"Next time I cash in my wolf—" Ward started to promise, but she cut him short.

"Do you mind if we stop at the Cove, Ward? Mommie wanted me to stop and get some currants. Marthy says they're ripe, and she has more than she knows what to do with."

"I don't mind-if you're dead sure it's the currants."

"You certainly are in a pestering mood to-day," Billy Louise protested, laughing. "You can't jump any game on that trail, smarty. Charlie Fox is a perfectly lovely young man, but he's got a girl in Wyoming. The stage-driver says there's never been a trip in that he didn't take a letter from the Cove box to Miss Gertrude M. Shannon, Elk Valley, Wyoming. So you needn't try —"

"Nice, mouthy stage-driver," Ward commented. "Foxy ought to land on him a few times and see if he'd take the hint."

"Well, I knew it before he told me. Marthy said last winter that Charlie's engaged. He's trying to get prosperous enough to marry her and bring her out to the Cove; it will be his when Marthy dies, anyway. I must say Charlie's a hustler, all right. He keeps a man all the time now, since he bought more cattle. Peter Howling Dog's working for him. Charlie's tried to range-herd his cattle so he and Peter can gather them alone; and he offered to look after mine, too, so I won't have so much riding to do this hot weather. He's awfully nice, Ward, really. I don't care if he is a rah-rah boy. And he isn't a bit in love with me."

"Is it possible," grinned Ward, "that any human man can come out West and not fall in love with the Prairie Flower —"

"Ward Warren, do you want me to —"

"But it's breaking all the rules of romance, Bill-the-Conk!" Ward persisted. "No story-sharp would ever stand for a thing like that. Don't you know that the nice young man from college always takes notice in the second chapter, says 'By Jove! What a little beauty!' in the third, and from there on till the wind-up spends most of his time running around in circles because the beautiful flower of the rancho gives him the bad eye?" He twisted sidewise in the saddle, took a half-hitch with the reins around the saddle-horn, and proceeded to manufacture a cigarette while he went on with the burlesque.

"It opened out according to Hoyle, a year ago, William. Nice young man comes west. Finds Flower of the Rancho first rattle of the box, with brave young buckaroo riding herd on her to beat four of a kind. Looks like there's no chance for our young hero. Brave buckaroo has to hie him forth to toil, however —" Ward paused long enough to light up, and afterwards blow out the match carefully before dropping it in the trail, " —at the humble sum of forty dollars per month. That leaves our young hero on the job temporarily. Stick in a few chapters of heart-burnings on the part of the brave buckaroo —"

"Oh, yes, no doubt!" from Billy Louise, who was trying not to giggle.

"Oh, he had 'em, far as that goes. Brave buckaroo had heart-burnings enough for a Laura Jean Libbey romance. All according to Hoyle. Young hero — Say, Bill, what's the matter with that gazabo, anyway? Hasn't he got good eyesight, or what? Can't the chump see he's over-looking a bet when —"

"Oh, you make me sick!" Billy Louise slashed at a ripening branch of service berries with her quirt and scared Blue so that he lunged against the romancer. "You men seem to think the girl has nothing to say about it! You think we just sit and smile and wait for somebody to snap his fingers, and we jump at him! You —"

"Didn't I say there would be several chapters where the haughty beauty keeps our young hero running around in circles, and the brave buckaroo can't figure out whether he ought to buy a ring or more shells for his six-gun?"

"With the inference that she flops into his arms in the last chapter and hides her maidenly blushes against the pocket where he keeps his sack of Bull Durham and papers —"

"Oh, you Bill-the-Conk! It would be the brave buckaroo in the last chapter then, would it?" Ward leaned close, swift tenderness putting the teasing twinkle to flight from his eyes. "Our young hero smokes a briar, Wilhemina-mine!"

"We-el—don't skip!" cried Billy Louise, backing away from him with more blushes than any girl could hope to hide behind a coat of tan. "There's lots of chapters before the last. And you've got to read them straight through and-no fair skipping!"

"Wilhemina-mine!" Ward repeated the newly invented appellation, which seemed to ap-proach satisfactorily close to the line of forbidden endearments.

"Oh, for pity's sake! I never knew you to act so." Billy Louise scowled unconvincingly at him from a safe distance.

"I never was kissed before," blurted Ward foolhardily, kicking Rattler closer.

"Well, if that's what ails you, I'll see it doesn't happen again," retorted Billy Louise squelch-ingly, and Ward's self-assurance was not great enough to lift him over the barrier of that rebuff.

They came upon Charlie Fox sitting on his horse beside the crude mail-box, reading avidly a letter of many crisp, close-written pages. Billy Louise flashed Ward an I-told-you-so glance.

"Why, how do you do?" Charlie came out of cloudland with a start and turned to them cordially, while he hastily folded the letter. "Going down into the Cove? That's good. I was just up after the mail. How are things up your way, Warren?"

"Fine as silk." Ward's eyes swung briefly toward what he considered the chief bit of fineness.

"That's good. Trail's a little narrow for three, isn't it? I'll ride ahead and open the gate."

"They've got a new gate down here," said Billy Louise trivially. "I forgot that important bit of news."

"Well, it is important-to us Covers," smiled Charlie, glancing back at them. "No more bars to be left down accidentally. This gate shuts itself, in case someone forgets."

"And you haven't lost any more cattle, have you?" The question was a statement, after Billy Louise's habit.

"Not out of the Cove, at any rate. I —can't speak so positively as to the outside stock-of course."

"You've missed some?" Billy Louise never permitted a tone to slip past her without tagging it immediately with plain English. Charlie's tone had said something to which his words made no reference.

"I don't like to say that, Miss Louise. Very likely they have stray-drifted, I mean-back toward their home ranch. Peter and I can't keep cases very closely, of course."

Billy Louise shifted uneasily in the saddle and pulled her eyebrows together. "If you think you've lost some cattle, for heaven's sake why don't you say so!" (Ward smiled to himself at her tone.) "If there's anything I hate, it's hinting and never coming right out with anything. Have you lost any?"

Charlie turned with a hand on the cantle and faced her with polite reproach. "Peter says we have," he admitted, with very evident reluctance. "I hardly think so myself. I'd have to count them. I know, of course, how many we've bought in the last year."

"Well, Peter knows more about it than you do," Billy Louise told him bluntly. "If he has missed any, they're probably gone."

"I was in hopes you would be on my side, Miss Louise." Charlie smiled deprecatingly. "I've argued with Aunt Martha and Peter until — But I didn't know you were a confirmed pessimist as well!"

"You didn't neglect to put your brand on them, did you?" asked Billy Louise cruelly.

Charlie flushed under the sunburn. "Really, Miss Louise, you've no mercy on a tenderfoot, have you?" he protested. "No, they are all branded, really they are. Peter and Aunt Martha saw to that," he confessed naïvely.

"It seems queer," said Billy Louise, thinking aloud. "Ward, there certainly is rustling going on around here; and no one seems to know a thing beyond the mere fact that they're losing cattle. Seabeck has lost some —"

"Oh, are you sure?" Charlie's eyes widened perceptibly. "I hadn't heard that. By Jove! It sort of makes a fellow feel shaky about going into cattle very strong, doesn't it? It-it knocks off the profits like the very deuce, to keep losing one here and there."

"A fellow has to figure on a certain percentage of loss," said Ward. "This the new gate?"

"Yes." Charlie seemed relieved by the diversion. "Just merely a gate, as you see; but we Covers are proud of every little improvement. Aunt Martha comes up here every day, I verily believe, just to look at it and admire it. The poor old soul never had any conveniences that she couldn't make herself, you know, and she thinks this is great stuff. I put this padlock on it so she can lock herself in, nights when I'm away. She feels better with the gate locked. And then I've got a dog that's as good as a company of soldiers himself. If either of you happen down here when there's no one about, you will have to introduce yourselves to Cerberus-so named because he guards the gates-not the gate to Hades, please remember. Surbus, Aunt Martha calls him, which is good Idahoese and seems to please him as well as any other. Just speak to him by name-Surbus if you like-and he will be all right, I think." He held open the gate for them to ride through and gave them a comradely look and smile as they passed.

Ward took in the details of the heavy gate that barred the gorge. He did not know that he betrayed the fact even to the sharp eyes of Billy Louise, but he could not quite bring himself to the point of meeting Charlie Fox anywhere near half-way in his overtures for friendship.

"The weight is so heavy that the gate shuts and latches itself, you see," Charlie went on, mounting on the inside of the barrier and following cheerfully after them. "But that doesn't satisfy Aunt Martha. She and Surbus make a special pilgrimage up here every night."

"She must be pretty nervous." Ward could not quite see why such precautions were necessary in a country where no man locked his door against the world.

"Well, she is, though you wouldn't suspect it, would you? When one thinks of the life she has lived, and how she pioneered in here when the country was straight wilderness, and all that. Of course, I didn't know her before Uncle Jason died-do you think she has changed since, Miss Louise?"

"Lots," Billy Louise assured him briefly. She was wondering why Ward was so stiff and unnatural with Charlie Fox.

"I think myself that the shock of losing him must have made the difference in her. There's Surbus; how's that for a voice? And he's just as blood-thirsty as he sounds, too. I'd hate to have him tackle me in the gorge, on a dark night. He's too savage, though it's only with strangers, and we don't see many of them. He almost ate Peter up, when he first came. And he gave you quite a scare last spring, didn't he, Miss Louise?"

"He came within an ace of getting his head shot off," Billy Louise qualified laconically. "Marthy came out just in the nick of time. I absolutely refuse to be chewed up by any dog; and I don't care who he belongs to."

"Same here, William," approved Ward.

Charlie laughed. "I see Surbus is not going to be popular with the neighbors," he said easily. "I do feel very apologetic over him. But Marthy wanted me to get a dog, and so when a fellow offered me this one, I took him; and as Surbus happened to take a fancy to me, I didn't realize what a savage brute he is, till he tackled Peter-and then Miss Louise."

"Well, Miss Louise was perfectly able to defend herself, so you needn't feel apologetic about that," said Billy Louise a trifle sharply. She hated Surbus, and she was quite open in her hatred. "If he ever comes at me again, and nobody calls him off, I shall shoot him." It was not a threat, as she spoke it, but a plain statement of a fact. "You'd better serve notice too, Ward. He's a nasty beast, and he'd just as soon kill a person as not. He was going to jump for my throat. He was crouched, just ready to spring-and I had my gun out-when Marthy saw us and gave a yell fit to wake the dead. Surbus didn't jump, and I didn't shoot. That's how close he came to being a dead dog."

She glanced at Ward and then furtively at Charlie Fox. If expression meant anything, Surbus was yet in danger of paying for that assault. She caught Ward's truculent eye, smiled, and shook her head at him. "We're pretty fair friends now," she said. "At least, we don't try to kill each other whenever we meet. 'Armed neutrality' fits our case fine."

"I think I'll volunteer under your flag," said Ward. "I'll leave Cerberus alone as long as he leaves me and my friends alone. But I'd advise him not to start anything."

"That's all Surbus or anyone else can ask. Come on, old fellow! Pardon me," he added to his companions and rode past them to meet the great, heavy-jowled dog. "Be still, Surbus. We're all friends, here."

The dog lifted a non-committal glance to Ward's face, growled deep in his chest, and dropped behind, nosing the tracks of Blue and Rattler as if he would identify them and fix them in his memory for future use.

Ward had never seen the Cove in summer. He looked about him curiously, struck by the atmosphere of quiet plenty. Over the crude fence hung fruit-laden branches from the jungle within. There was a smell of ripening plums in the air, and the hum of bees. Somewhere in the orchard a wild canary was singing. If he could live down here, he thought, with Billy Louise and none other near, he would ask no odds of the world or of heaven. He glanced at Charlie Fox enviously. Well, he had a fairly well-sheltered place of his own, up there in the hills. He could set out fruit and plants and things and have a little Eden of his own; though of course it couldn't be like this place, sheltered as it was from harsh winds by that high rock wall, and soaking in sunshine all day long. Still, he could fix his place up a lot, with a little time and thought and a good deal of hard work.

He looked at Billy Louise and saw how the beauty of the place appealed to her, and right there he decided to study horticulture so that he could raise plums and apples and hollyhocks and things.

"That old dame down there thinks a lot of you, William." Ward had closed the gate and was preparing to remount.

"Well, is there any reason why she shouldn't?" The tone of Billy Louise was not far from petulant.

"Not a reason. What's molla, Bill?"

"Nothing that I know of." Billy Louise lifted her eyes to the rock cabbages on the cliff above them and tried to speak convincingly.

"Yes, there is. Something's gone wrong. Can't you tell a pal, Wilhemina?"

There was no resisting that tone. Billy Louise looked at him, and though she still frowned, her eyes lightened a little.

"No, I can't tell a pal-or anybody else. I don't know. Something's different, down there. I don't know what it is, and I don't like it." She thought a minute and then smiled with that little twist of the lips Ward liked so much. "Maybe it's the dog," she guessed. "I never see his ugly mug that I don't feel like taking a shot at him. I like dogs, too, as a general thing. He's got a wicked heart! I know he has. He'd like nothing better than to take a chunk out of me."

"I'll go back and kill him; shall I, Bill Loo?"

"No. Some day maybe I'll get a chance at him myself. I've warned Marthy, so —"

"Are you dead sure it's the dog?" Ward looked at her with that keenness of glance which was hard to meet if one wanted to keep a secret from him.

"Why?" Billy Louise's tone did not invite further questioning.

"Oh, nothing! I just wondered."

"You don't like Charlie; anybody can see that."

"Yes? Foxy's a real nice young man."

"But you don't like him. You never do like anybody —"

"No?" Ward's smile dared her to persist in the accusation. "In that case I've no business to be fooling around here when there's work to be done. That Cove down there has roused a heap of brand-new wants in me, Wilhemina. Gotta have an orchard up on Mill Creek, lady-fair. Gotta have a flower garden and things that climb all over the house and smell nice. Gotta have four times as much meadow as I've got now, and a house full of books and pictures and things, and more cattle and horses, and a yellow canary in a yellow cage singing his head off out on the porch. Gotta work like one son-of-a-gun, Wilhemina, to get all those things and get 'em quick, so I can stand some show of-getting what I really do want."

"Well, am I keeping you?" Billy Louise was certainly in a villainous mood.

"You are," Ward affirmed quite calmly. "Only for you, I'd be hustling like the mischief right this minute along the get-rich trail. Say, Bill, I don't believe it's the dog!" He looked at her with the smile hiding just behind his lips and his eyes. And behind the smile, if one's insight were keen enough to see it, was a troubled anxiety. He shifted the pail of currants to the other arm and spoke again:

"What is it, Wilhemina? Something's bothering you. Can't you tell a fellow what it is?"

"No, I can't." Billy Louise spoke crossly. "I've got a headache. I've been riding ever since this morning, and I should think that's reason enough. I wish to goodness you'd let me alone. Go on back to work, if you're so crazy about working; I'm sure I don't want to hinder you in any of your get-rich-quick schemes!" She shut her teeth together with a click, jerked Blue angrily into the trail when he had merely stepped out of it to avoid a rock, and managed to make him as conscious of her mood as was Ward.

Ward eyed her unobtrusively with his face set straight ahead. He glanced down at the pail of currants, which was heavy, and at the trail, which was long and lonely. He twisted his lips in brief sarcasm-for he had a temper of his own-and rode on with his neck set very stiff and his eyes a trifle harder than they had ever been before when Billy Louise rode alongside. He did not turn off at the ford-and Billy Louise betrayed by a quick glance at him that she had half expected him to desert her there-but crossed it beside her and rode on up the hill.

He had made up his mind that he would not speak to her again until she wiped out, by apology or a change of manner, that last offensive remark of hers. He hoped she realized that he was only going with her to carry the currants, and he hoped she realized also that, if she had been any other person who had spoken to him like that, he would have dumped the currants on the ground and ridden off and left her to her own devices.

He did not once speak to Billy Louise on the way to the Wolverine; but his silence changed gradually from stubbornness to pure abstraction, as they rode leisurely along the dusty trail with the sunset glowing before them. He almost forgot the actual presence of Billy Louise, and he did actually forget her mood. He was planning just how and where he should plant his orchard, and he was mentally building an addition to the cabin and screening a porch wide enough to hang a hammock inside, and he was seeing Billy Louise luxuriously swinging in that hammock while he sat close, and smoked and teased and gloried in his possession of her companionship.

His thoughts shuttled to his little mine, though he seldom dignified it by that title. He speculated upon the amount of gold he might yet hope to wash out of that gravel streak, though he had held himself sternly back from such mental indulgence all the spring. He felt that he was going to need every grain of gold he could glean. He wanted his wife-he glowed at the mere thinking of that name-to have the nicest little home in the country. He decided that it would be pleasanter than the Cove, all things considered; he had a fine view of the rugged hills from his cabin, and he imagined the Cove must be pretty hot during the days, with that high rock wall shutting off the wind and reflecting the sun. His own place was sheltered, but still it was not set down in the bottom of a well. She had liked it. She had said...

They rode over the crest of the bluff and down the steep trail into the Wolverine. However cloudy the atmosphere between the two, the ride had seemed short-so short that Ward felt the jar of surprise when he looked down and saw the cabin below them. He glanced at Billy Louise, guessed from her somber face that the villainous mood still held her, and sighed a little. He was not deeply concerned by her mood. He understood her too well to descend into any slough of despondence because she was cross. Then he remembered the reason she had given-the reason he had not believed at the time. They were down by the gate, then.

"Head still ache, William?" he asked, in the tone which he could make a fair substitute for a caress.

"Yes," said Billy Louise, and did not look at him.

Ward was inwardly skeptical, but he did not tell her so. He swung off his horse, set down the pail of currants, and took Blue by the bridle.

"You go on in. I'll unsaddle," he commanded her quietly. And Billy Louise, after a perceptible hesitation, obeyed him without looking at him or speaking a word.

If Ward resented her manner, which was unreasonably uppish, he could not have chosen a more effective revenge. He talked with Mrs. MacDonald all through supper and paid no attention to Billy Louise. After supper he spied a fairly fresh Boise paper, and underneath that lay the *Butte Miner*. That discovery settled the evening, so far as he was concerned. If he and Billy Louise had been on the best of terms, it is doubtful if she could have dragged his attention from those papers.

Several times Billy Louise looked at him as though she meditated going over and snatching them away from him, but she resisted the temptation and continued to behave as a nice young woman should behave toward a guest. She left him sitting inside by the lamp, which her mother had lighted for his especial convenience, and went out and sat on the doorstep and stared at the dusky line of hills and at the Big Dipper. She was trying to think out the tangle of tiny, threadlike mysteries that had enmeshed her thoughts and tightened her nerves until she could not speak a decent word to anyone.

She felt that the lives of those around her were weaving puzzle-patterns, and that she must guess the puzzles. And she felt as though part of the patterns had been left out, so that there were ragged points thrusting themselves upon her notice-points that did not point to anything.

She sat with her elbows on her knees and her chin in her cupped palms, and scowled at the Big Dipper as if it held the answer away up there beyond her reach. Where did Ward get the money to do all the things he had done, this spring and summer? If he expected her to believe that wolf story —!

What became of the cattle that had disappeared, by twos and threes and sometimes more, in the last few months? Was there a gang of thieves operating in the country, and where did they stay?

Why had Ward hinted that she did not like Charlie Fox, and why didn't he himself like Charlie? Why had she felt that weight of depression creep over her when they were leaving the Cove? Why? Why?

Billy Louise tried to bring her cold, common sense to the front. She had found it a most effective remedy for most moods. Now it assured her impatiently that every question-save one-had been born in her own super-sensitive self. That one definite question was the first one she had tried to answer. It kept asking itself, over and over, until in desperation Billy Louise went to bed and tried to forget it in sleep.

Somewhere about midnight-she had heard the clock strike eleven a long while ago-she scared her mother by sitting up suddenly in bed and exclaiming relievedly: "Oh, I know; it's some new poison! He poisons them!"

"Wake up! For the land's sake, what are you dreaming about?" Her mother shook her agitatedly by the arm. "Billy Louise! Wake up!"

"All right, mommie." Billy Louise lay down and snuggled the light blanket over her shoulders. She had been awake and thinking, thinking till she thought she never could stop, but she did not tell mommie that. She went to sleep and dreamed about poisoned wolves till it is a wonder she did not have a real nightmare. The question was answered, and for the time being the answer satisfied her.

Ward was surely an unusual type of young man. He did not seem to remember, the next morning, that there had been any outbreak of bottled emotions on his part the day before, or any ill-temper on the part of Billy Louise, or anything at all out of the ordinary. Billy Louise had prepared herself to apologize-in some roundabout manner which would effect a reconciliation without hurting her pride too much-and she was rather chagrined to discover that Ward seemed neither to expect or to want any apology.

"Sorry I gotta go, William," he volunteered whimsically soon after breakfast. "But I gotta dig. Say, Wilhemina, if I stay away long enough, will you come after me again?"

"A wise man," said Billy Louise evasively, "may do a foolish thing once, but only a fool does it twice."

"I don't believe it's the dog." Ward shook his head at her in mock meditation. "It wouldn't last overnight, if it was just the dog." He looked at her with the hidden smile. "Are you sure —"

"I'm sure you know how to pester a person!" The lips of Billy Louise twisted humorously. "Lots of things bother me, and you ought to help me out instead of making it worse." She walked beside him down to the corral where Rattler was waiting, saddled and bridled for the homeward journey.

"Well, tell a fellow what they are. Of course, if it's the dog —"

"Ward Warren, you're awful! It isn't the dog. Well, it is, but there are heaps of other things I want to know, that I don't know. And you don't seem to care about any single one of them."

Ward leaned up against the fence and tilted his hat to shade his eyes from the sun. "Name a few of them, William Louisa. Not even a brave young buckaroo can be expected to mind-read a girl. If he could —"

"Well, is it poison you use?" Billy Louise thought it best to change Ward's trend of thought immediately. "Last night it just came to me all at once that you must have found some poison besides strychnine —"

"Eh? Oh, I see!" He managed a rather provoking slur on the last word. "No, William." His eyes twinkled at her. "It isn't poison. What's the other thing you want to know?"

Billy Louise frowned, hesitated, and, accepting the rebuff, went on to the next question:

"What went with Seabeck's cattle, and Marthy and Charlie's, and all the others that have disappeared? You don't seem to care at all that there seems to be rustling going on around here."

Ward gave her a quick look. His tone changed a bit:

"I don't know that there is any. I never yet lived in a cow-country where there wasn't more or less talk of-rustling. You don't want to take gossip like that too seriously. Anything more?"

Billy Louise glanced at him surreptitiously and looked away again. Then she tried to go on as casually as she had begun.

"Well, there's something about the Cove. I don't believe Marthy's happy. I couldn't quite get hold of the thing yesterday that gave me the blues-but it's Marthy. She's grieving, or something. She's different. She's changed more since last winter than she's changed since I can remember. You noticed something-at least you spoke about her coming up the gorge —"

"I said she thinks a lot of you, Wilhemina." Ward's tone and manner were natural again. "I noticed her looking at you when you didn't know it. She thinks a heap of you, I should say, and she's worrying about something. Maybe she'd rather have you in the Cove than Miss Gertrude M. Shannon. Don't you reckon an old lady that has had her own way all her life kind of dreads the advent of a brand-new bride in her domain?"

"Why, of course! Poor old thing! I never thought of that. And here you hit the nail on the head just with a chance thought. That shows what it means to be a brave young buckaroo, with heaps and piles of brains!" She laughed at him, but behind her bantering was a new respect for Ward's astuteness. "Go on. Tell me why you don't like Charlie Fox, or why you refuse to admit how nice and kind he is and —"

"But I don't refuse —"

"Well, I put it stupidly, of course, but you know what I mean. Tell me your candid opinion of him."

"I haven't any." Ward smoked imperturbably for a minute, so that Billy Louise began to think he would not tell her what she wanted to know. Ward could be absolutely, maddeningly dumb on some subjects, as she had reason to know. But he continued, quite frankly for him:

"Has it ever struck you, William Jane, that after all Foxy is not sacrificing such a hell of a lot?" He bit his lip because of the word he had let slip, but since Billy Louise took no notice, he went on: "He's got a pretty good thing, down there, if you stop to think. The old lady won't live always, and she's managed to build up a pretty fine ranch. It stands Foxy in hand to be good to her, don't you think? He'll have a pretty fine stake out of it. Far as I know, he's all right. I merely fail to see where he's got a right to wear any halo on his manly brow. He's got a good hand in the game, and he's playing it —a heap better than lots of men would. Dot's all, Wilhemina." He turned to her as if he would dismiss the subject. "Don't run off with the notion that I'm out after the heart's blood of our young hee-ro. I like him all right-far as he goes. I like him a heap better," he owned frankly, "since I glommed him devouring that letter from Miss Gertrude M. Shannon.

"Don't you want to ride a ways with me?" His eyes made love while he waited for her to speak. "Don't?" (When she shook her head.) "You're a pretty mean young person sometimes, aren't you? Wha's molla? Did I give you more mood than I wiped off the slate?"

"I don't know. You say a sentence or two, and it's like slashing a knife into a curtain. You show all kinds of things that were nicely covered before." Billy Louise spoke gloomily. "I'll see Marthy as a poor old lady waiting to be saddled with a boss, from now on. And Charlie Fox just simply working for his own interests and —"

"Now, William!"

"Oh, I can see it myself, now."

"Well, what if he is? We're all of us working for our own interests, aren't we?" He saw the gloom still deep in her eyes and flung out both hands impatiently. "All right, all right! I'll plead the cause of our young hee-ro, then. What would old Marthy do without him? He's made her more comfortable than she ever was in her life, probably. I noticed a big difference in the cabin, yesterday. And he's doing the work, and taking the responsibility, and making the ranch more valuable-even put a wire on the gate, that rings a bell at the house, so she'll know when company's coming, and can get the kitchen swept. He's done a lot —"

"For himself!" In her disillusionment Billy Louise went too far the other way. "And the cabin is more comfortable for that girl when he brings her there to run over Marthy!"

"Well, what of it? You don't expect him to put in his time for nothing, do you? In the last analysis we're all self-centered brutes, Wilhemina. We're thinking once for the other fellow and twice for ourselves, always. I'm working and scheming day and night to get a stake-so I can have what means happiness to me. Marthy's letting Foxy have full swing in the Cove, because that gives her an easier life than she's ever had. If she didn't want him there, she'd mighty quick shoo him up the gorge, or I don't know the old lady. We're all selfish."

"I think it's a horrid world!" rebelled the youthful ideals of Billy Louise. "I wish you wouldn't say you're just thinking of yourself—"

"I'm human," he pointed out. "I want my happiness. So do you, for that matter. We all want to get all we can out of life."

"And at the other fellow's expense!"

"Oh, not necessarily. Some of us want the other fellow to be just as happy as we are." His look pointed the meaning for him.

"I don't care; I think it's mean of Charlie Fox to bring—"

"Maybe not. The chances are the young lady will take to housework like a bear-cub to a syrup keg, and old Marthy will potter around with her flowers and be perfectly happy with the two of them. Cheer up, Bill Loo! Lemme have a smile, anyway, before I go. And I wish," he added quizzically, "you'd spare me some of that sympathy you've got going to waste. I'm a poor lonesome devil working away to get a stake, and you know why. I don't have nobody to give me a kind word, and I don't have no fun nor nothing, nohow. Come on and ride a mile or two!"

"I have to help mommie," said Billy Louise, which was not true.

"Well, if you won't, darn it, don't!" Ward reached down, caught her hand, and squeezed it, taking a chance on being seen. "Gotta go, Wilhemina-mine. Adios. I won't stay away so long next time." He turned away to his horse, stuck his foot in the stirrup; and went up into the saddle without any apparent effort. Then he swung Rattler close to where she stood beside the gate.

"Sure you want to be just pals, Wilhemina-mine?" he asked, bending close to her.

"Of course I'm sure," said Billy Louise quickly —a shade too quickly.

Ward looked at her intently and shrugged his shoulders. "All right," he said, in the tone which made plain his opinion of her decision. "You're the doctor."

Billy Louise watched him up the hill and out of sight over the top. When he was gone, she caught Blue and saddled him; then, with her gun buckled around her hips and her rope coiled beside the saddle-fork, she rode dismally up the canyon.

Chapter XII. The Little Devils of Doubt

Wolverine canyon, with the sun shining down aslant into its depths, was a picturesque gash in the hills, wild enough in all conscience, but to the normal person not in the least degree gloomy. The jutting crags were sunlit and warm. The cherry thickets whispered in a light breeze and sheltered birds that sang in perfect content. The service berries were ripening and hung heavy-laden branches down over the trail to tempt a rider into loitering. The creek leaped over rocks, slid thin blades of swift current between the higher bowlders, and crept stealthily down into shady pools, where speckled trout lay motionless except for the gently-moving tail and fins that held them stationary in some deeper shadow. Not a gloomy place, surely, when the peace of a sunny morning laid its spell upon the land.

Billy Louise, however, did not respond to the canyon's enticements. She brooded over her own discouragements and the tantalizing little puzzles which somehow would not lend themselves to any convincing solution. She was in that condition of nervous depression where she saw her finest cows dead of bloat in the alfalfa meadows-and how would she pay that machinery note, then? She saw John Pringle calling unexpectedly and insistently for his "time" —and where would she find another man whom she could trust out of her sight? John Pringle was slow, and he was stupid and growled at poor Phoebe till Billy Louise wanted to shake him, but he was "steady," and that one virtue covers many a man's faults and keeps him drawing wages regularly.

Her mother had been more and more inclined to worry as the hot weather came on; lately her anxiety over small things had rather gotten upon the nerves of Billy Louise. She felt ill-used and down-hearted and as if nothing mattered much, anyway. She passed her cave with a mere glance and scowl for the memories of golden days in her lonely childhood that clung around it. She passed Minervy's cave, and her lips quivered with self-pity because that childhood was gone, and she must not waste time or energy upon romantic "pretends," but must measure haystacks and allow so much for "settling," and then add and multiply and divide all over two sheets of tablet paper to find out how much hay she had to winter the stock on. She must hold herself rigidly to facts, and tend fences and watch irrigating ditches, and pay interest on notes three or four years old, and ride the hills and work her way through rocky canyons, keeping watch over the cattle that meant so much. She had meant to talk over things with Ward and ask his advice about certain details that required experienced judgment. But Ward had precipitated her thoughts into strange channels and so had unconsciously thwarted her counsel-seeking intentions. She had wanted to talk things over with Marthy, and Marthy had also unconsciously prevented her doing so and had filled Billy Louise with uneasiness and doubt which in no way concerned herself.

These doubts persisted, and so did the tantalizing little puzzles. They weaned Billy Louise's thoughts from her own ranch worries and nagged at her with the persistence of a swarm of buffalo gnats.

"Well, if he doesn't use poison, for goodness' sake, what does he use?" she asked indignantly aloud, after a period of deep thought. "I don't see why he wants to be so terribly secretive. He might be human enough to tell a person what he means. I'm sure I'd tell him, all right. I don't believe it's wolves at all. I don't see how-and still —I don't believe Ward would really lie to me."

She was in this particularly dissatisfied mood when she rode out of the canyon at its upper end, where the hills folded softly down into grassy valleys where her cattle loved best to graze. Since the grass had started in the spring, she had kept her little herd up here among the lower hills; and by riding along the higher ridges every day or so and turning back a wandering animal now and then, she had held them in a comparatively small area, where they would be easily gathered in the fall. A few head of Seabeck's stock had wandered in amongst hers, and some of Marthy's. And there was a big, roan steer that bore the brand of Johnson, over on Snake River. Billy Louise knew them all, as a housewife knows her flock of chickens, and if she missed seeing certain leaders in the scattered groups, she rode until she found them. Two old cows and one big, red steer that seemed always to have a following wore bells that tinkled pleasant little sounds in the alder thickets along the creek, as she passed by.

She rode up the long ridge which gave her a wide view of the surrounding hills and stopped Blue, while she stared moodily at the familiar, shadow-splotched expanse of high-piled ridges, with deep green valleys and deeper-hued canyons between. She loved them, every one; but to-day they failed to steep her senses in that deep content with life which only the great outdoors can give to one who has learned how satisfying is the draught and how soothing.

Far over to the eastward a black dot moved up a green slope and slid out of sight beyond. That might be Ward, taking a short-cut across the hill to his claim beyond the pine-dotted ridge that looked purple in the distance. Billy Louise sighed with a vague disquiet and turned to look away to the north, where the jumble of high hills grew more rugged, with the valleys narrower and deeper.

Here came two other dots, larger and more clearly defined as horsemen. From mere objects that stood higher than any animal and moved with a purposeful directness, they presently became men who rode with the easy swing of habit which has become a second nature. They must have seen her sitting still upon her horse in the midst of that high, sunny plateau, for they turned and rode up the slope toward her.

Billy Louise waited, too depressed to wonder greatly who they were. Seabeck riders, probably; and so they proved. At least one of them was a Seabeck man-Floyd Carson, who had talked with her at her own gate and had told her of the suspected cattle-stealing. The other man was a stranger whom Floyd introduced as Mr. Birken.

They had been "prowling around," according to Floyd, trying to see what they could see. Floyd was one of these round-faced, round-eyed, young fellows who does not believe much in secrecy and therefore talks freely whenever and wherever he dares. He said that Seabeck had turned them loose to keep cases and see if they couldn't pick up the trail of these rustlers who were trying to get rich off a running iron and a long rope. (If you are of the West, you know what that means; and if you are not, you ought to guess that it means stealing cattle and let it go at that.) It was not until he had talked for ten minutes or so that Billy Louise became more than mildly interested in the conversation.

"Say, Miss MacDonald," Floyd asked, by way of beginning a new paragraph, "how about that fellow over on Mill Creek? He worked for you folks a year or so ago, didn't he? What does he do?"

"He has a ranch," said Billy Louise with careful calm. "He's been working on it this summer, I believe."

"Uh-huh —we were over there this morning. Them Y6 cattle up above his place are his, I reckon?"

"Yes," said Billy Louise. "He's been putting his wages into cattle for a year or so. He worked for Junkins last winter. Why?"

"Oh, nothing, I guess! Only he's the only stranger in the country, and his prosperity ain't accounted for —"

"Oh, but it is!" laughed Billy Louise. "I only wish I had half as clear a ticket. When he isn't working out, he's wolfing; and every dollar he gets hold of he puts into that ranch. We've known him a long time. He doesn't blow his money, you see, like most fellows do."

Floyd found occasion to have a slight argument with his horse, just then. He happened to be one of the "most" fellows, and the occasion of his last "blow-out" was fresh in his mind.

"Well, of course, if you know he's all straight, that settles it. But it sure seems queer —"

"That fellow is straight as a string. Don't you suppose it's some gang over on the river, Floyd? I'd look around over there, I believe, and try to get a line on the unaccountables. There's a lot of new settlers come in, just in the last year or two, and there might be some tough ones scattered through the bunch. Better see if there has been any cattle shipped or driven through that way, don't you think?"

"We can try," Floyd assented without eagerness. "But as near as we can figure, it's too much of a drib-drab proposition for that. A cow and calf here and there, and so on. We got wind of it first when we went out to bring in a gentle cow that the deacon wanted on the ranch. We knew where she was, only she wasn't there when we went after her. We hunted the hills for a week and couldn't find a sign of her or her calf. And she had stuck down in the creek bottom all the spring, so it looked kinda funny." He twisted in the saddle and looked back at the pine-clotted ridge.

"There's a Y6 calf up there that's a dead ringer for the one we've been hunting," he observed. "But it's running with a cow that carries Junkins' old brand, So —" He looked apologetically into the calm eyes of Billy Louise. "Of course, I don't mean to say there's anything wrong up there," he hastily assured her. "But that's the reason I thought I'd ask you about that fellow."

"Oh, it's perfectly right to make sure of everybody," smiled Billy Louise. "I'd do the same thing myself. But you'll find everything's all straight up there. We know all about him, and how and where he got his few head of stock, and everything. But of course you could ask Junkins, if you have any doubt —"

"Oh, we'll take your word for it. I just wanted to know; he's a stranger to our outfit. I've seen him a few times; what's his name? Us boys call him Noisy. It's like pulling a wisdom tooth to get any kinda talk out of him."

"He is awful quiet," assented Billy Louise carelessly. "But he's real steady to work."

"Them quiet fellows generally are," put in Mr. Birken. "You run stock in here too, do you, Miss MacDonald?"

"The big Ds," answered Billy Louise and smiled faintly. "I've been range-herding them back here in these foothills this summer. Do you want to look through the bunch?"

Mr. Birkin blushed. "Oh, no, not at all! I was wondering if you had lost any."

"Nobody would rustle cattle from a lady, I hope? At any rate, I haven't missed any yet. The folks down in the Cove have, though."

"Yes, I heard they had. That breed rode over to see if he could get a line on them. It's hard luck; that Charlie Fox seems a fine, hard-working boy, don't you think?"

"Yes-s," said Billy Louise shyly, "he seems real nice." She looked away and bit her lip self-consciously as she spoke.

The two men swallowed the bait like a hungry fish. They glanced at each other and winked knowingly. Billy Louise saw them from the tail of her downcast eye, and permitted herself a little sigh of relief. They would be the more ready now to accept at its face value her statement concerning Ward, unless they credited her with the feat of being in love with the two men at the same time.

"Well, I'm sorry Charlie Fox has been tapped off, too. He's a mighty fine chap," declared Floyd with transparent heartiness, his round eyes dwelling curiously upon the face of Billy Louise.

"Yes, I must be going," said that young woman self-consciously. "I've quite a circle to ride yet. I hope you locate the rustlers, and if there's anything I can do-if I see or hear anything that seems to be a clew —I'll let you know right away. I've been keeping my eyes open for some trace of them, and-so has Char-Mr. Fox." Then she blushed and told them good-by very hastily and loped off up the ridge.

"Bark up that tree for awhile, you two!" she said, with a twist of her lips, when she was well away from them. "You-you darned idiots! To go prowling around Ward's place, just as if— Ward'll take a shot at them if he catches them nosing through his stock!" She scowled at a big D cow that thrust her head out of an alder thicket and sent Blue in after her. Frowning, she watched the animal go lumbering down the hill toward the Wolverine. "Just because he's a stranger and doesn't mix with people, and minds his own business and is trying to get a start, they're suspicious-as if a man has no right to — Well, I think I managed to head them off, anyway."

Her satisfaction lasted while she rode to the next ridge. Then the little devils of doubt came a-swarming and a-whispering. She had said she knew all about Ward; well, she did, to a greater extent than others knew. But-she wondered if she did not know too much, or if she knew enough. There were some things —

She turned, upon the crest of the ridge, and looked away toward the pine-dotted height locally known as the Big Hill, beyond which Ward's claim lay snuggled out of sight in its little valley. "I've a good mind to ride over there right now, and make him tell me," she said to herself. She stopped Blue and sat there undecided, while the wind lifted a lock of hair and flipped it across her cheek. "If he cares-like he says he cares-he'll tell me," she murmured. "I don't believe it's wolves. And of course it isn't —what those fellows seemed to think. But-where did he get the money for all that?" She sighed distressfully. "I hate to ask him; he'd think I didn't trust him, and I do. I do trust him!" There was the little head-devil of doubt, and she fought him fiercely. "I do! I do!" She thrust the declaration of faith like a sword through the doubt-devil that clung and whispered. "Dear Ward! I do trust you!" She blinked back tears and bit her lips to stop their quivering. "But, darn it, I don't see why you didn't tell me!" There it was: a perfectly human, woman-resentment toward a nagging mystery.

She headed Blue down the slope and as straight for the Big Hill as she could go. She would go and make Ward tell her what he had been doing; not that she had any doubt herself that it was perfectly all right, whatever it was, but she felt that she had a right to demand facts, so that she could feel more sure of her ground. And there would be more questions; Billy Louise was bright enough to see thus far into the future. Unless the rustlers were caught, there would be questions asked about this silent stranger who kept his trail apart from his fellows and whose prosperity was out of proportion with his opportunities. Why, even Billy Louise herself had been curious over that prosperity, without being in the slightest degree suspicious. Other people had not her faith in him; and they were not blind. They would wonder —

There was no trail that way, and the ridges were steep and the canyons circuitous. But Blue was a good horse, with plenty of stamina and much experience. He carried his lady safely, and he carried her willingly. Even her impatience could find no fault with the manner in which he climbed steep pitches, slid down slopes as steep, jumped narrow washouts, and picked his way through thickets of quaking aspens or over wide stretches of shale rock and lava beds. He was wet to his ears when finally he shuffled into Ward's trail up the creek bottom; but he breathed evenly, and he carried his head high and perked his ears knowingly forward when the corral and haystack came into view around a sharp bend.. He splashed both front feet into the creek just before the cabin and stopped to drink while Billy Louise stared at the silent place.

By the tracks along the creek trail she knew that Ward had come home, and she urged Blue across the ford and up the bank to the cabin. She slid off and went in boldly to hide her inward embarrassment-and she found nothing but emptiness there.

Billy Louise did not take long to investigate. The coffee-pot was still warm on the stove when she laid her palm against it, and she immediately poured herself a cup of coffee. A plate and a cup on the table indicated that Ward had eaten a hurried meal and had not taken time to clear away the litter. Billy Louise ate what was left, and mechanically she washed the dishes and made everything neat before she went down to look for Rattler. She had thought that Ward was out somewhere about the place and would return very soon, probably. Blue she had left standing in plain sight before the cabin, so that Ward would see him and know she was there —a fact which she regretted.

While she was washing dishes and sweeping, she had been trying to think of some excuse for her presence there. It was going to be awkward, her coming there on his heels, one might say. She remembered for the first time her statement that she had to help mommie and so could not take the time to ride even a mile with him! Being a young person whose chief amusement had always been her "pretends," she began unconsciously building an imaginary conversation between them, like this:

Ward would come out of the stable-or somewhere-see Blue and hurry up to the house. Billy Louise would be standing with her back to him, putting the dishes into neat little piles in the cupboard perhaps; anyway, doing something like that. Ward would stop in the doorway and say-well, there were several possible greetings, but Billy Louise chose his "'Lo, Bill!" as being the most probable. And then he would come up and take her in his arms. (Oh, she was human, and she was a woman, and she was twenty. And Ward had established a precedent, remember, and Billy Louise had not objected to any great extent.) And-and — (I'm going to tell on Billy Louise. She wiped a knife for at least five minutes without knowing what she was doing, and she stared at a sunny spot on the floor where a sunbeam came in through a crack in the wall, and she smiled absently, and her cheeks were quite a bit redder than usual.)

"I didn't expect to see you here, Wilhemina-mine."

"Oh, I was just riding around, and I came over to see how you dig dollars out of wolf-dens. You said you'd show me."

The trouble with the conversation began right there. Ward would be sure to remind her of the condition he had made, to tell her how he dug dollars out of wolf-dens when she was through with wanting to be just friends. That put it up to Billy Louise to say she would be engaged and marry him; and Billy Louise was not ready to say that or be that. Her woman-soul hung back from that decisive point. She would not shut the door upon her freedom and her girlish dreams and her ideals and all those evanescent bubbles which we try to carry with us into maturity. Billy Louise did not put it that way, of course. She only reiterated again and again: "I like you, but I don't want to marry anybody. I don't want to be engaged."

Well, that would probably settle Ward's telling her about digging dollars out of wolf-dens or anything else. He had a wide streak of stubbornness; no one could see the set of his chin when he was in a certain mood and doubt that. Billy Louise began to wish she had not come. She began to feel quite certain that Ward would be surprised and disgusted when he found her there, and would look at her with that faint curl of the lip and that fainter lift of the nostril above it, which made her go hot all over with the scorn in them. She had seen him look that way once or twice, and in spite of herself she began to picture his face with that expression.

Billy Louise was on the point of riding away a good deal more hastily than she had come, in the hope that Ward would not discover her there. Then her own stubbornness came uppermost, and she told herself that she had a perfect right to ride wherever she pleased, and that if Ward didn't like it, he could do the other thing.

She went to the door and stood looking out for a minute, wondering where he was. She turned back and stared around the room, which somehow held the imprint of his personality in spite of its rough simplicity.

There was a little window behind the bunk, and beside that a shelf filled with books and smoking material and matches. She knew by the very arrangement of that shelf and window that Ward liked to lie there on the bunk and read while the light lasted. Well, he was not there now, at any rate. She went over and looked at the titles of the books, though she had examined them with interest only yesterday. There was Burns; and she knew why it was he could repeat *Tam O'Shanter* so readily with never a moment's hesitation. There were two volumes of Scott —*Lady of the Lake* and other poems, much thumbed and with a cigarette burn on the front cover, and *Kenilworth*. There were several books of Kipling's, mostly verses, and beside it Morgan's *Ancient Society*, with the corners broken, and a fine-print volume of Shakespeare's plays. Then there was a pile of magazines and beyond them a stack of books whose subjects varied from Balzac to strange, scientific-sounding names. At the other end of the shelf, within easy reach from one lying upon the bunk, was a cigar-box full of smoking tobacco, a half-dozen books of cigarette papers, and several blocks of the small, evil-smelling matches which men of the outdoors carry for their compact form and slow, steady blaze.

At the head of the bed hung a flour-sack half full of some hard, lumpy stuff which Billy Louise had not noticed before. She felt the bag tentatively, could not guess its contents, and finally took it down and untied it. Within were irregular scraps and strips of stuff hard as bone —a puzzle still to one unfamiliar with the frontier. Billy Louise pulled out a little piece, nibbled a corner, and pronounced, "M-mm! Jerky! I'm going to swipe some of that," which she proceeded to do, to the extent of filling her pocket. For to those who have learned to like it, jerked venison is quite as desirable as milk chocolate or any other nibbly tid-bit.

The opposite wall had sacks of flour stacked against it, and boxes of staple canned goods, such as corn and tomatoes and milk and peaches. A box of canned peaches stood at the head of the bed, and upon that a case of tomatoes. Ward used them for a table and set the lantern there when he wanted to read in bed. "He's got a pretty good supply of grub," was the verdict of Billy Louise, sizing up the assortment while she nibbled at the piece of jerky. "I wonder where he is, anyway?" And a moment later: "He oughtn't to hang his best clothes up like that; they'll be all wrinkled when he wants to put them on."

She went over and disposed of the best clothes to her liking, and shook out the dust. She had to own to herself that for a bachelor Ward was very orderly, though he did let his trousers hang down over the flour-sacks in a way to whiten their hems. She hung them in a different place.

But where was Ward? Billy Louise bethought her that Blue deserved something to eat after that hard ride, and led him down to the stable. There was no sign of Rattler, and Billy Louise wondered anew at Ward's absence. It did not seem consistent with his haste to leave the Wolverine and his frequent assertion that he must get to work. From the stable door she could look over practically the whole creek-bottom within his fence, and she could see the broad sweep of the hills on either side. On her way back to the cabin, she tried to track Rattler, but there were several stock-trails leading in different directions, and the soil was too dry to leave any distinguishing marks.

She waited for an hour or two, sitting in the door-way, nibbling jerky and trying to read a magazine. Then she found a stub of pencil, tore out an advertising page which had a wide margin, wrote: "I don't think you're a bit nice. Why don't you stay home when a fellow comes to see you?" This she folded neatly and put in the cigar-box of tobacco over Ward's pillow. It never once occurred to her that Ward, when he found the note, would believe she had placed it there the day before, and would never guess by its text that she had made a second trip to his claim.

She resaddled Blue and rode away more depressed than ever, because her depression was now mixed with a disappointment keener than she would have cared to acknowledge, even to herself.

Chapter XIII. The Corral in the Canyon

Where the creek trail crossed the Big Hill and then swung to the left that it might follow the easy slopes of Cedar Creek, Blue turned off to the right of his own accord, as if he took it for granted that his lady would return the way she had come. His lady had not thought anything about it, but after a brief hesitation she decided that Blue should have his way; after all, it would simplify her explanations of the long ride if she came home by way of the canyon. She could say that she had ridden farther out into the hills than usual, which was true enough.

Billy Louise did not own such a breeder of blues as a lazy liver, her nerves were in fine working order, and her digestion was perfect; and it is a well-known fact that a trouble must be born of reality rather than imagination, if it would ride far behind the cantle. Billy Louise was late, and already the shadows lay like long draperies upon the hills she faced: long, purple cloaks ruffed with golden yellow and patterned with indigo patches, which were the pines, and splotches of dark green, which were the thickets of alder and quaking aspens. She couldn't feel depressed for very long, and before she had climbed over the first rugged ridge that reached out like a crooked finger into the narrow valley, she was humming under her breath and riding with the reins dropped loose upon Blue's neck, so that he went where the way pleased him best. Before she was down that ridge and beginning to climb the next, she was singing softly a song her mother had taught her long ago, when she was seven or so:

>"The years creep slowly by, Lorena,

>The snow is on the grass again;

>The sun's low down the sky, Lorena —"

Blue gathered himself together and jumped a washout three feet across and goodness knows how deep and jarred that melancholy melody quite out of Billy Louise's mind. When she had settled herself again to the slow climb, she broke out with what she called Ward's Come-all-ye, and with a twinkle of eye and both dimples showing deep, went on with a very slight interruption in her singing.

"'Oh, a ten-dollar hoss and a forty-dollar saddle'—that's you Blue. You don't amount to nothing nohow, doing jackrabbit stunts like that when I'm not looking! 'Coma ti yi youpy, youpy-a.'" She watched a cloud shadow sweep like a great bird over a sunny slope and murmured while she watched: "Cloud-boats sailing sunny seas-is that original, or have I cribbed it from some honest-to-goodness poet? Blue, if fate hadn't made a cowpuncher of me, I'd be chewing up lead-pencils trying to find a rhyme for alfalfa, maybe. And where would you be, you old skate? If the Louise of me had been developed at the expense of the Billy of me, and I'd taken to making battenburg doilies with butterflies in the corners, and embroidering corset covers till I put my eyes out, and writing poetry on Sundays when mommie wouldn't let me sew. I wonder if Ward — Maybe he'd have liked me better if I'd lived up to the Louise and cut out the Billy part. I'd be home, right now, asking mommie whether I should use soda or baking-powder to make my muffins with — Oh, gracious!" She leaned over and caught a handful of Blue's slatey mane and tousled it, till he laid his ears flat on his head and nipped his nose around to show her that his teeth were bared to the gums. Billy Louise laughed and gave another yank.

"You wish I were an embroidering young lady, do you? Aw, where would you be, if you didn't have me to devil the life out of you? Well, why don't you take a chunk out of me, then? Don't be an old bluffer, Blue. If you want to eat me, why, go to it; only you don't. You're just a-bluffing. You like to be tousled and you know it; else why do you tag me all over the place when I don't want you? Huh? That's to pay you back for jumping that washout when I wasn't looking." A twitch of the mane here brought Blue's head around again with all his teeth showing. "And this is for jarring that lovely, weepy song out of me. You know you hate it; you always do lay back your ears when I sing that, but-oh, all right-when I sing, then. But you've got to stand for it. I've been an indigo bag all day long, and I'm going to sing if I want to. Fate made me a lady cowpunch instead of a poet-ess, and you can't stop me from singing when I feel it in my system."

She began again with the "Ten-dollar hoss and forty-dollar saddle," and sang as much of the old trail song as she had ever heard and could remember, substituting milder expletives now and then and laughing at herself for doing it, because a self-confessed "lady cowpunch" is after all hedged about by certain limitations in the matter of both speech and conduct. She did not sing it all, but she sang enough to last over a mile of rough going, and she did not have to repeat many verses to do it.

Blue, because she still left the reins loose, chose his own trail, which was easier than that which they had taken in the forenoon, but more roundabout. Billy Louise, observing how he avoided rocky patches and went considerably out of his way to keep his feet on soft soil, stopped in the middle of a "Coma ti yi" to ask him solicitously if he were getting tender-footed; and promised him a few days off, in the pasture. Thereafter she encouraged the roundabout progress, even though she knew it would keep them in the hills until dusk; for she was foolishly careful of Blue, however much she might tease him and call him names.

Quite suddenly, just at sundown, her cheerful journeying was interrupted in a most unexpected manner. She was dreaming along a flat-bottomed canyon, looking for an easy way across, when Blue threw up his head, listened with his ears thrust forward, and sniffed with widened nostrils. From his manner, almost anything might lie ahead of them. And because certain of the possibilities would call for quick action if any of them became a certainty, Billy Louise twisted her gun-belt around so that her six-shooter swung within easy reach of her hand. With her fingers she made sure that the gun was loose in its holster and kicked Blue mildly as a hint to go on and see what it was all about.

Blue went forward, stepping easily on the soft sidehill. In rough country, whatever you want to see is nearly always around a sharp bend; you read it so in the stories and books of travels, and when you ride out in the hills, you find it so in reality. Billy Louise rode for three or four minutes before she received any inkling of what lay ahead, though Blue's behavior during that interval had served to reassure her somewhat. He was interested still in what lay just out of sight beyond a shoulder of the hill, but he did not appear to be in the least alarmed. Therefore, Billy Louise knew it couldn't be a bear, at any rate.

They came to the point of the hill's shoulder, and Billy Louise tightened the reins instinctively while she stared at what lay revealed beneath. The head of the gulch was blocked with a corral-small, high, hidden from view on all sides save where she stood, by the jagged walls of rock and heavy aspen thickets beyond.

The corral was but the setting for what Billy Louise stared at so unbelievingly. A horseman had ridden out of the corral just as she came into sight, had turned a sharp corner, and had disappeared by riding up the same slope she occupied, but farther along, and in a shallow depression which hid him completely after that one brief glimpse.

Of course, the gulch was dusky with deep shadows, and she had had only a glimpse. But the horse was a dark bay, and the rider was slim and tall and wore a gray hat. The heart of Billy Louise paused a moment from its steady beating and then sank heavily under a great weight. She was range-born and range-bred. She had sat wide-eyed on her daddy's knees and heard him tell of losses in cattle and horses and of corrals found hidden away in strange places and of unknown riders who disappeared mysteriously into the hills. She had heard of these things; they were a part of the stage setting for wild dramas of the West.

With a white line showing around her close-pressed lips and a horror in her wide-eyed glance, she rode quietly along the side of the bluff toward where she had seen the horseman disappear. He was riding a dark bay, and he wore a gray hat and dark coat, and he was slim and tall. Billy Louise made a sound that was close to a groan and set her teeth hard together afterwards.

She reached the hillside just above the corral. There were cattle down there, moving uneasily about in the shadows. Of the horseman there was of course no sign; just the corral, and a few restless cattle shut inside, and on the hilltops a soft, rose-violet glow, and in the sky beyond a blend of purple and deep crimson to show where the sun had been. Close beside her as she stood looking down a little, gray bird twittered wistfully.

Billy Louise took a deep breath and rode on, angling slightly up the bluff, so that she could cross at the head of the gulch. It was very quiet, very peaceful, and wildly beautiful, this jumble of hills and deep-gashed canyons. But Billy Louise felt as though something precious had died. She should have gone down and investigated and turned those cattle loose; that is, if she dared. Well, she dared; it was not fear that held her to the upper slopes. She did not want to know what brand they bore or whether an iron had seared fresh marks.

"Oh, God!" she said once aloud; and there was a prayer and a protest, a curse and a question all in those two words.

So trouble-trouble that sickened her very soul and choked her into dumbness and squeezed her heart so that the ache of it was agony-came and rode with her through the brooding dusk of the canyons and over the brighter hilltops.

Billy Louise did not remember anything much about that ride, except that she was glad the way was long. Blue carried her steadily on and on and needed no guiding, and though Wolverine canyon was black dark in most places, she liked it so.

John Pringle was standing by the gate waiting for her, which was unusual, if Billy Louise had been normal enough to notice it. He came forward and took Blue by the bridle when she dismounted, which was still more unusual, for Billy Louise always cared for her own horse both from habit and preference.

"Yor mommie, she's sick," he announced stolidly. "She's worry you maybe hurt yoreself. Yo better go, maybe."

Billy Louise did not answer, but ran up the path to the cabin. "Oh, has everything got to happen all at once?" she cried aloud, protesting against the implacableness of misfortune.

"Yor mommie's sick," Phoebe announced in a whisper. "She's crazy 'cause you been so long. She's awful bad, I guess."

Billy Louise said nothing, but went in where her mother lay moaning, her face white and turned to the ceiling. Billy Louise herself had pulled up her reserves of strength and cheerfulness, and the fingers she laid on her mother's forehead were cool and steady.

"Poor old mommie! Is it that nasty lumbago again?" she asked caressingly and did not permit the tiniest shade of anxiety to spoil the reassurance of her presence. "I went farther than usual, and Blue's pretty tender, so I eased him along, and I'm fearfully late. I suppose you've been having all kinds of disasters happening to me." She was passing her fingers soothingly over her mother's forehead while she explained, and she saw that her mother did not moan so much as when she came into the room.

"Of course I worried. I wish you wouldn't take them long rides. Oh, I guess it's lumbago-mostly-but seems like it ain't, either. The pain seems to be mostly in my side." She stirred restlessly and moaned again.

"What's Phoebe been doing for it? You don't seem to have any fever, mommie-and that's a good thing. I'll go fix you one of those dandy spice poultices. Had any supper, mommie?"

"Oh, I couldn't eat. Phoebe made a hop poultice, but it's awful soppy."

"Well, never mind. Your dear daughter is on the job now. She'll have you all comfy in just about two minutes. Head ache, mum? All right. I'll just shake up your pilly and bring you such a dandy spice poultice I expect you'll want to eat it!" Billy Louise's voice was soft and had a broody sweetness when she wished it so, that soothed more than medicine. Her mother's eyes closed wearily while the girl talked; the muscles of her face relaxed a little from their look of pain.

Billy Louise bent and laid her lips lightly on her mother's cheek. "Poor old mommie! I'd have come home a-running if I'd known she was sick and had to have nasty, soppy stuff."

In the kitchen a very different Billy Louise measured spices, and asked a question now and then in a whisper, and breathed with a repressed unevenness which betrayed the strain she was under.

"Tell John to saddle up and go for the doctor, Phoebe, and don't let mommie know, whatever you do. This isn't her lumbago at all. I don't know what it is. I wonder if a hot turpentine cloth wouldn't be better than this? I've a good mind to try it; her eyes are glassy with fever, and her skin is cold as a fish. You tell John to hurry up. He can ride Boxer. Tell him I want him to get a doctor here by to-morrow noon if he has to kill his horse doing it."

"Is she that bad?" Phoebe's black eyes glistened with consternation. "She's groaned all day and shook her head like this all time."

"Oh, stop looking like that! No wonder she's sick, if you've stood over her with that kind of a face on you. You look as if someone were dead in the house!"

"I'm skeered of sick folks. Honest, it gives me shivers."

"Well, keep out then. Make some fresh tea, Phoebe-or no, make some good, strong coffee. I'll need it, if I'm up all night. Make it strong, Phoebe. Hurry, and —" She stopped short and ran into the bedroom, called there by her mother's cry of pain.

That night took its toll of Billy Louise and left a seared place in her memory. It was a night of snapping fire in the cook-stove that hot water might be always ready; of tireless struggle with the pain that came and tortured, retired sullenly from Billy Louise's stubborn fighting with poultices and turpentine cloths and every homely remedy she had ever heard of, and came again just when she thought she had won the fight.

There was no time to give thought to the trouble that had ridden home with her, though its presence was like a black shadow behind her while she worked and went to and fro between bedroom and kitchen, and fought that tearing pain.

She met the dawn hollow-eyed and so tired she could not worry very much about anything. Her mother slept uneasily to prove that the battle had not gone altogether against the girl who had fought the night through. She had her reward in full measure when the doctor came, in the heat of noon, and after terrible minutes of suspense for Billy Louise while he counted pulse and took temperature and studied symptoms, told her that she had done well, and that she and her homely poultices had held back tragedy from that house.

Billy Louise lay down upon the couch out on the back porch and slept heavily for three hours, while Phoebe and the doctor watched over her mother.

She woke with a start. She had been dreaming, and the dream had taken from her cheeks what little color her night vigil had left. She had dreamed that Ward was in danger, that men were hunting him for what he had done at that corral. The corral seemed the center of a fight between Ward and the men. She dreamed that he came to her, and that she must hide him away and save him. But though she took him to Minervy's cave, which was secret enough for her purpose, yet she could not feel that he was safe, even there. There was something-some menace.

Billy Louise went softly into the house, tiptoed to the door of her mother's room, and saw that she lay quiet, with her eyes closed. Beside the window the doctor sat with his spectacles far down toward the end of his nose, reading a pale-green pamphlet that he must have brought in his pocket. Phoebe was down by the creek, washing clothes in the shade of a willow-clump.

She went into her own room, still walking on her toes. In her trunk was a blue plush box of the kind that is given to one at Christmas. It was faded, and the clasp was showing brassy at the edges. Sitting upon her bed with the box in her lap, Billy Louise pawed hastily in the jumble of keepsakes it held: an eagle's claw which she meant sometime to have mounted for a brooch; three or four arrowheads of the shiny, black stuff which the Indians were said to have brought from Yellowstone Park, a knot of green ribbon which she had worn to a St. Patrick's Day dance in Boise; rattlesnake rattles of all sizes; several folded clippings-verses that had caught her fancy and had been put away and forgotten; an amber bead she had found once. She turned the box upside down in her lap and shook it. It must be there-the thing she sought; the thing that had troubled her most in her dream; the thing that was a menace while it existed. It was at the very bottom of the box, caught in a corner. She took it out with fingers that trembled, crumpled it into a little ball so that she could not read what it said, straightened it immediately, and read it reluctantly from the beginning to the end where the last word was clipped short with hasty scissors. A paragraph cut from a newspaper, it was; yellow and frayed from contact with other objects, telling of things —

Billy Louise bit her lips until they hurt, but she could not keep back the tears that came hot and stinging while she read. She slid the little heap of odds and ends to the middle of the bed, crushed the clipping into her palm, and went out stealthily into the immaculate kitchen. As if she were being spied upon, she went cautiously to the stove, lifted a lid, and dropped the clipping in where the wood blazed the brightest. She watched it flare and become nothing-not even a pinch of ashes; the clipping was not very large. When it was gone, she put the lid back and went tiptoeing to the door. Then she ran.

Phoebe was down by the creek, so Billy Louise went to the stable, through that and on beyond, still running. Farther down was a grassy nook-on, beyond the road. She went there and hid behind the willows, where she could cry and no one be the wiser. But she could not cry the ache out of her heart, nor the rebellion against the hurt that life had given her. If she could only have burned memory when she burned that clipping! She could still believe and be happy, if only she could forget the things it said.

Phoebe called her, after a long while had passed. Billy Louise bathed her face in the cold water of the Wolverine, used her handkerchief for a towel, and went back to take up the duties life had laid upon her. The doctor's team was hitched to the light buggy he drove, and the doctor was standing in the doorway with his square medicine-case in his hand, waiting to give her a few final directions before he left.

He was like so many doctors; he seemed to be afraid to tell the whole truth about his patient. He stuck to evasive optimism and then neutralized the reassurances he uttered by emphasizing the necessity of being notified if Mrs. MacDonald showed any symptoms of another attack.

"Don't wait," he told Billy Louise gravely. "Send for me at once if she complains of that pain again, or appears —"

"But what is it?" Billy Louise would not be put off by any vagueness.

The doctor told Billy Louise in terms that carried no meaning whatever to her mind. She gathered merely that it was rather serious if it persisted-whatever it was-and that she must not leave her mommie for many hours at a time, because she might have another attack at any time. The doctor told her, however, in plain English that mommie was well over this attack-whatever it was-and that she need only be kept quiet for a few days and given the medicine-whatever that was-that he had left.

"It does seem as if everything is all muffled up in mystery!" she complained, when he drove away. "I can fight anything I can see, but when I've got to go blindfolded —" She brushed her fingers across her eyes and glanced hurriedly into the little looking-glass that hung beside the door. "Yes, mommie, just a minute," she called cheerfully.

She ran into her own room, grabbed a can of talcum, and did not wait to see whether she applied it evenly to her telltale eyelids, but dabbed at them on the way to her mother's room.

"Doctor says you're all right, mommie; only you mustn't go digging post-holes or shoveling hay for awhile."

"No, I guess not!" Her mother responded unconsciously to the stimulation of Billy Louise's tone. "I couldn't dig holes with a teaspoon, I'm that weak and useless. Did he say what it was, Billy Louise?" The sick are always so curious about their illnesses!

"Oh, your lumbago got to scrapping with your liver. I forget the name he gave it, but it's nothing to worry about." Billy Louise had imagination, remember.

"I guess he'd think it was something to worry about, if he had it," her mother retorted fretfully, but reassured nevertheless by the casual manner of Billy Louise. "I believe I could eat a little mite of toast and drink some tea," she added tentatively.

"And an egg poached soft if you want it, mom. Phoebe just brought in the eggs." Billy Louise went out humming unconcernedly under her breath as if she had not a care beyond the proper toasting of the bread and brewing of the tea.

One need not go to war or voyage to the far corners of the earth to find the stuff heroes are made of.

Chapter XIV. Each in his Own Trail

Since nothing in this world is absolutely immutable-the human emotions least of all, perhaps-Billy Louise did not hold changeless her broken faith in Ward. She saw it broken into fragments before the evidence of her own eyes, and the fragments ground to dust beneath the weight of what she knew of his past-things he had told her himself. So she thought there was no more faith in him, and her heart went empty and aching through the next few days.

But, since Billy Louise was human, and a woman-not altogether because she was twenty! — she stopped, after awhile, gathered carefully the dust of her dead faith, and, like God, she began to create. First she fashioned doubts of her doubt. How did she know she had not made a mistake, there at that corral? Other men wore gray hats and rode dark bay horses; other men were slim and tall-and she had only had a glimpse after all, and the light was deceptive down there in the shadows. When that first doubt was molded, and she had breathed into it the breath of life so that it stood sturdily before her, she took heart and created reasons, a whole company of them, to tell her why she ought to give Ward the benefit of the doubt. She remembered what Charlie Fox had said about circumstantial evidence. She would not make the mistake he had made.

So she spent other days and long, wakeful nights. And since it seemed impossible to bring her faith to life again just as it had been, with the glamor of romance and the sweetness of pity and the strength of her own innocence to make it a beautiful faith indeed, she used all her innocence and all her pity and a little of romance and created something even sweeter than her untried faith had been. She had a new element to strengthen it. She knew that she loved Ward; she had learned that from the hurt it had given her to lose her faith in him.

That was the record of the inner Billy Louise which no one ever saw. The Billy Louise which her little world knew went her way unchanged, except in small details that escaped the notice of those nearest her. A look in her eyes, for one thing; a hurt, questioning look that was sometimes rebellious as well; a droop of her mouth, also, when she was off her guard; a sad, tired little droop that told of the weight of responsibility and worry she was carrying.

Ward observed both, the minute he saw her on the trail. He had come across country on the chance that she might be riding out that way, and he had come upon her unawares while she and Blue were staring out over the desert from the height they had attained in the hills.

"'Lo, Bill!" he said, when he was quite close, and held himself ready to meet whatever mood she might present.

She turned her head quickly and looked at him, and the hurt look was still in her eyes, the droop still showed at her lips. And Ward knew they had been there before she saw him.

"Wha's molla, Bill?" he asked, in the tone that was calculated to invite an unburdening of her troubles.

"Ob, nothing in particular. Mommie's been awfully sick, and I'm always worried when I'm away from the ranch, for fear she'll have another spell while I'm gone. The doctor said she might have, any time. Were you headed for our place? If you are, come on; I was just starting back. I don't dare be away any longer." If that were a real unburdening, Ward was an unreasonable young man. Billy Louise looked at him again, and this time her eyes were clear and friendly.

Ward was not satisfied, for all the surface seemed smooth enough. He was too sensitive not to feel a difference, and he was too innocent of any wrongdoing or thinking to guess what was the matter. Guilt is a good barometer of personal atmosphere, and Ward had none of it. The worst of him she had known for more than a year; he had told her himself, and she had healed the hurt-almost-of the past by her firm belief in him and by her friendship. Could you expect Ward to guess that she had seen her faith in him die a violent death no longer than two weeks ago? Such a possibility never occurred to him.

For all that, he felt there was a difference somewhere. It chilled his eagerness a little, and it blanketed his enthusiasm so that he did not tell her the things he had meant to tell. He had ridden over with another nugget in his pocket —a nugget the size of an almond. He had come to give it to Billy Louise and to tell her how and where he had found it.

It is too bad that he changed his mind again and kept that lump of gold in his pocket. It would have explained so much, if he had given it to Billy Louise to put in her blue plush treasure box. It would even have brought to life that first faith in him. She might have told him-one never can foresee the lengths to which a woman's confessional mood will carry her-about that corral hidden in the canyon, and of her sickening certainty that she had seen him ride stealthily away from it. If she had, he would have convinced her that she was mistaken, and that he had that afternoon been washing gold a good ten miles from there, until it was too dark for him to work.

He took the nugget back home, and he took it sooner than he had intended to return. He also carried back a fit of the blues which seemed to have attacked him without cause or pretext, since he had not quarreled with Billy Louise, and had been warmly welcomed by "mommie." Poor mommie was looking white and frail, and her temples were too distinctly veined with purple. Ward told himself that it was no wonder his Wilhemina acted strained and unnatural. He meant to work harder than ever and get his stake so that he could go and make her give him the right to take care of her.

He began to figure the cost of commuting his homestead right away, so that he would not have to "hold it down" for another three years. Maybe she would not want to bring her mother so far off the main road. In that case, he would go down and put that Wolverine place in shape. He had no squeamishness about living on her ranch instead of his own, if she wanted it that way. He meant to be better "hooked up" financially than she was and have more cattle, when he put the gold ring on her finger. Then he would do whatever she wanted him to do, and he would not have to crucify his pride doing it.

You see, they could not have quarreled, since Ward carried castles as well as the blues. In fact, their parting had given Ward an uneven pulse for a mile, for Billy Louise had gone with him as usual as far as the corral, when he started home. And when Ward had picked up his reins and turned to put his toe in the stirrup, Billy Louise had come close-to his very shoulder. Ward had turned his face toward her, and Billy Louise-Billy Louise had impulsively taken his head between her two hands, had looked deep into his eyes, and then had kissed him wistfully on the lips. Then she had turned and fled up the path, waving him away up the trail. And though Ward never guessed that to her that kiss was a penitent vow of loyalty to their friendship and a slap in the face of the doubt-devils that still pursued her weaker moments, it set him planning harder than ever for that stake he must win before he dared urge her further toward matrimony.

It's a wonder that the kiss did not wipe out completely the somber mood that held him. That it did not, but served merely to tangle his thoughts in a most hopeless manner, perhaps proves how greatly the inner life of Billy Louise had changed her in those two weeks.

She changed still more in the next two months, however. There was the strain of her mother's precarious health which kept Billy Louise always on the alert and always trying to hide her fears. She must be quick to detect the first symptoms of a return attack of the illness, and she must not let her mother suspect that there was danger of a return. That much the doctor had made plain to her.

Besides that, there was an undercurrent of gossip and rumors of cattle stealing, whenever a man stopped at the ranch. It worried Billy Louise, in spite of her rebuilt belief in Ward. Doubt would seize her sometimes in spite of herself, and she did not see Ward often enough to let his personality fight those doubts. She saw him just once in the next two months, and then only for an hour or so.

A man rode up one night and stayed with them until morning, after the open-handed custom of the range-land. Billy Louise did not talk with him very much. He had shifty eyes and a coarse, loose-lipped mouth and a thick neck, and, girl-like, she took a violent dislike to him. But John Pringle told her afterwards that he was Buck Olney, the new stock inspector, and that he was prowling around to see if he could find out anything.

Billy Louise worried a good deal, after that. Once she rode out early with the intention of going to Ward's claim to warn him. But three miles of saner thought changed her purpose: she dared not leave her mother all day, for one thing; and for another, she could scarcely warn Ward without letting him see that she felt he needed warning; and even Billy Louise shrank from what might follow.

The stock inspector stopped again, on his way back to the railroad. Billy Louise was so anxious that she smothered her dislike and treated him nicely, which thawed the man to an alarming amiability. She questioned him artfully-trust Billy Louise for that! —and she decided that the stock inspector was either a very poor detective or a very good actor. He did not, for instance, mention any corral hidden in a blind canyon away back in the hills, and Billy Louise did not mention it, either. He had not found any worked brands, he said. And he did not appear to know anything further about Ward than the mere fact of his existence.

"There's a fellow holding down a claim, away over on Mill Creek," he had remarked. "I'll look him up when I come back, though Seabeck says he's all right."

"Ward is all right," asserted Billy Louise, rather unwisely.

"Haven't a doubt of it. I thought maybe he might have seen something that might give us a clew." Perhaps the stock inspector was wiser than she gave him credit for being. He did not at any rate pursue the subject any farther, until he found an opportunity to talk to Mrs. MacDonald herself. Then he artfully mentioned the fellow on Mill Creek, and because she did not know any reason for caution, he got all the information he wanted, and more, for mommie was in one of her garrulous humors.

He went away in a thoughtful mood, and I may as well tell you why. Do you remember that evening when Ward sat before the fire thinking so intently of a man that he pulled a gun on Billy Louise when she startled him? Well, this stock inspector was the man. And this man went away from the Wolverine thinking of Ward quite as intently as Ward sometimes thought of him. If Billy Louise had thrown a chip and hit the stock inspector on the back of the neck, it is very likely that he would have pulled a gun, also. I've an idea that Billy Louise might have done something more than throw a chip at him if she had known who he was; but she did not know, and she slept the sounder for her ignorance.

After that the days drifted quietly for a month and grew nippier at each end and lazier in the middle; which meant that the short summer was over, and that fall was getting ready to paint the wooded slopes with her gayest colors, and that one must prepare for the siege of winter.

It was some time in the latter part of September that Billy Louise got up in the middle of a frosty night because she heard her mother moaning. That was the beginning. She sent John off before daylight for the doctor, and before the next night she stood with her lips pressed together and watched the doctor count mommie's pulse and take mommie's temperature, and drew in her breath hardly when she saw how long he studied the thermometer afterwards.

There was a month or so of going to and fro on her toes and of watching the clock with a mind to medicine-giving. There were nights and nights and nights when the cabin window winked like a star fallen into the coulee, from dusk to red dawn. Ward rode over once, stayed all night, and went home in a silent rage because he could not do a thing.

There was a week of fluctuating hope, and a time when the doctor said mommie must go to a hospital-Boise, since she had friends there. And there was a terrible, nerve-racking journey to the railroad. And when Ward rode next to the Wolverine ranch, there was no Billy Louise to taunt or tempt him. John Pringle and Phoebe told him in brief, stolid sentences of the later developments and gave him a meal and offered him a bed, which he declined.

When the suspense became maddening, after that, he would ride down to the Wolverine for news. And the news was monotonously scant. Phoebe could read and write, after a fashion, and Billy Louise sent her a letter now and then, saying that mommie was about the same, and that she wanted John to do certain things about the ranch. She could not leave mommie, she said. Ward gathered that she would not.

Once when he was at the ranch, he wrote a letter to Billy Louise, and told her that he would come to Boise if there was anything he could do, and begged her to let him know if she needed any money. Beyond that he worked and worked, and tried to crowd the lonesomeness out of his days and the hunger from his dreams, with complete bone-weariness. He did not expect an answer to his letter-at least he told himself that he did not-but one day Phoebe gave him a thin little letter more precious in his eyes than the biggest nugget he had found.

Billy Louise did not write much; she explained that she could only scribble a line or two while mommie slept. Mommie was about the same. She did not think there was anything Ward could do, and she thanked him for offering to help. There was nothing, she said pathetically, that anybody could do; even the doctors did not seem able to do much, except tell her lies and charge her for them. No, she did not need any money, "thank you just the same, Ward." That was about all. It did not sound in the least like Billy Louise.

Ward answered the note then and there, and called her Wilhemina-mine —which was an awkward name to write and cost him five minutes of cogitation over the spelling. But he wanted it down on paper where she could see it and remember how it sounded when he said it, even if it did look queer. Farther along he started to call her Bill Loo, but rubbed it out and substituted Lady Girl (with capitals). Altogether he did better than he knew, for he made Billy Louise cry when she read it, and he made her say "Dear Ward!" under her breath, and remember how his hair waved over his left temple, and how he looked when that smile hid just behind his lips and his eyes. And he made her forget that she had lost faith in him. She needed to cry, and she needed to remember and also to forget some things; for life was a hard, dull drab in Boise, with nothing to lighten it, save a vicarious hope that did not comfort.

Billy Louise was not stupid. She saw through the vagueness of the doctors; and besides, she was so hungry for her hills that she felt like beating the doctors with her fists, because they did nothing to make her mommie well enough to go home. She grew to hate the nurse and her neutral cheerfulness.

That is how the fall passed for Billy Louise, and the early part of the winter.

Chapter XV. "You Won't get me Again"

One day late in the fall, Ward was riding the hills off to the north and west of his claim, looking at the condition of the range there and keeping an eye out for Y6 cattle. He had bought another dozen head of mixed stock, over toward Hardup, and they were not yet past the point of straying off their new range. So, having keen eyes and the incentive to use them, he paid attention to stock tracks in the soft places, and he saw everything within the sweep of his vision; and, since the day was clear and fine, his range of vision, when he reached a high point, extended to the Three Buttes away out in the desert.

By sheer accident he rode up to the canyon where the little corral lay hidden at the end, and looked down. And since he rode up at an angle different from the one Billy Louise had taken, the corral was directly beneath him-so directly, in fact, that half of it was hidden from sight. He saw that there were cattle within it, however, and two men at work there. And by chance he lifted his eyes and saw the nose of a horse beyond a jutting ledge sixty yards or so away, and the crown of a hat showing just above the ledge; a lookout, he judged instantly, and pulled Rattler behind the rock he had been at some pains to ride around.

Ward was a cowpuncher. He knew the tricks of the trade so well that he did not wonder what was going on down there. He knew. He was tempted to do as Billy Louise had done-ride on and pass up knowledge which might be disagreeable; for Ward was not one to spy upon his fellows, and the man whom he would betray into the hands of a sheriff must be guilty of a most heinous crime. That was his code: To let every fellow have a chance to work out his own salvation or damnation as he might choose. I don't suppose there was anything he hated worse than an informer.

He got behind the rock, since he had no great desire to be shot, and he discovered that his view of the corral was much plainer than from where he had first seen it. He looked behind him for an easy retreat to the skyline, and then before he turned to ride away, he glanced down again curiously.

A man walked out into the center of the corral and stood there in the revealing sunlight. Ward's eyes bored like gimlets through the space that divided them. Instinctively his hand went to the gun on his hip. It was a long pistol shot, and he was afraid he might miss; for Ward was not a wizard with a gun, much as I should like to misrepresent him as a dead shot. He was human, just like yourself. He could shoot pretty well, a great deal better than lots of men who do more boasting than he ever did, but he frequently missed. He measured the distance with his mind while the man stood there talking to someone unseen. To look at Ward's face, you would have sworn that the man was doomed; but something held Ward's finger from crooking on the trigger; the man had his back turned squarely toward the gun. Ward waited. The man did not move. He waited another minute, and then he opened his lips to shout. And when his lips parted for the call that would bring the fellow facing him, Ward's tricky brain snapped before his eyes the face of Billy Louise.

He lowered the gun. He could not shoot when he knew that the bullet would split a gulf between himself and the girl —a gulf that would separate him forever from that future where stood his air castles. Billy Louise had talked to him very seriously one day about this very possibility. She had made him see that shooting this man would be the worst thing he could possibly do.

He let down the hammer with his thumb, slid the gun back into his holster, and dismounted, with a glance toward the place where the lookout was stationed. He was sure he had not been seen, and so he crouched behind a splinter of rock and watched. He had no plan, but his instinct impelled him to closely watch Buck Olney.

Another man came into view, down there in the corral. He also stood plainly revealed, and Ward gave a little snort of contemptuous surprise when he recognized him. After that he studied the situation with scowling brows. This other man either upset his conclusions or complicated his manner of dealing with Buck Olney. Ward would not have hesitated one second about putting the sheriff on the trail of Buck, but if the second man were implicated, he could not betray one without betraying the other. And if the business down there in the corral were lawful, then he must think of some other means. At any rate, the thing to do now was to make sure.

The two in the corral came out and closed the gate behind them, and the first man kicked apart the embers of a small fire and afterward busied himself with the ground-either looking for tracks or covering them Up. They came a little way along the side of the bluff, mounted, and rode up toward where the lookout waited. And one of them rode a dark bay, and was slim and tall, and wore a gray hat.

Ward glanced at Rattler standing half asleep with reins dropped to the ground. He reached out, took the reins, and led the horse farther down under the shelter of the ledge. Rattler pricked up his ears at the sound of those other riders, but he did not show enough interest to nicker a greeting; he was always a self-centered beast and was content to go his way alone, like his master.

Ward stood up, where he could see the rim of the bluff over the ledge of lava rock. He might get a closer view and see who was the look out, and he might be seen; for that contingency he kept his fingers close to his gun. He heard their scrambling progress. Now and then one of the horses sent a little rock bounding down into the canyon, whereat the cattle on the corral moved restlessly around the small inclosure.

They came closer, after they had gained the top. Ward, leaning against the dull-gray rock before him, heard the murmur of their voices. Once he caught the unmistakable tones of the man he would like to kill. "I'll keep cases and git him." Plotting against some poor devil, as usual, Ward thought, and wondered if the man knew he lived in this part of the country; if he did, it might easily be —

"I'll keep cases some myself, you damned reptile," he muttered under his breath. "You won't get me again, if that's what you've got in mind."

They went on, and presently Ward was looking at their backs as they rode over the ridge. He stood for some time staring after them with what Billy Louise called his gimlet look. He was breathing shortly from the pressure he had put upon his self-control, and he was thinking-thinking.

The silence came creeping in on the heels of the faint, interrupted sound of their voices. Ward took a long breath, discovered that he was gripping his gun as though his life depended on hanging to it, and rubbed his numbed fingers absently. After a minute or so, he mounted and rode down to the corral.

Five dry cows and two steers snorted at his approach and crowded against the farther rails. Ward gave Rattler a touch of the spurs, rode close to the fence, and stood in his stirrups while he studied the bunch.

"Hell!" he said, when the inspection was over, and dropped back into the saddle while he gazed unseeingly at the canyon wall. It was a very real hell that his mind saw; a hell made by men, wherein other men must dwell in torment because of their sins or the sins of their fellows.

Seabeck's brand was a big V, a bad brand to own, since it favors revision at the hands of the unscrupulous. These cattle were Seabeck cattle, and their brand had been altered. For the right slant of the V had been extended a little and curled into a 6, so that in time the brand would stand casual inspection as a Y6 monogram-Ward's own brand. The work was crude-purposefully crude. The V bad not been reburned enough to make it look fresh, and the newly seared 6 had been added with a malevolent pressure that would make it stand out a fresh brand for a long time-in case of a delay in the proceedings, as Ward knew perfectly well.

So he sat there and looked over the fence and saw himself a convicted "rustler." There was the evidence, all ready to damn him utterly before a jury. They would be turned loose on the range near his claim, and they would be found before the scabs had haired over. It was a good time for rustling; round-ups were over for the winter, and the weather would confine range-riding to absolute necessity.

Of course, the work was coarse-so coarse as to reflect against his intelligence; but when brands are worked over and the culprit has been caught, the law is not too careful to give the prisoner credit for brains.

Ward stared at the altered brands and wondered what he had best do. He bethought him that perhaps it would be as well to put a little scenery between himself and that particular locality, and he started back up the hill. Once he pulled up as if he would go back, but he thought better of it. It was out of the question to turn those cattle loose. He could not kill them and dispose of the bodies-not when there were seven of them. He might go down and blotch the brands so that they would not read anything at all. He had thought of that before and decided against it. That would put those three on their guard and would probably not benefit him in the long run. They could work the brands on other cattle.

He hunched forward in the saddle and let Rattler choose his own trail up the hill. Though he did not know it, trouble had caught Billy Louise in that same place, and had sent her forward with drooping shoulders and a mind so absorbed that she gave no attention to her horse; but that is merely a trifling coincidence. The thing he had to decide was far more complicated than Billy Louise's problem.

Should he go straight to Seabeck and tell him what he had found out? He did not know Seabeck, except as he had met him once or twice on the trail and exchanged trivial greetings and a few words about the weather. Besides, Seabeck would very soon find out —

There it stood at his shoulder, grinning at him malevolently-his past. It tied his hands. Buck Olney he could deal with single-handed; for Olney had the fear of him that is born of a guilty conscience. He could send Buck "over the road" whenever he chose to tell some things he knew; he could do it without any compunctions, too. Buck Olney, the stock inspector, deserved no mercy at Ward's hands; and would get none, if ever they met where Ward would have a chance at him.

Olney he could deal with, alone. But with the evidence of those rebranded cattle, and the testimony of two men, together with the damning testimony of his past! Ward lifted his head and stared heavily at the pine slope before him. He could not go to Seabeck and tell him anything. In the black hour of that ride, he could not think of anything that he could do that would save him.

And then quite suddenly, in his desperation, he decided upon something. He laughed hardly, turned Rattler back from the homeward trail, and returned to the corral in the canyon. "They started this game, and they've put it up to me," he told himself grimly, "and they needn't squeal if they burn their own fingers."

He hurried, for he had some work ahead of him, and the sun was sliding past the noon mark already. He reached the corral and went about what he had to do as if he were working for wages and wanted to give good measure.

First, he rebuilt the little fire just outside the corral where the cattle could not trample it, but where one might thrust a branding iron into its midst from between the rails. When it was going properly, he searched certain likely hiding-places and found an iron still warm from previous service. He thrust it in to heat, led Rattler into the corral, and closed the gate securely behind him. Then he mounted, took down his rope and widened the loop, while his angry eyes singled out the animal he wanted first.

Ward was not an adept with a "running iron"; he was honest, whatever men might say of him. But he knew how to tie down an animal, and he sacrificed part of his lariat to get the short rope he needed to tie their feet together. He worked fast-no telling what minute someone might come and catch him-and he did his work well, far better and neater than had his predecessors.

When he left that corral, he smiled. Before he had ridden very far up the bluff, he stopped, looked down at the long-suffering cattle, and smiled again sardonically. One could read their brands easily from where he sat on his horse. They were not blotched; they were very distinct. But they were not Y6s within that corral. There were other brands which might be made of a Y6 monogram, by the judicious addition of a mark here and a mark there.

"There, damn yuh: chew on that awhile!" he apostrophized the absent three. He turned away and rode back once more toward home.

Rattler turned naturally into the trail which ran up the creek to the ranch, but Ward immediately turned him out of it. "We aren't going to overlook any bets, old-timer," he said grimly and crossed the creek at a point where it was too rocky to leave any hoof-prints behind them. He rode up the lower point of the ridge beyond and followed the crest of it on the side away from the valley. When he reached a point nearly opposite his cabin, he dismounted, unbuckled his spurs, and slipped their chains over the saddle-horn. Then he went forward afoot to reconnoitre. He was careful to avoid rock or gravelly patches and to walk always on the soft grass which muffled his steps.

In this wise he made his way to the top of the ridge, where he could look down upon the cabin and stable and corrals and see also the creek trail for a good quarter of a mile. The little valley lay quiet. His team fed undisturbed by the creek not far from the corral, which reassured Ward more than anything. Still, he waited until he had made reasonably sure that the bluff held no watcher concealed before he went back to where Rattler waited patiently.

"I guess they didn't plan to stir things up till they got those critters planted where they wanted them," he mused, while he rode down the bluff to his cabin. "But when they visit that bunch of stock again, I reckon things will begin to tighten!"

He was wary of exposing himself too much to view from the bluff while he did his chores that night, and he kept Rattler in the stable. Also, he slept very little, and before daybreak he was up and away. He had a rolled army blanket tied behind the saddle, a sack of grub and a frying-pan and a bucket for coffee. But he did not go any farther than the wolf-den, and he spent a couple of hours removing as well as he could any suspicious traces of having dug anything more than wolf pups from the bank on the ledge.

Chapter XVI. "I'm Going to Take You Out and Hang You"

The trouble with a man like Buck Olney is that you can never be sure of his method, except that it will be underhand and calculated to eliminate as much as possible any risk to himself. Ward, casting back into his memory-he had known Buck Olney very well, once upon a time, and in his unsuspecting youth had counted him a friend-tried to guess how Buck would proceed when he went down to that corral and found how those brands had been retouched.

"He'll be running around in circles for awhile, all right," he deduced with an air of certainty. "Blotched brands he'd know was my work; and he could have put it on me, too, with a good yarn about trailing me so close I got cold feet. As it is —" Ward smoked two cigarettes and scowled at the scenery. As it was, he did not know just what Buck Olney would do, except — "If he makes a guess I did that, he'll know I'm wise to the whole plant. And he'll get me, sure, providing I stand with my back to him long enough!" Ward had his back to a high ledge, at that moment, so that he did not experience any impulse to look behind him.

"Buck don't want to drag me up before a jury," he reasoned further. "He'd a heap rather pack me in all wrapped up in a tarp, and say how he'd caught me with the goods, and I resisted arrest."

The assurance he felt as to what Buck Olney would do did not particularly frighten Ward, even if he did neglect to go to bed in his cabin during the next few days. That was common sense, born of his knowledge of the man he was dealing with. He went to the cabin warily, just often enough to give it an air of occupancy. He frequently sat upon some hilltop and watched a lazy thread of smoke weave upward from his rusty stovepipe, but he slept out under the stars rolled in his heavy blanket, and he never crossed a ridge if he could make his way through a hollow. It is not always cowardice which makes a man extremely careful not to fall into the hands of his enemy. There is a small matter of pride involved. Ward would have died almost any death rather than give Buck Olney the satisfaction of "getting" him. For a few days he was cautious as an Indian on the war trail, and then his patience frazzled out under the strain.

At sunrise one morning, after a night of shivering in his blanket, he hunched his shoulders in disgust of his caution. If Buck Olney wanted anything of him, he was certainly taking his time about coming after it. Ward rubbed his fingers over his stubbly jaw, and the uncomfortable prickling was the last small detail of discomfort that decided him. He was going to have a shave and a decent cup of coffee and eat off his own table, or know the reason why, he promised himself while he slapped the saddle on Rattler.

He was camped in a sheltered little hollow in the hills, where the grass was good and there was a spring. It was a mile and more to his claim, straight across the upland, and it was his habit to leave Rattler there and walk over to the ridge, where he could watch his claim; frequently, as I have said, he stole down before daylight and lighted a fire in the stove, just to make it look as if he lived there. There was a risk in that, of course, granting that the stock inspector was the kind to lie in wait for him.

Ward rode to the ridge, with his blanket rolled and tied behind the cantle. His frying-pan hung behind his leg, and his rifle lay across the saddle in front of him. He was going home boldly enough and recklessly enough, but he was by no means disposed to walk deliberately into a trap. He kept his eye peeled, as he would have expressed it. Also, he left Rattler just under the crest of the ridge, took off his spurs, and with his rifle in his hands went forward afoot, as he had done every time he had approached his cabin since the day he found the corral and the cattle in the canyon.

In this wise he looked down the steep slope with the sun throwing the shadow of his head and shoulders before him. The cabin window blinked cheerfully in the sunlight. His span of mares were coming up from the meadow-in the faint hope of getting a breakfast of oats, perhaps. The place looked peaceful enough and cozily desirable to a man who has slept out for four nights late in the fall; but a glance was all Ward gave to it.

His eyes searched the bluff below him and upon either side. Of a sudden they sharpened. He brought his rifle forward with an involuntary motion of the arms. He stood so for a breath or two, looking down the hill. Then he went forward stealthily, on his toes; swiftly, too, so that presently he was close enough to see the carbuncle scar on the neck of the man crouched behind a rock and watching the cabin as a cat watches a mouse-hole. A rifle lay across the rock before the man, the muzzle pointing downward. At that distance, and from a dead rest, it would be strange if he should miss any object he shot at. He had what gamblers call a cinch, or he would have had, if the man he watched for had not been standing directly behind him, with rifle-sights in a line with the scar on the back of his thick neck.

"Throw up your hands!" Ward called sharply, when his first flare of rage had cooled to steady purpose.

Buck Olney jumped as though a yellow-jacket had stung him. He turned a startled face over his shoulder and jerked the rifle up from the rock. Ward raised his sights a little and plugged a round, black-rimmed hole through Buck's hat crown.

"Throw up your hands, I told you!" he said, while the hills opposite were still flinging back the sound of the shot, and came closer.

Buck grunted an oath, dropped the rifle so suddenly that it clattered on the rock, and lifted his hands high, in the quiet sunlight.

"Get up from there and go on down to the shack-and keep your hands up. And remember all the reasons I've got for wanting to see you make a crooked move, so I'll have an excuse to shoot." Ward came still closer as he spoke. He was wishing he had brought his rope along. He did not feel quite easy in his mind while Buck Olney's hands were free. He kept thinking of what Billy Louise had said to him about shooting this man, and it was the first time since he had known her that he disliked the thought of her.

Buck got up awkwardly and went stumbling down the steep slope, with his hands trembling in the air upon either side of his head. From their nervous quivering it was evident that his memory was good, and that it was working upon the subject which Ward had suggested to him. He did not give Ward the weakest imitation of an excuse to shoot. And so the two of them came presently down upon the level and passed around the cabin to the door, with no more than ten feet of space between them-so inexorably had Ward crowded close upon the other's stumbling progress.

"Hold on a minute!"

Buck stopped as still as though he had gone against a rock wall.

Ward came closer, and Buck flinched away from the feel of the rifle muzzle between his shoulder blades. Ward reached out a cautious hand and pulled the six-shooter from its scabbard at Buck's right hip.

"Got a knife? You always used to go heeled with one. Speak up-and don't lie about it."

"Inside my coat," grunted Buck, and Ward's lip curled while he reached around the man's bulky body and found the knife in its leather sheath. Evidently Buck was still remembering with disquieting exactness what reasons Ward might have for wanting to kill him.

"Take down your left hand and open the door."

Buck did so and put his hand up again without being told.

"Now go in and stand with your face to the wall." With the rifle muzzle, Ward indicated which wall. He noticed how Buck's fingers groped and trembled against the wall, just under the eaves, and his lip curled again in the expression which Billy Louise so hated to see.

Ward had chosen the spot where he could reach easily a small coil of rope. He kept the rifle pressing Buck's shoulders until he had shifted the knife into one hand, leaned, and laid its blade against Buck's cheek.

"Feel that? I'll jab it clear through you if you give me a chance. Drop your hands down behind you." He spent a busy minute with the rope before he pushed Buck Olney roughly toward a chair.

Buck sat down, and Ward did a little more rope-work.

"Say, Ward, you're making a big mistake if you —"

"Shut up!" snapped Ward. "Can't you see I'm standing all I can stand, just with the sight of you? Don't pile it on too thick by letting me hear you talk. I heard you once too often as it is."

Buck Olney caught his breath and sat very still. His eyes followed Ward as the eyes of a caged animal follow its keeper.

Ward tried to ignore his presence completely while he lighted a fire and fried bacon and made coffee, but the hard set of his jaw and the cold intentness of his eyes proved how conscious he was of Buck's presence. He tried to eat just to show how calm he was, but the bread and bacon choked him. He could feel every nerve in his body quiver with the hatred he felt for the man, and the bitterness which the sight of him called up out of the past. He drank four cups of coffee, black and sweetened at random, which steadied him a little. That he did not offer Buck food or drink showed how intense was his hatred; as a rule, your true range man is hospitable even to his enemies.

He rose and inspected the ropes to make sure that they were proof against twisting, straining muscles, and took an extra turn or two with the loose end, just to make doubly sure of the man's helplessness.

"Where did you leave your horse?" he asked him curtly, when he was through.

Buck told him, his eyes searching Ward's face for mercy-or at least for some clew to his fate-and dulling with disappointment because he could read nothing there but loathing.

Without speaking again, Ward went out and closed the door firmly behind him. He felt relieved to be away from Buck's presence. As he climbed the bluff and mentally relived the last hour, he wondered how he had kept from shooting Buck as soon as he saw him. Still, that would have defeated his main purpose, which was to make Buck suffer. He was afraid he could not make Buck suffer as Buck had made him suffer, because there were obstacles in the path of a perfect retribution.

Ward was not cruel by nature; at least he was not more cruel than the rest of us; but as he went after Rattler and Buck's horse, it pleased him to know that Buck Olney was tied hand and foot in his cabin, and that he was sick with dread of what the future held for him.

Ward was gone an hour. He did not hurry; there was no need. Buck could not get away, and a little suspense would do him good.

Buck's face was pasty when Ward opened the door. His eyes were a bit glassy. And from the congested appearance of his hands, Ward judged that he had tested to the full his helplessness in his bonds. Ward looked at him a minute and got out the makings of a smoke. His mood had changed in his absence. He no longer wanted absolute silence between them; instead, he showed symptoms of wanting to talk.

"If I turn you loose, Buck, what will you do?" he asked at last, in a curious tone.

"If you-Ward, I'll prove I'm a friend to yuh in spite of the idea you've got that I ain't. I never done nothing —"

"No, of course not." Ward's lip curled. "That was my mistake, maybe. You always used to say you were my friend, when —"

"And that's the God's truth, Ward!" Buck's face was becoming flushed with his eagerness. "I done everything I could for you, Ward, but the way the cards laid I couldn't —"

"Get me hanged. I know; you sure tried hard enough!" Ward puffed hard at his cigarette, and the lips that held it trembled a little. Otherwise he seemed perfectly cool and calm.

"Say, Ward, them lawyers lied to you."

"Oh, cut it out, Buck. I've seen you wriggle through a snake-hole before. I believe you're my friend, just the way you've always been."

"That's right, Ward, and I can prove it."

Ward snorted. "You proved it, old-timer, when you laid up there behind a rock with your sights on this shack, ready to get me when I came out. I sabe now how it happened Jim McGuire was found face down in the spring behind his shack, with a bullet hole in his back, that time. You were his friend, too!"

"Ward, I —"

"Shut up. I just wanted to see if you'd changed any in the last seven years. You haven't, unless it's for the worse. You've got to the end of the trail, old-timer. When you went laying for me, you fixed yourself a-plenty. Do you want to know what I'm going to do with you?"

"Ward, you wouldn't dare shoot me! With the record you've got, you wouldn't stand —"

"Who gave it to me, huh? Oh, I heap sabe; you've left word with your pardners that you were coming up here to arrest me single-handed. They will give the alarm, if you don't show up; and I'll go on the dodge and get caught and —" Ward threw away his cigarette and took a step toward his captive; a step so ominous that Buck squirmed in his bonds.

"Well, you can rest easy on one point. I'm not going to shoot you." Ward stood still and watched the light of hope flare in the eyes of his enemy. "I'm going to wash the dishes and take a shave-and then I'm going to take you out somewhere and hang you."

"My God, Ward! You-you —"

"I told you, seven years ago," went on Ward steadily, "that I'd see you hung before I was through with you. Remember? By rights you ought to hang by the heels, over a slow fire! You're about as low a specimen of humanity as I ever saw or heard of. You know what you did for me, Buck. And you know what I told you would happen; well, it's going to come off according to the programme.

"I did think of running you in and giving you a taste of hell yourself. But, as usual, you've gone and tangled up a couple of fellows that never did me any particular harm and I don't want to hand them anything if I can help it. So I'll just string you up-after awhile, when I get around to it-and leave a note saying who you are, and that you're the head push in this rustling business, and that you helped spend the money that Hardup bank lost awhile back; and that you're one of the gazabos —"

"You can't prove it! You —"

"I don't have to prove it. The authorities will do all that when they get the tip I'll give them. And you, being hung up on a limb somewhere, can't very well give your pardner the double-cross; so they'll have a fighting chance to make their getaway.

"Now I'm through talking to you. What I say goes. You can talk if you want to, Buck; but I'm going to carve a steak out of you every time you open your mouth." He pulled Buck's own knife out of its sheath and laid it convenient to his hand, and he looked as if he would do any cruel thing he threatened.

He relighted the fire, which had gone out long ago, and set the dish-pan on the stove with water to heat. He remade his bunk, spreading on the army blanket which he took from the saddle on Rattler. He swept the floor as neatly as any woman could have done it and laid the two wolf-skins down in their places where they did duty as rugs. He washed and wiped his few dishes, keeping Buck's knife always within reach and sending an inquiring glance toward Buck whenever that unhappy man made the slightest movement, though truth to tell, Buck did not make many. He brought two pails of water and set them on the bench inside, and in the meantime he had cooked a mess of prunes and set them in a bowl on the window-sill beside his bunk, where the air was coolest. He stropped his razor painstakingly and shaved himself in leisurely fashion and sent an occasional glance toward his prisoner from the looking-glass, which made Buck swallow hard at his Adam's apple.

And Buck, during all this time, never once opened his lips, except to lick his tongue across them, and never once took his eyes off Ward.

"I've sure put the fear of the Lord into you, haven't I, Buck?" Ward observed maliciously, wiping a blob of hairy lather upon a page torn from an old Sears-Roebuck catalogue. "I was kinda hoping you had more nerve. I wanted to get a whack at you, just to prove I'm not joshing."

Buck swallowed again, but he made no reply.

Ward washed his face in a basin of steaming water, got a can of talcum out of the dish cupboard, and took the soap-shine off his cheeks and chin. He combed his hair before the little mirror-trying unavailingly to take the wave out of it with water, and leaving it more crinkly over his temples than it had been in the first place-and retied the four-in-hand under the soft collar of his shirt.

"I wish you'd talk, Buck," he said, turning toward the other. He looked very boyish and almost handsome, except for the expression of his eyes, which gave Buck the shivers, and the set of his lips, which was cruel. "I've read how the Chinks hand out what they call the death-of-a-thousand-cuts; I was thinking I'd like to try it out on you. But-oh, well, this is Friday. It may as well go as a hanging." He made a poor job of his calm irony, but Buck was not in the mental condition to be critical.

The main facts were sufficiently ominous to offset Ward's attempt at facetiousness. Indeed, the very weakness of the attempt was in itself ominous. Ward might try to be coldly malevolent, but the light that burned in his eyes, and the rage that tightened his lips, gave the lie to his forced composure.

He went out and led up the horses to the door. He came back and started to untie Buck Olney's feet, then bethought him of the statement he had promised to write. He got a magazine and tore out the frontispiece-which, oddly enough, was a somber picture of Death hovering with outstretched wings over a battlefield-and wrote several lines in pencil on the back of it, where the paper was smooth and white.

"How's that?" he asked, holding up the paper so that Buck could read what he had written. "I ain't in the mood to sit down and write a whole book, so I had to boil down your pedigree. But that will do the business all right, don't you think?"

Buck read with staring eyes, looked into Ward's face, and opened his lips for protest or pleading. Then he followed Ward's glance to the knife on the table and shut his mouth with a snap. Ward laughed grimly, picked up the knife, and ran his thumb lightly over the edge to test its keenness. "Put a fresh edge on it for me, huh?" he commented. "Well, we may as well get started, I reckon. I'm getting almighty sick of seeing you around."

He loosened the rope that hound Buck to the chair and stood scowling down at him, drawing in a corner of his lip and biting it thoughtfully. Then he took his revolver and held it in his left hand, while with his right he undid the rope which hound Buck's hands.

"Stick your hands out in front of you," he commanded. "You'll have to ride a ways; there isn't any gallows tree in walking distance."

"For God's sake, Ward!" Buck's voice was hoarse. The plea came out of its own accord. He held his hands before him, however, and he made no attempt to get out of the chair. He knew Ward could shoot all right with his left hand, you see. He had watched him practice on tin cans, long ago when the two were friends.

"You know what I told you," Ward reminded him grimly and took up the knife with a deadly air that made the other suck in his breath. "Hold still! I'm liable to cut your throat if I make a mislick."

Really, it was the way he did it that made it terrible. The thing itself was nothing. He merely drew the back of the blade down alongside Buck's ear, and permitted the point to scratch through the skin barely enough to let out a thin trickle of blood. A pin would have hurt worse. But Buck groaned and believed he had lost an ear. He breathed in gasps, but did not say a word.

"Go ahead; talk all you want to, Buck," Ward invited, and wiped the knife-blade on Buck's shoulder before he returned the weapon to its sheath in his inside coat pocket.

Buck flinched from the touch and set his teeth. Ward tied his hands before him and told him to get up and go out to his horse. Buck obeyed with abject submissiveness, and Ward's lip curled again as he walked behind him to the door. He had not the slightest twinge of pity for the man. He was gloatingly glad that he could make him suffer, and he inwardly cursed his own humanity for being so merciful. He ought to have cut Buck's ear off slick and clean instead of making a bluff at it, he told himself disgustedly. Buck deserved it and more.

He helped Buck into the saddle, took the short rope in his hands, and hobbled Buck's feet under the horse, grasped the bridle-reins, and mounted Rattler. Without a word he set off up the rough trail toward Hardup, leading Buck's horse behind him.

Chapter XVII. "So-Long, Buck!"

"Before you go, Buck, I want to tell you that you needn't jolly yourself into thinking your death will be avenged. It won't. You noticed what I wrote; and there isn't a scrap of my writing anywhere in the country to catch me up—" Ward's thoughts went to Billy Louise, who had some very good samples, and he stopped suddenly. He was trying not to think of Billy Louise, to-day. "Also, when somebody happens to ride this way and sees you, I won't be anywhere around."

"This is the tree," he added, stopping under a cottonwood that flung a big branch out over the narrow cow-trail they were traveling. "The chances are friend Floyd will be ambling around this way in a day or two," he said hearteningly. "He can tend to the last sad rites and take charge of your horse. He's liable to be sore when he reads your pedigree, but I don't reckon that will make a great deal of difference. You'll get buried, all right, Buck."

Ward dismounted with a most businesslike manner and untied Buck Olney's rope from the saddle. "I can't spare mine," he explained laconically. He had some trouble in fashioning a hangman's noose. He had not had much practice, he remarked to Buck after the first attempt.

"How do you do it, Buck? You know more about these things than I do," he taunted. "You've helped hang lots of poor devils that will be glad to meet yuh in hell to-day."

Buck Olney moistened his dry lips. Ward glanced at his face and looked quickly away. Staring, abject terror is not nice to look upon, even though the man is your worst enemy and is suffering justly for his sins. Ward's fingers fumbled the rope as though his determination were weakening. Then he remembered some things, hunched his shoulders, impatient of the merciful impulse, and began the knot again. An old prospector had shown him once how it was done.

"Of course, a plain slip-knot would do the business all right," he said. "But I'll try and give you the genuine thing, same as you gave the other fellows."

"Ward, for God's sake, let me go!"

Ward started. He did not know that a man's voice could change so much in so short a time. He never would have recognized the tones as coming from Buck Olney's loose, complacent lips.

"Ward, I'll never—I'll leave the country—I'll go to South America, or Australia, or—"

"You'll go to hell, Buck," Ward cut in inexorably. "You've got your ticket."

"I'll own up to everything. I'll tell you where some of the money's cached we got in that Hardup deal, Ward. There's enough to put you on Easy Street. I'll tell you who helped—"

"You'd better not," advised Ward harshly, "or I'll make hanging a relief to you. I know pretty well, right now, all you could tell. And if I wanted to send your pardners up, I wouldn't need your help. It's partly to give them a chance that I'm sending you out this way, myself. I don't call this murder, Buck. I'm saving the State a lot of time and trouble, that's all; and your pardners the black eye they'd get for throwing in with you. I heap sabe who was the head push. You got them in to take whatever dropped, so you could get off slick and clean, just as you've done before, you-you—"

Buck Olney got it then, hot from the fires of Ward's wrath. A man does not brood over treachery and wrong and a blackened future for years, without storing up a good many things that he means to say to the friend who has played him false. Ward had been a happy-go-lucky young fellow who had faith in men and in himself and in his future. He had lived through black, hopeless days and weeks and months, because of this man who tried now to buy mercy with the faith of his partners.

Ward stood up and let the rope trail forgotten from his hands while he told Buck Olney all the things he had brooded over in bitterness. He had meant to keep it all down, but it was another instance of bottled emotions, and Buck, with his offer of a fresh bit of treachery, had pulled the cork. Ward trembled a little while he talked, and his face grew paler and paler as he dug deep into the blackest part of the past, until when he finished he was a tanned white. He was shaking at the last; shaking so that he staggered to the tree and leaned against it weakly, while he fumbled for tobacco and papers.

In the saddle Buck sat all hunched together as if Ward had lashed him with rawhide instead of with stinging words. The muscles of his face twitched spasmodically. His eyes were growing bloodshot.

Ward spilled two papers of tobacco before he got a cigarette rolled and lighted. He wondered a little at the physical reaction from his outburst, but he wondered more at Buck Olney sitting alive and unhurt on the horse before him —a Seabeck horse which Ward had seen Floyd Carson riding once or twice. He wondered what Floyd would do if he saw Buck now and the use to which the horse was being put.

Ward finished the cigarette, rolled another, and smoked that also before he could put his hand out before him and hold it reasonably steady. When he felt fairly sure of himself again, he lifted his hat to wipe off the sweat of his anger, gave a big sigh, and returned to the tying of the hangman's noose.

When he finally had it fixed the way he wanted it, he went close and flung the noose over Buck Olney's head. He could not trust himself to speak just then. He cast an inquiring glance upward, took Buck's horse by the bridle, and led him forward a few steps so that Buck was directly under the overhanging limb. Then, with the coil of Buck's rope in his hand, he turned back and squirmed up the tree-trunk until he had reached the limb. He crawled out until he was over Buck's bullet-punctured hat-crown, sliced off what rope he did not need, and flung it to the ground. He saw Buck wince as the rope went past him. The pinto horse shied out of position.

"Take the reins and bring him back here!" Ward called shortly, and gave a twitch of the rope as a hint.

Mechanically Buck obeyed. He did not know that the rope was not yet tied to the limb.

Ward tied the rope securely, leaving enough slack to keep Buck from choking prematurely. He fussed a minute longer, with his lip curled into a grin of sardonic humor. Then he crawled hack to the trunk of the tree and slid down carefully so that he would not frighten the pinto.

He went up and took the hobble off Buck Olney's feet, felt in the seam of his coat-lapel, and pulled out four pins, with which he fastened Buck's "pedigree" between Buck's shrinking shoulder-blades. Then he stood off and surveyed his work critically before he went over to Rattler, who stood dozing in the sunshine.

"Sorry I can't stay to see you off," he told Buck maliciously. "I've decided to let you go alone and take your own time about starting. As long as that cayuse stands where he is, you're safe as a church. And you've got the reins; you can kick off any time you feel like it. Sabe?" He studied Buck's horror-marked face pitilessly.

"You've got about one chance in a million that you can make that pinto stand there till some-one comes along," he pointed out impartially. "I'm willing to give you that chance, such as it is. And if you're lucky enough to win out on it-well, I'd advise you to do some going! South America is about as close as you'll be safe. Folks around here are going to know all about you, old-timer, whether they get to read what's on your back or not.

"And, on the other hand, it's a million-to-one shot you'll land where your ticket reads. I'd hate to gamble on that horse standing in one spot for two or three days, wouldn't you?" He wheeled Rattler unobtrusively, his eye on the pinto. "I hope he don't try to follow," he said. "I want you to have a little time to think about the things I said to you. Well, so-long."

Ward rode back the way he had come, glancing frequently over his shoulder at Buck, slumped in the saddle with a paper pinned to his back like a fire-warning on a tree, and his own grass rope noosed about his neck and connecting him with the cottonwood limb six feet above his hat crown.

Ward had not ridden a hundred yards before he heard Buck Olney scream hysterically for help. He grinned sourly with his eyebrows pinched together and, that hard, strained look in his eyes still. "Let him holler awhile!" he gritted. "Do him good, damn him!"

Until distance and the intervening hills set a wall of silence between, Ward heard Buck screaming in fear of death, screaming until he was so hoarse he could only whisper; screaming because he had not seen Ward take his knife and slice the rope upon the limb so that it would not have held the weight of a rabbit.

Chapter XVIII. Fortune Kicks Again

It was past noon when Ward rode down the steep slope to the creek bank just above his cabin. He was sunk deep in that mental depression which so often follows close upon the heels of a great outburst of passion. Mechanically he twitched the reins and sent Rattler down the last shelf of bank-and he did not look up to see just where he was. Rattler was a well-trained horse, since he was Ward's. He obeyed the rein signal and stepped off a two-foot bank into a nest of loose-piled rocks that slid treacherously under his feet. Sure-footed though he was, he stumbled and fell; and it was sheer instinct that took Ward's feet from the stirrups in time.

Ward sprawled among the rocks, dazed. The shock of the fall took him out of his fit of abstraction, and he pulled away from Rattler as the horse scrambled up and stood shaking before him. He tried to scramble up also....

Ward sat and stared stupidly at his left leg where, midway between his knee and his foot, it turned out at an unnatural angle. He thought resentfully that he had had enough trouble for once, without having a broken leg on top of it all.

"Now this is one hell of a fix!" he stated dispassionately, when pain had in a measure cooled his first anger. He looked around him like a man who is taking stock of his resources. He was not far from the cabin. He could get there by crawling. But what then?

Ward looked at Rattler, standing docilely within reach of his hand. He considered getting on-if he could, and riding-well, the nearest place was fifteen miles. And that was a good, long way from a doctor. He glanced again at the cabin and tried to study the situation impersonally. If it were some other fellow, now, what would Ward advise him to do under the circumstances?

He reached down and felt his leg gingerly. So far as he could tell, it was a straight, simple break-snapped short off against a rock, he judged. He shook his head over the thought of riding fifteen miles with those broken bones grinding their edges together. And still, what else could he do?

He reached out, took the reins, and led Rattler a step nearer, so that he could grasp the stirrup. With his voice he held the horse quiet while he pulled himself upright upon his good leg. Then, with pain-hurried, jerky movements, he pulled off the saddle, glanced around him, and flung it behind a buck-brush. He slipped off the bridle, flung that after the saddle, and gave Rattler a slap on the rump. The horse moved away, and Ward stared after him with set lips. "Anyway, you can look after yourself," he said and balanced upon his right leg while he swung around and faced the cabin. It was not far-to a man with two sound legs. A hundred yards, perhaps.

Ward crawled there on his hands and one knee, dragging the broken leg after him. It was not a nice experience, but it served one good purpose: It wiped from his mind all thought of that black past wherein Buck had figured so shamefully. He had enough to think of with his present plight, without worrying over the past.

In half an hour or so Ward rested his arms upon his own doorstep and dropped his perspiring face upon them. He lay there a long while, in a dead faint.

After awhile he moved, lifted his head, and looked about him dully at first and then with a certain stoical acceptance of his plight. He looked into the immediate future and tried to forecast its demands upon his strength and to prepare for them. He crawled farther up on the step, reached the latch, and opened the door. He crawled in, pulled himself up by the foot of his bunk, and sat down weakly with his head in his hands. Like a hurt animal, he had obeyed his instinct and had crawled home. What next?

If Ward had been a weaker man, he would have answered that question speedily with his gun. He did think of it contemptuously as an easy way out. If he had never met Billy Louise, he might possibly have chosen that way. But Ward had changed much in the past two years, and at the worst he had never been a coward. His hurt was sending waves of nausea over him, so that he could not concentrate his mind upon anything. Then he thought of the bottle of whisky he kept in his bunk for emergencies. Ward was not a man who drank for pleasure, but he had the Western man's faith in a good jolt of whisky when he felt a cold coming on or a pain in his stomach-or anything like that. He always kept a bottle on hand. A quart lasted him a long time.

He felt along the footboard of the bunk till his fingers touched the bottle, drew it out from its hiding-place —he hid it because stray callers would have made short work of it-and, placing the uncorked bottle to his trembling lips, swallowed twice.

He was steadier now, and the sickness left him like fog before a stiff breeze. His eyes went slowly around the cabin, measuring his resources, and his needs and limitations. He pulled his one chair toward him-the chair which Buck Olney had occupied so unwillingly-and placed his left knee upon it. It hurt terribly, but the whisky had steadied him so that he could bear the pain. He managed to reach the cupboard where he kept his dishes, and took down a bottle of liniment and a box of carbolized vaseline which he happened to have. He was near the two big, zinc water pails which he had filled that morning just to show Buck Olney how cool he was over his capture, and he bethought him that water was going to be precious in the next few weeks.

He lifted down one pail and swung it forward as far as he could, and set it on the floor ahead of him. Then he swung the other pail beside it. Painfully he hitched his chair alongside, lifted the pails and set them forward again. He did that twice and got them beside his bunk. He went back and inspected the tea-kettle, found it half full, and carried that also beside the bunk. Then he took another drink of whisky and rested awhile.

Bandages! Well, there was a new flour-sack hanging on a nail. He stood up, leaned and got it, and while he was standing, he reached for the cigar-box where he kept his bachelor sewing outfit; two spools of very coarse thread, some large-eyed needles to carry it, an assortment of buttons, and a pair of scissors. He cut the flour-sack into strips and sewed the strips together; his stitches were neater than you might think.

When the bandage was long enough, he rolled it as he had seen doctors do, and fished some pins out of the cigar-box and laid them where he could get his fingers on them quickly. He stood up again, reached across to a box of canned milk, and pried off the lid. "I'm liable to need you, too," he muttered to the rows of cans, and pulled the box close. He took Buck Olney's knife and whittled some very creditable splints from the thin boards, and rummaged in his "warbag" under the bunk for handkerchiefs with which to wrap the splints.

When he had done all that he could do to prepare for the long siege of pain and helplessness ahead of him, he moved along the bunk until he was sitting near the head of it with his broken leg extended before him, and took a last look to make sure that everything was ready. He felt his gun at his hip, removed belt and all, and threw it back upon the bed. Then he turned his head and stared, frowning, at the black butt where it protruded from the holster suggestively ready to his hand. He reached out and took the gun, turned it over, and hesitated. No telling what insane impulse fever might bring upon him-and still-no telling what Buck Olney might do when he discovered that he was not in any immediate danger of hanging.

If Buck came back to have it out with him, he would certainly need that gun. He knew Buck, a broken leg wouldn't save him. On the other hand, if the fever of his hurt hit him hard enough — "Oh, fiddlesticks!" he told himself at last. "If I get crazy enough for that, the gun won't cut much ice one way or the other. There are other ways of bumping off—" So he tucked the gun under the mattress at the head of his bed where he could put his hand upon it if the need came.

Then he removed his boots by the simple method of slitting the legs with Buck's knife, bared his broken leg in the same manner, swallowed again from the bottle, braced himself mentally and physically, gritted his teeth, and went doggedly to work.

A man never knows just how much he can endure or what he can do until he is making his last stand in the fight for self-preservation. Ward had no mind to lie there and die of blood-poisoning, for instance, and broken bones do not set themselves. So, sweating and swearing with the agony of it, he set his leg and bound the splints in place, and thanked the Lord it was a straight, clean break and that the flesh was not torn.

Then he dropped back upon the bed and didn't care whether he lived or not.

Followed days of fever, through which Ward lived crazily and lost count of the hours as they passed. Days when he needed good nursing, and did not get so much as a drink of water, except through pain and effort. Hours when he cursed Buck Olney and thought he had him bound to the chair in the cabin. Hours when he watched for him, gun in hand, through the window beside the bunk.

It was while he was staring glassy-eyed through the window that his attention wandered to the big, white bowl of stewed prunes. They looked good, with their shiny, succulent plumpness standing up like little wrinkled islands in the small sea of brown juice. Ward reached out with his left hand-he was gripping the gun in his right, ready for Buck when he showed up-and picked a prune out of the dish. It was his first morsel of food since the morning when he had tried to eat his breakfast while Buck Olney stared at him with the furtive malevolence of a trapped animal. That was three days ago. The prune tasted even better than it looked. Ward picked out another and another.

He forgot his feverish hallucination that Buck Olney was waiting outside there until he caught Ward off his guard. He lay back on his pillow, his fingers relaxed upon the gun. He closed his eyes and lay quiet. Perhaps he slept a little.

When he opened his eyes he was in the dark. The window was a transparent black square sprinkled with stars. Ward watched them awhile. He thought of Billy Louise; he would like to know how her mother was getting along and how much longer they expected to stay in Boise. He thought of the times she had kissed him-twice, and of her own accord. She would not have done it, either time, if he had asked her; he knew her well enough for that. She must be left free to obey the impulses of that big, brave heart of hers. A girl with a smaller soul and one less fine would have blushed and simpered and acted the fool generally at the mere thought of kissing a man of her own accord. Billy Louise had been tender as Christ Himself, and as sweet and pure. Was there another girl like her in the world? Ward looked at the stars and smiled. There was never such another, he told himself. And she "liked him to pieces"; she had said so. Ward laughed a little in spite of his throbbing leg. "Some other girl would have said, 'Ward, I lo-ove you,'" he grinned. "Wilhemina is different."

He lay there looking up at the stars and thinking, thinking. Once his lips moved. He was saying "Wilhemina-mine" softly to himself. His eyes, shining in the starlight, were very tender. After a long while he fell asleep, still thinking of her. A late moon came up and touched his face and showed it thin and sunken-eyed, yet with the little smile hidden behind his lips, for he was dreaming of Billy Louise.

Some time after daylight Ward woke and wanted a cigarette, which was a sign that he was feeling a little more like himself. He was feverish still, and the beating pain in his leg was maddening. But his brain was clear of fever-fog. He smoked a little of the cigarette he made from the supply on the shelf behind the bunk, and after that he looked about him for something to eat.

He had made a final trip to Hardup two weeks before, and had brought back supplies for the winter. And because his pay streak of gravel-bank had yielded a fair harvest, he had not stinted himself on the things he liked to eat. He lay looking over the piled boxes against the farther wall, and wondered if he could reach the box of crackers and drag it up beside the bunk. He was weak, and to move his leg was agony. Well, there was the dish of prunes on the window-sill.

Ward ate a dozen or so-but he wanted the crackers. He leaned as far as he could from the bed, and the box was still two feet from his outstretched fingers. He lay and considered how he might bring the box within reach.

At the head of the bunk stood the case of peaches and beneath that the case of canned tomatoes, the two forming a stand for his lantern. He eyed them thoughtfully, chewing a corner of his underlip. He did not want peaches or tomatoes just then; he wanted those soda-crackers.

He took Buck Olney's knife-he was finding it a most useful souvenir of the encounter! —and pried off a board from the peach box. Two nails stuck out through each end of the board. He leaned again from the bed, reached out with the board, and caught the nails in a crack on the upper edge of the cracker-box. He dragged the box toward him until it caught against a ridge in the rough board floor, when the nails bent outward and slipped away from the crack. Ward lay back, exhausted with the effort he had made and tormented with the pain in his leg.

After awhile he took the piece of board and managed to slide it under the box, lifting a corner of it over the ridge. That was hard work, harder than you would believe unless you tried it yourself after lying three days fasting, with a broken leg and a fever. He had to rest again before he took the other end of the board, that had the good nails, and pulled the box up beside the bunk.

In a few minutes he made another effort and pried part of the cover off the cracker-box with the knife. Then he pulled out half a dozen crackers and ate them, drank half a dipper of water, and felt better.

In an hour or so he believed he could stand it to fix up his leg a little. There was one splint that was poorly wrapped, or something. It felt as though it were digging slivers into his leg, and he couldn't stand it any longer.

He pulled himself up until he was sitting with his back against the wall at the head of his bunk and smoked a cigarette before he went any farther. Then he unwrapped the bandage carefully, removed the splint that hurt the worst, and gently massaged the crease in the bruised, swollen flesh where the narrow board had pressed so cruelly.

The crease itched horribly, and it was too sore to scratch. Ward cussed it and then got the carbolized vaseline and rubbed that on, wincing at the pain of his lightest touch. He did not hurry; he had all the time there was, and it was a relief to get the bandage off his leg for awhile. You may be sure he was very careful not to move those broken bones a hair's breadth!

He rubbed on the vaseline, fearing the liniment would blister and increase his discomfort, and replaced splint and bandage. He was terribly tired afterwards and lay in a half stupor for a long while. He realized keenly that he had a tough pull ahead of him, unless someone chanced to ride that way and so discovered his plight; which was so unlikely that he did not build any hopes upon it.

He had held himself aloof from the men of the country. He knew the Seabeck riders by sight; he had talked a little with Floyd Carson two or three times, and had met Seabeck himself. He knew Charlie Fox in a purely casual way, as has been related; and Peter Howling Dog the same.

None of these men were likely to ride out of their way to see him. And now that his mind worked rationally, he had no fear of Buck Olney's vengeful return. Buck Olney, he guessed shrewdly, was extremely busy just now, putting as many miles as possible between himself and that part of Idaho. Unless Billy Louise should come or send for him, he would in all probability lie alone there until he was able to walk. Ward did not try to comfort himself with any delusions of hope.

As the days passed, he settled himself grimly to the business of getting through the ordeal as comfortably as possible. He had food within his reach, and a scant supply of water. He worked out the question of diet and of using his resources to the best advantage. He had nothing else to do, and his alert mind seized upon the situation and brought it down to a fine system.

For instance, he did not open a can of fruit until the prunes were gone. Then he emptied a can of tomatoes into the bowl as a safeguard against ptomaine poisoning from the tin, and set the empty can on the floor. During the warm part of each day he slid open the window by his bunk and lay with the fresh air fanning his face and lifting the hair from his aching temples.

He tried to eat regularly and to make the fruit juice save his water supply. Sometimes he chewed jerked venison from the bag over his head, but not very often; the salt in the meat made him drink too much. On the whole, his diet was healthful and in a measure satisfying. He did not suffer from the want of any real necessity, at any rate. He smoked a good many cigarettes, but he was wise enough to leave the bottle of whisky alone after that first terrible time when it helped him through a severe ordeal.

He had his few books within reach. He read a good deal, to keep from thinking too much, and he tried to meet the days with philosophic calm. He might easily be a great deal worse off than he was, he frequently reminded himself. For instance, if he had been able to build another room on to his cabin, his bunk and his food supply would have been so widely separated as to cause him much hardship. There were, he admitted to himself, certain advantages in living in one small room. He could lie in bed and reach nearly everything he really needed.

But he was lonesome. So lonesome that there were times when life looked absolutely worthless; when the blue devils made him their plaything, and he saw Billy Louise looking scornfully upon him and loving some other man better; when he saw his name blackened by the suspicion that he was a rustler-preying upon his neighbors' cattle; when he saw Buck Olney laughing in derision of his mercy and fixing fresh evidence against him to confound him utterly.

He had all those moods, and they left their own lines upon his face. But he had one thing to hearten him, and that was the steady progress of his broken leg toward recovery. A long, tedious process it was, of necessity; but as nearly as he could judge, the bone was knitting together and would be straight and strong again, if he did not try to hurry it too much. He tried to keep count of the weeks as they passed. When the days slid behind him until he feared he could not remember, he cut a little notch on the window-sill each morning with Buck's knife, with every seventh day a longer and deeper notch than the others to mark the weeks. The first three days had been so hazy that he thought them only two and marked them so; but that put him only one day out of his reckoning.

He lay there and saw snow slither past his window, driven by a whooping wind. It worried him to know that his calves were unsheltered and unfed while his long stack of hay stood untouched-unless the cattle broke down his fence and reached it. He hoped they would; but he was a thorough workman, and in his heart he knew that fence would stand.

He saw cold rains and sleet. Then there were days when he shivered under his blankets and would have given much for a cup of hot coffee; days when the water froze in the pails beside the bed-what little water was left-and he chipped off pieces of ice and sucked them to quench his thirst. Days when the tomatoes and peaches were frozen in the cans, so that he chewed jerked venison and ate crackers rather than chill his stomach with the icy stuff.

Day by day the little notches and the longer ones reached farther and farther along the window-sill, until Ward began to foresee the time when he must start a new row. Day by day his cheek-bones grew more clearly defined, his eyes bigger and more wistful. Day by day his knuckles stood up sharper when he closed his hands, and day by day Nature worked upon his hurt, knitting the bones together.

But, though he was lean to the point of being skinny, his eyes were clear, and what little flesh he had was healthy flesh. Though he was lonesome and hungry for action and for sight of Billy Louise, his mind had not grown morbid. He learned more of the Bobbie Burns verses, and he could repeat *The Rhyme of the Three Sealers* in his sleep, and most of *The Lady of the Lake*. He used to lie and sing at the top of his voice, sometimes: *The Chisholm Trail* —unexpurgated-and *Sam Bass* and that doleful ditty about the *Lone Prairie*, and quaint old Scottish songs he had heard his mother sing, long and long ago. His leg would heal of itself if he let it alone long enough, he reminded himself often. His mind he must watch carefully, if he would keep it healthy. He knew that, and each day had its own little battle-ground. Sometimes he won, and sometimes the fight went against him-as is the way with the world.

Chapter XIX. The Brave Buckaroo

"BOISE, IDAHO, *December 23.*

"BRAVE BUCKAROO, —

"I wonder if you ever in your whole life got a Christmas present? I've been cultivating the Louise of me, and here are the first fruits of my endeavor; I guess that's the way they say it. I've spent so much time sitting by mommie when she's asleep, and I get tired of reading all the time, so a nurse in this ward-mommie has a room to herself of course, but not a special nurse, because I can do a lot of the little things-well, the nurse taught me how to hemstitch. So I got some silk and made some nice, soft neckerchiefs-one for you and one for me.

"This one I made last. I didn't want your eagle eyes seeing all the bobbly stitches on the first one. I hope you like it, Ward. Every stitch stands for a thought of the hills and our good times. I've brought Minervy back to life, and I try to play my old pretends sometimes. But they always break up into pieces. I'm not a kid now, you see. And life is a lot different when you get out into it, isn't it?

"Mommie doesn't seem to get much better. I'm worried about her. She seems to have let go, somehow. She never talks about the ranch much, or even worries about whether Phoebe is keeping the windows washed. She talks about when she was a little girl, and about when she and daddy were first married. It gets on my nerves to see how she has slipped out of every-day life. The nurse says that's common, though, in sickness. She says I could go home and look after things for a week or so just as well as not. She says mommie would be all right. But I hate to leave her.

"I'm awfully homesick for a good old ride on Blue. I miss him terribly. Have you seen anything of the Cove folks lately? Seems like I'm clear out of the world. I hate town, anyway, and a hospital is the limit for dismalness. Even the Louise of me is getting ready to do something awful if I have to stay much longer. Mommie sleeps most of the time. I believe they dope her with something. She doesn't have that awful pain so bad. So I don't have anything to do but sit around and read and sew and wait for her to wake up and want something.

"Pal, the Billy of me is at the exploding point! I believe I'll wind up by getting out in the corridor some day and shooting holes in all the steam radiators! Did you ever live with one, Ward? Nasty, sizzly things; they drive me wild. I'd give the best cow in the bunch for just one hour in front of our old stone fireplace and see the sparks go up the chimney, and hear the coyotes. Honest to goodness, I'd rather hear a coyote howl than any music on earth-unless maybe it was you singing a ten-dollar hoss an' a forty-dollar saddle. I'd like to hear that old trail song once more. I sure would, Ward. I'd like to hear it, coming down old Wolverine canyon. Oh, I just can't stand it much longer. I'm liable to wrap mommie in a blanket and crawl out the window, some night, and hit the trail for home. I believe I could cure her quicker right on the ranch. I wish I'd never brought her here; I believe it's just a scheme of the doctors to get money out of us. I know my poultices did just as much good as their old dope does.

"And this is Christmas, almost. I wonder what you'll be doing. Say, Ward, if you want to be a perfect jewel of a man, send me some of that jerky you've got hanging at the head of your bunk. I swiped some, that last time I was there. It would taste mighty good to me now, after all these hospital slops.

"And write me a nice, long letter, won't you? That's a good buckaroo. I've got to stop-mommie is beginning to wake up, and it's time for the doctor to come in and read the chart and look wise and say: 'Well, how are we to-day? Pretty bright, eh?' I'd like to kick him clear across the corridor-that is, the Billy of me would. And believe me, the Billy of me is sure going to break out, some of these days!

"I hope you like the neckerchief. I want you to wear it; if I come home and find it hasn't been washed a couple of times, there'll be something doing! Don't rub soap on it, kid. Make a warm lathery suds and wash it. And don't wave it by the corners till it dries. Hang it up somewhere. You'll have my stitches looking worse frazzled than my temper.

"Well, a merry Christmas, Pal-o'-mine-and here's hoping you and mommie and I will be eating turkey together at the Wolverine when next Christmas comes. Nummy-num! Wouldn't that taste good, though?

"Now remember and write a whole tablet full to

     "WILLIAM LOUISA,

     "WILHEMINA,

     "BILL-LOO,

     "BILL-THE-CONK,

     "BILLY LOUISE,

     "FLOWER OF THE RANCH-OH."

Phoebe put that letter on the mantel over the fireplace, the day after Christmas. Frequently she felt its puffy softness and its crackly crispness and wondered dully what Billy Louise had sent to Ward.

Billy Louise refrained from expecting any reply until after New Year's. Then she began to look for a letter, and when the days passed and brought her no word, her moods changed oftener than the weather.

Ward's literary efforts, along about that time, consisted of cutting notches in the window-sill beside his bunk.

On the day when the stage-driver gave Billy Louise's letter to Phoebe, Ward cut a deeper, wider notch, thinking that day was Christmas. Under the notch he scratched a word with the point of his knife. It had four letters, and it told eloquently of the state of mind he was in.

It was the day after that when Seabeck and one of his men rode up the creek and out into the field where Ward's cattle grazed apathetically on the little grass tufts that stuck up out of the snow. Ward was reading, and so did not see them until he raised himself up to make a cigarette and saw them going straight across the coulee by the line fence to the farther hills. He opened the window and shouted after them, but the wind was blowing keen from that direction, and they did not hear him.

Seabeck had been studying brands and counting, and he was telling Floyd Carson that everything was straight as a string.

"He must be out working this winter. I should think he'd stay home and feed these calves. The cows are looking pretty thin. I guess he isn't much of a stock hand; these nesters aren't, as a general thing, and if it's as Junkins says, and he puts all he makes into this place, he's likely hard up. Mighty nice little ranch he's got. Well, let's work over the divide and back that way. I didn't think we'd find anything here."

They turned and angled up the steep hillside, and Ward watched them glumly. He thought he knew why they were prowling around the place, but it seemed to him that they might have stretched their curiosity a little farther and investigated the cabin. He did not know that the snow of a week ago was banked over the doorstep with a sharp, crusty combing at the top, to prove that the door had not been opened for some time. Nor did he know that the two had ridden past the cabin on the other side of the creek and had seen how deserted the place looked; had ridden to the stable, noted there the unmistakable and permanent air of emptiness, and had gone on.

Floyd Carson alone might have prowled through both buildings, but Seabeck was a slow-going man of sober justice. He would not invade the premises of another farther than he thought it necessary. He had heard whispers that the fellow on Mill Creek might bear investigation, and he had investigated. There was not a shadow of evidence that the Y6 cattle had been gotten dishonestly. Therefore, Seabeck rode away and did not look into the snow-banked cabin, as another man might have done; and Ward missed his one chance of getting help from the outside.

Of course, he was doing pretty well as it was; but he would have welcomed the chance to talk to someone. Taciturn as Ward was with men, he had enough of his own company for once. And he would have asked them to make him a cup of coffee and warm up the cabin once more. Little comforts of that sort he missed terribly. If the room had not been so clammy cold, he could have sat up part of the time, now. As it was, he stayed in bed to keep warm; and even so he had been compelled to drag the two wolf-skins off the floor and upon the bed to keep from shivering through the coldest nights and days.

One day he did crawl out of bed and try to get over to the stove to start a fire. But he was so weak that he gave it up and crawled back again, telling himself that it was not worth the effort.

The letter with the silk neckerchief inside gathered dust upon the mantel, down at the Wolverine. When the postmark was more than two weeks old, another letter came, and Phoebe laid it on the fat one with fingers that trembled a little. Phoebe had a letter of her own, that day. Both were thin, and the addresses were more scrawly than usual. Phoebe's Indian instinct warned her that something was amiss.

This was Ward's letter:

"Oh, God, Ward, mommie's dead. She died last night. I thought she was asleep till the nurse came in at five o'clock. I'm all alone and I don't know what to do. I wish you could come, but if you don't get this right away, I'll see you at the ranch. I'm coming home as soon as I can. Oh, Ward, I hate life and God and everything. BILLY LOUISE."

"Please Ward, stay at the ranch till I come. I want to see you. I feel as if you're the only friend I've got left, now mommie's gone. She looked so peaceful when they took her away-and so strange. I didn't belong to her any more. I felt as if I didn't know her at all-and there is such an awful gap in my life-maybe you'll understand. You always do."

The day that letter was written, Ward drew a plan of the house he meant to build some day, with a wide porch on the front, where a hammock would swing comfortably. He figured upon lumber and shingles and rock foundation, and mortar for a big, deep fireplace. He managed to put in the whole forenoon planning and making estimates, and he was so cheerful afterwards that he whistled and sang, and later he tied a piece of jerky on the end of a string and teased a fat fieldmouse, whose hunger made him venturesome. Ward would throw the jerky as far as the string would permit and wait till the mouse came out to nibble at it; then he would pull the meat closer and closer to the bed and laugh at the very evident perturbation of the mouse. For the time being he was a boy indulging his love of teasing something.

And while Ward played with that mouse, Billy Louise was longing for his comforting presence while she faced alone one of the bitterest things in life-which is death. He had no presentiment of her need of him, which was just as well, since he was absolutely powerless to help her.

Chapter XX. "We Been Sorry for You"

Billy Louise, having arrived unexpectedly on the stage, pulled off her fur-lined mittens and put her chilled hands before the snapping blaze in the fireplace. Her eyes were tired and sunken, and her mouth drooped pitifully at the corners, but aside from that she did not seem much changed from the girl who had left the ranch two months and more before.

"I'll take a cup of tea, Phoebe, but I'm not a bit hungry," she said. "I ate just before I left town. How have you been, Phoebe?"

"We been fine. We been so sorry for you —"

"Never mind that now, Phoebe. I'd rather not talk about it. Has-anybody been here lately?"

"Charlie Fox, he come las' week-mebby week before las'. Marthy, she got rheumatis in her knee. Charlie, he say she been pretty bad one night. I guess she's better now. I tol' I wash for her if he brings me clo'es, but he says he wash them clo'es hisself. I guess Charlie pretty good to that old lady. He's awful p'lite, that feller is."

"Yes, he is. I'll go up and see her when I get rested a little. I feel tired to death, somehow; maybe it's the drive. The road is terribly rough, and it was awful tiresome on the train. Has-Ward been around lately?"

"Ward, he ain't been here for long time. I guess mebbe it's been six weeks I ain't seen him. Las' time he was here he wrote that letter. He ain't come no more. You let me drag this couch up to the fire, and you lay down and rest yo'self. I'll put on more wood. Seems like this is awful cold winter. We had six little pigs come, and four of 'em froze. John, he brung 'em in by the fire, but it's no good; they die, anyway."

Billy Louise dropped apathetically upon the couch after Phoebe had helped her pull off her coat. She did not feel as though anything mattered much, but she must go on with life, no matter how purposeless it seemed. To live awhile and work and struggle and know the pain of disappointment and weariness, and then to die: she did not see what use there was in struggling. But one had to go on just the same. She had borrowed money for mommie's sickness, and she would have to repay it; and it was all so purposeless!

"How are the cattle wintering?" She forced herself to make some show of interest in things.

"The cattle, they're doing all right. One heifer, she got blackleg and die, but the rest they're all right. John, he couldn't find all; two or three, they're gone. He says mebby them rustlers got 'em. He looked good as he could."

"Are-has there been any more trouble about losing stock?" Billy Louise shut her hand into a fist, but she spoke in the same tired tone as before.

"I dunno. Seabeck, he told John they don't catch nobody yet. That inspector, he come by long time ago. I guess he stopped with Seabeck. He ain't come back yet. I dunno where he's gone. Seabeck, he didn't say nothing to John about him, I guess. Maybe he went out the other way."

"I —did you do what I told you, Phoebe, about-mommie's things?"

For once Phoebe did not answer garrulously. "Yes, I done it," she said softly. "The boxes is in the shed when you want 'em."

"All right, Phoebe. Is the tea ready?"

While she sipped creamy tea from a solid-silver teaspoon which had been a part of mommie's wedding-set, Billy Louise looked around the familiar room for which she had hungered so in those deadly, monotonous weeks at the hospital. The fire snapped in its stone recess, and the cheerful warmth of it comforted her body and in a measure soothed her spirit. She was chilled to the bones with facing that bitter east wind for hours, and she had not seen a fireplace in all the time she had been away.

But the place was empty, with no mommie fussing about, worrying over little things, gently garrulous. If mommie had come back well, she would have asked Phoebe about everything in the house and out of it. There would have been a housewifely accounting going on at this minute. Phoebe would be apologetic over those grimy windows, instead of merely sympathetic over the sorrow in the house. Billy Louise wondered wherein she lacked. For the life of her she could not feel that it mattered whether the windows were clean or dirty; life was drab and cheerless outside them, anyway.

Billy Louise in the last few months had tried to picture herself alone, with mommie gone. Her imagination was too alive and saw too clearly the possibilities for her never to have dwelt upon this very crisis in her life. But whenever she had tried to think what it would be like, she had always pictured Ward beside her, shielding her from dreary details and lightening her burden with his whimsical gentleness. She had felt sure that Ward would ride down every week for news of her, and she had expected to find him there waiting for her, after that last letter. Whatever could be the matter? Had he left the country?

Billy Louise's faith had compromised definitely with her doubts of him. Guilty or innocent, she would be his friend always; that was the condition her faith had laid down challengingly before her doubts. But unless he were innocent and proved it to her, she would never marry him, no matter how much she loved him. That was the concession her faith had made to her doubts.

Billy Louise had a wise little brain, for all she idealized life and her surroundings out of all proportion to reality. She told herself that if she married Ward with her doubts alive, her misery would be far greater than if she gave him up, except as a friend. Of course, her ideals stepped in there with an impracticable compromise. She brought back the Ward Warren of her "pretend" life. She dreamed of him as a mutely adoring friend who stood and worshiped her from afar, and because of his sins could not cross the line of friendship.

If he were a rustler, she would shield him and save him, if that were possible. He would love her always-Billy Louise could not conceive of Ward transferring his affections to another less exacting woman-and he would be grateful for her friendship. She could build long, lovely scenes where friendliness was put to the front bravely, while love hid behind the mask and only peeped out through the eyes now and then. She did not, of course, plan all this in sober reason; she just dreamed it with her eyes open.

It had been in such a spirit that she had written to Ward; though he would undoubtedly have read love into the lines and so have been encouraged in the planning of that house with the wide porch in front! She had dreamed all the way home of seeing Ward at the end of the journey. Perhaps he would come out and help her down from the stage, when it stopped at the gate, and call her Bill-Loo —never once had Ward spoken her name as others spoke it, but always with a twist of his own which made it different, stamped with his own individuality-and he would walk beside her to the house and comfort her with his eyes, and never mention mommie till she herself opened the way to her grief. Then he would call her Wilhemina-mine in that kissing way he had —

Someone came upon the doorstep and stood there for a moment, stamping snow off his feet. Billy Louise caught her breath and waited, her eyes veiled with her lashes and shining expectantly. A little color came into her cheeks. Ward had been delayed somehow, but he was coming now because she needed him and he wanted her —

It was only John Pringle, heavy-bodied, heavy-minded, who came in and squeaked the door shut behind him. Billy Louise gave him a glance and dropped her head back on the red cushion. "Hello, John!" she greeted tonelessly.

John grinned, embarrassed between his pleasure at seeing Billy Louise and his pity for her trouble. His white teeth showed a little under his scraggy, breath-frosted mustache.

"Hello! You got back, hey? She's purty cold again. Seems like it's goin' storm some more." He pulled off his mittens and tugged at the ice dangling at the corners of his lips. "You come on stage, hey? I bet you freeze." He went over and stood with his back to the fire, his leathery brown hands clasped behind him, his face still undecided as to the most suitable emotion to reveal. "Well, how you like town, hey? No good, I guess. You got plenty trouble now. Phoebe and me, we stick by you long as you want us to."

"I know you will, John." Billy Louise bit her lips against a sudden impulse to tears. It was not Ward, but the crude sympathy of this old halfbreed was more to her than all the expensive flowers that had been stacked upon mommie's coffin. She had felt terribly alone in Boise. But her chilled soul was beginning to feel the warmth of friendship in these two half-savage servants. Even without Ward, her home-coming was not absolutely cheerless, after all.

"Well, we make out to keep things going," John announced pridefully. "We got leetle bad luck, not much. One heifer, she die-blackleg. Four pigs, they froze-leetle fellers. I save the rest, all right. Ole Mooley, she goin' have a calf purty queeck now. I got her in leetle shed by hog-pen. Looks like it storm, all right."

"Felt like it, too." Billy Louise made an effort to get back into the old channels of thought. "We'll milk old Mooley, John; I feel as if I could live on cream and milk for the next five years. You ought to see the watery stuff they call milk in Boise! Star must be pretty near dry now, isn't she?"

"Purty near." John's voice was beginning to ooze the comfort that warmth was giving his big body. "She give two quart, mebby. Spot, she give leetle more. I got that white hog fat. I kill him any time now you say."

"If it doesn't storm, you might kill him to-morrow or next day, John. I'll take a roast up to Marthy when I go. I'll go in a day or two." She glanced toward the kitchen end of the long room. Phoebe was busy in the pantry with the door shut. "Have you seen or heard anything of Ward lately?" she asked carelessly.

"No. I ain't seen Ward for long time. I thought mebbe he be down long time ago. He ain't come." John shifted a little farther from the blaze and stood teetering comfortably upon the balls of his feet, like a bear. "Mebbe he's gone out other way to work."

"Did he say anything?"

"No, he don't say nothin' las' time he come. That's —" John rolled his black eyes seekingly at the farther wall while he counted mentally the weeks. "I guess that mus' be fo' or five weeks now. Charlie Fox, he come las' week."

"John, you better kill a chicken for Billy Louise. I bet she ain't had no chicken since she's gone." Phoebe came from the pantry with her hands all flour. "You go now. That young speckled rooster be good, mebby. He's fat. He's fightin' all the chickens, anyway."

"All right. I kill him." John answered with remarkable docility. Usually he growled at poor Phoebe and objected to everything she suggested.

His ready compliance touched Billy Louise more than anything since her return. She felt anew the warm comfort of their sympathy. If only Ward had been there also! She got up from the couch and went to the window where she could look across at the bleak hilltop. She stood there for some minutes looking out wistfully, hoping that she would see him ride into view at the top of the steep trail. After awhile she went back and curled up on the wide old couch and stared abstractedly into the fire.

John had gone out after the young speckled rooster that fought the other chickens and must now do his part toward salving the hurt and cheering the home-coming of Billy Louise. John returned, mumbled with Phoebe at the far end of the room, and went out again. Phoebe worked silently and briskly, rattling pans now and then and lifting the stove lids to put in more wood. Billy Louise heard the sounds but dimly. The fire was filled with pictures; her thoughts were wandering here and there, bridging the gap between the past and the misty future. After awhile the savory odor of the young speckled rooster, that had fought all the other chickens but was now stewing in a mottled blue-and-white granite pan, smote her nostrils and won her thoughts from dreaming. She sat up and pushed back her hair like one just waking from sleep.

"I'll set the table, Phoebe, when you're ready," she said, and her voice sounded less strained and tired. "That chicken sure does smell good!" She rose and busied herself about the room, setting things in order upon the reading-table and the shelves. Phoebe was good as gold, but her housekeeping was a trifle sketchy.

"Ward, he borried some books las' time," Phoebe remarked, lifting the lid of the stew kettle and letting out a cloud of delicious-smelling steam. "I dunno what they was. He said he'd bring 'em back nex' time he come."

"Oh, all right," said Billy Louise, and smiled a little. Even so slight a thing as borrowed books made another link between them. For a girl who means to be a mere friend to a man, Billy Louise harbored some rather dangerous emotions.

She picked up the two letters she had written Ward, brushed off the dust, and eyed them hesitatingly. It certainly was queer that Ward had not ridden down for some word from her. She hesitated, then threw the thin letter into the fire. Its message was no longer of urgent, poignant need. Billy Louise drew a long breath when the grief-laden lines crumbled quickly and went flying up the wide throat of the chimney. The other letter she pinched between her thumbs and fingers. She smiled a little to herself. Ward would like to get that. She had a swift vision of him standing over there by the window and reading it with those swift, shuttling glances, holding the handkerchief squeezed up in his hand the while. She remembered how she had begun it —"Brave Buckaroo" —and her cheeks turned pink. He should have it when he came. Something had kept him away. He would come just as soon as he could. She laid the letter back upon the mantel and set a china cow on it to keep it safe there. Then she turned brightly and began to set the table for Phoebe and John and herself, and came near setting a fourth place for Ward, she was so sure he would come as soon as he could. Mommie used to say that if you set a place for a person, that person would come and eat with you, in spirit if not in reality.

Phoebe glanced at her pityingly when she saw her hesitating, with the fourth plate in her hands. Phoebe thought that Billy Louise had unconsciously brought it for mommie. Phoebe did not know that love is stronger even than grief; for at that moment Billy Louise was not thinking of mommie at all.

Chapter XXI. Seven Lean Kine

"And you looked good, all up above here?" Billy Louise held Blue firmly to a curved-neck, circling stand, while she had a last word with John before she went off on one of her long rides.

"All up in the hills, and round over by Cedar Creek, and all over." John's mittened gesture was even more sweeping than his statement. "I guess mebby them rustlers git 'em."

"Well, I'm going up to the Cove. I may not be back before dark, so don't worry if I'm late. Maybe I'll look along the river. I know one place where I believe cattle can get down to the bottom, if they're crazy enough to try it. You didn't look there, did you?"

"No, I never looked down there. I know they can't git down nohow."

"Well, all right; maybe they can't." Billy Louise slackened the reins, and Blue went off with short, stiff-legged jumps. It had been a long time since he had felt the weight of his lady, and his mood now was exuberant, especially so, since the morning was clear, with a nip of frost to tingle the skin and the glow of the sun to promise falsely the nearness of spring. The hill trail steadied him a little, though he went up the steepest pitch with rabbit-jumps and teetered on his toes the rest of the way.

Billy Louise laughed a little, leaned, and grabbed a handful of slatey mane. "Oh, you Blue-dog!" she said, for that was his full name. "Life is livable, after all, as long as a fellow has got you and can ride. You good-for-nothing old ten-dollar hoss! I —wonder would it be wicked to sing? What do you think, Blue? You'd sing, I know, at the top of your voice, if you could. Say, Blue! Don't you wish, you were a donkey, so you could stick out your neck and go *Yee-ee*-haw! *Yee-ee* —haw? Try it once. I believe you could. It's that or a run, one or the other. You'll bust, if you don't do something. I know you!"

At last on the high level, seeing Blue could not bray his joy to the world, Billy Louise let him go. She needed some outlet, herself, after those horrible, dull weeks weighted with tragedy. She had been raised on horseback, almost; and for two terrible months she had not been in the saddle. And there is nothing like the air of the Idaho hills to stir one's blood and send it singing.

Through the sagebrush and rocks, weaving in and out, slacking speed a little while he went down into deep gullies, thundering up the other side, and racing away over the level again, went Blue. And with him, laughing, tingling with new life, growing pinker-cheeked every minute, went Billy Louise. Her mother's death did not oppress her then. She thought of her as she raced, but she thought of her with a little, tender smile. Her mother was resting peacefully, and there was no more pain or worry for the little, pale, frail woman who had lived her life and gone her way.

"Dear old mommie!" said Billy Louise under her breath. "Your kid is almost as happy as you are, right now. Don't be shocked, there's a dear, or think I'm going to break my neck. Blue and I have just simply got to work off steam. You, Blue!" She leaned another inch forward.

Blue threw up his head, lifted his heels, and ran like a scared jackrabbit over the uneven ground. They were not keeping to the trail at all; trails were too tame for them in that mood. They ran along the rim-rock at the last, where Billy Louise could glance down, now and then, at the river sliding like a bright-blue ribbon with icy edges through the gray, snow-spotted hills.

"Hold on, Blue!" Billy Louise pulled up on the reins. "Quit it, you old devil! A mile ought to be enough for once, I should think. There's cattle down there in that bottom, sure as you live. And we, my dear sir, are going down there and take a look at them." She managed to pull Blue down to stiff-legged jumps and then to a walk. Finally she stopped him, so that she could the better take in her surroundings and the possibilities of getting down.

In the country it is as in the cities. One forms habits of journeying. One becomes perfectly familiar with every hill and every little hollow in certain directions, while some other, closer part remains practically unexplored. Billy Louise had always loved the Wolverine canyon, and its brother, Jones canyon, which branched off from the first. As a child she had explored every foot of both, and had ridden the hills beyond. As a young woman she had kept to the old playground. Her cattle ranged at the head of the canyons.

The river bottoms came as near being unknown territory as she could have found within forty miles of her home. For one thing, the river bottom was narrow, except where was the Cove, and pinched in places till there seemed no way of passing from one to another. Little pockets there were, tucked away under the rocky bluff with its collar of "rim-rock" above. One might climb down afoot, but Billy Louise was true to her range breeding; she never went anywhere afoot if she could possibly get there on a horse. And down there by the river she never had happened to find it necessary to go, either afoot or a-horseback. Still, if cattle could get down there —

"I guess we'll have to ride back a way," she said, after a brief inspection, during which Blue stood so close to the rim that Billy Louise must have had a clear head to feel no tremor of nerves or dizziness.

She turned and rode slowly back along the edge, looking for the place where she believed cattle could get down if they were crazy enough to try.

"Don't look very encouraging, does it, Blue?" Billy Louise stared doubtfully at the place, leaning and peering over the rim. "What d'ye think? Reckon we can make it?"

Blue had caught sight of the moving specks far down next the river and up the stream half a mile or more. He was a cow-horse to the bone. He knew those far-off specks for cattle, and he knew that his lady would like a closer look at them. That's what cattle were made for: to haze out of brush and rocks and gullies and drive somewhere. So far as Blue knew, cattle were a game. You hunted them out of ungodly places, and the game was to make them go somewhere else against their wishes. He prided himself on being able to play that game, no matter what were the odds against him.

Now he tilted his head a little and looked down at the bluff beneath him. The game was beginning. He must get down that bluff and overtake those specks and drive them somewhere. He glanced up and down the bluff to see if a better trail offered. Billy Louise laughed understandingly.

"It's this or nothing, Blue. Looks pretty fierce, all right, doesn't it? Of course, if you're going to make a perfect lady get off and walk —"

Blue snuffed at the ledge with his neck craned. The rim-rock had crumbled and sunk low into the bluff, like a too rich pie-crust when the oven is not quite hot enough. From a ten- or fifteen-foot wall it shrunk here to a three-foot ledge. And below the rocks and bowlders were not actually piled on top of one another; there were clear spaces where a wary, wise, old cow-horse might possibly pick his way.

Blue chose his trail and crumpled at the knees with his hoofs on the very edge of the ledge; went down with a cat-jump and landed with all four feet planted close together. He had no mind to go on sliding in spite of himself, and the bluff was certainly steep enough to excuse a bungle.

"So far so good." Billy Louise glanced ruefully back at the ledge. "We're down; but how the deuce do you reckon we'll get up again?"

Blue was not worrying about that part. He went on, picking his way carefully among the bowlders, with his nose close to earth, setting his hindlegs stiffly and tobogganing down loose, shale slopes. Billy Louise sat easily in the saddle and enjoyed it all. She was making up in big doses for the drab dullness of those hospital weeks. She ought to walk down the bluff, for this was dangerous play; but she craved danger as an antidote to that shut-in life of petty rules and regulations.

It was with a distinct air of triumph that Blue reached the bottom, even though he slid the last forty feet on his haunches and landed belly-deep in a soft snow-bank. It was with triumph to match his perky ears that Billy Louise leaned and slapped him on the neck. "We made it!" she cried, "and I didn't have to walk a step, did I, Blue? You're there with the goods, all right!"

Blue scrambled out of the bank to firm footing on the ripened grass of the bottom, and with a toss of his head set off in a swinging lope, swerving now and then to avoid a badger hole or a half-sunken rock. They had done something new, those two; they had reached a place where neither had ever been before, and Blue acted as if he knew it and gloried in the escapade quite as much as did his lady.

The cattle spied them and went trotting away up the river, and Blue quickened his stride a little and followed after. Billy Louise left the reins loose upon his neck. Blue could handle cattle alone quite as skillfully as with a rider, if he chose.

The cattle dodged into a fringe of bushes close to the river and disappeared, which was queer, since the bluff curved in close to the bank at that point. Blue pricked up his ears and went clattering after, slowed a little at the willow-fringe, stuck his nose straight out before him, and went in confidently. The cattle were just ahead. He could smell them, and his listening ears caught their heavy breathing. It was very rocky there in the willows, and he must pick his way with much care. But when he crashed through on the far side, and Billy Louise straightened from leaning low along his neck to avoid the stinging branches, the cattle gave a snort and went lumbering away, still following the river.

This was another small, grassy bottom. Blue went galloping after them, indignant that they should even attempt to elude him. They were making for the head of that pocket, and Billy Louise twitched the reins suggestively. Blue obeyed the hint, which proved that the human brain is greater in strategy than is brute instinct, and raced in an angle from the fleeing cattle. Billy Louise leaned and called to him sharply for more speed; called for it and got it. They jumped a washout that the cattle went into and out of with great lunges, farther down toward its mouth. They gained a little there, and by a burst of hard running they gained more on the level beyond.

The cattle began to swerve away from them, closer to the river. Blue pulled ahead a little, swerving also, and as Billy Louise tightened the reins, he slowed and circled them craftily until they huddled on the steep bank, uncertain which way to go. Billy Louise pulled Blue down to a walk as she drew near and eyed the cattle sharply. They did not look like any of hers, after all. There were five dry cows and two steers.

One of the steers stood broadside to Billy Louise. The brand stared out from his dingy red side, the most conspicuous thing about him. Billy Louise caught her breath. There was no faintest line that failed to drive its message into her range-trained brain. She stared and stared. Blue looked around at her inquiringly, reproachfully. Billy Louise sent him slowly forward and stirred up the huddled little bunch. She read the brand on each one; read the story they shouted at her, of bungling theft. She could not believe it. Yet she did believe it, and she went hot with anger and disappointment and contempt. She sat and thought for a minute or two, scowling at the cattle, while she decided what to do.

Finally she swung Blue on the down-stream side and shouted the range cattle-cry. The animals turned awkwardly and went upstream, as they had been going before Billy Louise stopped them. Blue followed watchfully after, content with the game he was playing. Where the bluffs drew close again to the river, the cattle climbed to a narrow, shelving trail through the rocks and went on in single file, picking their way carefully along the bluff. Below them it fell sheer to the river; above them it rose steeply, a blackened jumble, save where the snow of the last storm lay drifted.

Billy Louise had never known there was a trail up this gorge. She eyed it critically and saw where bowlders had been moved here and there to make its passage possible. Her lips were set close together and they still bore the imprint of her contempt.

She thought of Ward. Mentally she abased herself before him because of her doubts. How had she dared think him a thief? Her brave buckaroo! And she had dared think he would steal cattle! Her very remorse was a whip to lash her anger against the guilty. She hurried the cattle along the dangerous trail, impatient of their cautious pace.

When finally they clattered down to the level again, it was to plunge into willow thickets whose branches reached out to sweep her from the saddle. Blue went carefully, stopping now and then at a word from his lady, to wait while she put a larger, more stubborn branch out of her way. She could not see just where she was going, but she knew that she was close upon the cattle, and that they seemed familiar with the trail. Now and then she caught sight of a rough-haired rump and switching tail in the thicket before her. Then the whip-like branches would swing close, and she could see nothing but their gray tangle reaching high above her head. She could hear the crackling progress of the cattle close ahead, and the gurgling clamor of the river farther away to her right. But she could not see the bluff for the close-standing willows, and she did not know whether it was near or far to its encircling wall.

Then, just as she was beginning to think the willows would never end, she came quite suddenly out into the open, and Blue lifted himself and jumped a dry ditch. The cattle were before her, shambling along the fenced border of a meadow.

Since she had closed up on the cattle and had read on their sides the shameful story of theft, Billy Louise had known that she would eventually come out at the lower end of the Cove; and that in spite of the fact that the Cove was not supposed to have any egress save through the gorge. What surprised her was the short distance; she had not realized that the bluff and the upland formed a wide curve, and that she had cut the distance almost in half by riding next the river.

She seemed in no doubt as to what she would do when she arrived. Billy Louise was not much given to indecision at any time. She drove the cattle into the corral farthest from the house, rode on to the stable, and stopped Blue with his nose against the fence there and with his reins dragging. Then, tight-lipped still, she walked determinedly along the path to the gate that led through the berry-jungle to the cabin.

She opened the gate and stepped through, closing it after her. She had not gone twenty feet when there was a rush from the nearest thicket, and Surbus, his hair ruffed out along his neck, growled and made a leap at her with bared fangs.

Billy Louise had forgotten about Surbus. She jumped back, startled, and the dog missed landing. When he sprang again he met a thirty-eight calibre bullet from Billy Louise's gun and dropped back. It had been a snap shot, without any particular aiming; Billy Louise retreated a few steps farther, watching the dog suspiciously. He gathered himself slowly and prepared to spring at her again. This time Billy Louise, being on the watch for such a move, aimed carefully before she fired. Surbus dropped again, limply —a good dog forever more.

Billy Louise heard a shrill whistle and the sound of feet running. She waited, gun in hand, ready for whatever might come.

"Hey! Charlie! Somebody's come; the bell, she don't reeng." Peter Howling Dog, a pistol in his hand, came running down the path from the cabin. He saw Billy Louise and stopped abruptly, his mouth half open.

From a shed near the stable came Charlie, also running. Billy Louise waited beside the gate. He did not see her until he was close, for a tangled gooseberry bush stood between them.

"What was it, Peter? Somebody in the Cove? Or was it you —"

"No, it wasn't Peter; it was me." Billy Louise informed him calmly and ungrammatically. "I shot Surbus, that's all."

"Oh! Why, Miss Louise, you nearly gave me heart failure! How are you? I thought —"

"You thought somebody had gotten into the Cove without your knowing it. Well, someone did. I rode up from below, along the river."

"Oh-er-did you? Pretty rough going, wasn't it? I didn't think it could be done. Come in; Aunt Martha will be —"

"I don't think she'll be overjoyed to see me." Billy Louise stood still beside the gooseberry bush, and she had forgotten to put away her gun. "I drove up those cattle you had down below. You're awfully careless, Charlie! I should think Peter or Marthy would have told you better. When a man steals cattle by working over the brands, it's very bad form to keep them right on his ranch in plain sight. It-isn't done by the best people, you know." Her voice stung with the contempt she managed to put into it. And though she smiled, it was such a smile as one seldom saw upon the face of Billy Louise.

"What's all this? Worked brands! Why, Miss Louise, I —I wouldn't know how to —"

"I know. You did an awful punk job. A person could tell in the dark it was the work of a greenhorn. Why didn't you let Peter do it, or Marthy? You could have done a better job than that, couldn't you, Marthy?"

Poor old Marthy, with her rheumatic knees and a gray hardness in her leathery face, had come down the path and stood squarely before Billy Louise, her hands knuckling her flabby hips, her hair blowing in gray, straggling wisps about her bullet head.

"Better than what? Come in, Billy Louise. I'm right glad to see ye back and lookin' so well, even if yuh do 'pear to be in one of your tantrums. How's yer maw?"

Billy Louise gasped and went white. "Mommie's dead," she said. "She died the ninth." She drew another gasping breath, pulled herself together, and went on before the others could begin the set speeches of sympathy which the announcement seemed to demand.

"Never mind about that, now. I'm talking about those Seabeck cattle you folks stole. I was telling Charlie how horribly careless he is, Marthy. Did you know he let them drift down the river? And a blind man could tell a mile off the brands have been worked!" Billy Louise's tone was positively venomous in its contempt. "Why didn't you make Charlie practise on a cowhide for awhile first?" she asked Marthy cuttingly.

Marthy ignored the sarcasm. Perhaps it did not penetrate her stolid mind at all. "Charlie never worked any brands, Billy Louise," she stated with her glum directness.

"Oh, I beg his pardon, I'm sure! Did you?"

"No, I never done such a thing, neither. I don't know what you're talkin' about."

"Well, who did, then?" Billy Louise faced the old woman pitilessly.

"I d'no." Marthy lifted her hand and made a futile effort to tuck in a few of the longest wisps of hair.

"Well, of all the —" The stern gray eyes of Billy Louise flew wide open at the effrontery of the words. If they expected her to believe that!

"That's it, Miss Louise. That's the point we'd like to settle, ourselves. I know it sounds outrageous, but it's a fact. Peter and I found those cattle up in the hills, with our brand worked over the V. On my word of honor, not one of us knows who did it."

"But you've got them down here —"

"Well —" Charlie threw out a hand helplessly. His eyes met hers with appealing frankness. "We couldn't rub out the brands; what else could we do? I figured that somebody else would see them if we left them out in the hills, and it might be rather hard to convince a man; you see, we can't even convince you! But, so help me, not one of us branded those cattle, Miss Louise. I believe that whoever has been rustling stock around here deliberately tried to fix evidence against us. I'm a stranger in the country, and I don't know the game very well; I'm an easy mark!"

"Yes, you're that, all right enough!" Billy Louise spoke with blunt disfavor, but her contemptuous certainty of his guilt was plainly wavering. "To go and bring stolen cattle right down here —"

"It seemed to me they'd be safer here than anywhere else," Charlie observed naïvely. "Nobody ever comes down here, unknown to us. I had it sized up that the fellow who worked those brands would never dream we'd bring the stock right into the Cove. Why, Miss Louise, even I would know better than to put our brand on top of Seabeck's and expect it to pass inspection. If I wanted to steal cattle, I wouldn't go at it that way!"

Billy Louise glanced uncertainly at him and then at Marthy, facing her grimly. She did not know what to think, and she showed it.

"How do you mean-the real rustlers?" She began hesitatingly; and hesitation was not by any means a mental habit with Billy Louise.

"I mean just what I said." Charlie's manner was becoming more natural, more confident. "I've been riding through the hills a good deal, and I've seen a few things. And I've an idea the fellow got a little uneasy." He saw her wince a little at the word "fellow," and he went on, with an impulsive burst of confidence. "Miss Louise, have you ever, in your riding around up above Jones Canyon, in all those deep little gulches, have you ever seen anything of a —corral, up there?"

Billy Louise held herself rigidly from starting at this. She bit her lips so that it hurt. "Where-abouts is it?" she asked, without looking at him. And then: "I thought you would go to any length before you would accuse anybody."

"I would. But when, they deliberately try to hand me the blame-and I'm not accusing any-body-anybody in particular, am I? The corral is at the head of a steep little canyon or gulch, back in the hills where all these bigger canyons head. Some time when you're riding up that way, you keep an eye out for it. That," he added grimly, "is where Peter and I ran across these cattle; right near that corral."

The heart of Billy Louise went heavy in her chest. Was it possible? Doubts are harder to kill than cats or snakes. You think they're done for, and here they come again, crowding close so that one can see nothing else.

"Have you any idea at all, who-it is?" She forced the words out of her dry throat. She lifted her head defiantly and looked at him full, trying to read the truth from his eyes and his mouth.

Charlie Fox met her look, and in his eyes she read pity-yes, pity for her. "If I have," he said, with an air of gently deliberate evasion, "I'll wait till I am dead sure before I name the man. I'm not at all sure I'd do it even then, Miss Louise; not unless I was forced to do it in self-defense. That's one reason why I brought the cattle down here. I didn't want to be placed in a position where I should be compelled to fight back."

Billy Louise ran her gloved fingers down the barrel of her gun, and stuck the weapon back in its holster. "I killed Surbus, Marthy," she said dully. "I had to. He came at me."

Marthy turned heavily toward the spot which Billy Louise indicated with her downward glance. She had not seen the dog lying there half hidden by a berry bush. Marthy gave a grunt of dismay and went over to where Surbus lay huddled. Her hard old face worked with emotion.

"You shot him, did yuh?" Marthy's voice was harsh with reproach. "What did he do to yuh, that you had to go t' work and shoot him? He warn't your dog, he was mine! I must say you're gittin' high-an'-mighty, Billy Louise, comin' here shootin' my dog and accusin' Charlie and me to our faces uh bein' thieves. And your maw not cold in 'er grave yit! I must say you're gitting too high-an'-mighty fer old Marthy. And me payin' fer your schoolin' and never gitting so much as a thankye fer it, and scrimpin' and savin' to make a lady out of yuh. And here you come in a tantrum, callin' me a thief right in my face! You knowed all along who worked them brands. If yuh don't, I kin mighty quick tell ye —"

"Now, Aunt Martha, never mind scolding Billy Louise; you know you think as much of her as you do of me, and that's throwing a big bouquet at myself!" Charlie went up and laid his arm caressingly over the old woman's shoulder. "You don't want to let this upset you, Aunt Martha. Surbus was a mean-tempered brute with strangers. You know that. I don't blame Miss Louise in the least. She was frightened when he came at her, and she hadn't presence of mind enough to see he was only bluffing and wouldn't hurt —"

"Bluffing, was he?" Billy Louise roused herself to meet this covert attack upon her courage. "So are you bluffing. And so is Marthy, when she says she paid for my —" She stopped, confronting an accusing memory of mommie's mysterious silence about the school money, and her own passing curiosity which had never been satisfied. "Even if she did, I don't know why she need throw it up to me now. I never asked her for money. Nobody ever did. And that has nothing to do with Surbus, anyway. He's a nasty, mean brute that ought to have been killed long ago. I'm not a bit sorry. I'm glad I did kill him."

"Yes, I know yuh be. You're hard as —"

"I wouldn't talk about hardness, if I were you, Marthy! What are you, right now-and always? Was I to blame for thinking those cattle had been stolen? They're in the Cove, with your brand on. And unless you pay Seabeck for them, you're stealing them if you keep them. It doesn't matter who put the brand on; you're keeping the cattle. What do you call that, I'd like to know? They're down here in the big corral now. If you mean to do what's square, you'll take them up to Seabeck's and explain —"

"Explain who it was ran our brand on?" Charlie's voice was silk over iron. "I'm afraid if I were forced into explanations, I'd have to tell all I know, Miss Louise. Do you advise that-really?"

"I don't advise anything." Baffled and angry and hurt to the very soul of her, Billy Louise opened the gate and went out. "It strikes me you Cove folks are not wanting advice these days, or needing it. If you know anything to tell, for heaven's sake don't hold back on my account! It's nothing to me, one way or the other. I'm no rustler, and no friend of rustlers, if that's what you're hinting at." She left them with a proud lift to her chin and a very straight back, went to

Blue, and mounted him mechanically. Billy Louise was "seeing red" just then. She rode back past the gate, the three were still standing there close together, talking. Billy Louise swung round in the saddle so that she faced them.

"You needn't worry, Marthy, about that school-money," she called out angrily. "I'll take your word for it and pay you back every cent, with legal rate of interest. And I'm darned glad I did shoot Surbus!"

"Oh, say, Miss Louise!" Charlie called placatingly. "Please don't go away feeling —"

"You go to the devil!" Billy Louise flung back at him and touched Blue with her heel. "I hope that shocked some of the politeness out of him, anyway," she added grimly to herself. "Oh, I hate everything-Ward and God and all! I hate life —I hate it!"

She pulled Blue down to a walk and rode slowly for a couple of rods, fighting against the reaction that crept inexorably over her anger, chilling it and making it seem weak and unworthy. With a sudden impulse born of her stern instincts of justice, she jerked Blue around and galloped back. Charlie had disappeared, and Peter Howling Dog was walking sullenly toward the corraled cattle. Marthy was going slowly up the path to the cabin, looking old and bent and broken-spirited because of her bowed shoulders and stiff, rheumatic gait, but harsh and unyielding as to her face. Billy Louise stopped by the fence and called to her. Marthy turned, stared at her sourly, and stood where she was.

"Wall, what d'yuh want now?" she asked uncompromisingly.

Billy Louise fought back an answering antagonism. She must be just; she could not blame Marthy for feeling hard toward her. She had insulted them horribly and killed Marthy's dog.

"I want to tell you I'm sorry I was so mean, Marthy," she said bravely. "I haven't any excuse to make for it; only you must see yourself what a shock it would be to a person to find those cattle down here. But I know you're honest, and so is Charlie. And I know you'll do what's right. I'm sorry I told Charlie to go to the devil, and I'm sorry I shot your dog, Marthy."

Apologies did not come easily to Billy Louise. She wheeled then and rode away at a furious gallop, before Marthy could do more than open her grim lips for reply.

Chapter XXIII. Billy Louise Gets a Surprise

Frightened, worried, sick at heart because her crowding doubts and suspicions had suddenly developed into black certainty just when she had thought them dead forever, Billy Louise rode up the narrow, rocky gorge. She had come to have a vague comprehension of the temptation Ward must have felt. She had come to accept pityingly the possibility that the canker of old influences had eaten more deeply than appeared on the surface. She had set herself stanchly beside him as his friend, who would help him win back his self-respect. She felt sure that he must suffer terribly with that keen, analytical mind of his, when he stopped to think at all. He had no warped ethics wherewith to ease his conscience. She knew his ideas of right and wrong were as uncompromising as her own, and if he stole cattle, he did it with his eyes wide open to the wrong he was doing. And yet —

"That's bad enough, but to try and fasten evidence on someone else!" Billy Louise gritted her teeth over the treachery of it. She believed he had done that very thing. How could she help it? She had seen the corral and had seen Ward ride away from it in the dusk of evening; or she believed she had seen him, which was the same thing. She knew that Ward's prosperity was out of proportion with his visible resources. And she knew what lay behind him. Was his version of the past after all the correct one? Might not the paragraph she had burned been nothing more than the truth?

Billy Louise fought for him; fought with her stern, youthful judgment which was so uncompromising. It takes years of close contact with life to give one a sure understanding of human weakness and human endeavor.

At the ford, when Blue would have crossed and taken the trail home, Billy Louise reined him impulsively the other way. Until that instant she had not intended to seek Ward, but once her fingers had twitched the reins against Blue's neck, she did not hesitate; she did not even argue with herself. She just glanced up at the sun, saw that it was not yet noon-so much may happen in two or three hours! —and sent Blue up the hill at a lope.

She did not know what she would do or what she would say when she saw Ward. She knew that she was full of bitterness and disappointment and chagrin. She had accused innocent persons of a crime. Ward had placed her in that position and compelled her to recant and apologize. She had offended Marthy beyond forgiveness-and Charlie Fox. Her face burned with shame when she remembered the things she had said to them. Ward was the cause of that humiliation; and Ward was going to know exactly what she thought of him; beyond that she did not go.

The two mares fed dispiritedly at the lowest corner of the field, their hair rough with exposure to the winter winds and the storms, their ribs showing. With all the hay he had put up, Ward might at least keep his horses in better shape, Billy Louise censured, as she passed them by. A few head of cows and calves wandered aimlessly among the thinnest fringe of willows along the creek; they showed more ribs than did the mares. Billy Louise pulled her lips tight. They did not look as though they had been fed a forkful of hay all winter; your true range man or woman gets to know these things instinctively.

Farther along, Billy Louise heard a welcoming nicker and turned her head. Here came Rattler, thin-flanked and rough-coated, trotting down a shallow gulley to meet Blue. The two horses chummed together whenever Ward was at the Wolverine. Billy Louise pulled up and waited till Rattler reached her. He and Blue rubbed noses, and Blue laid back his ears and shook his head with teeth bared, in playful pretense of anger. Rattler kicked up his heels in disdain at the threat and trotted alongside them.

Billy Louise rode with puckered eyebrows. Ward might neglect his stock, but he would never neglect Rattler like this. And he must be at home, since here was his horse. Or else...

She struck Blue suddenly with her rein-ends and went clattering up the trail where the snow lay in shaded, crusty patches rimmed with dirt. The trail was untracked save by the loose stock. Where was Ward? What had happened to him? She looked again at Rattler. There was no sign of recent saddle-marks along his side, no telltale imprint of the cinch under his belly. Where was Ward?

Blind, unreasoning terror filled Billy Louise. She struck Blue again and plunged into the icy creek-crossing near the stable. She stopped there just long enough to see how empty and desolate it was, and how the horses and cattle had huddled against its sheltering wall out of the biting winds; and how the door was shut and fastened so that they could not get in. She opened it and looked in, and shut it again. Then she turned and ran, white-faced, to the cabin. Where was Ward? What had happened to Ward? Thief or honest man, treacherous or true-what had happened to him?

Billy Louise saw the doorstep banked over with old, crusted snow. Her heart gave a jump and stopped still. She felt her knees shake under her. Her face seemed to pinch together, the flesh clinging close to the bones. Her whole being seemed to contract with the deadly fear that gripped her. It was like that chill morning when she had crept out of her cot and gone over to mommie's bed and had lifted mommie's hand that was hanging down....

She came to herself; she was running up the creek, away from the cabin. Running and stumbling over rocks, and getting tripped with her riding-skirt. She stopped, as soon as she realized what she was doing; she stopped and stood with her hands pressed hard against each side of her face, forcing herself to calmness again-or at least to sanity. She had to go back. She told herself so, many times. "You've got to go back!" she repeated, as if to a second person. "You can't be such a fool; you've got to go back. And you've got to go inside. You've got to do it."

So Billy Louise went back to the cabin, slowly, with shaking legs and a heart that fluttered and stopped, fluttered and jumped and stopped, and made her stagger as she walked. She reached the doorstep and stood there with her palms pressing hard against her cheeks again. "You've got to do it. You've got to!" she whispered to herself commandingly.

She never doubted that Ward was inside. She thought she would find him dead-dead and horrible, perhaps. No other solution seemed to fit the circumstances. He was in there, dead. He had been dead for some time, because there were no saddle-marks on Rattler, and because the snow was crusted over the doorstep with never a mark to break its smooth roundness. She had to go in. She was the person who must find him and do what she could. She must do it, because he was Ward-her Ward.

It took courage to open that door, but Billy Louise had courage enough to open it, and to step inside and close the door after her. She did not look at anything in the cabin while she did it, though. She kept her eyelids down so that she only saw the floor directly in front of the door. She had a sense of relief that it looked perfectly natural, though dusty.

"Throw up your hands!" came hoarsely from the bunk. Billy Louise gasped and pulled her gun, and dropped crouching to the floor. Also she looked up. She had not recognized that voice, and while she had never except in imagination faced an emergency like this, she had played robbers and rescues too often not to have formed a mental habit to fit the situation. What she did she had done many, many times in her "pretend" world, sitting somewhere dreaming.

From her crouching position she looked into Ward's fever-wild eyes. He was sitting up in the bunk, and he was pointing his big forty-five at her relentlessly. "Get up from there!" he ordered sternly. "Don't try any game like that on me, Buck Olney! Get up and go over and sit in that chair. I've got a few things to say to you."

Billy Louise somehow grasped the truth, up to a certain point. Ward was sick; so sick he didn't know her. She thought she would better humor him. She got up and went and sat in the chair as he directed.

Ward, keeping the gun pointing her way, sneered at her in a way that made the soul of Billy Louise crimple. She faced him big-eyed, too amazed at the change in him to feel any fear that he would harm her. He had whiskers two inches long. She wouldn't have known him except for his hair-and that was terribly tousled; and his eyes, though they were wild and angry. His voice was hoarse, and while he glared at her, he coughed with a hard, croupy resonance.

"So you came back, did yuh?" he asked grimly at last. "Well, you didn't get a chance to plug me in the back. How long did you lay up there on the bluff this time, waiting to catch me when I wasn't looking? I've been wishing I'd loft that rope so it would have hung you, you damned — — —!" (Billy Louise listened round-eyed to certain man-sized epithets strange to her ears.)

"I suppose you and Foxy and that halfbreed have been fixing up some more evidence, huh? You figure that I can't catch 'em this time and work the brands over, so they'll stand Y6es, and I'll get railroaded to the pen. Well, you've overplayed your hand, old-timer. I let you fellows down easy, last time. I don't reckon Foxy objected much to those few I turned back to him, and I don't reckon you did any kicking when you found I'd cut the rope so it wouldn't hold your rotten carcass. You can't let well enough alone, though. You thought you'd raise me, did you? You thought you'd come back and try another whack at me behind my back. You knew damned well I wasn't the kind of man that would jump the country. You knew you'd find me right here, attending to my business like I've always done.

"But you've overplayed your hand. This time I'm going to get you-and Foxy and the breed along with you. It was a damned, rotten trick, running Y6es over Seabeck's brand. If I hadn't caught you in the act, you'd have planted them cattle where all hell couldn't have saved me when they were found. If I hadn't caught you at it and run MK monograms over the whole cheese, I'd have been up against it for fair. So now you're going to get what's coming to yuh. I won't take any chances on your not trying it again. I'm going to protect myself right.

"You throw that gun on the bed." (Billy Louise did so, her eyes still upon Ward's flushed face.) "Now, get down that tablet from the shelf. Here's a pencil." He drew one from under his pillow and tossed it toward her. "Now you write the truth about all this rustling. It's a bigger thing than shows right in this neighborhood. I know that. And I know too that Foxy has been pulling down some on the side. He never paid for all the stock that's running around vented and rebranded MK. I've got that sized up. Pretty smooth trick, too; a heap better than working brands. He ought to have been satisfied with that-but a crook never is satisfied. I knew he wasn't the tenderfoot he tried to make out, and when I saw some of his stock and that gate fixed to ring a bell when it was opened, I knew he was a crook. But he made a big mistake when he threw in with you, you —

"I want you to write down the truth about that Hardup deal; who was in with you. I know, all right, but I want it down on paper. And I want to know how long Foxy's been in with you, and who's working the game on the outside. Get busy; write it all down. I'll give you all the time you need; don't leave out anything. Dates and all, I want the whole graft. Don't try to get away. I've got this gun loaded to the guards, and you know I'm aching for an excuse —" He stopped and coughed again, hoarsely, rackingly. Then he lay quiet, except for his rasping breath and watched.

Billy Louise, with the tablet on her trembling knees, pretended to write. From under her lashes she watched Ward curiously. She saw his attention waver, saw his eyes wander aimlessly about the room. She sat very still and waited, making scrawly marks that had no meaning at all. She saw Ward's fingers loosen on the revolver, saw his head turn wearily on the pillow. He was staring out through the window at the brilliant blue of the sky with the dazzling white clouds drifting like bits of cotton to the northward. He had forgotten her.

Chapter XXIV. The Hookin'-Cough Man

Billy Louise waited another minute or two, weighing the possibilities. She saw Ward's fingers drop away from the gun, but they remained close enough for a dangerously quick gripping of it again, if the whim seized him. Still-surely to goodness, Ward would never get crazy enough to hurt her! Perhaps her feminine assurance of her hold on him, more than her courage, kept her nerves fairly steady. She bit the pencil absently, watching him.

Ward turned his head restlessly on the pillow and coughed again. Billy Louise got up quietly, went close to the bed, and laid her hand on his forehead. His head was hot, and the veins were swollen and throbbing on his temples.

"Brave Buckaroo got a headache?" she queried softly, stroking his temples soothingly. "Got the hookin'-cough, too. Get every measly thing he can think of. Even got a grouch against the Flower of the Ranch-oh!" Her voice was crooningly soft and sweet, as if she were murmuring over a sleepy baby.

Ward closed his eyes, opened them, and looked up into her face. One hand came up uncertainly and caught her fingers closely. "Wilhemina-mine!" he said, in his hoarse voice. His eyes cleared to sanity under her touch.

Billy Louise drew a small sigh of relief and reached unobtrusively with her free hand for the gun. She slid it down away from his fingers, and when he still paid no attention, she picked it up quite openly and laid it against the footboard. Ward did not say anything. He seemed altogether occupied with the amazing reality of her presence. He clung to her fingers and looked at her with that intent stare of his, as if he were trying to hold her there by the sheer power of his will.

"Well, how am I going to doctor you and feed you and make you all comfy, with one hand?" asked Billy Louise with quavering flippancy.

"Kiss me!"

"Ah-might catch the hookin'-cough," bantered Billy Louise, leaning a bit closer.

"Kiss me!"

"Oh, well, I s'pose sick folks have to be humored." Billy Louise leaned closer still. "Mighty few kissy places left," she observed with the same shaky flippancy, a minute later. "Say, Ward, you look for all the world like old Sourdough Williams!" Sourdough Williams, it may be remarked, was a particularly hairy and unkempt individual who lived a more or less nomadic life in the hills, trapping.

"You look like —" Ward groped foggily for a simile. Angel was altogether too commonplace.

"Like the lady who's going to get busy right now, making you well. What have you been doing to yourself? Never mind; I don't want you talking yourself crazy again. Do you know you tried to shoot me up when I came in? And you made me start in to write a record of my sins. But that's all right, seeing you've got the hookin'-cough, I'll forgive you this once. Lie still-and let go my hand. I want to put a wet cloth on your head."

"Did I —"

"You did; and then some. Forget it. You've got a terrible cold; and from the looks of things, you've had it for about six months." Her eyes went comprehensively about that end of the cabin, with the depleted cracker-box, the half-emptied boxes of peaches and tomatoes, and the buckets that were all but empty of water. She was shocked at the pitiful evidence of long helplessness. She did not quite understand. Surely Ward's cold had not kept him in bed so long.

"Well, this is no time for mirth or laughter," she said briskly, to hide how close she was to hysteria, "since it looks very much like 'the morning after.' First, we've got to tackle that fever of yours." She picked up a water-pail and started for the door. As she passed the foot of the bunk, she confiscated the two revolvers and took them outside with her. She had no desire to be mistaken again for Buck Olney.

When she came back, Ward's eyes were wild again, and he started up in bed and glared at her. Billy Louise laughed at him and told him to lie down like a nice buckaroo, and Ward, recalled to himself by her voice, obeyed. She got the wash-basin and a towel and prepared to bathe his head. He wanted a drink. And when she held a cup to his lips and saw how greedily he drank, a little sob broke unexpectedly from her lips. She gritted her teeth after it and forced a laugh.

"You're sure a hard drinker," she bantered and wet her handkerchief to lay on his brow.

"That's the first decent drink I've had for a month," he told her, dropping back to the pillow, refreshed to the point of clear thinking. "Old Lady Fortune's still playing football with me, William. I've been laid up with a broken leg for about six weeks. And when I got gay and thought I could handle myself again, I put myself out of business for awhile, and caught this cold before I came to and crawled back into bed. I'm —sure glad you showed up, old girl. I was-getting up against it for fair." He coughed.

"Looks like it." Billy Louise held herself rigidly back from any emotional expression. She could not afford to "go to pieces" now. She tried to think just what a trained nurse would do, in such a case. Her hospital experience would be of some use here, she told herself. She remembered reading somewhere that no experience is valueless, if one only applies the knowledge gained.

"First," she said cheerfully, "the patient must be kept quiet and cheerful. So don't go jumping up and down on your broken leg, Ward Warren; the nurse forbids it. And smile, if it kills you."

Ward grinned appreciatively. Sick as he was, he realized the gameness of Billy Louise; what he failed to realize was the gameness of himself. "I'm a pretty worthless specimen, right now," he said apologetically. "But I'm yours to command, Bill-the-Conk. You're the doctor."

"Nope, I'm the cook, right now. I've got a hunch. How would you like a cup of tea, patient?"

"I'd rather have coffee-Doctor William."

"Tea, you mean. I'll have it ready in ten minutes." Then she weakened before his imploring eyes. "You really oughtn't to drink coffee, with that fever, Ward. But, maybe if I don't make it very strong and put in lots of cream — We'll take a chance, buckaroo!"

Ward watched her as intently as if his life depended on her speed. He had lain in that bunk for nearly six weeks with the coffee-pot sitting in plain sight on the back of the stove, twelve feet or so from his reach, and with the can of coffee standing in plain sight on the rough board shelf against the wall by the window. And he had craved coffee almost as badly as a drunkard craves whisky.

The sound of the fire snapping in the stove was like music to him. Later, the smell of the coffee coming briskly to the boiling-point made his mouth water with desire. And when Billy Louise jabbed two little slits in a cream can with the point of a butcher knife and poured a thin stream of canned milk into a big, white granite cup, Ward's eyes turned traitor to his love for the girl and dwelt hungrily upon the swift movements of her hands.

"How much sugar, patient?" Billy Louise turned toward him with the tomato-can sugar-bowl in her hands.

"None. I want to taste the coffee, this trip."

"Oh, all right! It's the worst thing you could think of, but that's the way with a patient. Patients always want what they mustn't have."

"Sure-get it, too." Ward spoke between long, satisfying gulps. "How's your other patient, Wilhemina? How's mommie?"

"Oh, Ward! She's dead-mommie's dead!" Billy Louise broke down unexpectedly and completely. She went down on her knees beside the bed and cried as she had not cried since she looked the last time at mommie's still face, held in that terrifying calm. She cried until Ward's excited mutterings warned her that she must pull herself together. She did, somehow, in spite of her sorrow and her worry and that day's succession of emotional shocks. She did it because Ward was sick-very sick, she was afraid-and there was so much that she must do for him.

"You be s-still," she commanded brokenly, fighting for her former safe cheerfulness. "I'm all right. Pity yourself, if you've got to pity somebody. I —can stand-my trouble. I haven't got any broken leg and-hookin'-cough." She managed a laugh then and took Ward's hand from her hair and laid it down on the blankets. "Now we won't talk about things any more. You've got to have something done for that cold on your lungs." She rose and stood looking down at him with puckered eyebrows.

"Mommie would say you ought to have a good sweat," she decided. "Got any ginger?"

"I dunno. I guess not," Ward muttered confusedly.

"Well, I'll go out and find some sage, then, and give you sage tea. That's another cure-all. Say, Ward, I saw Rattler down the creek. He's looking fine and dandy. He came whinnying down out of that draw, to meet us; just tickled to death to see somebody."

"Don't blame him," croaked Ward. "It's enough to tickle anybody." Her voice seemed to steady his straying fancies. "How're-the cattle-looking?"

"Just fine," lied Billy Louise. "You're the skinniest thing I've seen on the ranch. Now do you think you can keep your senses, while I go and pick some nice, good meddy off a sage bush?"

"I guess so." Ward spoke drowsily. "Give me some more coffee and I can."

"Oh, you're the pesteringest patient! I told you coffee isn't good for what ails you, but I suppose —" She poured him another cup of coffee, weakened it with hot water, and let him drink it straight. After all, perhaps the hot drink would induce the perspiration that would break the fever. She pulled up the wolf-skins and the extra blankets he had tossed aside in his feverish restlessness and covered him to his chin.

"If you don't move till I come back," she promised, "I'll maybe give you another cup-after you've filled up on sage tea." With that qualified hope to cheer him, she left him.

She did not spend all her time picking sage twigs. A bush grew at the corner of the cabin within easy reach. She went first down to the stable and led Blue inside and unsaddled him. Rattler was standing near, and she tried to lead him in also, but he fled from her approach. She found the pitchfork and managed to scratch a few forkfuls of hay down from a corner of the stack; enough to fill a manger for Blue and to leave a little heap beside the stable for Rattler.

When she was leaving the stable to return to the house, however, she changed her plan a little. She went back, carried the small pile of hay into the stable, and filled another manger. Then she took down the wire gate of the hay corral and laid it flat alongside the fence. Rattler would go in to the stack, and she would shut him in. That would simplify the catching of him when he was needed. She would find something in which to carry water to him, if he was too frisky to lead to the creek. Billy Louise was no coward with horses, but she recognized certain fixed limitations in the management of a snuffy brute like Rattler. He was not like Blue, whom she could bully and tease and coax. Rattler was distinctly a man's saddle-horse. Billy Louise had never done more than pat his shoulder after he was caught and saddled and, therefore, prepared for handling. She foresaw some perturbation of spirit in regard to Rattler.

Ward was lying quiet when she went in, except that he was waving her handkerchief to and fro by the corners to cool it. Billy Louise took it from him, wet it again with cold water, and scolded him for getting his arms from under the covers. That, she said, was no nice way for a hookin'-cough man to do.

Ward meekly submitted to being covered to his eyes. Then he wriggled his chin free and demanded that she kiss him. Ward was fairly drunk with happiness because she was there, in the cabin. The dreary weeks behind him were a nightmare to be forgotten. His Wilhemina-mine was there, and she liked him to pieces. Though she had not affirmed it with words, her eyes when she looked at him told him so; and she had kissed him when he asked her to. He wanted her to repeat the ecstasy.

"Ward Warren, you're a perfectly awful hookin'-cough man! There. Now that's going to be the very last one — Oh, Ward, it isn't!" She knelt and curved an arm around his face and kissed him again and yet again. "I do love you, Ward. I've been a weak-kneed, horrid thing, and I'm ashamed to the middle of my bones. You're my own brave buckaroo always-always! You've done what no other man would do, and you don't whine about it; and I've been weak and-horrid; and I'll have to love you about a million years before I can quit feeling ashamed." She kissed him again with a passion of remorse for her doubts of him.

"Are you through being pals, Wilhemina?" Ward broke rules and freed an arm, so that he could hold her closer.

"No, I'm just beginning. Just beginning right. I'm your pal for keeps. But —"

"I love you for keeps, lady mine." Ward stifled another cough. "When are you going to-marry me?"

"Oh, when you get over the hookin'-cough, I s'pose." Once more Billy Louise, for the good of her patient, forced herself into safe flippancy-that was not flippant at all, but merely a tender pretense.

"Now it's up to you to show me whether you are in any hurry at all to get well," she said. "Keep your hands under the covers while I make some tea. That fever of yours has got to be stopped immediately-to once."

She went over and busied herself about the stove, never once looking toward the bed, though she must have felt Ward's eyes worshiping her. She was terribly worried about Ward; so worried that she put everything else into the background of her mind and set herself sternly to the need of breaking the fever and lessening the evident congestion in his lungs.

She hunted through the cupboards and found a bottle of turpentine; syrupy and yellowed with age, but pungent with strength. She found some lard in a small bucket and melted half a teacupful. Then she tore up a woolen undershirt she found hanging on a nail and bore re-lentlessly down upon him.

"You gotta be greased all over your lungs," she announced with a matter-of-factness that cost her something; for Billy Louise's innate modesty was only just topped by her good sense.

Ward submitted without protest while she bared his chest-as white as her own-and applied the warm mixture with a smoothly vigorous palm. "That'll fix the hookin'-cough," she said, as she spread the warm layers of woolen cloth smoothly from shoulder to shoulder. "How does it feel?"

"Great," he assured her succinctly, and wisely omitted any love-making.

"Will your game leg let you turn over? Because there's some dope left, and it ought to go between your shoulders."

"The game leg ought to stand more than that," he told her, turning slowly. "If I hadn't got this cold tacked onto me, I'd have been trying to walk on it by now."

"Better give it time-since you've been game enough to lie here all this while and take care of it. I don't believe I'd have had nerve enough for that, Ward." She poured turpentine and lard into her palm, reached inside his collar and rubbed it on his shoulders. "Good thing you had plenty of grub handy. But it must have been awful!"

"It was pretty damned lonesome," he admitted laconically, and that was as far as his com-plainings went.

Billy Louise then poured the water off the sage leaves she had been brewing in a tin basin, carefully fished out a stem or two, and made Ward drink every bitter drop. Then she covered him to the eyes and hardened her heart against his discomfort, while she kept the handkerchief cool on his head and between times swept the floor with a carefully dampened broom and wiped the dust off things and restored the room to its most cheerful atmosphere of livableness.

"Wan' a drink," mumbled Ward, with a blanket over his mouth and a raveled thread tickling his nose so that he squirmed.

Billy Louise went over and laid her fingers on his neck. "I can't tell whether it's grease or perspiration," she said, laughing a little. "What are you squinting up your nose for? Surely to goodness you don't mind that little, harmless raveling? If you wouldn't go on breathing, it wouldn't wiggle around so much!" Nevertheless, she plucked the tormenting thread and threw it on the floor.

"Gimme-drink," Ward mumbled again.

"There's more sage tea —"

"Waugh!"

"I suppose that means you aren't crazy about sage tea! Well, I might give you a teenty-weenty speck more of coffee. You can't have water yet, you know. You've-you've got to sweat like a nigger in a cotton patch first." (Billy Louise could talk very nicely when she wanted to do so. The Billy of her could also be humanly inelegant when she felt like it, as you see.)

Ward grunted something and afterwards signified that he would take the coffee and call it square.

The next time she went near him, he was wrinkling his lean nose because beads of perspiration were standing there and slipping occasionally down to his cheeks.

"Fine! You're two niggers in a cotton patch now," she announced cheeringly. "And Mr. Hookin'-cough will have to hunt another home, I reckon. You weren't half as hoarse when you swore that last time."

It was physically impossible for Ward to blush, since he was already the color of a boiled beet; but he looked guilty when she uncovered the rest of his face and wiped off the gathered moisture. "I didn't think you'd hear," he grinned embarrassedly.

"I was listening for it, buckaroo. I'd have been scared to pieces if you hadn't cussed a little. I'd have thought sure you were going to die. A man," she added sententiously, "always has a chance as long as he's able to swear. It's like a horse wiggling his ears."

The comparison reminded her that she intended to shut Rattler in the hay corral; she dried Ward's hands hastily, pulled the wolf-skins off the bed, and commanded him to keep covered until she came back. She ran down bareheaded to the stable, saw Rattler industriously boring his nose into the stack, and put up the gate.

When she went into the cabin again, Ward gave a start and opened his eyes like one who has been dozing. Billy Louise smiled with gratification. He was better. She knew he was better. She did not speak, but went over to the stove and pretended to be busy there, though she was careful to make no noise. When she turned finally and glanced toward the bed, Ward was asleep.

Billy Louise took a deep breath, tiptoed over to the bench beside the table, sat down, and pillowed her head on her folded arms. She wanted to cry, and she needed to think, and she was deadly, deadly tired.

Chapter XXV. The Wolf Joke

Billy Louise stayed all night. She was afraid to leave Ward until his cold was safely better, and there was no one living near enough to summon; no one whom she wanted to summon, in fact, however close they might have been. She spent most of the night curled comfortably on the wolf-skins beside the stove, with a sack of flour for a pillow and Ward's fur coat for covering. Ward slept more unbrokenly than he had done for a long time, while Billy Louise lay cuddled under the smelly fur and thought and thought.

In the morning, if Ward were well enough, she meant to ask him about those cattle he had mentioned when he thought her Buck Olney. They were the same ones which she had seen in the Cove, she knew. Ward had told enough to prove that. He had, in fact, told nearly all she needed to know-except the mystery of his prosperity. He had not mentioned that, and Billy Louise was more curious than ever about his "wolf hunting."

At sunrise she rebuilt the fire and made fresh coffee and a stew from the pieces of jerky she had soaked overnight for the purpose. She wanted eggs, and bread for toast, and fresh cream; but she did not have them, and so she managed a very creditable breakfast for her patient without these desirables.

"Say, that's great. A fellow doesn't appreciate coffee and warm food until he's eaten out of cans and boxes for a month or so. You're a great little lady, Wilhemina. I wish you'd happened along sooner-about six weeks sooner. I'd have got some pleasure out of my broken leg then, maybe."

"Was it-did Buck Olney break it?" Billy Louise knew he had not, but she had been waiting for a chance to open the subject.

"No. I broke it myself, pulling Rattler off a bank into some rocks. I believe I could walk on it, doctor, if you could rustle me something to use for crutches. That's what held me in bed so long. Beckon you could manufacture a pair for me?" His eyes made love. "You've done everything else." He caught her hand and kissed the palm of it. "Can't the Billy part turn carpenter?"

"I'll see. Say, Ward, do you think you could shave off those whiskers if I got everything ready for you? I don't like you to look like old Sourdough. Or maybe I could do it. I —I used to shave daddy's neck, sometimes."

Ward ran his fingers thoughtfully over his hairy cheeks. "I expect I do look like a prehistoric ancestor. I'll see what I can do about it. I set my own leg; I guess I can shave myself. You're a great doctor, Wilhemina. You knocked that cold up to a peak, all right. But —I don't believe you'd better tackle barbering, my dear girl."

Billy Louise pouted her lips at him. She could afford to pout now: Ward was so like himself that she did not worry over him at all. She also felt that she could afford to badger him into telling her some of the things she wanted to know.

"Where did you hang Buck?" she asked naïvely.

"Huh?" Ward's eyes bored into hers with his intent look, trying to read her thoughts.

"Where was it you hanged Buck Olney?"

"Nowhere. I put the fear of the Lord into him, that's all. How did you hear about it?"

"From you." Billy Louise was maddeningly calm. "You told me all about it yesterday. And about those cattle in the corral up here. I found them yesterday myself, Ward-only it seems a month ago! —down in the Cove."

"Did you?"

"Yes, and I drove them up to the corral and read the riot act to Marthy and Charlie Fox —"

"Huh! What did they say?"

"Oh, they denied it, of course! What are we going to do about it, Ward?"

"Nothing, I guess. What did you want to do?"

"I don't know. I don't want to hurt them, and I don't want them to hurt anyone else. Do you know Seabeck? He's an awfully square old fellow. I believe —" An idea formed vaguely in the back of Billy Louise's mind. "I believe I could persuade him —"

"I believe you could persuade the devil himself, if you took a notion to try," Ward affirmed sincerely, when she hesitated. "What do you want to persuade him into?"

"Oh, nothing, I guess! How do you feel, Ward? We've got to stick to the job of getting you fit to leave here and go on down to the ranch with me. When do you think you could manage to ride?"

Ward looked longingly out of the window, just as he had been looking for six weeks. "I think I could manage it now," he said doggedly, because of his great longing. "I set my own leg —"

"Yes, and I'm willing to admit you're a wonder, and have gotten the stoics beaten at their own game. Still, there's a limit to what the human body will stand. I'm going down to tend the horses, and if you think you can walk without hurting your leg, I'll hunt some forked sticks for crutches. We'll see how you make out with them, first, before we talk about riding twenty miles on horseback. Besides, you'd catch more cold if you went out to-day."

While she talked, her plans took definite shape in the back of her mind. She took Buck Olney's knife that was lying on the window-sill and went in search of crutches among the willows along the creek. Forked sticks were plentiful enough, but it was not so easy to find two that would support even so skinny a man as Ward. She compromised by cutting four that seemed suitable and binding them together in couples.

When she went in with her makeshifts, Ward was sitting upon the side of the bunk, clothed and in his right mind-but pitifully wobbly and ashamed of his weakness.

"You shouldn't have tried to get up yet," she scolded. "Do you want to be worse, so I'll have to cure you all over again?" Then, woman-like, she proceeded to annul the effect by petting and sympathy.

It was while she was sitting in the one chair, padding the sticks crudely enough but effectively, that Ward, gazing at her with the light of love in his eyes, thought of something he had meant to tell her.

"Oh, by the way, I've got something for you, Wilhemina," he said. "Put down that thing and come over here. I want to shave before I take a try at walking, anyway. See here, lady-mine. How would you like these strung on a gold chain?"

From under his pillow he drew out a tobacco sack and emptied the contents into her palm. "Those are your Christmas present, Bill-Loo. Like 'em?"

"Do I!" Billy Louise held up the biggest one and stared at it round-eyed. "Gold nuggets! Where in the world —"

"That's what I'm going to tell you-now you're through being just pals. Oh, I'd have told you, anyway, I reckon, only the play never came right, after that first little squabble we had over it." He put an arm around her, pulled her down beside him, and rubbed his bristly chin over her hair. "That's the wolf joke, William. I did make a lot of money wolfing-on the square. I dug out a den of pups and struck a little pocket of pretty rich gravel. I've been busy panning it out all the time I could spare, till the creek froze up."

"You found a gold mine?" Billy Louise gasped. "Why, whoever would have thought —"

"Oh, I wouldn't call it a gold mine, exactly," he hastened to assure her, before her imagination dazzled her. "There isn't enough of it. It's just a pocket. I've cleaned up about eighteen hundred dollars, this summer, besides these nuggets. Maybe more. And there's some left yet. I found both ends of the streak; it lies along a ledge on the side of a gully. I couldn't find anything except in that one streak of gravel; and when that's gone she's done, as near as I can figure. But it isn't all gone yet, lady mine. There's enough left to pay the preacher, anyway. That big fellow I found along toward the last, just before I quit working." He kissed her gravely. "Poor old girl! She's dead game, all right, and she's kind of had the cards stacked against her from the start. But things are going to come easier from now on, if I'm any prophet. It's too bad —"

Billy Louise read his thought.

"Mommie looked so peaceful, Ward. At the last, I mean. If I could have waked her up, I don't believe I'd have had the heart to do it. She never was very happy; you know that. She couldn't seem to see the happiness in little things. So many are like that. And she looked happier-at the last-than I ever saw her look before. So —I'm happier, too-since yesterday."

"Are you?" Ward dropped his face against her hair and held it there for a minute. It was not his cold altogether that had made his voice break hoarsely over those two words.

"Do you know —" Billy Louise was lifting the nuggets one after the other and letting them drop to her lap —"happiness is like gold, Ward. We've got to pan it out of life ourselves. If we try to steal it from someone else, we pay the penalty, don't you think? And so many go looking and looking for great big chunks of it all-all-whatever they do to it." She laughed a little at her ignorance of the technical process. "You see what I mean, don't you? We get a streak of gravel; that's life. And we can pan out happiness if we try-little nuggets and sometimes just colors-but it keeps us hoping and working."

"Doctor of philosophy!" Ward kissed her hair. "You're a great little girl, all right. And I'm the buckaroo that has struck a mighty rich streak of pay dirt in life, Wilhemina. I'm panning out happiness millions to the pan right now."

Billy Louise, attacked with a spasm of shyness, went abruptly back to padding the makeshift crutches and changed the subject.

"I'm going home, soon as I fix you comfy," she said.

Whereupon Ward protested most strenuously and did not look in the least like a man who has just announced himself a millionaire in happiness.

"What for?" he demanded, after he had exhausted himself to no purpose in telling her that she should not leave the cabin until he could go along.

"I want eggs-for you, you ungrateful beast. And some bread for toast. And I want to tell Phoebe and John where I am."

"You think those Injuns are going to hurt themselves worrying? I don't want any eggs and toast. I've managed all right on crackers and jerky for six weeks, so I guess I can stand it a few hours longer. Still, if you're crazy to go —" He dropped back on the pillow and turned his face away.

Billy Louise worked silently until she had made the crutches as soft on top as she could. Then she hunted for Ward's razor and shaving-cup and after one or two failures-through using too much water-she managed to make a cup of very nice lather.

"Now, buckaroo, don't be a sulky kid," she said, firmly as she could. "You know it's hard enough for me to go off and leave you here like this. But, as you say, you've managed to get along for six weeks without me, so —"

"Sure. I could do it again, I reckon." Ward turned a gloomy pair of eyes upon her. "What's the rush? Do you think it isn't proper —"

"It's always proper to do what is right and helpful and kind," said Billy Louise with dignity, because she had made up her mind and was trying not to weaken. "I've lived in this country all my life, and I guess my reputation will stand this little strain," she went on lightly, "even if anyone finds it out. I've got to go, that's all. Those people in the Cove —" It was eloquent of her stern justice that she could not bring herself to speak them by name.

"You aren't going to turn them over to the sheriff, are you, William? Good Lord, girl! If I can —"

"Your lather is getting cold," Billy Louise said evenly. "I ought to have known better than mention the subject at all. I'm going to do what's right. I believe I have some faint idea of right and wrong, Ward Warren. And I'm not going to do anything that I don't feel is right, or anything that I'll be sorry for. You might trust me, I think. It's early yet —"

"You'll come back before night, won't you?" From his tone, Ward had yielded the point-and was minded to yield with what graciousness he could command. It had occurred to him that he was behaving like a selfish booby. Billy Louise should not call him weak-kneed; whatever happened.

"No, I don't think I can, Ward. I might send John."

"You needn't bother. I don't want John."

"Well, I don't suppose he would be much comfort. I'll make a pot of coffee, Ward, and I'll fill the lantern and fix it so you can heat a cup when you want to; how will that be?" She brightened a little at the idea. "And I'll fix your lungs up again before I go and bake some nice, hot biscuits and put here, and butter, and fix you just as comfy as possible. Or, if you can manage to get around with the crutches, all the better. I'll leave things so you won't have to go outside for a thing.

"And, Ward" —she bent over him anxiously —"I'm going because I must. For all our sakes I must go right away. And I'll come back to-morrow just as early as I can get here. So if you are real good, and take care of your cold, and get a little strong about walking, you can go back with me. And to-morrow night you can sit in daddy's chair before the fireplace, and we'll have chicken and —"

"All right-all right!" Ward laughed suddenly. "Will you give me a lump of sugar and let me look at all the pitty pittys in the album? Oh, you William the Conqueror!" He caught her close, when he saw that he had hurt her feelings a little, and held her a minute. "When I get two good legs under me, Wilhemina," he promised softly, "I'm going to stake myself to the job of taking care of you. Your cheeks are pretty thin, little lady-girl. Damn the luck, anyway!"

"Here's the lather. I'm going down and saddle up," said Billy Louise. "When I come back, we'll see how the crutches work."

"Oh, say!" Ward called after her. "My saddle's behind a buck bush up along the trail where the bank is cut straight. I forgot about that. And would you mind bringing the looking-glass, William? How the deuce do you think a man's going to shave without a glass? And that old paper to wipe the lather on, while you're at it. I see the Billy of you hasn't got to the shaving-point yet, at any rate!"

Billy Louise took down the glass and flung it on the bed, threw the newspaper after it, and departed with her chin in the air to find his saddle and bridle and carry them to the stable.

Ward, sitting up in bed, stared at the closed door remorsefully. When he was convinced that she did not intend to return even for the last word which is so tempting to a woman, he reached for the glass, held it up, and looked within.

"Sufferin' saddle blankets!" he grunted and dropped the glass. "And she could kiss a mug like that!"

Floyd Carson was a somewhat phlegmatic young man, but he swore an astonished oath when he saw Billy Louise galloping along the lane that led nowhere except to the womanless abode of Samuel Seabeck. He walked very fast to the stable, which was the first logical stopping-place, and so he met Billy Louise before she had time to dismount, even supposing she intended to do so.

"Hello, Floyd! Is Mr. Seabeck at home?" Billy Louise was not one to waste time in the superfluities of speech when she had anything on her mind.

"Sure. Get off, and I'll put up your horse. We're just through eatin', but our grub carpenter will rustle something for yuh, all right."

"No, I can't stop this time. I'm not hungry, anyway. Just give a yell for Mr. Seabeck, will you? I want to see him a minute."

Floyd eyed her uncertainly, decided that Billy Louise was not in the mood to yield to persuasion, and tactfully hurried off to find Seabeck without shouting for him-lest he bring others also, who were evidently not wanted at all. He took it that Billy Louise felt some diffidence about visiting a strictly bachelor outfit, and he set himself to relieve her of any embarrassment.

Presently Seabeck himself came from the dirt-roofed, rambling cabin which was his home and strode down the path, buttoning his coat as he came. Floyd's face showed for a minute in the doorway before he effaced himself completely, and not another man was in sight anywhere. Billy Louise was grateful to circumstance; she had dreaded this visit, though not for the reason Floyd Carson believed.

"How de do, Miss MacDonald? Pretty nice day, but I'm afraid it's a weather-breeder. The wind's trying to change, I notice."

"Yes, and so I mustn't stop. Could you ride part way home with me, Mr. Seabeck? I —want to talk with you about something. And I can't stop a minute. I must get home."

"Why, certainly, I'll go. If you'll wait just a minute while I saddle up-or if you'd rather ride on, I'll overtake you."

"I'll ride on, I think. Blue hates standing around, and he's a little warm, too. You're awfully good, Mr. Seabeck —"

"Oh, not at all!" Seabeck stubbed his toe on the stable doorsill in his confusion at the praise. "I'll be right along, soon as I can slap a saddle on." He disappeared, and Billy Louise turned and loped slowly down the lane.

So far, so good. Billy Louise tried to believe that it was all going to be as plain sailing as this fortuitous beginning, but she was aware of a nervous fluttering in her throat while she waited, and she knew that she positively dreaded hearing Seabeck gallop up behind her on the frozen trail. "Why will people do things that make a lot of trouble for others?" she cried out petulantly. And then she heard the steady *pluck, pluckety-pluck* of Seabeck's horse, and twisted her lips with a whimsical acceptance of the part she had set herself to play. She might smash things, she told herself, but at the worst it would be only a premature smash. "Come, Bill," she adjured herself, pretending it was what Ward would have said, had he looked into her mind. "Be a Bill-the-Conk —and a good one! Shove in your chips and play for all there is in it."

"You must have some lightning method of saddling, Mr. Seabeck," she smiled over her shoulder at him when he came up.

"We learn to do things quick when we've handled cattle a few years," he admitted. He had a diffident manner of receiving compliments which pleased Billy Louise and gave her confidence a needed brace. She was not a skilled coquette; she was too honest and too straightforward for that. Still, nature places certain weapons in the hands of a woman, and instinct shows her how to use them. Seabeck, from his very unaccustomedness to women, seemed to her particularly pliable. Billy Louise took her courage in both hands and went straight to the point.

"Mr. Seabeck, I've always heard that you're an awfully square man," she said. "Daddy seemed to think that you could be depended on in any kind of a pinch. I hope it's true. I'm banking a lot on your squareness to-day."

"Why, I don't know about my being any better than my neighbors," he said, with a twinkle of humor in his eyes, which were a bright, unvarying blue. "But you can bank on my doing anything I can for you, Miss MacDonald. I think I could be even better than square-to help a plucky little girl who —"

"I don't mean just the ordinary squareness," Billy Louise put in quietly. "I mean bigness, too; a bigness that will make a man be more than square; a bigness that will let him see all around a thing and judge it from a bigger viewpoint than mere justice —"

"Hm-mm —if you could trust me enough to —"

"I'm going to, Mr. Seabeck. I'm going to take it for granted you're bigger than your own squareness. And if you're not-if you're just a selfish, weak, letter-perfect, honest man, I'll-feel like-thrashing you." Without a doubt that was the Billy of her which spoke.

"I'll take the thrashing if you think I need it," he promised, looking at her with something more than admiration. "What have you done, Miss MacDonald? If I can help you hide the body —"

"There!" Billy Louise dared to wrinkle her nose at him-and I don't know which of her did it. "I knew you'd play up like a good sport. But what if it isn't a body? What if-what if you found some of your cattle with-with a big D —run over your brand?" She had a perfectly white line around her mouth and nostrils then, but she faced him squarely.

"Hm-mm!" Seabeck gave her a quick, sidewise glance and pulled thoughtfully at the graying whiskers that pointed his chin. "I would have been glad to lend you money, or help you in any way."

"Yes, I know." Billy Louise snapped her reins impatiently. "But what would you do about the-cattle?"

"What could I do? What would you want me to do? I should do whatever would help you. I would —"

"Would you-be as ready to help somebody else? Somebody I —thought a —lot-of?"

Seabeck, evidently, saw light. He cleared his throat and spat gravely into a bush. "I see you don't trust me, after all," he said.

"I do. I've got to; I mean, I'd have to whether I did or not. It's like this, Mr. Seabeck. It isn't the big D brand; of course you knew it couldn't be. But it isn't yours, either. Someone was tempted and was weak. They're sorry now. They want to do the right thing, and it rests with you whether they can do it. You can shut them up in jail if you like; you have a perfect right to do it. Some men would do that and be able to sleep after it, I suppose. But I believe you're bigger than that. I believe you're big enough to see that if a person goes wrong and then sees the mistake and wants to pull back into the straight trail, a man-even the one who has been wronged-would be committing a moral crime to prevent it. To take a person who wants to make a fresh, honest start, and shut that person up amongst criminals and brand him as a criminal, seems to me a worse wrong than to steal a few head of cattle; don't you think so, Mr. Seabeck?"

What Mr. Seabeck thought did not immediately appear in speech. He was pulling a little harder at his whiskers and staring at the ears of his horse.

"That would depend on the person," he said at last. "Some men are born criminals."

"Oh, we aren't talking about that kind of a man. Surely to goodness you don't call Charlie Fox a born criminal, or Marthy Meilke?"

"Charlie Fox! Is that the person you mean, who has been —"

"Yes, it is! And he is horribly sorry, and so is Marthy, and they'll pay you for the cattle. And if you do anything mean about it, it will simply kill poor old Marthy. You couldn't send her to the pen, Mr. Seabeck. Think how she's worked there in the Cove; and Charlie has worked like a perfect slave; and he was trying to get a start so he-could-get married —"

"Hm-mm!" Rumors had reached Seabeck, thanks to Billy Louise's dropped lashes upon a certain occasion, which caused him to believe he saw further light.

"And if you're going to be horrid —"

"Will the-lady he wants to marry give him another chance?"

"Don't you think she ought to-if she l-loves him?" Billy Louise studied the skyline upon the side farthest from Seabeck.

"You say he wants to pay for the cattle and —"

"He'll do anything he can to make amends," said Billy Louise, with conviction. "He'll take his medicine and go to jail if you insist," she added sorrowfully. "It will ruin his whole life, of course, and break a couple of women's hearts, but —"

"It's a bad thing, a mighty bad thing, when a man tries to get ahead too fast."

"It's a good thing when he learns the lesson without having to pay for it with his whole future," Billy Louise amended the statement.

Seabeck smiled a little behind his fingers that kept tugging at his whiskers.

"Did Charlie Fox send Miss Portia —"

"He doesn't know I had any intention of coming," Billy Louise assured him quickly and with perfect truth. "They'll both be awfully surprised when they find it out" —which was also perfectly true —"and when they see you ride up, they'll think you've got the sheriff at your back. I haven't a doubt they —"

"There are a few points I'd like to clear up, if you can help me," Seabeck interrupted. "All this rustling that has been going on for the past year and a half: are Fox and the Meilke woman mixed up in that? I want," he said, "to help the young man-and her. But if they have been operating on a large scale, I'm afraid —"

"I believe Charlie must have been influenced in some ways by bad acquaintances," Billy Louise answered more steadily than she felt. "But his-rustling-has been of a petty kind. I won't apologize for him, Mr. Seabeck. I think it's perfectly awful, what he has done. But I think it would be more awful still not to give him a chance. The other rustling is some outside gang, I'm sure. If Charlie was mixed up with them, it's very slightly-just enough to damn him utterly if he were arrested and tried. He isn't a natural criminal. He's just weak. And he's learned his lesson. It's up to you, Mr. Seabeck, to say whether he shall have a chance to profit by the lesson. And there's poor old Marthy in it, too. She just worships Charlie and would do anything-even steal for him."

Seabeck meditated for a mile, and Billy Louise watched him uneasily from the tail of her eye. To tell the plain truth, she was in a panic of fear at what she had done. It had looked so simple and so practicable when she had planned it; and now when the words were out and the knowledge had reached Seabeck and was beyond her control, she could not think of any good reason for telling him.

Last night, when she lay curled up by the stove under Ward's wolf-skin coat, this seemed the only possible way out: To tell Seabeck and trust to his kindness and generosity to refrain from pushing the case. To have Charlie Fox give back what he had stolen or pay for it-anything that would satisfy Seabeck's sense of justice-and let him start honestly. She had thought that Seabeck would be merciful, if she told him in the right way; but now, when she stole a glance at his bent, brooding face, she was frightened. He did not look merciful, but stern and angry. She remembered then that stealing cattle is the one crime a cattleman finds it hard to forgive.

Billy Louise might have spared herself some mental anguish if she could have known that Seabeck was brooding over the wonder of a woman's love that pardons and condones a man's sins. He was wishing that such a love as Billy Louise's had come to him, and he was wondering how a man could be tempted to go wrong when such a girl loved him. He was laboring under a misapprehension, of course. Billy Louise had permitted him to misunderstand her interest in the matter. If he had known that she was pleading solely for Marthy-poor, avaricious, gray, old Marthy-perhaps his mercy would have been less tinged with that smoldering resentment which was directed not so much at the wrongdoer, as at fate which had cheated him.

"I'm glad you came and told me this," he said at last. "Very glad, indeed, Miss MacDonald. Certain steps have been taken lately to push this-wipe out this rustling and general lawlessness, and if you had not told me, I'm afraid the mills of justice would have ground your-friends. Of course the law would be merciful to Mrs. Meilke. No jury would send an old woman like that — By the way, that breed they have had working for them-he is in the deal, too, I take it."

"Yes, of course. They had to have someone to help. Marthy can't do any riding." Billy Louise spoke with a dreary apathy that betrayed how the reaction had set in. "She stayed in the Cove, in case anyone came prowling down there. It seems there's a wire fastened to the gate, and it rings a bell down at the house somewhere when the gate is opened. And besides that she had a dog that would tackle strangers. I don't believe," she went on, after a little silence, "that Marthy would have turned dishonest for herself. She was grasping, and all she cared for was getting ahead. It-sort of grew on her, after the years of trying to dig a bare living out of the ground. I —can understand that; and I can see how she would go to any length almost for-Charlie. But —"

"Well, let's not think any more about them until we have to." There was a certain crude attempt at soothing her anxieties. "You've trusted me, Miss MacDonald. I'll try and not disappoint you in the matter, though, unless they are quite separate from the gang which is being run down, it may be hard to protect them. Do you know-whether-any other cowman has suffered from their-mm-mm-haste to get rich?"

"I don't think there's anyone but you," Billy Louise replied lifelessly.

"Hm-mm —do you know, Miss MacDonald, whether there was any intimacy between-your friends-and the man we had for stock inspector, Mr. Olney?"

"I —can't say, as to that." Billy Louise, you see, did not know much about details, but the little she did know made her hedge.

"There's a queer story about Olney. You know he has left the country, don't you? It seems he rode very hurriedly up to the depot at Wilmer to take the train. Just as he stepped on, a fellow who knew him by sight noticed a piece of paper pinned on the back of his coat. He jerked it loose. It was a —m-m —very peculiar document for a man to be wearing on his back." Seabeck pulled at his whiskers, but it was not the pulling which quirked the corners of his lips. "The man said Olney seemed greatly upset over something and had evidently forgotten the paper until he felt it being pulled loose. He said Olney looked back then, and he was the color of a pork-rind. The train was pulling out. The man took the paper over to a saloon and let several others read it. They-mm-mm-decided that it should be placed in the hands of the authorities. Have —m-m —your-friends ever mentioned the matter to you?"

"No," said Billy Louise, and her eyes were wide.

"Hm-mm! We must discover, if we can, Miss MacDonald, whether they are in any way implicated with this man Olney. I believe that this is at present more important than the recovery of any —m-m —cattle of mine which they may have appropriated."

Billy Louise looked at him for a minute. "Mr. Seabeck, you're awfully dear about this!" she told him. "I haven't been as square as you; and I've been — Listen here, Mr. Seabeck! I don't love Charlie Fox a bit. I love somebody else, and I'm going to marry him. He's so square, I'd hate to have him think I even let you believe something that wasn't true. It's Marthy I'm thinking of, Mr. Seabeck. I was afraid you wouldn't let Charlie off just for her sake, but I thought maybe if you just thought I —wanted you to do it for mine, why, maybe-with two women to be sorry for, you'd kind of —"

"Hm-mm!" Seabeck sent her a keen, blue, twinkling glance that made Billy Louise turn hot all over with shame and penitence. "Hm-mm!" he said again-if one can call that a saying-and pulled at his graying whiskers. "Hm-mmm!"

Billy Louise led the way down the gorge, through the meadow, and along the orchard to the little gate. The Cove seemed empty and rather forlorn, with the wind creeping up the river and rattling the dry branches of the naked fruit trees. Not much more than twenty-four hours had slid into the past since Billy Louise had galloped away from the place, yet she felt vaguely that life had taken a big stride here since she last saw it. Nothing was changed, though, as far as she could see. A few cattle fed in the meadow next the river, a fattening hog lifted himself from his bed of straw and grunted at them as they passed. A few chickens were hunting fishworms in the thawed places of the garden, and a yellow cat ran creepingly along the top rail of the nearest corral, crouched there with digging claws and pounced down into a flock of snowbirds. A drift of dead apple leaves stirred uneasily beside the footpath through the berry bushes. Billy Louise started nervously and glanced over her shoulder at Seabeck. For some reason she wanted the comfort of his presence. She waited until he came up to her-tall, straight like a soldier, and silent as the Cove itself.

"I'm —scared," said Billy Louise. She did not smile either when she said it. "I —hate empty-feeling places. I'm —afraid of emptiness."

"Yet you are always riding alone in the hills." Seabeck looked down at her with a puzzled expression in his eyes.

"The hills aren't empty," she told him impatiently. "They're just big and quiet. This is —" She flung out a hand and did not try to find a word for what she felt.

"Shall I go first? I thought you would rather —"

"I would." Billy Louise pulled herself together, angry at her sudden impulse to run, as she had run from Ward's quiet cabin. She remembered that unreasoning panic-was it really only yesterday? —and went steadily up the path and across the little ditch which Marthy had dug. Why must sordid trouble and dull misery hang over a beauty-spot like this? she thought resentfully.

She stopped for a minute on the doorstep, hesitating before she opened the door. Behind her, Seabeck drew close as if he would shield her from something; perhaps he, too, felt the deadly quiet and emptiness of the place.

Billy Louise opened the door and stepped into the kitchen. She stopped and stood still, so that her slim figure would have hidden the interior from the eyes of Seabeck had he not been so tall. As it was, she barred his way so that he must stand on the step outside.

By the kitchen table, with her elbows on the soiled oilcloth, sat Marthy. Her uncombed hair hung in wisps about her head; her hard old face was lined and gray, her hard eyes dull with brooding. Billy Louise, staring at her from the doorway, knew that Marthy had been sitting like that for a long, long time.

She went over to her diffidently. Hesitatingly she laid her gauntleted hand on Marthy's stooped shoulder. She did not say anything. Marthy did not move under her touch, except to turn her dull glance upon Seabeck, standing there on the doorstep.

"C'm in," she said stolidly. "What'd yuh come fer?"

"Miss MacDonald will perhaps explain —"

"She ain't got nothin' to explain," said hard old Marthy with grim finality. "I'll do what explainin's to be done. C'm in. Don't stand there like a stump. And shut the door. It's cold as a barn here, anyway."

"Oh, Marthy!" cried Billy Louise, with the sound of tears in her voice.

"Don't oh Marthy me," said the harsh voice flatly. "I don't want no Marthyin' nor no sympathy. Well, old man, you're here to colleck, I s'pose. Take what's in sight; 'tain't none of it yourn, far's I know, but anything you claim you kin have, fer all me. I've lived honest all my days an' worked fer what I got. I've harbored thieves in my old age and trusted them that wa'n't fit to be trusted. I've allus paid my debts, Seabeck. I'm willin' to pay now fer bein' a fool."

"W-where's Charlie?" Billy Louise leaned and whispered the question.

"I d'no, and I don't care. He's pulled out-him an' that breed. I'll have t' pay yuh for seven growed cattle I never seen till yist'day, Seabeck. You can set yer own price on 'em. I ain't sure, but I've got an idee they was shot las' night an' dumped in the river. You c'n set yer price. I've got rheumatiz so bad I couldn't go 'n' put a stop to nothin' —but —"

"Oh, Marthy!" Billy Louise was shivering and crying now. "Marthy! Don't be so-so hard. It was all Charlie —"

"Yes," said Marthy harshly, "it was all Charlie. He was a thief, an' I was sech a simple-minded old fool I never knowed what he was. I let him go ahead, an' I set in the house with a white apurn tied on me an' thought I was havin' an easy time. I set here and let him rob my neighbors that I ain't never harmed er cheated out of a cent, and soon's he thought he was found out, he-left ole Marthy to look after herself. Never so much as fed the hogs or done the milkin' first! Looky here, Seabeck! You'll git paid back, an' I'll take your figgers fer what I owe, but if you git after Charlie, I'll-kill yuh. You let 'im go, I'm the one he hurt most-and I ain't goin' —" She laid her frowsy old head on her arms, like one who is utterly crushed and dumb.

"Oh, Marthy!" Billy Louise knelt and threw her arms around Marthy's shoulders.

"You've got to come and lie down, Marthy," said Billy Louise, after a long, unbroken silence.

"Mr. Seabeck, if you'll start a fire, I'll make some tea for her. Come, Marthy-just to please me. Do it for Billy Louise, Marthy."

The old woman rose stiffly, and with a feebleness that seemed utterly foreign to her usual energy, permitted Billy Louise to lead her from the kitchen. In the sitting-room that Charlie had built and furnished for her, Marthy lay and stared around her with that same dull apathy she had shown from the first. Only once did she manifest any real emotion, and that was when Billy Louise came in with some tea and toast.

"You take all them books outa them shelves an' burn 'em up," she commanded. "An' you take them two pictures off'n that shelf, of him an' her, an' bring 'em t' me."

Billy Louise set the toast and tea down on a chair and brought the pictures. She did not say a word, but she looked a little scared and her eyes were very big, just as they had been when Ward mistook her for Buck Olney and so let her see into another one of the dark places of life. It seemed to Billy Louise that she was being compelled to look into a good many dark places, lately.

Marthy took the two photographs and looked at the first with hatred. "The Jezebel! She won't git to run it over ole Marthy," she muttered with sullen triumph and twisted the cardboard spitefully in her gnarled old fingers. "She can't come here an' take all I've got an' never give me a thankye for it. I'm shet uh her, anyway." She twisted again and yet again, till the picture was a handful of ragged scraps of cardboard. Then she raised herself to an elbow and flung the fragments far from her and lay down again with glum satisfaction.

Her fingers touched the other picture, which had slid to the couch. Mechanically she picked it up and held it so that the light from the window struck it full. This was Charlie's face-Charlie with the falsely frank smile in his eyes, and with his lips curved as they did when he was just going to say, "Now, Aunt Martha!" in tender protest against her too eager industry.

Marthy's chin began to quiver while she looked. Her lips sagged with the pull of her aching heart. For the third time in her life Billy Louise saw big, slow tears gather in Marthy's hard blue eyes and slide down the leathery seams in her cheeks. Billy Louise looked, found her vision blurring with her own tears, and turned and tiptoed from the room.

Seabeck was gone somewhere on his horse. Billy Louise guessed shrewdly that he was down in the meadows, looking over the cattle and trying to estimate the extent of the thievery. She put Blue in the stable and fed him, with that half-mechanical habit of attending to the needs of one's mount which becomes second nature to the range-bred. She would not go on to the Wolverine; that needed no decision; she accepted it at once as a fact. Marthy needed her now more than anyone. More even than Ward, though Billy Louise hated to think of him up there alone and practically helpless. But Marthy must have her to-night. Marthy was facing her bitterest sorrow since Minervy died, and Marthy was old. Ward, Billy Louise reminded herself sternly, was not old, and he was facing happiness-so far as he or anyone knew. She wanted very much to be with Ward, but she could not delude her conscience into believing that he needed her more than did Marthy.

Seabeck returned after awhile, and Billy Louise, who was watching from the doorway, met him at the little gate as he was coming up to the house.

"Well, how bad is it, Mr. Seabeck?" she asked sharply, just because she felt the imperative need of facts-she who had struggled so long in the quicksands of suspicion and doubts and fears and suspense.

"Hmm-mm —how bad is it-in the house?" he countered. "The real crime has been committed there, it seems to me. A few head of cattle, more or less, don't count for much against the broken heart of an old woman."

"Oh!" Billy Louise, her hands clenched upon the gate, stared up wide-eyed into his face. And this was the real Seabeck, whom she had known impersonally all her life! This was the real man of him, whom she had never known; a flawless diamond of a soul behind those bright blue eyes and that pointed, graying beard; poet, philosopher, gentleman to the bone. "Oh! You saw that, too! And they're your cattle that were stolen! You saw it-oh, you're-you're —"

"Hmm-mm —a human being, I hope, Miss MacDonald, as well as a mere cattleman. How is the old lady?"

"Crying," said Billy Louise, with brief directness. "Crying over the picture of that-swine. Think of his running off and leaving her here all alone-and not even doing the chores first!" (Here, you must know, was broken an unwritten law of the ranch.) "And Marthy's got rheumatism, too, so she can hardly walk —"

"I'll attend to the chores, Miss MacDonald." Seabeck's lips quirked under the fingers that pulled at his whiskers. "You say-over his picture?"

"Yes, over his picture!" Billy Louise spoke with a suppressed fury. "With that honest look in his eyes-oh, I could kill him!"

"Hmm-mm —it does seem a pity that one can't. But if she can cry —"

"I see. You believe too that tears are a necessary kind of weakness for a woman, like smoking tobacco is for a man-or swearing. Well, I can just tell you, Mr. Seabeck, that some tears pull the very soul out of a person; they're the red-hot pinchers of the torture-chamber of life, Mr. Seabeck. Every single, slow tear that Marthy sheds right now is taking that much away from her life. Why, she-she idolized that-that devil. She hadn't much that was lovable in poor old Jase; he was just her husband; he wasn't even a real man. And she never had any children to love, except a little girl that died. And she's worked here and scrimped and saved till she got just fairly comfortable, and then Charlie Fox came and patted her on the back and called her a game little lady, and poor old Marthy just poured out all the love and all the trust she had in her, on him! And she's old, and she had starved all her life for a little love —a little affection and a few kind words. I don't suppose Jase kissed her once in twenty years; I couldn't imagine him getting up steam enough to kiss anybody! And Charlie petted her and did little things for her that nobody had ever done in her life. It meant a whole lot to Marthy to have a man take the water bucket away from her and give her a little hug and tell her she mustn't think of carrying water; oh, you're a man, and I don't suppose you can realize; I didn't myself, till lately —" Billy Louise blushed and then twisted her lips, wondering if love had taught her all this.

"And so Marthy just leaned more and more on him and let him take care of her and pet her; and she never once dreamed he was doing anything crooked. I thought she did, I know, Mr. Seabeck. I thought she was in it, too; but I see now that Marthy has been living the woman in her, these last two years; she'd never had a chance before. And now to have him-to know he's just a common thief and to have him go off and leave her-Mr. Seabeck, I'd be willing to bet all I've got that Marthy would have forgiven his stealing cattle, if he had just stayed. She'd have done anything on earth for him; and the bigger the sacrifice she made for him, the more she would have loved him; women are like that. But to have him go off-and-leave her-and not bother his head about what happened to her, just so he got out of it-Mr. Seabeck, that's going to kill Marthy. It's going to kill her by inches."

"I —see," he assented, looking thoughtfully at the flushed face and big, shining eyes of Billy Louise. (I wonder if Seabeck was not thinking how he had known Billy Louise impersonally all her life and yet had never met the real Billy Louise until to-day!)

"And yet," she added bitterly, "she's going to protect him if it takes every cent she's managed to rake together these last thirty years. You heard what she told you. She said she'd kill you if you hurt Charlie. She'd try it, too."

"Hmm-mm, yes! My life has been threatened several times to-day." Seabeck looked at her with eyes a-twinkle, and Billy Louise blushed to the crown of her Stetson hat. "Do you think, Miss MacDonald, she would feel like talking business for a few minutes?"

"Oh, yes; if she's like me, she'll want to get the agony over with." Billy Louise turned with a twitch of the shoulders. She felt chilled, somehow. She had not quite expected that Seabeck would want to talk about his stolen stock at all. She had rather taken it for granted that he would let that subject lie quiet for awhile. Oh, well, he was a cattleman, after all.

Marthy did not attempt to rise when Seabeck followed Billy Louise into the sitting-room. She caught up her apron and wiped her eyes and her nose, however, and she also slid Charlie's picture under the cheap cushion. After that she faced Seabeck with harsh composure and waited for the settlement.

"Hm-mm! I have been looking over the cattle," he began, sitting on the edge of a chair and turning his black hat absently round and round by the brim. "You-mm-mm-you tell me there were seven head of grown stock —"

"That they shot and throwed in the river, with the brands cut out," interpolated Marthy stolidly. "I heard 'em say that's how they would git rid of 'em, an' I heard 'em shootin' down there."

"Hmm-mm, yes! Do you know just what —"

"Five dry cows 'n' two steers-long two-year-oles, I jedged 'em to be." Marthy was certainly prompt enough and explicit enough. And her lips were grim, and her faded blue eyes hard and steady upon the face of Seabeck.

"Hmm-mm —yes! I find also," he went on in his somewhat precise voice that had earned him the nickname of "Deacon" among his punchers, "that there are more young stock vented and rebranded than I —er-sold your nephew. Fourteen head, to be exact. With the cattle you tell me which were-mm-m —disposed of last night, that would make twenty-one head of stock for which-mm-mm —I take it you are willing to pay."

"I ain't got the money now," Marthy stated, too apathetic to be either defiant or placating. "You c'n fix up the papers t' suit yerself. I'll sign anything yuh want."

"Hmm-mm —yes! A note covering the amount, with legal rate of interest, will be-quite satisfactory, Mrs. Meilke. I shall make a lump sum at the going price for mixed stock. If you have a blank note, I —"

"You kin look in that desk over there," permitted Marthy. "If yuh don't find any there, there ain't none nowhere."

Seabeck did not find any blank notes. He found an eloquent confusion of jumbled letters and accounts and papers, and guessed that the owner had done some hasty sorting and straightening of his affairs. He sighed, and his blue eyes hardened for a minute. Then Billy Louise moved from the door and went over to kneel comfortingly beside Marthy, and Seabeck looked at the two and sighed again, though his eyes were no longer stern. He pulled a sheet of paper toward him and wrote steadily in a prim, upright chirography that had never a flourish anywhere, but carefully crossed t's and carefully dotted i's and punctuation marks of beautiful exactness.

"You will please sign here, Mrs. Meilke," he said calmly, coming over to them with the sheet of paper laid smoothly upon a last-year's best-seller and with Charlie's fountain pen in his other hand. "And if Miss MacDonald will also sign, as an endorser, I think I can safely do away with any mortgage or other legal security."

Billy Louise stood up and gave him one look-which Seabeck did not appreciate, because he did not see it.

"I'd ruther give a mortgage," Marthy said uneasily, sitting up suddenly and looking from one to the other. "I don't want Billy Louise to git tangled up in my troubles. She's got plenty of her own. Her maw's just died, Mr. Seabeck. And I'll bet there was a hospital 'n' doctor's bill bigger 'n this cattle note, to be paid. I don't want to pile on —"

"Now, Marthy, you be still. I'm perfectly willing to sign this note with you. If it will satisfy Mr. Seabeck, I'm sure it's the very least we can do-or-expect." Billy Louise, bless her heart, was trying very hard to be grateful to Seabeck in spite of the slump he had suffered in her estimation.

"Well, I'll want your written word that yuh won't prosycute Charlie nor help nobody else prosycute him," stipulated Marthy, with sudden shrewdness. "If me 'n Billy Louise signs this note, we'll pay it; and we want some pertection from you, fer Charlie."

"Hmm-mm —I see!" He turned and went back to the littered desk and wrote carefully again upon another sheet of paper. "I think this will be quite satisfactory," he said, and handed the paper to Marthy.

"Git my specs, Billy Louise-off 'n the shelf over there," she said, and read the paper laboriously, her lips forming the letters of every word which contained more than one syllable. Marthy, remember, was a plainswoman born and bred.

"I guess that'll do," she pronounced at last, pushing the spectacles up on her lined forehead. "You read it, Billy Louise, 'n' see what yuh think."

"I think it's all right, Marthy," said Billy Louise, after she had read the document twice. "It's a bill of sale; and it also wipes the slate clean of any possible —I think Mr. Seabeck is very c-clever."

Whereupon Marthy signed the note, with a spluttering of the abused pen in her stiffened old fingers and a great twisting of her grim mouth as she formed the capitals. Then Billy Louise wrote her name with a fine, schoolgirl ease and a little curl on the end of the last d. Seabeck took the paper from the tips of Billy Louise's supercilious fingers, returned with it to the desk for a blotter, hunted an envelope, folded the note carefully, and laid it away inside.

"I believe that is all, Mrs. Meilke. I hope you will suffer no further uneasiness on account of your-nephew."

"I'm liable t' suffer some gittin' that five hundred dollars paid up," Marthy returned with some acerbity. "I'm much obleeged to yuh, Mr. Seabeck, fer bein' so easy on us. If yuh hadn't drug Billy Louise into it, I'd say yer too good to be human."

"Hmm-mm —not at all," Seabeck stammered deprecatingly and left the room with what haste his natural dignity would permit.

That ended the Seabeck part of the whole sordid affair, except that he remained for another hour, doing chores and making everything snug for the night. Also he filled the kitchen woodbox as high as he could pile the sticks and brought water to last overnight-since Charlie's plan to pipe water into the cabin had remained a beautiful plan and nothing more. Billy Louise thanked Seabeck, when he was ready to go.

"I knew you were square, and you're really big-souled, too. I'll remember it always, Mr. Seabeck."

"Will you?" Seabeck looked down at her, with his hand upon the latch. "Even if you are put in a position where you must pay that note-you will still — Hm-mm! I see. Before I go, Miss MacDonald, I should like your permission to send a man down here to look after things."

"No, you mustn't." Billy Louise spoke with prompt decision. "Marthy might think you were-you see, it wouldn't do. I'll see about getting a man. If you will take this note up and leave it in the mail-box for me, John Pringle will come up to-morrow. We'll manage all right."

"You're quite right. But, Miss MacDonald, there is something else. I —er-should like to give you a little-wedding gift, since you honored me with the news of your approaching-mm-m — marriage. As an old neighbor, and one of your most sincere admirers, who would feel greatly honored by your friendship, I —should like to have you accept this —" He held something out to Billy Louise and pulled open the door for instant escape. "Good night, Miss MacDonald. I think it will storm." Then he was gone, hurrying down the narrow path with long strides, his tall figure bent to the wind, his coat napping around his lean legs.

Billy Louise closed the door and her half-open mouth and let down her lifted eyelids. Standing with her back against the wall, she turned that something-an envelope-over twice, then tore off the end and pulled out the contents. It was the note she and Marthy had signed no longer than an hour ago, and written large across the face of it were the words: "Paid, Samuel Seabeck."

"The-old-darling!" said Billy Louise under her breath and went straight in to show it to Marthy.

Chapter XXVIII. All Right and Comfy

Seabeck was a fine weather prophet, for that time at least. It did storm that night and the next day and the next; a howling, tearing blizzard that carried the snow so far and so fast that it almost wore it out; so that when the spasm was over, the land lay bleaker and raggeder than ever, with hard-packed drifts in all the hollows and bare ground between. Of course it was out of the question for Billy Louise to leave the Cove while the storm lasted, so she took care of Marthy and the pigs and chickens and cows, and between whiles she tormented herself with direful pictures of Ward up there alone on Mill Creek. Sometimes she saw him raving in fever and wanting a drink which he could not get, so that thirst tortured him; then calling for her, when she could not come. Sometimes she saw him trying to hobble somewhere on those crutches, and falling exhausted-breaking more bones, perhaps; or catching more cold, or something. She was a most distressed Billy Louise, believe me, and she wished a hundred times a day that she had stayed with Ward; she wished that, in spite of Marthy's need of her. She was terribly sorry for Marthy; but Marthy had not broken any leg, and besides, she was not in love with Marthy.

On the second day John Pringle battled through the storm to see what Billy Louise would have him do. And Billy Louise gave him instructions about finding a man and sending him up to the Cove at once, and looking after the Wolverine ranch until she came, and having Phoebe send up some clothes for her. She felt better when she had set the wheels in motion again, and as she stood in the door and watched John's broad, stolid back out of sight on his homeward journey, she made up her mind that she would start at daylight for Mill Creek, and she didn't care whether it stormed or not. She simply would not leave Ward there alone any longer. She almost wished that she had told Seabeck about Ward; he would have sent a man over to look after him. But she was selfish, and she wanted Ward to herself; so she had not so much as mentioned his name to Seabeck.

She milked the two cows by lantern light, next morning; and the pigs did not seem to want to leave their nests when she poured their breakfast into the trough by the wavering light she carried. She made coffee for Marthy and took it to her in bed, and told her that she would leave plenty of wood and kindling, and that Marthy must sleep as long as she could and not worry about a single, living thing. She said she must get an early start, because it might be "bad going" and she meant to bring Ward back with her if he were able to travel at all.

"I can't be in two places at once, Marthy, so if you don't mind, I'll bring him down here where I can look after the two of you at the same time. You'll let me, won't you? Or else," she added hopefully, "I'll take you both down home. Would you rather —"

"I'd ruther stay here where I b'long," said Marthy dully. "But I don't want you should go t' any trouble about me, Billy Louise. I've rustled fer m'self all my life, and I guess I kin yit. If it wa'n't fer my rheumatiz, I'd ask no odds of anybody. I ain't goin' t' leave, anyway. Charlie might come back, er —"

"Well, you needn't leave." Billy Louise told herself that she was not disappointed, because she had not hoped to persuade Marthy to leave the Cove. "You don't mind if I bring Ward down here, do you, Marthy?"

"No, I don't mind nothin' you kin do," said Marthy in the same dull tone, pouring her saucer full of coffee and spilling some on her pillow, because her hands were not as steady as they used to be. "He kin sleep in Charlie's room, if yuh want he should." She took two big swallows that emptied the saucer, handed the dish to Billy Louise, and lay down again. "I don't seem to care about nothin'," she remarked tonelessly. "I'd jest as soon die as live. I wisht you'd send word to Seabeck I want t' see him, Billy Louise. Oh, it ain't about Charlie," she added harshly. "He's shet uh me, and I'm shet uh him. I —got some other business with Seabeck. Tell him to bring a couple uh men along with him."

"Is there any hurry, Marthy?" Billy Louise stood holding the cup and saucer in her two hands, and stared down anxiously at the lined old face on the pillow. A faint, red glow was in the sky, and the lamp-light dimmed with the coming of day. "You don't feel-badly, do you, Marthy?"

"Me? No, Why should I feel bad? But I want t' see Seabeck and a couple of his men, jest as quick as you kin git word to 'em."

"Which ones?" Billy Louise was plainly puzzled. Was Marthy going to make him take those cattle back? It was like her. Billy Louise did not blame her for feeling that way, either. If she had had the money, she would have paid him herself for the cattle.

"It don't matter which ones. You send 'im word, Billy Louise, like the good girl yuh always have been. You've always kinda took the place of my Minervy to me, Billy Louise; and I won't bother yuh much longer."

"Oh, of course I will! The stage will go up this forenoon. I'll send a note to Seabeck. It won't be any bother at all. What shall I say? Just that you want to see him?"

"I kin write it m'self, I guess, if you'll bring me a pencil and paper. I can't seem t' git used to a pen. I kin write all I want t' say."

Billy Louise let it go at that. She brought the paper and pencil and went after Blue, while Marthy, sitting up in bed, wrote her note. Billy Louise was eager to start; and I don't think anyone should blame her if she hurried Marthy a little, and if her parting words were few, and her manner slightly abstracted. She knew just how Marthy was feeling-or thought she did; and she was simply wild with anxiety over Ward.

Blue discovered before she was out of the gorge that his lady was wild over something. Never had she come so near to being a merciless rider as on that nippy morning. There were drifts: Blue went through them in great lunges. There were steep hills: but there was no stopping at the top to breathe awhile and admire the view. Billy Louise rode with an eye upon the climbing sun, and with her mind busy adding up miles and minutes.

She rode up the creek trail at a long lope, and she pulled up at the stable and slid off Blue, who was wet to his ears and moving every rib when he breathed. (Blue was a good horse, with plenty of speed and stamina, but Billy Louise had given him all he wanted, that morning.) She went straight to a corner of the hay corral and stopped with her hands clutching the top wire.

"Ward Warren, for heaven's sake, what are you doing?" You couldn't have told from her tone that she had been crying, a mile back, from sheer anxiety, or that she "loved him to pieces." She sounded as if she did not love him at all and was merely disgusted with his actions.

"I'm trying to sink my loop on this damned buzzard-head of a horse," Ward retorted glumly. "I've been trying for about an hour," he added, grinning a little at his own plight.

"Well, it's a lucky thing for you he won't let you," Billy Louise informed him sternly, stooping to crawl under the bottom wire. "You've got about as much sense as —" She did not say what. "Give me that rope, and you take yourself and your crutches out of the corral, Mr. Smarty. I just had a hunch you couldn't be trusted to behave yourself."

"Brave Buckaroo got lonesome," Ward said, looking at her with eyes alight, as he hobbled slowly toward her. "You'll have to open the gate for me, William. Rattler'll make a break for the open if he sees a crack as wide as your little finger."

By then he was near enough to reach out an arm and pull her close to him. "Oh, William girl, I'm sure glad to see you once more. I got scared. I thought maybe I just dreamed you were here; so I tackled —"

"You tackled more than you could handle," Billy Louise finished with her lips close to his. "You haven't got any sense at all. You might have known I'd come the very first minute I could."

"I know —I know."

"And you ought to know you mustn't try to ride Rattler, Ward. What if he'd pitch with you?"

"In that case, I'd pile up, I reckon. Say, William, a broken leg does take a hell of a time to get well. But all the same, I'll top old Rattler, all right. I'd top anything rather than spend another night in that jail."

"You'll ride Blue," Billy Louise told him calmly "I'm going to ride Rattler myself."

"Yes, you are-not!"

"Do you mean to say I can't? Do you think —"

"Oh, I guess you can, all right, but —"

"Well, if I can, I'm going to. If you think I can't handle a measly old skate like that —"

"He's been running out for nearly two months, Wilhemina —"

"And look at his ribs! If you'll just kindly go in the house while I saddle —"

"I'll kindly stay right here, lady-girl. You don't know Rattler —"

"And you don't know Billy Louise MacDonald." She wrinkled her nose at him and turned back to unsaddle Blue. "I really didn't intend to go back right now," she said, "but seeing you've got your heart set on it, I suppose we might as well." Then she added: "We're only going as far as the Cove, anyway; and I really ought to hurry back to look after Marthy. Charlie Fox and Peter pulled out and left her there all solitary alone. I've been staying with her since I left here. I told her we'd be down there, and stay till-further notice."

Billy Louise did not give Ward much opportunity for argument. He was too awkward with his crutches to keep up with her, and she managed to be on the move most of the time.

I may as well admit that she was horribly afraid of Rattler, and horribly afraid that he and Ward would find it out. She did not hurry much. She took plenty of time to put Ward's saddle on Blue, and when she finally took her rope and went in after Rattler, who was regarding her from the corner of the stack where he might run either way, she wished that Ward was elsewhere-and she did not much care where.

But Ward was anxious, and he stayed where he was by the corner of the stable and swore in violent undertones because he was condemned to look on while his Wilhemina took long chances on getting hurt. Not a move of hers escaped his fear-sharpened eyes, while she went carelessly close to Rattler, and then, with a quick flip, landed the loop neatly over his head. Ward would have felt less pleased if he had known how her heart was thumping. He saw only the whimsical twist of her lips and thought that she was enjoying a distinctly feminine sense of triumph at her success.

Billy Louise led Rattler boldly up to where lay her saddle and Ward's bridle. She hoped she did not look scared, but she was wondering all the time what Rattler would do when she "piled on"; pile her off, probably, her pessimism told her, for Billy Louise was no lady broncho-fighter, for all she rode so well on horses that she knew. There is a difference.

"Sure you want to tackle him, lady-girl?" Ward asked her, after he had himself attended to the bridling-since Rattler was touchy about the head. "Of course, he isn't bad, when you know him; but he's liable to be pretty snuffy after running out so long. And he never had a woman on him. You better let me ride him."

"Don't be silly. You couldn't even mount him, with that game leg. And besides, don't you see I've been wanting an excuse to ride Rattler ever since I knew you? You must have a very poor opinion of my riding."

"Oh, if you put it that way —" Ward yielded, just as she knew he would. "I haven't a doubt but what you can handle him if you take a notion. Only-if you got hurt —"

"But I won't." Billy Louise braced her courage with a smile and picked up the saddle blanket. But Ward took it from her and hobbled close enough to adjust it.

"He knows me," he explained meaningly. "Better let me saddle up. He don't know but what I can cave a rib or two in, if he don't behave. Just hand me the saddle, William, please."

"You're only trying to scare me out," Billy Louise accused him, with a vast relief well hidden. "I'm not a bit afraid of him."

"All right; that'll help some." He steadied himself by the horse's twitching shoulder while he reached carefully for the cinch. "I guess I'm more scared than you are."

"I know you are. I've taken too many tumbles to let the prospect of another one worry me, anyway. Why, Blue ditched me himself, three different times when I first began to ride him. And even yet the old devil would like to, once in a while." Billy Louise was actually talking herself rapidly into a feeling of confidence.

She needed it. When she had helped Ward upon Blue-and that was not easy, either, considering that he only had one leg fit to stand on-and had gone to the cabin for her bag of nuggets and Ward's roll of money which he had forgotten, and had exhausted every other excuse for delay, she picked up Rattler's reins and wound her fingers in his mane, and took hold of the stirrup as nonchalantly as if she were mounting Blue.

She went up at the instant when Rattler jumped sidewise from her. She got partly into the saddle, clung there for a few harrowing seconds, and then went over his head and plump into a snowdrift beside the stable.

"Good God!" groaned Ward and went white and weak as he watched.

"Good gracious!" grumbled Billy Louise, righting herself and digging snow out of her collar and sleeves. "Stop your laughing, Ward Warren!" (Ward was not laughing, and she knew it.) "I'll ride that ornery cayuse, just to show him I can. You Rattler, I'll fix you for that!" She turned to Ward and twisted her lips at him. "I see now why you named him that," she said. "Because he rattles your teeth loose."

"You keep off him!" Ward shouted sternly.

"You keep still!" Billy Louise shouted back at him. "We're going to find out right now who's boss."

Whether she referred to Rattler or to his master she did not stipulate; perhaps she meant both of them. At any rate, she caught the horse again and mounted, a great deal more cautiously than she had at first, in spite of Ward's threats and entreaties. She got fairly into the saddle and stayed there-with the help of the horn and the luck that had thus far carried her through almost anything she undertook. She was not a bit ashamed of "pulling leather."

"Now we're all right and comfy," she announced breathlessly, when the first fight was over and Rattler, like his master, had yielded to the inevitable. "And we know who's boss, and we're all of us squindiciously happy, because we're headed for home. Aren't we, buckaroo?"

"I suppose so," Ward mumbled doubtingly, for a moment eyeing her sidelong. He was not quite over his scare yet.

"And say, buckaroo!" Billy Louise reined close, so that she could reach out and pinch his arm a little bit. "Soon as your leg is all well, and you're every speck over the hookin'-cough, why-you can be the boss!"

"Can I?"

"Honest, you can. I've" —Billy Louise had the grace to blush a little —"I've always thought I'd love to have somebody bully me and boss me and 'buse me. And I —" Her lips twitched a little. "I think you can qualify. What was that you said just as I was getting on the second time? I was too busy to listen, but —"

"But what? I don't remember that I said anything." Ward got hold of her free hand and held it tight.

"Oh, yes, you did! It was sweary, too."

"Was it?"

"Yes, it was. You sweared at Flower of the Ranch-oh."

Billy Louise stopped at that, since Ward refused to be baited. She sensed that there were bigger things than a "sweary" sentence in the forefront of her buckaroo's mind. She waited.

They came to the gate, and Billy Louise freed her hand from his clasp and dismounted, since it was a wire gate and could not be opened on horseback. She closed it after him, looked to her cinch, tightened it a little, patted Rattler forgivingly on the neck, caught the horn with one hand and the stirrup with the other, and went up quite like a man, while Ward watched her intently.

"'In sooth, I know not why you are so sa-ad,'" murmured Billy Louise, when she swung alongside in the trail.

Ward caught her hand again and did not let go; so they rode hand in hand down the narrow valley.

"I was wondering —" he hesitated, drawing in a corner of his lip, biting it, and letting it go. "Wilhemina, if old Lady Fortune takes a notion to give me another kick or two, just when life looks so good to me —"

"Why, we'll kick back just as hard as she does," threatened Billy Louise courageously. "Don't let happiness get on your nerves, Ward."

"If I wasn't crippled, it wouldn't. But when a man's down and out, he-thinks a lot. The last three days, I've lived a whole lifetime, lady-girl. Everything seems to be coming my way, all at once. And I'm afraid; what if I can't make good? If I can't make you happy" —he squeezed her fingers so that Billy Louise had to grit her teeth to keep from interrupting him —"or if anything should happen to you-Lord! I —I never knew what it was to be crazy scared till I saw you fall off Rattler. I —"

"You've got nerves, buckaroo. You've been shut up there alone so long you see things all distorted. We're going to be happy, because we'll be together, and we've so much to do and so much to think of. You must realize, Ward, that we've got three places to take care of, and you and me and poor old Marthy. She hasn't anybody, Ward, but us. And she's changed so-got so old-just in the last few days. I never knew a person could change so much in such a little while. She's just let go all holds and kind of sagged down, mentally and physically. We'll have to take care of her, Ward, as long as she lives. That's why I'm taking you there-so we can look after her. She won't leave the Cove. I —I was hoping," she added shyly, "that we could sit in front of our own fireplace, Ward, and have nice cozy evenings; but —-well, there always seems to be something for me to do for somebody, Ward."

"Oh, you Wilhemina!" Ward slipped his arm around her, to the disgust of Rattler and Blue, and made shift to kiss her twice. "Long as you live, you'll always be doing something for some-body; that's the way you're made. And nobody's been doing things for you; but if the Lord lets me live, that's going to be my job from now on."

He said a great deal more, of course. They had nearly fifteen miles to go, and they rode at a walk; and a man and a maid can say a good deal at such a time. But I don't think they would like to have it all repeated. Their thoughts ranged far: back over the past and far into the future, and clung close to the miracle of love that had brought them together. There is one thing which Billy Louise, even in her most self-revealing mood, did not tell Ward, and that is her doubts of him. Never once did he dream that she had suspected him and wrung her heart because of her suspicions-and in that I think she was wise and kind.

They found Seabeck and Floyd Carson and another cowboy at the Cove, just preparing to leave. Marthy, it transpired, had wanted to make her will, so that Billy Louise would have the Cove when Marthy was done with it. Billy Louise cried a little and argued a good deal, but Marthy had not lost all her stubbornness, and the will stood unchanged.

When Ward understood all of the circumstances, he hobbled into the kitchen and signaled Seabeck to follow him; and there he counted out five hundred dollars from his last gold-harvest and with a few crisp sentences compelled Seabeck to accept the money. (At that, Seabeck stood a loser by Charlie's thievery, but no one knew it save himself, since he never mentioned the matter.)

Billy Louise and Ward were married just as soon as Ward was able to make the trip to the county-seat, which was just as soon as he could walk comfortably with a cane.

They stayed the winter in the Cove, and a part of the spring. Then they buried grim, gray old Marthy up on the side hill near Jase, where she had asked them to lay her work-worn body when she was gone.

They were very busy and very happy and pretty prosperous with their three ranches and what gold Ward washed out of the gravel-bank while they were living up on Mill Creek, so that he could prove up on his claim. They never heard of Charlie Fox again, or of Buck Olney-and they never wanted to.

If you should some time ride through a certain portion of Idaho, you may find the tiny valley of the Wolverine and the decaying cabins which prove how impossible it is for a couple to live in three places at once. If you should be so fortunate as to meet Billy Louise, she might take you through the canyon and point out to you her cave and Minervy's. It is possible that she might also show you the washout which always made her and Ward laugh when they passed it. And if you ride up over the hill and along the upland and down another hill, you cannot fail to find the entrance to the Cove; and perhaps you will like to ride down the gorge and see the little Eden hidden away there. You may even ride as far as Mill Creek; but you will be told, very likely, that no one ever found any gold there. And if you should meet them, give my regards to Billy Louise and Ward-who never calls himself a football these days.

THE END

www.ingramcontent.com/pod-product-compliance
Lightning Source LLC
Chambersburg PA
CBHW071426300726
48976CB00004B/1254